THE SHIFT

Discovering Inner Evolution

J.W. Pressler

YJ Press Publishing LLC

As Above, So Below

The stars that burn through endless night,
Reflect the soul's unspoken light.
A rhythm pulses, bold and deep,
In stone and seed, in breath and sleep.

The tides obey the silent moon,
As hearts align in a hidden tune.
The galaxy's unending spin,
Resounds beneath the human skin.

A thought ignites, unseen yet true—
A wave that bends, a voice that knew.
The mind—a mirror, shaped by will,
A frequency the soul makes ever still.

The All is Mind, the ancient say,
A truth now written in DNA.
Entangled threads, unseen, but known—
The past still hums within our own.

What's far is near, what's gone remains—
We carry stars within our veins.
No wall divides the dark from glow;
We rise and fall in mirrored flow.

For form and fire, for root and wind,
Are joined by what we hold within.
For space and soul, for ebb and flow,
Are one—the law of As Below.

CONTENTS

One

Shadows of Ambition

Luna Zephyr's heels echoed through the corridors of GenovaTech Solutions' Chicago headquarters, a rhythm as precise and commanding as the woman herself.

The building was a testament to modern ambition—steel, glass, and angles designed to inspire awe. From her office on the thirty-seventh floor, she often gazed at the Willis Tower looming over the city, a constant reminder of the heights she had climbed. Now, she moved through the space with effortless authority, her tailored blazer catching the light in the glow of sleek, modern fixtures. To her team, she was a force of nature: brilliant, composed, unyielding.

But as Luna reached the glass-walled conference room, a peculiar unease tugged at her—a shadow in the corner of her mind that refused to be ignored. She smoothed a stray strand of hair and adjusted the stack of documents in her arms, brushing the feeling aside.

Inside, the room was tense. Her team sat in a neat line on one side of the polished table, their notepads open and pens poised. Opposite them, the client—a tech mogul with a reputation for cutting through mediocrity like a scalpel—waited with arms crossed. Luna didn't falter. She lived for this. Pressure wasn't an obstacle; it was the air she breathed.

"This campaign," she began, her voice smooth and commanding, "isn't just a solution. It's the evolution your brand has been waiting for."

Her presentation flowed like clockwork. The visuals were stunning, the data airtight. Every word was calculated to anticipate objections before they could form. When she reached the slide titled *Adaptive Pathways*, the client leaned forward, his expression softening.

"This isn't just another predictive model," Luna continued, gesturing toward the streamlined interface on the screen. "It's built on principles inspired by quantum processing—real-time adaptability, multi-path projections. Imagine what that could mean for industries beyond tech—like human medicine, where personalized treatments could be designed before symptoms even appear."

The client's eyes flickered with interest. Approval was imminent, as Luna had known it would be.

But as the meeting concluded, handshakes exchanged and praise murmured, Luna felt... nothing. The usual adrenaline, the high of victory, was absent.

Instead, the shadow of unease returned, heavier now, coiling in the pit of her stomach. She glanced at her reflection in the polished glass wall, catching a flicker of something foreign in her own eyes.

The rest of the week passed in a blur of routine—morning strategy calls, performance reviews, late-night emails answered with mechanical efficiency. The campaign, supposedly the highlight of her quarter, barely caused a ripple among her peers. Even the client's verbal approval didn't trigger the usual celebratory buzz.

Luna moved through it all with practiced grace, her heels clicking across marble floors and her smile perfectly calibrated—professional, approachable, untouchable. It was the armor she had built over years of climbing the ranks, each success another polished plate shielding the soft spots beneath.

By Friday afternoon, the stillness became suffocating. Too quiet. Too smooth. That's when the email arrived.

The chime snapped her attention to the screen. She leaned forward, brows knitting as she opened the message: *Executive Leadership Realignment.* Her pulse quickened as she read the words: *Your position has been eliminated due to restructuring.*

For a moment, she stared at the screen, uncomprehending. The email was cold, impersonal—a single paragraph that undid years of her life. Her vision blurred as the words burned into her mind: *The Board has determined your direction is no longer aligned with the company's goals.*

The office, her sanctuary, suddenly felt oppressive. The accolades on the shelves mocked her, relics of a success that had been reduced to a footnote.

Her chest tightened as the weight of the moment pressed down. Luna's hand hovered over her phone, instinctively reaching for action—an appeal, a confrontation—but she stopped herself.

This wasn't a fight she could win. Logic, her most reliable ally, whispered the truth: *the corporate world had no room for sentiment.* She had been deemed expendable. *I should have seen this coming. I saw it in his eyes. He loved my plan... he just didn't love me.* She thought, reading over the words once again. *Nice severance package.* A final thought on the rejection before she closed her laptop.

Luna moved mechanically, gathering the few personal items she had allowed herself to display in the sterile space: her personal laptop, a crystal nameplate, a sleek pen set from her first promotion, and a small potted plant whose only saving grace was the natural light streaming through the floor-to-ceiling windows. Each item felt heavier than it should as she tucked them into a plain cardboard box. The silence in the office was painful, punctuated only by the soft rustle of her movements. With the box balanced in her arms, she walked the familiar hallways one last time, her heels echoing like a countdown. Heads turned, some offering polite smiles, others quickly averting their gaze, as if her misfortune might be contagious. By the time she reached the elevator, the weight in her chest was unbearable, her reflection in the doors an unwelcome reminder of all she had lost.

That evening, Luna sat in her apartment, the remnants of her day swirling in her mind like a storm. The wine in her glass offered little solace, its warmth doing nothing to dull the ache in her chest. She stared at the city lights outside her window, trying to make sense of what had happened, of what came next.

Her phone buzzed, the sudden noise breaking the silence. Without looking at the caller ID, she answered, her voice hoarse.

"Hello?"

"Luna, it's Miriam."

Her aunt's voice was steady but carried a weight that immediately set Luna on edge. She hadn't spoken to Miriam in years, not since she'd left the community and severed ties from her past.

"Miriam," Luna said, the word a question and an accusation all at once. "Why are you calling?"

"Oh, I'm... sorry, Luna. I don't know how to say this," Miriam began, her voice faltering. "It's about your mother."

Luna's chest tightened. She gripped the phone, her knuckles white.

"She's gone, Luna... A heart attack... It was sudden."

The words hit like a physical blow. The wine glass slipped from her hand, shattering against the floor.

"She's... gone?" Luna's voice cracked, disbelief warring with the reality sinking in.

"The funeral is in three days," Miriam continued. "You should come home."

Home. The word hung in the air, heavy with memories she had spent years burying. That community, Everwood... wasn't a home—it was a wound, a reminder of everything she had fought to escape. The cornerstone to the walls built around her heart.

"I don't know if I can," Luna whispered, her voice faltering.

"Luna," Miriam said softly. "She left something for you. Something important."

A hard lump formed in Luna's throat as she fought to steady her voice. "I'll... try," she said, the words heavy with hesitation, a fragile promise teetering on the edge of doubt.

As the call ended, Luna remained frozen, the shards of glass at her feet a reflection of the cracks forming in her carefully constructed life. Memories began to resurface: her mother's radiant smile, the vibrant murals of the community, the hidden pain that had driven her away.

Sleep that night was elusive. When it finally claimed her, it brought vivid dreams, an experience she hadn't had in years. She saw her mother, radiant and alive, standing beneath an ancient oak tree. Its branches twisted into intricate patterns of a faint glow, like veins of light pulsing with life. Her mother reached out, her eyes filled with knowing.

"*Come home, Luna,*" she said, her voice echoing like a melody. "*The answers are waiting.*"

Luna woke with a start, her mother's words lingering in the stillness. It felt so real... so real that for the first time in ages, she felt a pull—an undeniable force drawing her back to the place she had vowed never to return.

The wine glass shards were gone by morning, swept into a dustpan with the same mechanical efficiency Luna used to handle every obstacle in her life. She was a woman of action, not indulgent in grief or sentimentality. But as she stood in her spotless kitchen, clutching her phone and staring at Miriam's number in her call history, the usual logic that guided her next move faltered.

Her instinct was to stay in Chicago. Fight for what she built. There had to be a way to claw her way back into the company—an appeal, a reapplication, something to reassert her worth to the Board. She'd made it once before; she could make it again. But another part of her, quieter yet insistent, whispered that staying would be futile, a desperate clinging to a life that had already unraveled.

Luna stared at her reflection in the hallway mirror. The woman staring back at her was polished, sophisticated, and in control. But the longer she looked, the more she saw the cracks beneath the surface. Her mind wandered to the towering glass building she'd left the previous evening. *Could I really walk back in, plead my case, and restore what had been taken?*

She sighed and turned away from the mirror, pacing toward her bedroom. The sprawling apartment—a symbol of her success—felt emptier than usual, its minimalist design mocking her with its lack of warmth. She grabbed her suitcase from the closet, its pristine leather exterior untouched since her last business trip, and set it on the bed. If there was ever a good time to get out of town, it was now.

Pack, then decide. The thought steadied her trembling hands as she opened her wardrobe. Business suits, pencil skirts, silk blouses—her carefully curated armor for the corporate battlefield—hung in precise rows. She hesitated, her fingers brushing over the fabric, their familiar textures suddenly foreign. None of it felt right. None of it felt like her somehow. The realization hit unexpectedly, as did the hollow ache of her mother's absence, a void that seemed to echo louder in the stillness of the room.

She closed the wardrobe with a frustrated snap and turned to the drawers. A pair of well-worn jeans and an old, oversized sweater—a relic from her college days—caught her eye. She hadn't worn them in years, yet they felt like a small rebellion against the polished persona she had curated. She couldn't help but smile, holding them up to herself in the mirror. *This feels right.*

She threw them in the suitcase with toiletries and a few other essentials. But then, staring at the half-filled suitcase, doubt crept in. If she left Chicago, it would be a concession—a final admission that her career, the life she'd worked tirelessly to build, was over. If she wanted it back, she would have to counter them quickly.

Luna sat on the bed's edge, staring at the suitcase. Frustrated, she yanked out the clothes and shoved them back into the drawers. *This is ridiculous.* She didn't have time for nostalgia.

But the stillness of the apartment pressed on her, her thoughts spiraling. She moved to the closet, pulling down an old box she hadn't touched since the day she moved in. The edges of the cardboard were worn, the lid covered in dust. She set it on the bed and hesitated, her hand hovering over it.

When she finally opened it, the smell of aged paper and forgotten memories hit her. Inside were remnants of a life she had tried to leave behind: a bracelet woven from multicolored threads, its frayed ends a silent echo of her mother's warmth. Beneath it, a journal—the leather cover scuffed and soft from years of handling—waited patiently for her touch, grounding her as emotions surged, raw and unyielding.

Luna's breath hitched as she picked up the journal. It was hers—she recognized the loopy handwriting on the first page, the exuberant swirls of a girl who hadn't yet learned to guard her emotions. She flipped through it, catching glimpses of poems, sketches of the oak tree she had loved as a child, and snippets of dreams she could barely remember now.

Then, tucked between the pages, she found it: a faded photograph of her mother, arms outstretched in front of a mural she had painted. Her fingers hovered over the image before brushing it lightly, as though afraid to disturb its fragile edges. Her hand rose instinctively to her mouth, muffling a whimper that escaped despite her resolve. Her chin quivered, and the first tears slipped free, warm trails she hadn't allowed herself to feel until now. A shaky breath, a wipe of her cheeks, and she set the photo aside with trembling fingers, willing the emotions back into the cracks she had carefully sealed.

Still fighting to steady herself, Luna looked down at the page where the faded photo rested. Her eyes caught on an entry scrawled just beneath it, the date at the top drawing her attention. It was from her fifteenth year—a time when the community had been both her sanctuary and her prison. She tried to focus, but the words blurred as fresh tears welled up, spilling over despite her effort to contain them.

She snapped the journal shut and set it on the bed next to the empty suitcase. The past she had buried was clawing its way back, and despite her instincts to resist, she couldn't bring herself to leave the journal behind.

This time, when she packed, it was deliberate. Comfortable clothes—jeans, sweaters, sneakers—items that would suit the rugged paths and casual pace of the community. She grabbed her toiletries, a book for the road, and finally zipped the suitcase shut.

Standing in the doorway, she looked back at the apartment. It was immaculate, a shrine to the life she had built, and yet it felt hollow. She had fought for this life, sacrificed for it. And now, it felt like it was slipping through her fingers. *I'll figure it out when I return.* She thought, shaking her head unsure of the future.

She exhaled deeply, grabbed her keys, and stepped into the hallway.

The decision weighed on her, but the pull to return to her roots was stronger.

As she eased onto the highway, the city skyline receded into the horizon, its glittering edges softened by distance. The tension in her chest began to loosen, replaced by an uneasy stillness she wasn't sure how to name. The open road stretched ahead, winding through hills and valleys, offering the kind of solitude that begged for reflection.

She thought of the life she was leaving behind—the sharp lines of corporate ambition, the relentless chase for success that had filled her days and hollowed her nights. The city apartment, the accolades, the carefully maintained image of control—it all felt strangely distant now, like someone else's life she had only been borrowing.

But the life she was driving toward wasn't simple either. Everwood was a place steeped in contradictions—vivid murals, vibrant laughter, and a sense of belonging she had longed for as a child, tangled with the suffocating pain of rejection and unspoken truths. The thought of returning made her chest tighten again, but it also stirred something deeper, something she couldn't quite name.

The road ahead was long, winding through familiar landscapes that felt both inviting and foreboding. For the first time in years, Luna had no clear direction—only the weight of everything she'd lost and the uneasy pull of everything unknown.

TWO

CROSSROADS

Luna slid the key card across the motel's counter, offering a faint smile to the clerk who barely glanced up from his phone. The roadside motel just outside of Springfield, Missouri, was a far cry from the high-rise luxury she was used to, but it had served its purpose: a quiet night to gather her thoughts. The coffee in her hand was bitter and lukewarm, but she sipped it anyway, hoping it might wake her from the strange limbo she'd been floating in since leaving Chicago. Stepping outside, she took a deep breath of crisp morning air, the swish of the passing cars on the highway nearby reminding her of how far she'd already come—and how much farther she had to go. With a final glance at the motel, she climbed back into her Audi Q7 to join the symphony of engines, tires, and wind, creating a rhythmic, ever-changing white noise. The route to Eureka Springs blinking steadily on the GPS screen.

The luxury SUV hummed softly as it wound along the two-lane highway, each turn pulling Luna further from the city's sleek, unrelenting pace and closer to a past she had spent years trying to forget. The vibrant autumn landscape framed the road ahead, golden leaves falling in slow spirals to carpet the ground. Luna had always thought the changing seasons in this part of the country were beautiful, but now they felt distant, their beauty dimmed by the weight pressing on her chest. The closer she came, the emptier she felt. Knowing her mother would not be there to greet her.

The narrow highway stretched on, winding through rolling hills that grew steeper and more imposing as she neared her destination. Each curve felt familiar, as though the landscape were whispering her name, beckoning her back to a time when she had felt free. But that sense of freedom had been an illusion. Beneath the laughter, the art, and the vibrant Everwood community, shadows had always lingered. And one of those shadows had driven her away.

She shook her head, as if to dislodge the memories. Now wasn't the time to spiral into the past. Her mother was gone, and the thought of facing that reality—no chance for reconciliation, no final words—gnawed at her composure. Luna had rehearsed the conversation she might have had with her mother a thousand times in the years since she'd left, but none of those imaginary dialogues had prepared her for this. The finality of death was unforgiving.

The road curved sharply, revealing the valley below. Luna's breath caught as the familiar sight of the small community, appropriately named Everwood, unfolded before her. Nestled amidst the wooded hills, it looked like a place plucked from a dream. Vibrant murals adorned the sides of buildings, their colors vivid even from a distance. The open fields near the gathering hall were dotted with sculptures—an ever-changing display of the community's creativity. Beyond it all, the forest loomed, its dense canopy concealing the trails she had once known so well.

As she descended into the valley, the tension in her chest tightened further. Everwood looked the same, yet it wasn't. Luna's SUV bumped along the dirt road leading into the heart of the community, the sound of gravel under her tires jarring her from her thoughts. As she pulled into the small parking area near the gathering hall, a wave of nervous energy coursed through her. Faces turned toward her as she stepped out, their expressions curious but cautious. She didn't recognize many of them—new members, likely—but their presence only deepened her unease.

"Luna!" a voice called, warm and familiar.

She turned to see her Aunt Miriam hurrying toward her, her silver-streaked braid swinging with each purposeful step. The flowing, earth-toned clothes she wore seemed to meld with the surrounding landscape, as though she had stepped straight out of the forest itself. There was a quiet grace in her movements, a resilience that mirrored the natural world she so clearly belonged to. When Miriam drew closer, Luna caught the unmistakable echo of her mother in her features—the sharp green eyes, the gentle curve of her smile, and the way her expression held both strength and softness. Grief had etched lines into her face, but the warmth of her smile was genuine, and its familiarity unwound some of the tension coiled in Luna's chest.

"Aunt Miriam," Luna said softly, allowing herself to be enveloped in her aunt's embrace. For a moment, the rest of the world faded, and Luna clung to one of the few people who had believed her when the community had turned its back.

"Before we head to the cabin," Miriam said gently, stepping back, "there's something I want you to see."

Luna followed her aunt through the gathering hall's arched entrance. Inside, the air was warm and tinged with the faint scent of dried herbs and wood smoke. The large, open space was a hive of quiet activity, with members setting up chairs, arranging flowers, and draping tables in soft fabrics. A woman with kind eyes and a gentle smile approached, her hands dusted with petals.

"You must be Margaret's daughter," she said softly, her voice laced with sympathy. "I'm so sorry for your loss, Dear. Your mother meant the world to all of us—she had such a gift for making people feel seen."

Luna hesitated, unsure how to respond. Before she could find the words, the woman turned to Miriam with a knowing look. "You've done so much, Miriam. Let me take care of the rest."

Miriam nodded, offering a small smile of gratitude before guiding Luna farther into the room. But it wasn't the preparations or the murmured condolences that caught Luna's attention—it was the painting that seemed to dominate the far corner.

It was a symphony of color and motion, a swirling depiction of energy and light that seemed to shift as Luna approached. She felt her breath catch in her throat as her eyes narrowed and traced its intricate patterns: spirals that echoed galaxies, waves that seemed to pulse with rhythm, and threads of gold that tied everything together. "It's beautiful."

"It's called *The Shift*," Miriam said, her voice low but reverent. "She finished it just a week before she passed. Margaret said it was the most important work she'd ever done."

Luna reached out, her fingers hovering near the frame. "It feels... alive," she whispered.

Miriam nodded. "Your mother believed it held meaning for those who were ready to see it." She gave a slight chuckle. "I guess that means I'm not ready. I'm having a hard time finding meaning in anything with her gone."

Luna continued her reach, and the moment her fingertips grazed the edge of the frame, a jolt of energy shot through her hand. It wasn't painful, but startling—a gentle static pulse that rippled through her, leaving her heart racing.

She yanked her hand back, breath quickening. *What was that?* Her fingers still tingled.

Miriam's voice cut through her confusion. "Are you okay? Did you feel something too?" She said curiously.

Luna nodded, unsure what to say. The sensation lingered in her fingertips, an echo of something she couldn't name.

Miriam frowned thoughtfully. "Stephen said the same thing happened to him," she murmured, almost to herself.

Luna blinked, her focus narrowing on the painting as the words registered, but she said nothing. The sensation coursing through her made it difficult to tune into anything else, as if the painting itself demanded her attention.

Miriam stepped closer, holding a small leather-bound book. "She... wanted you to have this," she said, offering it to Luna. "It's one of her journals. She said it was meant for you."

"For me?" A moment of confusion as she took it into her hands. The journal felt heavier than it should have, its worn cover soft against Luna's palm. She flipped it open, her eyes landing on the first page. The neat handwriting was unmistakable, each letter deliberate and steady.

To Luna,
The answers you seek are already within you. Trust the rhythm.

Luna's breath caught as she read the words. Her fingers traced the ink, the letters somehow alive with her mother's presence.

"She always knew you'd come back," Miriam said softly. "She believed you'd find what you needed when the time was right."

Luna closed the journal, clutching it to her chest as the weight of the moment settled over her. The painting, the journal, her mother's cryptic words—it was too much to process. But beneath the confusion, a flicker of something stirred. Hope, perhaps. Or maybe something older, something deeper.

"I'm so glad you came," Miriam said, pulling back to study Luna's face. Her sharp green eyes, a mirror of Luna's own, were filled with concern. For a moment, Luna hesitated, the weight of Miriam's words settling over her. She felt a flicker of something unfamiliar—a quiet warmth stirring in the space she had long kept closed. Her throat tightened, but she managed a small, genuine smile, the first she had allowed herself in what felt like years. "You've been driving for hours. Come, let me take you to the cabin. You need to rest before tomorrow."

Luna nodded, the lump in her throat making it hard to speak. She followed Miriam to the edge of Everwood, where a small cabin stood nestled against the trees. It was rustic but well-kept, with a small porch and a view of the forest that stretched endlessly behind it. As they neared, her eyes caught on a familiar trail winding into the woods. A shallow breath escaped her—she knew exactly where it led. Pyramid Hill, a place she had once loved, with its distinct shape and sweeping views, but also the path to a memory she had spent years trying to bury. The collision of joy and pain welled up unexpectedly, tugging at her resolve. The sight stirred a flicker of something—nostalgia, maybe, or something darker—but she pushed it aside before it could take root.

"I thought you'd like some space," Miriam said, unlocking the door and stepping inside.

The cabin's interior was modest but inviting, an open layout that blended living and sleeping areas seamlessly. A sturdy wooden table stood near the center, flanked by a pair of mismatched chairs. Against one wall, a narrow bed with a colorful quilt was tucked neatly under a window. Shelves filled with books, trinkets, stones, crystals, and jars of herbs lined the far corner, while a small fireplace with a blackened hearth promised warmth on colder nights. The adjoining kitchenette, though compact, was functional, with enough space for basic cooking.

Luna scanned the space, taking it in slowly. At first, it seemed untouched, as if no one had stepped inside for weeks. But then she noticed the subtle signs of life—an empty tea cup on the windowsill, a half-burned candle beside a worn sketchbook, a folded blanket draped over the arm of a wooden chair. Traces of her mother lingered here, woven into the fabric of the place. The sight of it made something tighten in her chest.

Miriam stepped aside, letting Luna take it all in. "She spent a lot of time here," she said softly. "When she needed quiet. When she needed to think."

Luna nodded, swallowing hard. She didn't trust herself to speak.

Without thinking, she set the leather-bound journal on the table, her fingers lingering on its cover before pulling away. She wasn't ready to open it yet. Just knowing it was there felt like enough for now.

Miriam, watching her closely, hesitated before speaking again. "I'll put on some tea."

Luna blinked, pulled from her thoughts. "You don't have to—"

"I want to," Miriam said simply, already moving to the kitchenette. "Besides, you look like you could use something warm."

Luna sighed but didn't argue. Instead, she lowered herself into one of the mismatched chairs, exhaustion pressing down on her now that she had finally stopped moving. The journal sat inches away, silent and waiting. She resisted the urge to touch it again.

Miriam worked in silence, the quiet hum of the kettle filling the space between them. After a moment, she set two steaming mugs on the table and took the chair across from Luna.

They sat in easy quiet for a while, the kind that only grief and shared history could create. The tea's warmth seeped into Luna's palms, grounding her, though she still felt untethered.

"She never stopped believing in you, you know," Miriam said at last.

Luna's fingers tightened around her mug. She glanced at the journal but didn't pick it up. "I don't know if that makes me feel better or worse."

Miriam sighed, studying her niece's face. "She understood why you left. But she always knew you'd find your way back."

Luna took a slow sip of tea, letting the words settle, but she didn't respond. She wasn't ready to.

Miriam didn't push. Instead, she reached across the table, squeezing Luna's hand briefly before rising. "I'm so happy to have you here. Get some rest," she said gently. "We'll talk more tomorrow."

Luna nodded, waiting until the door clicked shut behind her before exhaling deeply. The cabin settled into silence, the only sound the faint rustling of trees outside.

She looked at the journal again, tracing its worn edges with her eyes. Not yet, she thought.

The cabin was still.

Miriam's presence had left a warmth in the air, but now, in the silence, it felt fragile—like something that would disappear if Luna let herself think too much. She sat motionless in the chair, staring at the half-empty mug in her hands, her body heavy with exhaustion.

The journal remained where she had placed it on the table, untouched. Yet, despite her exhaustion, Luna's gaze kept drifting back to it. The worn leather cover seemed to breathe in the dim light, waiting—patient, expectant. She told herself she wasn't ready, that sleep was what she needed. But even as she let her head fall back against the chair, a quiet restlessness settled in her chest, a whisper at the edge of her thoughts.

Her phone buzzed.

The sharp vibration against the wooden surface made her flinch. A tether to the outside world she wasn't sure she wanted to hold onto right now.

With a reluctant sigh, she reached for it. The preview grabbed her attention. It was from a close friend and colleague.

Vanessa: You Need to Read This.

Luna frowned, her thumb hovering over the notification. A flicker of unease curled in her stomach as she tapped the email open.

Luna,

I just found out what really happened. You need to fight this.

The CEO of HelixCore was completely sold on your pitch, but—get this—he told the Board he didn't believe a woman could actually deliver on what was promised. They fired you to save the deal.

I'm disgusted. If you want to come back and fight, I'll back you up. You could get a settlement—maybe even your job back. Call me.

Luna's breath left her in a sharp exhale.

For a moment, she just stared at the words, as if reading it again might change them. But they stayed the same, glaring at her from the glowing screen.

The betrayal was like a punch to the ribs. She had worked for that company for years, built her reputation from nothing, outperformed every expectation. And still, it wasn't enough. Not because of her skill, not because of her work—because she was a woman.

Her grip on the phone tightened.

She pushed back from the table, standing abruptly as if the movement could shake off the anger curling hot in her chest.

She paced, her bare feet pressing into the worn wooden floor, the quiet of the cabin only amplifying the storm inside her. Back and forth in the dim light of the cabin, past the journal that sat unopened, waiting. Outside, the wind stirred the trees, whispering against the windows, but it wasn't enough to drown out the thoughts clashing in her mind.

This wasn't just about her job. It was about control. About how people in power got to decide who was allowed to succeed, who was deemed worthy.

A shiver passed through her, the weight of those words settling over her anger like a heavy hand pressing on her chest. Her shoulders began to soften.

She had spent so long fighting—clawing for respect, for success, for something that felt solid beneath her feet. And now, standing here, surrounded by the remnants of a life she had abandoned, she felt an unfamiliar pull.

A question.

What if the fight she thought she needed, wasn't the one she was supposed to have?

She exhaled sharply, glancing around the cabin—the uneven wooden beams, the scent of old books and dried herbs, the quiet hum of the forest pressing in from the outside. This place should have felt small, suffocating, like a cage she had once broken free from. Instead, it felt... real.

Unlike the high-rise office where she had spent years convincing herself she belonged. Unlike the boardroom where every victory had felt fleeting, where her successes had been measured in figures and contracts, never in meaning. The corporate world had given her status, but it had taken something from her too—something she hadn't realized she had lost until now.

Her mother's passing had pulled her from that hollow dream, shaken her awake from a life that, in the end, had given her nothing of substance. And for once, she wasn't mourning its end—she was relieved.

Her phone screen dimmed, Vanessa's name disappearing into the darkness. Luna exhaled, pressing the device face-down onto the table. For now, Chicago could wait.

She turned back to the journal, the leather soft beneath her fingertips. This fight—wasn't about a job. It was about something deeper. Something she had spent years refusing to see.

Taking a breath, she pulled the journal closer.

Luna traced the journal's worn cover, running her fingers along the edges as if preparing herself. The anger from Vanessa's email still simmered beneath her skin, but something deeper had taken hold now—a quiet pull, insistent and unshakable.

Finally, she opened it.

The scent of aged paper rose to meet her—a faint blend of dried ink and something earthy, like the remnants of sage or pressed petals trapped between the pages. The journal's spine creaked softly, as if stretching after years of silence.

Her mother's handwriting filled the pages, precise yet fluid, each letter carrying the familiar rhythm of her touch. Some words were underlined with firm, deliberate strokes. Others slanted slightly, as if written in a rush, too urgent to be contained by neatness.

Luna skimmed the first few entries, her eyes tracing notes on energy, consciousness, and the unseen threads that wove through existence. The words didn't feel still—they pulsed. They whispered. As if the ink itself held echoes of her mother's voice.

Then, her gaze snagged on a passage underlined twice, the pressure of the pen slightly indented in the paper, as if her mother had wanted to make sure she wouldn't overlook it.

"The Principle of Mentalism: All is mind. The Universe is mental. What you perceive as reality begins within."

The words seemed to hum.

Luna exhaled, sinking deeper into the chair.

Her mother had always spoken of thoughts as living things—seeds planted in the mind that grew into the world around them. She could almost hear her now, the soft cadence of her voice threading through memory.

"Every thought is a ripple," she had said once, brushing paint onto a canvas in sweeping, effortless arcs. *"If you want to change your world, start from thought."*

Back then, Luna had dismissed it—another poetic idea from a woman who spent more time painting visions than facing reality. But now, in the quiet of the cabin, the words settled into her bones, filling the hollow spaces she hadn't realized were empty.

She turned the page.

"The Principle of Correspondence: As above, so below; as within, so without."

Beneath the words, a sketch sprawled across the page—an oak tree, its roots tangled deep beneath the earth, mirroring the branches stretching skyward.

Luna ran her fingers over the drawing, feeling the slight grooves where the pen had pressed firmly into the paper. The ink had bled in places, as if her mother had lingered too long on certain lines, tracing and retracing the curves.

The image stirred something long buried.

She could still hear her mother's voice, steady and warm:

"Everything in life has its reflection. The way you feel inside shapes the world you see outside. That's why it's so important to understand yourself—to be rooted and strong, like the oak."

A lump rose in Luna's throat.

How many times had she tried to shape her world through force? Through control? Power, logic, success—these were the things she had chased, believing they were the only things that made her strong. But had she ever truly looked inward? Had she ever been rooted? Or had she been grasping, reaching for branches that were never meant to hold her?

Her fingers lingered on the page before she turned it again.

Near the bottom of the next entry, a phrase stood out, written in a looser, almost hurried script:

"The journey of discovery is long and weightless. You must let go of the things that no longer serve you to travel it."

Luna inhaled sharply.

Let go.

The words pressed against her, heavier than she expected.

Her career had been everything—her identity, her security, the foundation she had built her life upon. And yet, she had felt so lost, so hollow in it. She had gritted her teeth through boardroom meetings, silenced her instincts for the sake of professionalism, clawed her way to success only to find that the air at the top was thin and suffocating.

She curled her fingers around the edge of the journal, gripping it tightly—then, just as quickly, loosened her hold.

Perhaps it is time to let go of what no longer serves me.

Luna exhaled shakily and closed the journal, but she didn't let go of it. Her hands stayed wrapped around its edges, gripping it as if it might steady her. But she wasn't meant to be steady. Not here. Not now.

The journal wasn't just full of lessons—it was full of *her mother*. The way she saw the world, the wisdom she had tried to pass down, the pieces of her mind and soul carefully etched into ink. And Luna had spent so many years running from it, from *her*.

Now, it was too late.

A sudden, crushing ache welled up inside her.

She could feel her mother in the words, in the soft curls of her hand-writing, in the underlined passages that hinted at what she had thought was important, what she might have wanted Luna to understand. But no matter how many times she read them, no matter how many pages she turned, she could never *ask*. Never hear her mother's voice explain what it *really* meant.

She had wasted so much time.

Her lungs forgot to move as the grief surged forward, raw and unre-lenting.

Luna pressed the heels of her hands into her eyes, willing the tears away—but they came anyway, slipping hot and silent down her cheeks. Her shoulders shook as she pulled the journal to her chest, holding it tightly, as if somehow, *someway*, it could bring her mother back.

But it couldn't.

And for the first time since arriving in Everwood, she let herself mourn.

For the mother she had lost.

For the mother she had pushed away.

For the questions she would never get to ask.

Her body curled inward as sobs wracked through her, years of distance collapsing in an instant. It felt endless—like she could cry forever and still not touch the depths of all she had lost.

But slowly, the storm quieted. The sobs faded into trembling breaths.

The tears slowed.

She wiped at her damp cheeks, exhaling hard, trying to find her way back to herself. But the cabin suddenly felt too small, too suffocating. The air was thick with memory, with the scent of old paper and her mother's lingering presence.

She needed to breathe.

Luna stood, pushing the chair back, the wood scraping softly against the floor. She didn't think—just moved.

She stepped toward the door, drawn by something she couldn't yet name.

Outside, the night was vast and quiet, the forest stretching endlessly before her. She stepped barefoot onto the cool earth, her breath curling in the crisp air. The trees stood tall, their dark silhouettes swaying gently in the breeze.

She closed her eyes and listened.

The rustling of leaves. The distant hoot of an owl. The faint trickle of a stream she had forgotten was there.

Had the world always been this alive? Or was she just beginning to notice?

A slow exhale left her lips, and she felt lighter than she had in ages.

She wasn't ready to let go completely. Not yet. But maybe it was time she loosen her grip.

And that, she realized, was a start.

THREE

ECHOES OF THE PAST

T he dream began slowly, like a ripple in still water. Luna was standing in a field of wildflowers, the colors vibrant and impossibly vivid. The air was warm and sweet, carrying the faint hum of bees and the distant rustle of leaves. She turned in a slow circle, her eyes scanning the horizon until they settled on a familiar figure.

Her mother stood beneath a towering oak tree, her back to Luna as she worked on a canvas. The brush in her hand moved with purpose, her strokes fluid and confident. Luna took a step closer, the ground soft beneath her bare feet.

"Mom?" Luna called out with uncertainty.

Her mother paused, turning just enough for Luna to see her profile. A soft smile played on her lips, her eyes sparkling with warmth.

"You found the journal," she said, her voice carrying across the field as if she were standing beside her.

Luna nodded, her throat tightening. "I don't understand it," she admitted, her voice barely above a whisper.

Her mother's smile widened, and she gestured to the canvas. "You will. In time. But you have to trust yourself, Luna. The answers are already within you. Open your heart. It's time to feel again."

Luna stepped closer, her gaze shifting to the painting. It was unfinished, its swirls of color and light echoing the patterns she'd seen in *The Shift*. She reached out to touch it, her fingers brushing the edge of the canvas—

Luna woke with a fright, her breath catching in her throat. The room was dark, the faint glow of moonlight filtering through the curtains. She sat up slowly, her heart pounding in her chest as the remnants of the dream clung to her like cobwebs.

Her eyes moved to the journal on the bedside table, its presence grounding her in the moment. The dream had felt so real, her mother's voice so clear that it lingered in the air around her. She reached for the journal, her fingers brushing its cover.

The answers are already within you.

The words echoed in her mind, a mantra that both comforted and challenged her. She didn't know what her mother had intended for her to find, but her curiosity began to outweigh her reason.

The morning sunlight poured through the cabin's small windows, casting golden patterns across her face. Luna stretched beneath the quilt, her body slow to respond after a restless night. The dream still lingered at the edges of her thoughts, its vividness unlike anything she had experienced before. It wasn't just a dream, she decided—it was something more, though she couldn't yet name what.

Rising from the bed, she padded to the small kitchenette and filled the kettle with water. The cabin felt different in the morning light, its coziness more welcoming than confining. She glanced at the journal on the table, its cover catching the sunlight. A part of her wanted to dive back into its pages, to uncover more of her mother's cryptic wisdom, but another part hesitated. The words were heavy, demanding, and she wasn't sure she was ready for what they might reveal.

Something about her mother's words—or maybe it was the dream—gave her an epiphany. She needed to let go of what no longer served her. Before she could second-guess herself, she reached for her phone.

Luna's fingers hovering over Vanessa's name. She had drafted responses in her mind already—ones filled with righteous fury, legal threats, demands for justice. But now, it feels different. This was weight she no longer needed to carry.

Her fingers moved, slow but deliberate. She tapped the reply button.

Subject: Re: You Need to Read This
Vanessa,

Thank you for telling me the truth. A few days ago, I would have fought this with everything I had. But now, I see it clearly. That fight was never mine to win.

I spent years building a version of myself that fit into GenovaTech's world, playing by rules I didn't write. And now that they've erased me from their story, I realize I don't belong in it anymore.

They didn't fire me because I couldn't deliver. They fired me because I was never meant to be part of their vision. And honestly? I don't want to be.

I'll find a life that feels real. A life that doesn't need to be won or defended—only lived.

Let them have their deal. I have something better.

Take care,

Luna

She hovered over the send button, exhaling slowly. Luna, didn't quite know what that *something better* was yet, but she felt she would find it. So, with a quiet certainty, she tapped it. The message vanished, and with it, the last tether to the life she had outgrown.

Letting go. Check! A small but certain accomplishment. A familiar feeling—one she knew well—a brave step into the unknown.

As the kettle began to whistle, a soft knock at the door startled her. Setting the kettle aside, she moved to the door and opened it to find Miriam standing on the porch, her expression kind but serious.

"Good morning," Miriam said, holding up a basket filled with fresh bread and fruit. "I thought you might want some breakfast."

"Thank you," Luna said, stepping aside to let her aunt in. The smell of warm bread filled the cabin as Miriam set the basket on the table and took a seat. It was abundantly clear that Miriam was going the extra mile to make Luna as comfortable as possible. *Had Miriam been watching the cabin for signs of life?* The idea sat strangely in Luna's chest—comforting and unsettling all at once. She wasn't used to being looked after anymore. Luna poured two cups of tea and joined her, the silence between them comfortable but expectant.

Miriam studied her for a moment, her sharp green eyes seeming to see more than Luna was ready to share. "How are you feeling this morning?" she asked.

Luna hesitated, her fingers curling around the warm mug. "I'm... not sure," she admitted. "The journal, a dream I had—it's a lot to process."

Miriam nodded, her expression softening. "Dreams huh, that sounds about right. Your mother's teachings were always... layered. She believed that the answers would come when you were ready for them."

Luna frowned, her gaze dropping to the journal on the table. "She always talked about rhythms and connections, about finding balance, but I never really understood what she meant. It all felt so... abstract."

"It is, in a way," Miriam said. "But it's also deeply practical. Your mother used to say that understanding the principles wasn't about memorizing them—it was about feeling them, living them. She wanted you to see the world as she did, not just with your eyes, but with your heart."

Luna's chest tightened at the words, recalling what her mom had said in the dream. *What a coincidence, her words.* The weight of her mother's expectations pressing down on her. "And what if I can't?" she asked, her voice barely above a whisper. "What if I'm not the person she thought I was?"

Miriam reached across the table, her hand warm and steady as it rested on Luna's. "You are," she said simply. "You always have been. It's not about being perfect, Luna. It's about being open, about trusting yourself enough to try. That's why your mother never tried to convince you to stay. She knew the experiences you needed were out there, waiting for you. From what I know, you've done wonderful things, and you've become exactly who you were meant to be—for today. Tomorrow will take care of itself."

The words settled over Luna like a blanket, their warmth both comforting and challenging. They felt too big to absorb all at once, brushing against parts of her heart she hadn't acknowledged in years. She didn't know if she believed them, but she wanted to. That desire, tentative and fragile, felt like a door she hadn't realized was locked beginning to creak open.

Miriam stood, her movements fluid and unhurried, like the gentle sway of a tree in the breeze. She gathered the empty mugs and walked them to the sink. Her presence, still grounding the space. "I'll let you have some time to yourself," she said, her voice a soft melody of understanding. "But I think it might help to visit the gathering hall again. The formal service is at noon, and your father will be there too."

Luna's breath locked tight in her chest at the mention of him, a knot of unease tightening in her chest.

"If it's too much, you don't have to go," Miriam added, her tone kind but resolute. "But I hope you will. There's something healing in being part of this, in being seen by others and seeing them in return." She paused, meeting Luna's gaze.

Luna nodded, her throat too tight to respond. As Miriam left, the cabin felt quieter than before, the silence filled with possibilities she wasn't sure she was ready to face.

FOUR

REFLECTIONS IN THE VOID

While she had a slight hesitation getting dressed that morning, Luna had not come all this way to skip the service. Standing in front of the mirror, she adjusted the simple black dress she had chosen, its smooth fabric a stark contrast to the weight pressing on her chest. For a moment, she caught her own reflection, the tension in her jaw betraying the calm facade she was trying to maintain. A long breath later, she reached for the bracelet she had found among her mother's belongings—a small token of connection—and slipped it onto her wrist before heading out the door.

The morning air was cool and crisp, carrying with it the faint scent of pine and damp earth. Luna walked the familiar paths toward the gathering hall, the crunch of gravel underfoot the only sound accompanying her thoughts. The community around her seemed to hum with quiet purpose, neighbors passing by with nods of recognition or murmured condolences. Each interaction was a reminder of the shared loss that had brought them all together, though it felt heavier to Luna, more personal.

Luna found herself standing once again in the gathering hall ahead of the service. The space was quieter now, the gentle bustle of preparation replaced by a reverent stillness. She looked toward the far wall, where the painting, *The Shift*, called to her. There it was, dominating the space, its colors and patterns as mesmerizing as they had been the day before.

She stepped closer, her breath catching as the light streaming through the windows seemed to make the painting glow. The swirling forms within it seemed almost alive, shifting subtly as her eyes traced the patterns. It was as if the painting held secrets she couldn't yet understand, something just out of reach but profoundly familiar.

So she reached. Her fingers hovered just above the frame, her hand trembling slightly. The memory of the jolt she'd felt the day before made her hesitate, the ghost of the sensation lingering in her mind like a warning. But curiosity, insistent and unrelenting, pushed her forward. Slowly, deliberately, her fingertips brushed the edge of the canvas.

This time, the sensation was different. It wasn't a sharp jolt but a warmth—a steady, comforting hum that radiated through her fingers and traveled up her arm. The warmth expanded, resonating in her chest, her breath catching as it seemed to sync with the rhythm of her own heartbeat. It was impossible, and yet it felt so undeniably real. Her mind scrambled for an explanation. *How is this possible?* Logic faltered, leaving her senses untethered.

Closing her eyes, Luna let herself sink into the sensation. The world around her began to dissolve, its edges softening until it was replaced by something vast and infinite. The warmth became a pulse, deep and steady, a rhythm that seemed to echo in her very bones.

Behind her closed lids, images began to bloom—flickering, fragmented, yet vivid. She saw her mother's hands moving with purpose across the canvas, each stroke of paint imbued with a life of its own. A spiral of stars whirled into view, a galaxy alive with color and light, its energy radiating outward in infinite waves. Then the spiral folded inward, becoming fractals of vivid hues, cascading into patterns too intricate to follow.

The vision shifted again. She saw the roots of a great tree, twisting and reaching deep into the earth, their veins glowing faintly with an otherworldly light. The roots pulsed with the same rhythm, as if drawing life from something primal and ancient.

Luna's inhale stuttered. The sensation was overwhelming—a kaleidoscope of images, emotions, and energy that she couldn't fully grasp, and yet it felt like it was a part of her.

When she opened her eyes, the room around her felt sharper, brighter. The sunlight streaming through the windows seemed more alive, catching motes of dust that swirled like galaxies in the air. The painting itself hadn't changed, but something within her had shifted, like a locked door cracking open for the first time.

She stumbled back, her heart racing, as though she'd just glimpsed a truth too vast and too intricate to comprehend.

"*Everything is connected,*" her mother's voice whispered in her mind, soft but clear. "*You might not see it now, but one day you will.*"

Luna blinked, her mind racing to reconcile what had just happened. *Is this me? Or... is this her...* She trailed off, unable to complete the thought. The sensation lingered, and for once, she allowed herself to feel it—completely, without restraint.

Her hand hovered near the painting again, her pulse pounding. There was no logic, no reason to explain what she'd felt. Yet in the absence of answers, she found herself questioning everything she had once believed. The possibilities stretched before her, vast and uncharted, like the infinite spirals she had seen in her vision.

A tremor ran through her as she slowly turned, scanning the room with wary eyes. *Empty.*

Relief flooded her chest, though it did little to steady her nerves. Had anyone been there—had anyone seen her stumble, seen the raw disbelief etched across her face—she wasn't sure how she would have explained it. Even she didn't know what had just happened.

Her breath was still uneven, her pulse an erratic drumbeat in her ears. The gathering hall, though unchanged, suddenly felt too small, its walls pressing in with quiet expectation. The hum of her mother's whispered words still lingered in her mind, curling around her thoughts like unseen threads.

She needed air.

Without another glance at the painting, Luna turned on unsteady feet and strode toward the door. The cool metal handle grounded her as she pushed it open, stepping into the crisp morning light. The moment the fresh air hit her skin, she exhaled sharply, as if she'd been holding her breath without realizing it.

She placed her hands on her knees, inhaling deeply, willing herself back to the present. But no matter how hard she tried, she could still feel the warmth of the vision pulsing in her bones, an aftershock of something far greater than she could comprehend.

The gathering hall filled slowly as noon approached, the quiet hum of voices mingling with the soft shuffle of footsteps. Luna stood near the back, feeling both detached and overly aware of her surroundings. People moved with purpose, arranging flowers, adjusting chairs, and exchanging whispered condolences. Their faces were familiar, yet distant—figures from a life she had left behind.

Miriam approached, her steps measured and deliberate. "It's almost time," she said softly, placing a hand on Luna's arm.

Luna nodded, her throat tight as she followed her aunt toward the rows of chairs. The seats were filling quickly, with community members of all ages taking their places, their expressions a mix of grief and reverence. Quiet murmurs filled the air, the soft rustle of fabric and the occasional comforting touch between neighbors speaking volumes about the closeness of the community.

At the front of the hall, a table draped in soft linen held a collection of photographs, candles, and a small vase of wildflowers. At the center was a framed photo of her mother, her smile radiant and serene.

But it wasn't the photo that made Luna's breath hitch—it was the urn beside it.

Sleek and unassuming, it sat among the memories like it had always been there. Luna wasn't sure when it had arrived or who had placed it, but the sight of it made her heart sink, heavy with the weight of reality. *She's really gone.*

Luna's chest tightened at the sight. She hesitated, her steps faltering as her gaze lingered on the photograph. Her mother looked so alive, so present, that it was hard to reconcile the image with the stark reality of her absence. Tears pricked at her eyes, and though she fought to maintain her composure, the wave of loss was undeniable.

As she passed down the aisle, a young woman seated near the edge caught her eye. Without a word, the woman gently placed a small packet of tissues into Luna's hand, her eyes filled with quiet sympathy. The simple gesture, so unassuming yet so full of care, nearly undid her. Luna's chin quivered as she gave a faint nod of gratitude, her fingers curling tightly around the packet as she continued to her seat.

"Come," Miriam said gently, guiding her toward an empty seat near the middle. "You'll want to be here when it begins."

Luna followed, the tension in her shoulders easing just slightly as she sank into the chair. She had expected to be led to the front, to sit in full view of everyone, where grief felt performative. But here, nestled among familiar faces, she wasn't on display—just present. For that, she was quietly grateful.

Luna sat, her hands gripping the edges of the chair as though anchoring herself to the moment. The room grew quieter, the murmur of voices fading into a respectful hush as an elder stepped forward. Eleanor. Her sharp features and piercing eyes swept over the crowd, her presence commanding even in mourning.

Eleanor's late husband, a founding member of the community, had been instrumental in shaping its earliest days. Though Eleanor's ideals didn't always align with many of the current members, her connection to its history and her husband's legacy had earned her a seat of respect and power among the elders. She wielded her influence with precision, her words cutting through debates like a blade, and few dared to challenge her.

As Eleanor's gaze passed over her, Luna felt a flicker of unease settle in her chest. The elder's piercing eyes reminded her of another time, years ago, when those same eyes had seemed colder, harder—when they had looked at her not with sympathy, but judgment. The memory was faint, but its edges were sharp enough to sting. Eleanor had been one of the voices that had spoken out after her assault, questioning Luna's account in hushed conversations that never quite stayed out of earshot.

Now, as Eleanor's gaze lingered for a moment before moving on, Luna gripped the chair tighter, willing herself to stay grounded. The room seemed smaller, heavier, as if the weight of the past was pressing down on her.

"Thank you all for being here today," Eleanor began, her voice steady and formal. "Margaret was a cornerstone of this community, a guiding light who touched each of our lives in profound ways. Her wisdom, her art, her boundless compassion—these are gifts she shared with us, and they are gifts we will carry forward."

Luna felt a pang of resentment at Eleanor's words, her mind flashing back to moments when that same woman had dismissed her; belittled her pain. She shifted in her seat, her fingers tightening on the chair as Eleanor continued, her words polished and impersonal. The same tone Luna had once perfected in the boardroom—measured, detached, a way to keep control of the conversation.

A tactic. A shield.

The thought unsettled her.

The ceremony moved forward with a series of heartfelt tributes. Members of the community stood to share memories of Margaret, their voices filled with admiration and love. Some spoke of her art, describing how her vibrant murals had brought life to the gathering hall and beyond. Others reflected on her teachings, the wisdom she had shared in quiet moments that had rippled through the community. A few recalled small acts of kindness—words of encouragement, a gentle hand on a shoulder that had left lasting impressions.

Luna sat still, listening as the knot of emotions inside her twisted tighter. She wiped at her cheeks with trembling fingers, the tears coming and going as the memories spoken aloud stirred something raw within her. She tried to keep her breathing steady, her composure intact, but occasionally she had to reach for the tissues the young woman had given her, dabbing at her nose and the corners of her eyes.

The words felt sincere, yet they skimmed the surface of who her mother truly was. As tribute after tribute unfolded, Luna's chest tightened—not with frustration, but with curiosity. No one mentioned her mother's journals, those leather-bound books filled with cryptic messages and intricate philosophies. The depth of her ideas, the way she explored truths that seemed to dance just beyond reach, was absent from their words. Luna began to wonder if the journals were something her mother had kept only for her, a part of herself she had never shared with anyone else.

She dabbed at her eyes, her mind swirling. *Did she write them just for me?* The thought was equal parts humbling and unsettling, a quiet realization that perhaps her mother had left her not just memories, but pieces of a puzzle meant to guide her. The idea carried weight, but not entirely unwelcome. Beneath the sorrow, there was a flicker of something else—a quiet yearning to understand her mother in a way no one else had, to follow the threads her journals had begun to weave.

Luna hadn't noticed him during the service. It wasn't until he stood to speak that her attention shifted. A man in his mid-thirties rose from his seat, his movements unhurried yet deliberate. He was tall, with a lean, wiry frame and hair that curled just slightly at the edges. His paint-stained hands betrayed his work before he even opened his mouth. When he spoke, his voice carried the weight of someone who thought deeply before he chose his words. Luna breathed heavily and sighed in the moment she recognized him "*Ezra*," she whispered.

"Margaret wasn't just an artist," Ezra began, his voice warm and steady. "She was a creator. A weaver of connections—between colors, between people, and between the seen and unseen."

The room fell silent as he continued, his words drawing everyone in. "She once told me that art is a conversation, not a monologue. It's about asking questions, inviting others to see the world through your eyes, and being willing to see through theirs in return. Margaret lived her life that way—always creating, always asking, always inviting."

Luna felt the sting of unshed tears as she listened. There was something about his tone, the quiet reverence in his voice, that made her chest ache. His words weren't just about her mother; they were a reflection of the community she had left behind, a mirror held up to a part of herself she had long ignored.

As he finished, the hall filled with a respectful silence, heavy with shared emotion. Ezra stepped down from the front, his expression somber but warm, and began making his way back to his seat.

When their eyes met, something unexpected stirred in Luna—a flicker of recognition that went deeper than the years they had been apart. For a fleeting moment, she saw not the man standing before her, but the boy he had been: carefree and grinning, his hand outstretched to help her climb Pyramid Hill after she had stumbled, still grinning as he carried her sketchpad the rest of the way.

Now, those boyish features were framed by lines of experience, his eyes steadier but no less familiar. The connection was brief, but it lingered, weaving itself into the fabric of her thoughts as he slipped back into his seat. Luna looked away, her chest tight, unsure whether the ache that followed was from grief or something she had buried even deeper.

As the ceremony drew to a close, Miriam leaned over and whispered, "Would you like to say something?"

Luna's heart skipped... a rare moment for her, she is unprepared, the idea never even considered. "I... I don't know what to say," she admitted, her voice trembling.

"You'll know when you stand," Miriam said, her tone gentle but firm. "If you feel ready."

Dread curled in her stomach at the thought of addressing the community, but as she looked at her mother's photograph, a quiet resolve began to build within her. Slowly, she rose, her legs unsteady as she made her way to the front.

The hall grew silent, all eyes turning toward her. Luna hesitated, her gaze dropping to the floor as she took a deep breath. When she looked up, her mother's painting, The Shift, loomed behind her, its colors vibrant and alive.

"I didn't know if I should speak," Luna began, her voice trembling, her eyes scanning the room as if searching for permission. "I didn't know if I could. My relationship with my mother was... complicated. I left this place because I didn't think I belonged here. I thought if I could just get far enough away, I could outrun the parts of myself that didn't make sense. But coming back, standing here today, I've realized something: she never stopped believing in me. Not once. Even when I stopped believing in myself."

Her voice cracked, and she paused, gripping the edges of the podium as though it might anchor her. She looked toward her mother's photograph on the table, her gaze softening. "My mother... she saw the world in ways I couldn't, or maybe just refused to. She saw connections where I saw chaos. She found beauty in the smallest things—the shimmer of light through leaves, the imperfect edges of a broken shell. And she believed, more than anything, that we are all capable of something extraordinary. That even in our messiest, most flawed moments, there's still something worth creating."

Luna drew in a shaky breath, her emotions surfacing with every word. "I didn't understand her when I was younger. I thought she was naïve. I thought her optimism—her way of pouring herself into everything she did—was misplaced, wasted even. I was so certain the world wasn't like that. That it didn't work that way. But now..." She hesitated, her words faltering as she felt the weight of the moment settle over her. "Now, I'm starting to think she was right. That maybe it's not about the way the world works—it's about the way we *choose* to perceive it. She wasn't just painting or teaching. She was trying to show us something bigger. Something we're all a part of, if we're brave enough, or even ready, to see it."

She wiped her cheek with the back of her hand, her voice steadier now but no less raw. "I don't know if I'll ever fully understand her. This place. Or even myself. But what I do know is that she believed in me. And maybe... maybe she saw something in me that I couldn't see in myself."

Her voice softened, a brief realization that in her successful career, she had lost something deeper within... a hint of resolve threading through her final words. "I think it's time I start trying. For her. And maybe, just maybe... for me too."

As Luna returned to her seat, the room remained silent for a long moment before a soft murmur of approval swept through the crowd. Miriam reached over and squeezed her hand, her expression filled with quiet pride.

The ceremony ended shortly after, the community members dispersing in hushed groups. Luna lingered near the back, her thoughts a whirlwind as she watched the others file out. She felt drained, yet lighter, as though something within her had shifted—a small but significant step toward healing.

And then she saw him. Her father, Silas Zephyr, standing near the door, his expression unreadable. Their eyes met briefly before he hung his head low, turned and walked out, leaving Luna with a flood of emotions she wasn't ready to confront.

Luna lingered by the door of the gathering hall, her thoughts heavy as she watched her father disappear into the distance. His hunched shoulders and hesitant steps seemed to mirror the weight she felt in her own chest. It had been years since they had been in the same space, and now, when faced with the reality of him standing just a few feet away, she wasn't sure how she felt.

Anger? Regret? Longing?

She pressed a hand to her temple, closing her eyes against the storm of emotions. Silas had been silent when she needed him most, absent in all the ways that mattered. And yet, seeing him now, she couldn't deny the flicker of something softer—something that whispered forgiveness might be possible, even if she didn't yet know how to offer it.

The sound of footsteps pulled her back, and she turned to see Miriam approaching, her expression careful and observant.

"I saw him," Miriam said simply, folding her arms as she leaned against the doorway.

Luna nodded, her jaw tightening. "He didn't even—" Luna, unsure how to finish that sentence.

Miriam tilted her head, her gaze thoughtful. "Maybe he didn't know how. Grief has a way of silencing people, making them unsure of their place. He loved her dearly and proved it to her every day, but your dad... he's always struggled with finding the right words in moments like this."

"That's putting it lightly," Luna muttered, her voice tinged with bitterness. She shook her head, trying to push back the frustration bubbling to the surface. "He didn't stand up for me back then, had no words to give in my defense either. When I needed him to believe me, to fight for me, he stayed quiet."

Miriam didn't respond immediately. Instead, she stepped closer, her hand resting gently on Luna's shoulder. "You're right," she said softly. "He failed you when it mattered most. And that pain doesn't just disappear. But people are more complicated than we give them credit for. Silas... Your father, he's carried that guilt every day since you left."

Luna's throat tightened, her breath catching. She didn't want to hear this—not now, not when her anger felt so justified. But Miriam's words planted a seed of doubt, one that made her chest ache in ways she wasn't prepared for.

"What am I supposed to do with that?" Luna asked, her voice low and uncertain. "How am I supposed to face him after all this time?"

"You start by facing yourself," Miriam said, her tone gentle but firm. "You're here, Luna. That's already a step forward. The rest... it will come when you're ready."

Luna exhaled shakily, her gaze dropping to the ground. The idea of confronting her father—of unraveling years of resentment and pain—felt insurmountable. But deep down, a part of her wanted to try, if only to find some sense of closure.

"I need some air," she said finally, stepping past Miriam and out into the open.

The sunlight was warm against her skin, a sharp contrast to the chill that had settled in her chest. She walked aimlessly, her feet carrying her toward the edge of the community. The forest loomed ahead, its shadows inviting but foreboding.

She paused at the tree line, her gaze drawn to the towering oak before her. Its presence was steady, unchanging, as though it had been waiting for her.

Luna approached slowly, her fingers brushing against the rough bark of the old oak tree. The texture was familiar, a living connection to the past, each groove and scar a silent witness to countless seasons and stories. She sank to the ground beneath its sprawling canopy, the cool earth pressing against her palms and grounding her in the moment.

The early autumn sunlight filtered through the canopy, where the first hints of gold and amber touched the leaves. Shifting patterns danced across the ground—patterns that reminded her of the ripples she had once read about in her mother's journal. Every cause has its effect; every effect has its cause. Nothing happens by chance. The words circled in her mind, their meaning deepening with each repetition.

Her thoughts turned to her father. Had he been part of that rhythm? A ripple set into motion by choices made long before she was born? She remembered the coldness in his eyes when she had left, the way he had withdrawn even further after the incident. At the time, it had felt like abandonment, a cutting-off that she had blamed him for, but now... she wondered.

What decisions had led him there, to that distance? Had his own pain, his own regrets, shaped the way he'd handled hers? The principle her mother had written about wasn't just about events—it was about people, too. Choices, feelings, actions—they all sent ripples outward, affecting not just the present but the years that followed. Her father's silence, his failure to stand by her when she needed him, had left scars, but maybe... maybe it had come from a place she didn't yet understand. *How am I piecing this all together?* The thoughts felt foreign, as if it belonged to someone else.

Luna closed her eyes and leaned back against the tree, its solid presence steadying her. The rhythm of the world seemed to hum through the roots beneath her, a quiet reminder that nothing existed in isolation. Every moment, every decision, was part of a web, its effects rippling outward like waves on a still pond.

The ache in her chest softened, not disappearing entirely but shifting into something else—a quiet determination. If she was going to find peace—real peace—it would have to start with understanding. Not just of her father's role in her life, but of her own. She wasn't just caught in the ripples; she was creating them, too.

Her hand pressed against the bark again, this time with a sense of purpose. The tree, with its deep roots and sprawling branches, had weathered countless storms and still stood. Luna let its strength flow through her, its enduring rhythm a quiet assurance that the ripples of the past didn't have to define her future.

For the first time since arriving, Luna allowed herself to consider the possibility that coming home wasn't just about mourning her mother. It was about rediscovering herself, and perhaps, find a way to mend what had been broken.

A light breeze ticked the hair on the back of her neck, as it carried a faint scent of aftershave to her nose.

"I thought I might find you here."

The voice startled her, and she turned to see him approaching. His hands were tucked into the pockets of his worn jeans, and a small, tentative smile played at the corners of his mouth.

"Ezra." His name slipped from her lips, barely above a whisper, as their eyes met. Any lingering anger or hesitation melted under the weight of his steady, familiar gaze. It was the same unwavering presence that had once been her refuge, a quiet strength that reminded her of a time when she had felt safe, even in her most uncertain moments.

Before she could stop herself, she stepped forward and embraced him. The gesture was instinctive, her arms wrapping around him as if seeking the comfort she hadn't realized she needed. In that moment, the walls she had so carefully built around her heart crumbled, leaving her vulnerable in a way that felt both terrifying and liberating. She felt the warmth of his arms encircle her, the solid reassurance of someone who had always seen her for who she truly was.

But the rawness of the moment caught up with her, and she pulled back quickly, her breath unsteady and a flush of embarrassment crept up her cheeks. She averted her eyes, her fingers fidgeting at her sides as she tried to make sense of the flood of emotion that had broken free.

Regaining her composure, she said, "You spoke beautifully," her voice softer than she intended.

He stepped closer, his movements careful, as though he didn't want to disturb the fragile moment. "Thank you," he said. "I meant every word. Your mother... she was remarkable."

Luna nodded, her gaze dropping to the ground. "She was," she murmured. "Sometimes I wonder if I ever really understood her."

He tilted his head, studying her with a quiet intensity. "Understanding isn't always about knowing," he said. "Sometimes it's about feeling. And from what I saw there..." He gestured toward the gathering hall. "I think you understand her more than you realize."

Luna breathed in a sense of true peace she hadn't felt in a long time. She searched her mind for the answers, mistakenly asking the question aloud. "How long has it been?"

"Fifteen, give or take," he said, his tone light but tinged with something deeper. "You haven't changed much."

She laughed softly, the sound surprising even herself. "I think I've changed more than you know." Nodding her head, she recalled a moment from her corporate life—standing in a polished conference room, her voice calm and measured as she dismantled a competitor's proposal with surgical precision. There had been no hesitation, no warmth, only the calculated execution of strategy. The memory felt distant now, like watching someone else's life play out.

His gaze softened, and he nodded. "Maybe. But some things don't change—not really."

For a moment, they stood in silence, the weight of the years between them both present and distant. Luna glanced at the oak tree, her fingers trailing along its bark. "This place... it feels different now," she said. "Like it's waiting for something."

Ezra's smile faded slightly, his expression thoughtful. "It always does," he said. "That's what makes it special. It has a way of holding on to things—memories, energy, hope. Maybe that's why you're here."

His words lingered in the air, and Luna felt the familiar pull of doubt and longing in her chest. She didn't know what she was searching for, but she smiled as she wondered if Ezra might have a part to play in helping her find it.

Her eyes trailed off into the distance as she processed the whirlwind of emotions of the day.

While he was pleased to see her, Ezra could read in her face that she needed some alone time.

"Well, I will leave you to your thoughts for now." he said, stepping back but not before offering her a small, knowing smile. "But Luna? Don't be a stranger." His lips curled as his profile turned away.

She watched him go, his steps unhurried as he disappeared down the path. The silence that followed felt heavier, yet somehow more comforting. Turning back to the oak tree, she pressed her palm against its trunk once more, letting its steady rhythm match her own.

Luna lingered at the oak tree after Ezra's departure, her hand tracing the grooves in the bark as her mind replayed their exchange. His presence had stirred something within her—a mixture of comfort, familiarity, and an unsettling vulnerability she wasn't sure she was ready to face. He had always been her refuge in childhood, the steady rock she leaned on when life felt chaotic. And now, after all these years, he seemed both unchanged and entirely new, as if time had preserved his essence while adding a quiet depth she couldn't ignore.

The emotions swirling inside her begged for the cold walls to go back up, to shield her heart from the ache of feeling too much. *If I leave today, I could...* The thought flickered—a fleeting escape plan tied to Vanessa's email, one she had already dismissed. It was a tempting retreat, a way to reclaim the life she had built—a life of order, control, and predictable moves. But she couldn't finish the thought. She had already made her choice, and she wouldn't pick up that weight again.

The pull of her mother's wishes was too strong—the breadcrumbs she had left, the mystical experience woven into the painting—too compelling to ignore. Luna's fingers stilled against the bark, the texture grounding her as a quiet resolve began to settle in her chest. Leaving might be easier, but something about staying felt *right*. It wasn't just an obligation; it was a deep, instinctive knowing that the answers she needed were here, waiting for her to find them.

The forest around her was alive with the whispers of the wind and the faint rustle of leaves. The stillness of the moment brought her back to her mother's journal and the principle she had read the night before: *"Opposites are identical in nature but different in degree. Heat and cold, love and hate, light and darkness—they are the same, existing on a spectrum."*

Ezra and her—what were they now? Opposites grown from the same soil, their lives diverging only to intersect again here, under the canopy of their shared past?

She sighed and rose to her feet, brushing dirt from her hands as she turned back toward the path. The sun hung low in the sky, casting long shadows across the community. As she walked, her thoughts returned to the service, to the faces she hadn't seen in years, and to the one face she couldn't stop thinking about—her father.

Miriam was waiting for her on the porch of the cabin, a mug of tea in her hands. She offered Luna a small smile as she approached, her sharp eyes catching the tension in Luna's expression.

"Walks can be good for sorting through things," Miriam said, gesturing to the empty chair beside her. "But they don't always give you answers."

Luna sat down heavily, the weight of the day pressing on her shoulders. "I saw Ezra," she said after a moment, her voice tentative.

Miriam raised an eyebrow, her smile widening. "He had beautiful words at the service, didn't he"

Luna nodded, her gaze dropping to her hands. "It was... beautiful. He always had a way with words."

"That he does," Miriam agreed, her tone light but knowing. "Ezra's always had a gift for seeing things as they are—and for helping others see them too. I imagine he's missed you."

Luna's chest tightened at the thought. "I don't know how to feel about seeing him again," she admitted. "It's like... everything I tried to leave behind is staring me in the face. Ezra, Dad, this place—none of it feels real, and yet it's all so much more real than anything I found out there."

Miriam nodded, her expression thoughtful. "Coming home has a way of doing that. It makes you question what's real, what's worth holding on to. But Luna, you don't have to decide everything right now. Let yourself feel it. Let yourself be here."

Luna leaned back in her chair, the mug of tea warm in her hands. She wanted to push back, to say she wasn't sure if she could let herself feel anything without falling apart. But the truth was, she didn't have the energy to fight anymore.

The sun dipped lower on the horizon, the sky painted in hues of gold and pink. The quiet between them was comfortable, filled with the unspoken understanding that came from shared loss.

Miriam broke the silence. "Your father—He's been carrying this for a long time," Miriam said gently. "You might not see it now, but he's trying in his own way."

Luna exhaled sharply. Miriam's choice of topic sparking a storm of anger within. "Trying doesn't change the past."

"No," Miriam agreed. "But it might change the future."

The words hung in the air between them, and Luna felt the ache in her chest deepen. She wanted to believe it was possible—to mend what had been broken, to find some way forward. But forgiveness felt like an impossible task, a bridge too far to cross.

As the first stars began to appear in the darkening sky, Miriam rose from her chair, her movements unhurried. "Get some rest, Luna," she said, her voice kind but firm. "Tomorrow's another day. And who knows? It might surprise you."

Luna watched her go, the warmth of the tea slowly fading in her hands. The forest beyond the cabin was a silhouette against the night, its shadows beckoning her toward something she couldn't yet name.

She stayed there for a long time, her thoughts circling back to Ezra's words, to the steady hum of the oak tree, to the principle of polarity that had echoed in her mind all day.

Opposites are identical in nature but different in degree.

Perhaps that was true of her and her father. Perhaps it was true of Ezra.

The stars above seemed to shimmer with quiet purpose, their light reaching across vast distances to illuminate the darkness. Luna closed her eyes and let the cool night air wash over her, a quiet determination settling in her chest.

Whatever tomorrow held, she would face it. One step, one choice, one truth at a time.

FIVE

THE RHYTHM OF RETURNING

The morning broke quietly, the light creeping in, filtered through the thin curtains of the cabin and painting soft patterns on the wooden floor. Luna stirred, her sleep fitful but deep enough to offer a sense of clarity she hadn't felt in days. The tea mug from the night before still rested on the small table by the chair, a faint reminder of her conversation with Miriam.

She swung her legs over the side of the bed, her bare feet meeting the cool wood. The journal sat where she'd left it, its worn cover catching the morning light. The principles her mother had so lovingly written about filled her thoughts again. Cause and effect, polarity, vibration—all of it felt like pieces of a puzzle she didn't yet know how to assemble. She looked at her watch. 9:30, Luna's eyes widened. She couldn't recall the last time she had slept in so late. Her fast paced life often demanded her to be at full speed before sunrise.

Outside, the sounds of the community at work drifted through the open window: the rhythmic chop of wood, soft laughter, and the gentle clinking of dishes. It was a symphony of life that seemed worlds away from the hum of office chatter and the sharp click of her heels on corporate floors.

After a quick wash, Luna dressed in the most comfortable clothes she'd packed—jeans and a light sweater that felt almost foreign compared to the sharp tailoring she was used to. She tied her hair loosely and stepped outside, the crisp morning air filling her lungs.

Miriam seemed to be waiting for her again, lingering near the edge of the garden with a basket of fresh herbs and flowers. "Good morning," she called, her smile warm but subdued.

"Good morning," Luna replied, her voice still husky from sleep. She walked over to join Miriam, the scent of rosemary and lavender greeting her as she approached with an arm around her waist.

"I thought you might like to help with these," Miriam said, holding up the basket. "It always clears my head to work with my hands. Then maybe later I can take you to your moms art studio."

Luna nodded, taking the basket from her, smiling at the thought of her mothers studio, a place that held so many memories. They moved to a small table near the porch, where an assortment of twine and scissors awaited. Miriam began weaving the stems together, her hands deft and sure. Luna watched for a moment before mimicking her movements, her fingers clumsy but determined.

As they worked, Miriam glanced up. "Ezra stopped by early this morning," she said casually, her tone light but probing.

Luna's hands stilled for a fraction of a second before she resumed weaving. "What did he say?"

"Not much," Miriam said, her eyes fixed on her work. "But he asked how you were. Said he might swing by later."

Luna's chest tightened, a flutter of something unnamable rising within her. She kept her gaze on the bundle of herbs in her hands, her voice carefully neutral. "He doesn't have to check on me. I'm fine."

Miriam's lips twitched, the hint of a smile. "I don't think he's checking on you, Luna. I think he's just... glad you're here."

Luna swallowed hard, the herbs in her hands suddenly feeling heavier. She wanted to brush off Miriam's words, to shrug off the significance of Ezra's presence. But deep down, she couldn't deny the warmth that had spread through her at the thought.

Before she could respond, a voice called out from the path leading toward the cabin.

"Am I interrupting?"

Both women looked up to see Ezra approaching, his hands tucked into the pockets of his jeans. He wore a plain gray T-shirt, its simplicity somehow amplifying his presence.

"Not at all," Miriam said, her smile widening. "We were just putting together bundles for the kitchen. Care to lend a hand?"

Ezra stepped closer, his grin easy and familiar. "You know I'm not much of a gardener," he said, but his tone was warm.

"You're here now. You might as well make yourself useful," Miriam teased, gesturing towards the simple tools and twine.

Luna looked down at her hands, suddenly hyper aware of the way her fingers trembled slightly. She focused on the task in front of her, refusing to meet Ezra's gaze as he settled into the chair beside her. This lack of confidence perplexed Luna. Only days ago she sat across the table of powerful men discussing million dollar deals, without a hint of hesitation in her eyes. And today, she struggles to look a man in the eye after a casual 'good morning'.

For a moment, the three of them worked in companionable silence, the rhythm of their movements filling the space. It was Ezra who broke the quiet.

"Your mom used to do this every morning," he said softly, his tone nostalgic. "I remember watching her from the workshop. She always looked so peaceful."

Luna glanced at him then, her throat tight. "I remember. She always said it helped her think," she said, her voice barely above a whisper.

Ezra nodded, his expression thoughtful. "She had a way of finding the quiet in things. Even in chaos."

The words hung between them, their weight both comforting and heavy. Miriam rose, brushing off her hands as she glanced toward the path leading to the far side of the garden. "Oh, I just remembered—I promised to help Eleanor gather some flowers for the evening. You know how particular she is about her arrangements," she said lightly, her knowing smile lingering. "You two take your time."

With that, she turned and strolled toward the tree line, her figure disappearing into the soft dappled light of the morning.

Luna hesitated, her gaze fixed on the bundle of herbs in her hands. "You didn't have to come," she said finally, her voice careful.

Ezra leaned back slightly, his gaze steady. "I wanted to."

Something in his tone disarmed her, and she looked up, meeting his eyes. The vulnerability she saw there mirrored her own, and for the first time, she allowed herself to acknowledge the space he had always held in her life—a quiet, steady presence that felt like home.

She exhaled softly, a small smile tugging at the corners of her mouth. "You're still as thoughtful as ever," she said, her voice lighter now.

Ezra's grin widened. "And you're still impossible to forget."

Luna rolled her eyes, but the blush on her cheeks gave her away.

The tension between them eased, replaced by the gentle rhythm of shared laughter. It had been a long time, but the feeling returned—subtle yet unmistakable. A sense of belonging. Of connection. Of home.

The two spent a few moments together, simply enjoying the subtle presence of something more. The moment lingered, warm and unhurried, until Ezra glanced at the watch on his wrist. "I hate to leave," he said, his expression softening, "but I made a promise to help James in town this morning. There's always something to be done, it seems."

Luna nodded, her fingers brushing the herbs absently. "You should go. I'm sure he'll be wondering where you are," she said, her tone calm but tinged with reluctance.

Ezra hesitated for a beat, his eyes lingering on her. "I'll see you later, though?"

Her lips curved into a faint smile. "Maybe," she said, the word holding more meaning than she intended.

Ezra returned her smile, the warmth in his gaze making her chest tighten. "Take care, Luna," he said gently, before turning and walking toward the path that led back to town.

She watched him go, the sound of his footsteps fading into the distance. The quiet of the garden settled over her, the weight of their exchange still lingering in the air. Her gaze drifted to the herbs in her hand, their faint, earthy scent grounding her in the present even as her mind churned.

What am I even doing here? The question echoed in her thoughts, sharp and unrelenting. The emotions stirred by Ezra, by this place, were impossible to ignore. Should she stay and face the uncertainty of these new possibilities, of connections she had long since buried? Or was life pulling her in a new direction all together?

Her gaze lifted to the treetops swaying gently in the breeze, as if the answer might be hidden there. But instead of clarity, she felt only the ache of indecision. Her thoughts turned to her mother's journal, to the words she had read the night before: *Look within for answers.*

The phrase felt like a whisper, as though her mother were speaking directly to her. Luna swallowed hard, the memory of her mother's teachings stirring something deep within. It had been years since she'd last tried. As a child, she had practiced regularly under her mother's guidance, learning to steady her mind and connect to the rhythms of the world around her. But those practices had fallen away as she built her new life, replaced by sharp focus and ambition that left little room for introspection.

Now, she felt the pull again—a quiet but insistent nudge to seek the answers not in the world outside, but within herself.

Luna's mind in the distance, her footsteps leading her way.

The cabin was still as Luna settled onto the floor, the rough wood pressing against her legs as she crossed them beneath her. The journal lay on the table nearby, its words still echoing in her mind. *Look within for answers.* Her mother's voice felt so clear in her memory, almost as if Margaret herself were in the room, urging her forward.

She hesitated, her fingers brushing against the edge of her sweater. *What if I've forgotten how?* The thought lingered, but she shook it off, inhaling deeply as she straightened her back.

Her eyes fluttered closed, and she let her hands rest lightly on her knees. The steady rhythm of her breath filled the silence, each inhale and exhale drawing her a step closer to stillness.

At first, her mind raced, thoughts colliding in a discord of doubt and distraction. Snippets of the day resurfaced—Ezra's voice at the service, the painting's hum beneath her fingertips, the flicker of tension in her father's eyes. She tried to watch them, to let them drift past like clouds in the sky, but they clung stubbornly, pulling her deeper into their storm.

Her mother's words came to her then: "*Become the observer of your thoughts, not their captive.*"

Luna's focus shifted, her breath steadying as she tried to detach from the chaos in her mind. For a moment, the noise softened, her awareness narrowing to the gentle rise and fall of her belly. A faint warmth bloomed in her core, subtle but distinct, like the first flicker of a candle's flame in the infinite darkness of a large lightless room.

She leaned into the sensation, her body relaxing as the hum of the world seemed to shift around her. She felt lighter, almost as though she were floating, her mind brushing against something vast and serene.

And then it was gone.

The thoughts surged back, sharper and louder than before. A pointless to-do list from a job she no longer had, the sting of her last fight with her father, the ache of unresolved pain—all pressing against her, demanding attention. As if her mind refused to step into the unknown, grasping instead for the comfort of chaos.

Her chest tightened, frustration prickling at the edges of her focus. She clenched her fists, her breathing quickening. *Why can't I do this?*

She opened her eyes abruptly, the cabin's warm light greeting her like a reproach. Her body felt heavy now, weighed down by the harsh feeling of failure. She let out a harsh exhale, rubbing her temples as the tension in her shoulders refused to release.

"Some observer." She muttered to herself, the bitterness in her voice surprising even her.

She paced, agitation simmering. Her mother had made it look effortless—insight flowing as naturally as breath. *What am I missing?*

Luna's mind flashed back to being fifteen, watching her mother sit cross-legged beneath the old oak tree, eyes closed, face serene. Back then, she'd thought it was just theatrics—another one of her mother's dreamy rituals. But now, standing here with nothing but her restless thoughts, Luna wondered if she'd overlooked something real.

Her gaze landed on the journal, its cover worn and familiar. It seemed to call to her, a quiet reminder of the journey she had only just begun. With a sigh, she picked it up and sank into the chair by the window, letting the stillness of the room settle around her.

She opened the journal to a new page, her eyes scanning the elegant script. The words felt like they were written just for her, their meaning resonating deeper than the ink on the page.

"There is rhythm in all things, my darling. The rise and fall, the ebb and flow. To fight the rhythm is to fight yourself, for it is the rhythm that carries us, that connects us to the universe itself. When you find the rhythm, you will find your place within it."

Luna closed her eyes, the words swirling in her mind like a melody she couldn't quite catch. Her breath slowed as she considered their meaning, her earlier frustration softening into a quiet resolve.

The rhythm was there—she could feel it, even if only faintly. She just needed to learn how to listen again.

Her mind drifted to memories of her mother painting in the garden. She could still see her there, sunlight streaking her hair, her hands moving with intuitive precision as though guided by an unseen force. The image brought a small, bittersweet smile to Luna's lips.

She thought about her life in the city—the relentless pace, the constant pressure to produce, to win. It had all felt so important then. But now, with distance, she could see it clearly: a rhythm, yes, but one that fed on urgency rather than purpose. Movement without meaning. Progress without peace.

She closed the journal gently, her hand lingering on its cover. A faint hum of resolve settled in her chest, quiet but steady. She wasn't ready to dive fully into what her mother had left behind, but the pull was undeniable. The path was real.

The need to move, to clear her thoughts, rose within her. Setting the journal aside, Luna stepped out of the cabin into the warm afternoon air. The community buzzed softly around her, its members tending to their daily tasks. She passed a woman painting a mural on the side of a building, the vibrant swirls of color catching her eye. Nearby, a group of children laughed as they ran barefoot through the grass, their joy unrestrained and infectious.

For the first time in years, she felt a pang of longing—not for the life she had left behind, but for the simplicity of the life she had once known.

Her feet carried her toward the central garden, a vibrant hub of activity surrounded by flowerbeds and shaded by the sprawling branches of an old sycamore tree. Several people greeted her with polite nods or warm smiles, their familiarity with her mother evident in their gazes. The scent of lavender and earth wrapped around her, grounding her in a place that still carried traces of her mother's touch. From the carefully arranged beds to the small sculptures tucked among the greenery, she could feel it in the air.

As she wandered deeper into the garden, she found herself standing at the edge of a small clearing. In the center stood Eleanor, her sharp features softened slightly by the dappled sunlight. She was speaking to a small group of community members, her tone measured but commanding.

Luna's eyes narrowed, her stomach twisted at the sight of her. Eleanor had been a looming presence in her childhood, her authority unquestioned but often unkind. The memories of their last confrontation flashed through Luna's mind, the sting of disbelief and dismissal still raw even after all these years.

Their eyes met briefly, and Eleanor's expression hardened, her words faltering for a fraction of a second before she resumed speaking. Luna turned away, her chest tight with unspoken words.

She walked aimlessly, her feet leading her toward the outskirts of the community. The tension in her chest eased as the noise of daily life faded, replaced by the rustle of leaves and the distant chirping of birds. She found herself at the edge of the forest, the same path she had followed as a child stretching before her like a whispered invitation.

Luna hesitated, her gaze drifting to the sun-dappled trail. The pull was strong, but so was the fear—of what she might find, of what might find her.

She took a step forward, the sound of her footfall barely audible against the soft earth. The forest seemed to hold its breath, its energy shifting as though it recognized her presence.

Luna exhaled slowly, her resolve steadying. Whatever lay ahead, she would face it.

The forest welcomed Luna with a quiet embrace, its shadows cool and inviting as she stepped onto the familiar path. The air was thick with the scent of moss and damp earth, the whispers of leaves brushing against one another carried on a gentle breeze. Each step felt deliberate, the crunch of twigs beneath her feet grounding her in a way that words couldn't.

As a child, this trail had been her refuge—a sanctuary where she could escape the noise of the community and lose herself in the rhythm of the natural world. Now, it felt like walking into a memory, each twist and turn of the path sparking a flicker of recognition.

Her pace slowed as she neared the old clearing, the place where she had spent countless afternoons lying in the grass, staring up at the endless expanse of sky. The trees here seemed taller, their trunks gnarled and ancient, their roots weaving into the earth like veins. At the center stood a hill, its pyramid-like shape covered in soft green grass and dotted with wildflowers that swayed lazily in the light breeze.

Luna paused at the edge of the clearing, her chest tightening as a wave of nostalgia washed over her. She could almost hear the echoes of her younger self laughing, the sound mingling with the faint rustle of the leaves. She stepped forward, her gaze drawn to the hill's peak.

The sunlight streaming through the canopy seemed brighter here, its golden rays illuminating the clearing like a spotlight. Luna felt an inexplicable pull toward the center, as though the hill itself were calling her.

Climbing slowly, she let her fingers graze the grass, the soft blades brushing against her skin. The hum she had felt the night before—the faint vibration deep in her chest—returned, stronger now, as though the forest's energy was answering something within her.

At its peak, she lowered herself onto the soft ground, her legs folding beneath her. The view was breathtaking, the trees surrounding the clearing forming a natural cathedral that seemed to stretch endlessly outward. She closed her eyes, the warmth of the sun on her skin grounding her as she let her breath steady.

"*Every cause has its effect; every effect has its cause.*" Her mother's voice whispered through her mind, the words from the journal weaving seamlessly with her surroundings. The principle of rhythm, of polarity, of correspondence —it was all here, written into the fabric of the forest, the cycles of growth and decay that sustained life. Luna began to recognize it all for what it is.

She placed her hands on the earth, her palms pressing into the cool soil. A faint pulse seemed to rise beneath her touch, subtle yet undeniable—as if the ground recognized her, responding in kind. She didn't understand it—not fully—but she felt it, the connection her mother had spoken of, the hum of the vibration in all that she had written about.

Luna sat in stillness, letting the late afternoon sun seep into her skin, its warmth grounding her. A memory surfaced, unbidden: her mother sitting cross-legged in this very spot, her hands resting lightly on her knees, her eyes closed in serene concentration. Luna had watched from the edge of the clearing, too young to understand the significance of what her mother was doing but captivated nonetheless.

"Find the rhythm, feel the frequency at which life vibrates" her mother had said when she'd finally noticed Luna's presence. "It's always there, in everything, waiting for you to listen with closed ears."

Luna opened her eyes, the memory fading but its impact lingering. She leaned back, her gaze drifting to the sky. The memory stirred something long dormant within her—peace, perhaps, or maybe hope.

Her reverie was broken by the sound of footsteps on the trail. She sat up, her body tensing instinctively as she turned toward the noise. A figure emerged from the shadows, tall and familiar, his movements unhurried yet deliberate.

Ezra.

He paused at the edge of the clearing, his gaze meeting hers. There was no hesitation in his expression, only quiet understanding. "I thought I might find you here," he said, his voice warm and steady as he climbed the hill.

Luna's heart quickened, but she forced herself to remain composed. "Is that so?" she said lightly, her tone masking the emotions that swirled beneath the surface. "You seem to have a knack for knowing where to find me." She laughed softly, the sound more an attempt to steady herself than an expression of amusement.

He stepped closer, exhaling as he reached the peak. "Damn," he muttered with a half-smile, still catching his breath. "You always pick the spots that make me work for it." His gaze flicked across the horizon before settling on her. "You seemed deep in thought this morning. I took a guess that this is where you come to sort things out?" He hesitated for a beat, then added, "Hope I'm not interrupting."

Her gaze shifted back to the horizon, the weight of his words settling over her. "No," she murmured, her voice quieter now, raw with honesty. "You're not interrupting. I just..." She hesitated, her fingers brushing against the thick grass beside her. "I don't know what I need right now."

Ezra lowered himself to the ground a few feet away, his presence steady and unassuming. "That's the thing about this place," he said after a moment. "It doesn't ask you to know. It just asks you to be."

The simplicity of his words struck something deep within her. She didn't respond, but she didn't need to. The silence that followed was comfortable, the kind that didn't demand to be filled.

For a while, they sat together in the clearing, the sounds of the forest weaving around them like a gentle symphony. Luna closed her eyes again, letting the rhythm of the moment settle over her.

Luna suddenly felt like she wasn't running anymore—not from her past, her pain, or herself. She was just present, with herself, with him.

As the sun dipped lower in the sky, the clearing grew quieter, its golden hues softening into shades of amber and rust. Luna remained seated at the crest of the hill, her knees tucked loosely to her chest, while Ezra stretched out on the grass beside her. His presence was calming, a steady rhythm that echoed the hum of the forest around them.

"Do you ever feel like this place is... alive?" Luna asked suddenly, her voice breaking the comfortable silence. Her gaze was fixed on the horizon, her expression pensive. "Like it's not just a backdrop, but a... participant?"

Ezra propped himself up on one elbow, studying her with quiet curiosity. "I think your mother would have agreed with you," he said. "She always talked about the energy of this land, how it resonated with people who were open to feeling it."

Luna nodded slowly, her fingers brushing the grass beneath her. "I used to feel it too, I think. When I was younger. But now... it feels different. Distant, somehow. Or maybe I've just forgotten what it feels like to notice."

Ezra smiled faintly, his gaze drifting to the trees. "You've been away for a long time, Luna. But this place—it's patient. It waits for people to come back to it, to themselves."

His words washed over her, soothing as an ocean tide, both comforting and challenging. She tilted her head, a wry smile tugging at her lips. "You sound a lot like her, you know, my mother. Always so sure that everything has a purpose, that every moment is part of some grand design."

"And you don't think it is?" Ezra asked gently, his tone free of judgment.

Luna hesitated, her gaze dropping to her hands. "I don't know what I think anymore," she admitted. "I've spent so many years trying to control everything, to plan every step. And now... now I don't even know who I am without all of that. And I question whether or not I was in control at all."

Ezra didn't respond immediately, his thoughtful silence encouraging her to continue.

"I thought I'd find answers in her journal," she said, her voice softer now. "But all it's done is make me realize how far I've drifted from the person I used to be. The person she wanted me to be."

"Maybe that's the point," Ezra said finally. "Sometimes we have to lose ourselves completely before we can find who we are meant to be."

Luna looked at him then, her eyes searching his face for something she couldn't name. His steady gaze met hers, and for a moment, the air between them seemed to hum with an unspoken understanding.

"Do you ever think about leaving?" she asked abruptly, her voice laced with curiosity. "About going somewhere else, starting over?" A wishful thought that maybe she can still escape this place without giving up on something... missing in her life.

Ezra chuckled softly, shaking his head. "I've thought about it," he admitted. "But this place... it's a part of me, just like it's a part of you. I think we both know you can't really outrun something that's in your bones."

Luna's chest tightened at his words, a quiet ache she couldn't quite place. She turned her gaze back to the horizon, her thoughts swirling like the leaves at her feet as she sank into silent contemplation.

As the light continued to fade, Ezra pushed himself to his feet, brushing grass from his jeans. "I will let you be. You won't find answers with me hanging around" he laughed, his voice warm but tinged with reluctance. "Maybe next time you can come find me." He teased.

Luna nodded, rising slowly to stand beside him. He was wrong, she did find answers in his presence, but she didn't protest. "Thank you," she said, her voice barely above a whisper.

"For what?" he asked, his brow furrowing slightly.

"For reminding me of who I used to be," she said. "And for not giving up on who I might be still."

Ezra's smile was small but genuine, his eyes soft as they met hers. "You don't need anyone else to remind you of that, Luna," he said. "It's all still there. You just have to trust yourself enough to look."

With that, he turned and began walking back down the trail, his steps steady and unhurried. Luna watched him go, her heart heavy with gratitude and something else she wasn't ready to name.

When he disappeared into the trees, she turned back toward the clearing. The hill's quiet presence seemed to hum with approval, as though it had witnessed something significant and was holding the memory in its roots.

Luna sank back to the ground, the journal's words replaying in her mind. The rhythm, the vibration, the interconnectedness of it all—it was beginning to make sense, not in her mind but in her heart.

As the first stars began to appear in the darkening sky, Luna closed her eyes and let the night envelop her. She didn't have all the answers yet, but she found hope in a subtle feeling that it was all rising to the surface.

The walk back to the cabin was quiet, the forest enveloping Luna in a cocoon of soft shadows and muted sounds. The rhythm of her steps matched the cadence of her thoughts, both steady and measured. The encounter with Ezra lingered, his words weaving themselves into her mind alongside her mother's teachings.

She paused just before the cabin came into view, her gaze drifting back toward the path that had led her to the clearing. Something about that space—its energy, its quiet wisdom—felt like a piece of her mother still lived there. The hum of the hill, the way it resonated within her, was unlike anything she had experienced in the city. *How could I have forgotten the magic of this place?*

Crossing the threshold of the cabin, she immediately noticed how the space felt different than it had in the morning. It was quieter now, the muted light casting long shadows across the floor. The journal lay where she had left it, its worn cover catching the soft glow from the lamp.

She sank into the chair by the window, the journal heavy in her hands. She hadn't planned to open it again tonight—her emotions were already raw—but the pull was undeniable. Turning to a new page, she found her mother's familiar handwriting, the words looping gracefully across the paper.

"As above, so below; as within, so without. The universe is a mirror, reflecting the truths we carry within ourselves. To understand it, you must first understand yourself."

Luna ran her fingers over the text, her mother's voice echoing in her mind. She thought of the clearing, of the way the hill had seemed to breathe with her, and the flicker of peace she had felt under Ezra's steady gaze.

Could this be what her mother meant? That the answers she sought weren't somewhere out there, but inside her all along?

The thought was both comforting and terrifying. She had spent so long running—from her past, from her pain, from the person she had been. Facing herself now felt like standing at the edge of a vast chasm, unsure if she would fall or fly.

Luna leaned back in the chair, her gaze drifting to the ceiling. The stillness of the cabin pressed in around her, amplifying the quiet rhythm of her breath. She closed her eyes, letting the words from the journal replay in her mind like a mantra.

"As *within, so without.*"

The principle of correspondence, her mother had called it. The idea that everything was connected, that the patterns within mirrored the patterns without. She remembered her mother explaining it once, her voice soft yet firm as she painted swirls of color on a canvas.

"*It's like music, Luna,*" her mother had said. "*The same rhythm exists in a single note as it does in an entire symphony. Once you learn to hear it, you'll see it everywhere.*"

The memory brought a lump to Luna's throat. She had dismissed her mother's words back then, too focused on her own ambitions to see the wisdom in them. But now, as the journal lay open in her lap, those words felt like a lifeline.

She closed the journal gently, her hands resting on its cover. Her mother had always been trying to show her something, to guide her toward a truth she hadn't been ready to see.

But now... now she was ready to try.

Rising from the chair, Luna moved to the small table by the window, where Miriam had left a candle earlier that day. She lit it carefully, the flame flickering to life with a quiet whoosh. The soft glow illuminated the room, casting long shadows that danced across the walls.

She sat cross-legged on the floor, her hands resting lightly on her knees. The act of meditation felt foreign and familiar all at once, a muscle long unused but still remembered. Closing her eyes, she let her breath steady, her focus narrowing to the gentle rise and fall of her chest.

The stillness came slowly, her thoughts swirling like leaves caught in a breeze. She let them come, observing each one without judgment before letting it drift away. It was harder than she expected—not to engage, not to follow—but in brief moments, she felt the beginnings of something. A quiet hum, a faint connection to the vibration her mother had always spoken of.

The moments were fleeting, slipping through her fingers like grains of sand. Frustration began to creep in, tightening her chest and quickening her breath. She opened her eyes abruptly, the glow of the candle a stark contrast to the darkness beyond the window.

"I can't do this," she muttered, her voice breaking the silence.

But even as she said the words, a part of her knew she had to keep trying.

Luna leaned forward, blowing out the candle. The room plunged into darkness, but the hum of the forest outside reminded her that she was not alone.

Tomorrow, she thought, as she climbed into bed, a gentle rain began to patter across the roof, promising a pleasant night's sleep. *Tomorrow I will try again.*

U NFINISHED C ONVERSATIONS

T he next morning dawned with a soft mist clinging to the edges of the forest, the air cool and heavy with the scent of rain-soaked earth. Luna woke slowly, the quiet hum of the community beginning its day drifting in through the cabin window. She lay still for a moment, her gaze fixed on the wooden beams above her, her mind tracing the fragments of dreams that lingered at the edges of her consciousness.

There was a clarity to the morning that hadn't been there the day before—a faint but persistent tug urging her forward. She wasn't sure if it was the journal, the hill, or her conversation with Ezra that had planted the seed, but something within her had shifted.

Deciding to stay a little longer, Luna drove to a small strip mall along the highway near Everwood, the mist still clinging to the trees. The modest collection of shops and market stands blended practicality with charm, a quiet hub where locals sold handcrafted goods alongside every-day necessities. As she stepped inside, familiar faces emerged—members of the Everwood community tending small storefronts and kiosks, their work reflected in the carefully arranged displays of hand-woven scarves, herbal tinctures, and intricately carved wooden trinkets.

She browsed slowly, selecting a few essentials—a soft sweater, a pair of sturdy jeans, and a notebook to replace the tablet she had left behind. Each purchase felt oddly grounding, a small act of settling into a life she hadn't yet decided to embrace.

At a small shop filled with candles and soaps, the warm scent of laven-der and cedar stirred something deep within her. She traced her fingers over a carved wooden incense holder, its intricate design reminding her of the patterns in her mother's paintings. Without hesitation, she brought it to the counter, along with a bundle of sage and a candle infused with wild herbs. By the time she returned to the cabin, her arms were full, her heart unexpectedly lighter, and the morning mist had burned away, leaving the day clear and open.

After a late lunch, Luna stepped outside, her boots crunching softly against the damp earth. The path toward the heart of the community was alive with motion: people chatting in small groups, children running barefoot through the grass, the rhythmic clatter of tools and laughter mixing with the sounds of nature. The day seemed to pass her by, leaving her in peace.

She passed a mural on the side of a building, its vibrant colors striking against the muted tones of the morning. The image depicted a tree with sprawling roots and branches that seemed to reach for the stars. Beneath the canopy, figures danced in a circle, their forms abstract yet evocative. Luna paused, her gaze tracing the intricate patterns. Her mother's hand was unmistakable in the brushstrokes, the balance of movement and stillness within the painting resonating deeply.

A warmth spread through her chest, an openness she hadn't felt in years—an unfamiliar, almost startling vulnerability. It was as if the mural had unlocked something inside her, another door to emotions she had kept at arm's length. Yet, with it came an undercurrent of unresolved pain, memories of the past still sharp and raw. But Luna's determination hardened. *Now's the time*, she thought, her determination kicking in. She wouldn't let the past dictate her future.

The shed was tucked away near the edge of the forest, its wooden structure weathered but sturdy. The scent of sawdust and pine filled the air, mingling with the faint hum of activity inside. Luna hesitated at the doorway, her hand hovering just above the latch. Her heart raced as memories flooded back, sharp and unwelcome.

Taking a deep breath, she pushed the door open.

Her father was there, hunched over a workbench, his hands steady as they guided a chisel along the edge of a wooden plank. The lines of his face were etched deeper than she remembered, his hair more gray than brown. But his movements were the same—precise, deliberate, a quiet rhythm that spoke of years spent crafting things with care.

Luna clenched her fists, her nails digging into her palms as she forced herself to step forward. The creak of the floorboards announced her presence, and her father stilled, his hand pausing mid-motion.

"Luna," he said with startled fright, "I wasn't sure you'd come," he said, his voice low and rough, as though he had been rehearsing the line.

Luna hesitated before perching on the edge of the bench, her back stiff and her gaze fixed on the piece of wood in his lap. He studied her for a moment, then picked up a strip of sandpaper and began smoothing the newly chiseled surface, the rhythmic motion filling the silence, steadying his nerves as the dreaded moment approached.

"You've been avoiding me," she said finally, her voice sharper than she intended.

He paused, his hand hovering over the wood. "Not avoiding," he said carefully. "Just... giving you space."

"Space!" she repeated, her tone dripping with disbelief and a hint of anger. "Is that what you call it? Because from where I'm sitting, it looks a lot like guilt."

Silence...

"Look, I didn't come for you," Luna continued, her tone sharper than she intended. She saw him flinch slightly, but he didn't turn to face her.

The silence stretched between them, heavy and suffocating. "I came for me, because if I don't work through this, I...." Luna's chest tightened as the anger she had buried for years began to rise. "Why didn't you believe me?" she blurted out, her voice trembling. "Why didn't you protect me? That man stole my innocence, but you... you silenced my voice."

Her father flinched, the sandpaper slipping from his grasp. His lips pressed into a thin line as he sat back, his gaze hardening. "I did what I thought was best at the time, Luna," he said sharply, his voice rising. "You think it was easy for me? You think I didn't lie awake every night wondering if I'd failed you?"

"You did fail me!" Luna's voice cracked, the words tearing from her throat like a wound ripped open. She stood abruptly, her fists clenched at her sides. "You were supposed to protect me, but you let them bury the truth like it didn't matter—**like I didn't matter!**"

Her father shot to his feet, his own frustration spilling over. "Do you think I don't know that? Do you think I don't live with that every single day?" His voice was raw now, trembling with equal parts anger and anguish. "I've been carrying this guilt for years, Luna—years! And I know nothing I say can ever make it right, but I... I didn't know what else to do!"

The air between them vibrated with the force of their emotions, the tension threatening to boil over. Luna's chest heaved, her pulse pounding in her ears as his words echoed in the silence that followed.

Her father set the chisel down with deliberate care, his movements slow and measured. He turned to face her, his expression a mixture of weariness and something deeper—regret, maybe, or shame. "Look, Luna..."

"No," she interrupted, her voice rising. "You don't get to just say my name like that and think it makes everything okay. Do you have any idea what it was like? To go through that and then have you—my own father—stand there and say nothing?"

His jaw tightened, his hands gripping the edge of the workbench. "I didn't know what to do," he said finally, his voice barely above a whisper.

"You didn't know what to do?" Luna repeated, her tone incredulous. The heat of her anger bubbled over, spilling into her words. "You didn't know what to do, so you did nothing? You let them dismiss me—let them paint me as a liar. Your daughter! And you let him go on with his life as if nothing..." The final words caught in her throat, unable to form.

"They kicked him...." He paused knowing that such a fact wouldn't mend her wounds. Silas closed his eyes briefly, to find the words he should be saying. "I failed you," he said, his voice breaking. "I know that. I've known it every single day since you left."

"Do you?" Luna shot back, her voice trembling with the weight of her pain. "Do you have any idea what it felt like to leave everything behind because I couldn't bear to stay? To cut myself off from everything I knew, because staying meant facing your silence every day?"

Her father's hands trembled slightly as he stepped toward her, his gaze heavy with guilt. "I was weak, Luna," he admitted, his voice cracking. "I trusted the wrong people. I believed in the community, in its leaders, when I should have believed in you."

The rawness of his confession stopped her in her tracks, her breath hitching in her throat. The anger that had burned so brightly within her began to flicker, replaced by something else—confusion, sorrow, a longing she couldn't name.

She turned away from him, her gaze fixed on the open sky. Her mother's voice echoed in her mind, soft and steady: "*Opposites are identical in nature but different in degree. Anger and joy, light and darkness—they are the same, existing on a spectrum. To change the polarity is to change your perspective.*"

The principle of polarity. Her mother had spoken of it often, using it to explain everything from the changing seasons to the shifts within one's heart. Luna closed her eyes, the memory of her mother's words calming the storm within her.

She took a deep breath, her voice quieter when she spoke again. "I don't know if I can listen to moms lessons of forgiveness," she said, her tone steadier now. "Not yet. But I can't carry this anger anymore. It's too heavy, and I won't let it drive me away again."

Her father's shoulders sagged, as though the weight of his own guilt had finally been acknowledged. "I don't deserve your forgiveness," he said, his voice thick with emotion. "But I want you to know—I never stopped loving you. Not for a moment."

The words hit her like a wave, washing over the cracks in her armor and leaving her exposed. She turned to face him, her eyes shimmering with unshed tears. "You should have fought for me," she said softly. "You should have been someone I could count on."

"I know," he said, his voice barely audible. "And if I could do it all over again, I would."

The silence that followed was thick with unspoken words, but it was no longer suffocating. It was the kind of silence that held space for healing, for the possibility of something new.

Luna stepped back, her hands trembling as she wiped at her eyes. "I need time," she said simply.

Her father nodded, his own eyes glistening. "Take all the time you need, Luna," he said.

Without another word, she turned and walked away, her steps unsteady but purposeful. The forest welcomed her back, its cool embrace soothing the raw edges of her emotions. As she made her way back to the cabin, her mother's words echoed in her mind once more.

"To change the polarity is to change your perspective. In every shadow, there is light."

Luna exhaled slowly, the tightness in her chest easing as the stars began to peek through the now darkening sky. Healing would take time, but somehow, she felt like it was possible.

The cabin was quiet when Luna returned, the air thick with a silence that clung like morning fog. She sat at the small wooden table, her hands tracing the edges of her mother's journal. The encounter with her father had left her shaken, the rawness of their exchange replaying in her mind. Anger and sorrow churned within her, battling for dominance, but beneath it all, there was something quieter. A small but steady whisper of possibility.

She opened the journal, her fingers pausing on a page she hadn't yet read. The ink was slightly smudged, the handwriting looser than usual, as though her mother had written in haste. Luna's eyes scanned the text, the words pulling her in.

"Chaos and order are two sides of the same coin—one cannot exist without the other. Chaos offers the opportunity for growth; order creates the space to heal. To resist one is to reject the other, and in doing so, we deny ourselves the fullness of life."

Luna leaned back in her chair, the words settling heavily in her chest. Her mother had always spoken in riddles, her teachings layered with meanings that only became clear in hindsight. But this—this felt different. The timing was too precise, the message too perfectly aligned with the turmoil stirring inside her. It was as if the universe itself had nudged her toward this page, guiding her to read these words in the only moment she would truly hear them.

She exhaled, her fingers tracing the edge of the worn paper. Chaos and order. Anger and forgiveness. Light and shadow. The principle of polarity. Had her mother known she would struggle with this balance? Or was something greater at play, weaving meaning into the spaces between past and present, turning coincidence into certainty?

She closed her eyes, her mother's voice echoing in her mind like a melody she had forgotten the tune of. "*Opposites are not enemies, Luna. They are partners, dancing together to create the rhythm of life. Know that when there is one, you can follow its path to the other.*"

Her thoughts drifted to the encounter with her father, the weight of his confession mingling with the pain of her own memories. He had failed her, yes, but his guilt had been palpable, his regret as raw as her anger. For years, she had carried the belief that his silence was indifference, but now she wondered if it had been something else entirely. **"There is no truth on this plane, only half-truths."** A subtle phrase passing through her mind as if her mother was guiding her understanding.

Luna opened her eyes, her gaze falling on the journal again. The words seemed to shimmer in the dim light, their meaning just out of reach. Her mother had always been able to see the connections, to weave together the threads of meaning that others overlooked. Luna had dismissed it as naivety, but now she wondered if it had been wisdom all along.

She turned the page, her breath catching as she read the next passage.

"Forgiveness is not a gift we give to others, but a gift we give to ourselves. It is the act of releasing the chains that bind us, freeing our hearts to beat in harmony with the rhythm of the universe. To forgive is not to forget, but to acknowledge the pain and choose to move forward anyway."

The words hit her like a wave, their wisdom undeniable. She thought of her father, of the years they had spent apart, each of them bound by their own pain. She wasn't ready to forgive him—not yet—but, she felt it would come, in time. The weight of her anger was exhausting, a burden she was no longer sure she wanted to carry.

Luna closed the journal gently, her hands trembling slightly. The path ahead was uncertain, but she felt the first stirrings of something she needed desperately: hope.

She rose from the table, her gaze drifting to the small window. The forest outside was bathed in darkness, its shadows deepening as the sun sank below the horizon. The clearing called to her, its quiet presence a balm for her restless spirit.

Grabbing her new soft sweater, she stepped outside, the cool fall air brushing against her skin. The path to the clearing was familiar now, its twists and turns etched into her memory. As she walked, her thoughts quieted, the rhythmic crunch of her boots against the earth grounding her in the present.

When she reached the hill, she paused, her gaze sweeping over the clearing. The wildflowers glowed softly in the fading light, their delicate petals swaying in the breeze. She climbed to the top, her steps slow and deliberate, and sank onto the grass.

The silence of the forest enveloped her, its stillness broken only by the distant call of a bird and the rustle of leaves. Luna closed her eyes, her hands pressing into the cool earth. She focused on her breath, the rise and fall of her chest syncing with the rhythm of the world around her.

Her mother's words echoed in her mind once more. "Find the rhythm, Luna. Feel the frequency at which life vibrates."

She let herself sink into the moment, her thoughts drifting like leaves on a stream. Luna allowed herself to be still—not searching, not striving, just being. The hum of the earth beneath her seemed to grow stronger, resonating with something deep within.

Luna's breath hitched as a memory surfaced, unasked. She was a child again, sitting cross-legged in this very spot as her mother painted the horizon. "What are you painting?" she had asked, her voice filled with innocent curiosity.

"Not what, my love," her mother had replied, her eyes alight with a joy that seemed otherworldly. "How... The rhythm, the connection, the dance of light and shadow. It's all there, if you look closely enough." She had traced the air with her fingertips as if guiding an unseen current, her gaze drifting toward the canvas with quiet intent. "A painting is more than color on a surface—it's a vessel. If you listen, if you truly see, it will remember."

The memory faded, but its impact lingered. Luna opened her eyes, the clearing around her bathed in the soft glow of the moon. She wasn't sure what she was searching for, but for the first time, she felt like she was moving closer to it.

As she sat in the clearing, the stars above beginning to shimmer in the deepening sky, Luna allowed herself a moment of peace. The path ahead was uncertain, but for now, she was content to simply exist within the rhythm of the moment.

SEVEN

PATTERNS AND PORTENTS

T he next morning, Luna skipped breakfast. Her stomach had been in knots since yesterday. It wasn't just the argument with her father; it was the heaviness of ignoring the true source of her trauma. As she stepped down the beaten path toward pyramid hill, she paused. This morning, she chose a less-traveled path to the left. The air was crisp, the sunlight cutting through the lingering fog with sharp precision. Luna soon found herself standing at the edge of an abandoned woodworking shed deep in the woods, her fingers brushing against the weathered wood of the doorframe. The scent of rotting, moldy wood mingled faintly with damp earth, filling her senses.

The shed looked smaller now than she remembered, its walls hunched as though burdened by the weight of time. But it wasn't the space that made her chest tighten; it was the memories bound within these walls. Memories she had spent years escaping.

Her hand hovered over the latch, hesitating. She told herself it was just a building, just wood and nails. Yet the thought of crossing the threshold made her stomach churn. With a deep breath, she pushed the door open, the creak of the hinges breaking the stillness.

The interior was dim, the light filtering through cracks in the walls casting long shadows across the room. Tools hung neatly on the far wall, their edges dulled by years of disuse. The workbench sat in the center, its surface marred with scratches and stains that told the story of countless projects. Everything was as it had been—except for the feeling.

Luna stepped inside, her movements tentative, as though crossing an invisible threshold into a space she no longer recognized. The air felt heavier here, thick with echoes of the past, each breath laced with an unease that pressed down on her chest. Her gaze wandered to the far corner of the shed, where shafts of light broke through the wooden slats, illuminating motes of dust swirling aimlessly in the stillness.

Her eyes caught on a small carving perched on the edge of the workbench—a figurine of a bird, its wings poised as though ready to take flight. She remembered being a child, running carefree through the forest, the weight of the world still years away. That bird, so small and delicate, now felt like a cruel reminder of the innocence she had lost.

A shallow breath escaped her as the memories surged forward, relentless and sharp. She saw herself as a teenager, standing frozen in this very spot, the laughter she'd carried as a child forever silenced. Then the truth she had spoken, trembling and desperate, had hung in the air like fragile glass, shattering under the weight of disbelief. The betrayal in their silence—those who should have protected her—cut deeper than the event itself, teaching her how easily the truth could be dismissed and how quickly the world could turn cold.

The room seemed even smaller now, the walls closing in as her heart raced. Her fingers brushed against the edge of the workbench, the rough wood biting into her palm as if grounding her to a painful moment. She remembered the months, years even, after that day—how she had learned to bury everything, to build walls so thick and high that even she couldn't climb them.

Her breaths came faster, shallow and ragged, as the storm inside her grew louder. The soft hum of the forest outside, the birdsong and rustling leaves, all faded into a muffled haze. She stumbled back, her hand catching the edge of the workbench as though it might anchor her, but the weight of her emotions threatened to pull her under.

Above her, the shafts of light seemed almost brighter now, cutting through the dim space like thin blades. They illuminated the dust still dancing in the air, a swirl of movement within the silence. Luna's gaze followed the gentle patterns, the chaos of the whirling particles strangely mesmerizing. Her chest tightened, her throat constricting as a single tear traced a hot path down her cheek. She surrendered to it—the grief, the anger, the raw ache that had waited too long to be felt.

Breathe, Luna. Her mother's voice whispered in her mind, soft and steady, as if carried on the air around her. *Feel the rhythm, the ebb and flow. Let it carry you.*

Her trembling fingers curled against the edge of the workbench, the wood grounding her as she closed her eyes and forced herself to focus on her breathing. Inhale. Exhale. In. Out. The words from the journal surfaced in her mind, their meaning sharper now than ever before: *Chaos and order are two sides of the same coin. One cannot exist without the other.*

The storm within her began to ease, its jagged edges softening as her breaths slowed. Each inhale seemed to draw strength from the shafts of light above her, each exhale releasing fragments of the darkness that had long weighed her down. *Chaos is not the end, but a beginning,* her mother's voice seemed to whisper. *Even in brokenness, there is a chance to create something new.*

When Luna opened her eyes, her gaze fell on the bird figurine once more. It seemed to watch her, its carved wings poised mid-flight, frozen in the moment before it would take to the air. She reached out, brushing her fingers gently against its surface. The bird, a symbol of freedom she had once thought lost to her, now felt like a quiet promise—a reminder that she could choose to rise, even from the deepest shadows.

Luna straightened, her grip on the workbench steadying her as her breath settled into an easy rhythm. The shed hadn't really changed, but she had. She could feel it in the way her chest no longer felt hollow, in the way her thoughts no longer spiraled. The shadows of the past were still here, lingering at the edges, but they no longer felt insurmountable, no longer needed to be held under lock and key. They were part of her story, but they no longer defined her present.

The morning sun rising higher in the sky as Luna retraced her steps toward the cabin. Her hands were unsteady, the echoes of the woodworking shed still swirling in her mind, but the calm she had managed to grasp held firm. She knew she couldn't stop here. The shadows of her past demanded more light, and her mother's art studio felt like the next place to seek it.

Miriam had mentioned the studio the day before, the memory of this place floating at the back of her mind since. Though hesitant, Luna knew the time had come. With a deep breath, she followed the winding path toward the small structure on the outskirts of the community. It was a modest building, its wooden walls covered in ivy, but it stood tall against the backdrop of the forest—a place of creation amidst nature's embrace. She could feel her mothers growing presence as she came near.

The door creaked softly as she pushed it open. Inside, the air was thick with the smell of turpentine and dried paint. The studio was exactly as she remembered: canvases leaned against every available surface, their abstract forms alive with color and movement. Jars of brushes and palette knives crowded a table in the corner, their bristles stiff with dried pigment. Light streamed through the tall windows, illuminating the space with a warm, golden glow.

Luna stepped inside, her fingers trailing along the edge of a nearby easel. A half-finished painting rested on it, the strokes bold and deliberate. Her mother's presence was everywhere—in the meticulous organization of tools, in the riot of colors that filled the room, in the small details that spoke of a life dedicated to creation.

Luna thought stepping inside would bring her to tears; it was one of the reasons she had hesitated so long to enter. But the overwhelming grief she expected didn't come. Instead, she felt something quieter, deeper—a sense of presence that made her breath catch. It wasn't absence that filled the room; it was her mother's essence, as though Margaret had been walking beside her these past few days, guiding her steps. Luna realized she felt closer to her mother now than she ever had, as if the walls they'd both built in life had crumbled, leaving only connection in their place.

She moved to the center of the room, her gaze falling on stacks of journals arranged on a writing table. Miriam had given her one, but there were more—dozens, maybe, each one a potential treasure trove of her mother's thoughts. Luna reached for the nearest one, its leather cover soft beneath her fingers. She opened it carefully, the pages brittle with age.

The first entry was dated the year Luna was born. Her mother's handwriting was steady, the words flowing across the page like a river. As she read, Luna felt the youth in her mothers pen strokes.

"To create is to connect. Art is the bridge between the seen and the unseen, a language that speaks to the soul. In every stroke, there is meaning. In every color, there is truth."

Luna swallowed hard, the words striking a chord deep within her. Her mother's art had always seemed otherworldly, imbued with a magic Luna had never fully understood. Reading her thoughts, she could see it clearly now—it was deeper than magic. It was intention, purpose, and something undeniably real. A deliberate, almost sacred act of weaving the threads of the universe into something tangible.

She turned the page, her breath catching at a delicate sketch of the oak tree. Its roots sprawled into intricate patterns, mirroring the stars above. Below the drawing, her mother had written:

"The oak holds the rhythm of the earth. Its roots mirror the heavens, its branches reach for the cosmos. It reminds us to stay grounded while seeking the infinite."

Luna traced the lines with her finger, the memory of sitting beneath that very tree only yesterday fresh in her mind. Her mother's voice seemed to whisper through the room, her teachings unfolding in ways Luna had never expected.

Her gaze drifted to the opposite page. The handwriting there was bolder, more deliberate.

"Balance is never found in solitude but in union. One half is powerless

without the other."

The phrase was underlined twice, with a faint, almost hesitant scrawl beside it:

"Trust the roots you know."

Luna frowned, the words stirring something unspoken. Her mind flickered to Ezra—the boy who had once walked these forest paths with her, who spoke her mother's language of symbols and secrets. Could her mother have meant him?

She flipped through more pages, skimming sketches, musings, and snippets of poetry. Then, near the middle of the journal, a passage stopped her cold.

To *Luna*, In every question, there is a rhythm. In every answer, a vibration. You are the key, my love. Trust yourself.

Luna's breathing fractured under the moment's pressure. This wasn't abstract philosophy; it was personal. A message, not just for understanding the world, but for understanding herself.

Her hands trembled as she read the words, her chest tightening. Luna checked the most recent date once more. *I was only 7 months old... How?— These aren't just journals—they're guides.* Luna suddenly realized. Messages left behind for her to find when she was ready. Luna couldn't place the feeling of knowing, but she felt her mother had a different sense for time then she understood. And though Luna didn't feel ready, the journal seemed to suggest otherwise.

She closed the book gently, her heart heavy with emotion and confusion of the possible and impossible. The studio felt alive around her, its energy humming in tune with her own. In that moment, she allowed herself to believe that her mother had known her better than she knew herself.

Luna fumbled, an unusually clumsy moment, as she went to place the old journal back, tripping over her own foot, she bumped the table. A short stack of journals tumble over, a few dropping to the ground. "Sorry, sorry, sorry." Luna shouted to her mothers presence, as she rushed to pick them up. On the ground in front of her, one of the journals laid open. A simple but purposeful sketch.

A circle inside a square, inside a triangle, inside a circle—

But, It wasn't the symbol that caught her eye. She lifted the journal for a closer look, it was the note underneath the circle that sent a shiver down her spine.

"Find Elias to make sense of it."

This note wasn't addressed to her, but she understood that this was a message from her mother, and it was of great importance. A resonating pulse rippled through her body as she read the note once more through the filter of tearing eyes, she confirmed the deeper meaning as it resonated in her, in the rhythm of her heart.

Taking a deep breath, Luna rose and held the journal close to her chest. She wasn't sure what the next step would be, but for now, she would let the message, and symbol settle, their meaning unfolding in its own time, this she was sure of.

The sun dipped lower, casting long shadows across the studio floor. Luna stepped outside, the cool evening air grounding her. She looked back at the studio, its windows glowing softly in the fading light. It was a place of creation, of connection, of truth. And she knew she would return.

Luna carried the journal close to her chest as she walked back toward the cabin, the quiet of the evening pressing softly around her. Her steps were measured, deliberate, as though the weight of what she had found required care to bear. The sun dipped lower in the sky, the golden light softening into a warm amber glow that filtered through the trees.

The geometric sketch and the name "Elias" burned in her mind, repeating like a quiet drumbeat. Who was Elias? The name stirred something familiar, though she couldn't place it. A fragment of memory lingered at the edge of her thoughts, frustratingly out of reach.

Back at the cabin, Luna settled into the small chair by the window, placing the journal carefully on the table. She stared at the cover for a long moment before flipping it open again, her fingers tracing the lines of the sketch. The shapes—the circle, square, and triangle—seemed simple, but their arrangement felt deliberate, like a key waiting for the right lock.

Her mother's words echoed in her mind: "*Find Elias to make sense of it.*"

Luna sighed, leaning back in the chair as her thoughts swirled. She pulled the first journal Miriam had given her closer, flipping through its pages for any mention of the name. The entries were rich with her mother's reflections on art, philosophy, and the principles that seemed to govern her life, but there was no sign of Elias.

Frustration prickled at the edges of her mind, but she forced herself to breathe deeply, her mother's teachings grounding her once more: "*Every question has its rhythm; every answer, a vibration.*"

The hum that had settled beneath her skin since arriving in the community grew stronger as she closed her eyes, a subtle vibration that seemed to echo in her very bones. She let the steady rhythm of her breath guide her, slow and deliberate, each inhale pulling her deeper into the quiet and each exhale releasing the noise of her thoughts. The chaos of her mind began to still, replaced by a calm so profound it felt almost tangible, like the hush before a storm.

As the calm deepened, a faint pressure began to build behind her forehead, subtle at first but growing with each passing moment. It wasn't painful, but insistent, as though something within her was straining to break free, pushing against the barriers she had long since erected.

Images began to rise, unbidden and fragmented, as if her mind were drawing them from a hidden well: the oak tree standing resolute against the sky, its roots reaching deep into the earth; the studio, light streaming through dusty windows, illuminating her mother's easel; the clearing at Pyramid Hill, bathed in soft twilight, the air charged with a sense of something just beyond her grasp.

Her breath hitched as the visions shifted. Her mother's hands appeared, deft and confident, painting broad strokes on a canvas. Each stroke seemed alive, the colors glowing faintly as they merged into a swirling geometric pattern—precise yet organic, like it had grown naturally from the canvas itself. The symbol pulsed with light, its meaning tantalizingly close, and then it dissolved into flashes.

A face emerged, blurred at first, but carrying a sense of deep familiarity. The features teased at the edges of recognition—a warm smile, eyes that held understanding—but before Luna could place it, the image wavered and shifted. Was it a dream? A memory? Or something else entirely?

Her eyes snapped open, the connection breaking like a thread pulled too taut. She gasped, the room around her suddenly too solid, too still. Her chest rose and fell with sharp breaths as she ran a hand through her hair, trying to ground herself.

The answers felt so close, brushing against the edges of her consciousness, but they remained elusive, like water slipping through her fingers. The hum beneath her skin softened, fading into the background, but its echo lingered, a quiet reminder that something greater was waiting to be found.

Her gaze drifted back to the journal, and a thought struck her. *Perhaps Miriam might know something about Elias. If her mother had confided in anyone, it would have been her.*

The community was quieter now, the sounds of the day giving way to the softer murmurs of evening. Luna found Miriam near the gathering hall, refreshing the flowers at her sister's memorial. Her aunt looked up as she approached, her expression warm but tinged with curiosity.

"Luna," Miriam greeted her, setting down a bundle of wildflowers. "What brings you out here?"

Luna hesitated, clutching the journal in her hands. "I found something in the studio," she said slowly. "A sketch, and... a name. Elias. Does that mean anything to you?" Luna said, flipping the journal towards Miriam for a closer look.

Miriam's smile faltered, her brow furrowing as she leaned against the table. "Elias," she repeated, the name rolling off her tongue like a distant memory. "I haven't heard that name in years. Your mother mentioned him a few times, but she was always... vague."

"Vague how?" Luna pressed, her pulse quickening.

Miriam crossed her arms, her gaze distant, as if sifting through old memories. "It always struck me as odd. On the rare occasions she mentioned his name, it was almost by accident, like a footnote to a thought she hadn't meant to share. All she ever told me was that he was someone she had studied with, someone who helped her make sense of what she thought she knew. But, that was long before you were born. I don't know if she ever kept in touch with him after that."

The air hitched behind her ribs. "Do you know where he is? Or how I can find him?"

Miriam shook her head, her expression softening into something that bordered on regret. "I wish I did. For a time, I wondered..." She hesitated, her voice dropping slightly. "I wondered if there was something more between them, but now I think it was something else entirely. Your mother was wise, but she was protective—not just of her knowledge, but of him. As if even speaking his name too often might disrupt... something." Miriam's eyes narrowed slightly, her tone taking on a note of quiet certainty. "But if she left you that message, Luna, it means she believed you would find him when the time was right."

Luna's grip on the journal tightened as the weight of her mother's faith pressed against her doubts. The questions burned brighter now, their answers hidden just beyond her grasp.

Miriam reached out, her hand resting lightly on Luna's shoulder. "Trust yourself," she said softly. "Your mother believed in you. You need to believe in yourself too."

Luna nodded, though the uncertainty in her chest didn't fade. As she made her way back toward the cabin, the name Elias repeated in her mind, each syllable carrying with it the promise of something she couldn't yet understand. "I have to figure this out. Maybe the answer is in the other journal, and I just didn't see it." As her mind wandered in thought, she looked up to see that her feet had not taken her to the cabin as intended.

The air beneath the old oak tree was cool and still, its roots sprawling like veins across the earth. "Hmm... ok. I get it, not in the journal." Finally trusting in the path, the rhythm of life.

Luna lowered herself to the ground, folding her legs beneath her in a quiet, deliberate motion. She rested her hands lightly on her knees, her palms facing upward as if inviting the energy of the earth and sky to meet within her. The rough bark of the oak pressed against her back, grounding her in its ancient strength as she closed her eyes, letting the stillness of the moment settle over her. She placed the journal beside her, its presence a silent companion as she prepared herself.

Luna closed her eyes and inhaled deeply, letting the rhythm of her breath match the gentle sway of the tree's branches above. Her mother's voice lingered in her memory, soft yet insistent: "Find the rhythm, Luna. Feel the frequency at which life vibrates."

The name, Elias, whispered through her mind, mingling with fragments of her mother's teachings. Luna imagined her mother's steady hands guiding her, imagined the connection they had shared when she was young, before everything had unraveled. She clung to that feeling now, reaching within herself as though searching for a thread that could lead her to understanding.

Her breathing slowed, the world around her fading as she turned her focus inward. She visualized the geometric symbol from the journal—the circle, square, and triangle—its lines glowing faintly in her mind's eye. She let it guide her, drawing her deeper into the quiet expanse of her thoughts. For a moment, she felt weightless, the hum of the forest around her blending with the rhythm of her own pulse.

And then the shadows crept in.

Memories surfaced: the shed, the pain, the disbelief in her father's eyes. Her chest tightened, the rhythm of her breath faltering as her thoughts spiraled out of control. She struggled to pull herself back, to quiet the chaos, but the harder she tried, the more elusive the calm became.

Her mother's voice flickered faintly: "*Opposites are identical in nature but different in degree. Anger and joy, chaos and serenity—they are the same.*"

The words steadied her momentarily, but the connection slipped away like sand through her fingers. Her breathing quickened, frustration bubbling to the surface. She opened her eyes abruptly, the serene energy of the tree now a stark contrast to the storm within her.

She pressed her palms against the cool earth, her head bowing forward as she tried to calm herself. *Why can't I do this? Why can't I reach her?* The questions tore through her, their weight leaving her breathless.

"You won't find answers in this state," a voice interrupted, low and melodic, yet firm.

Luna's head snapped up, her eyes meeting those of a woman standing a few feet away. She was tall and willowy, her presence both grounding and ethereal. Her skin glowed faintly in the dappled sunlight, her dark hair cascading over her shoulders in loose waves. She wore a simple linen dress, and in her hands, she held a small bundle of herbs tied with twine.

"I didn't mean to startle you," the woman said, her tone gentle but unwavering. She stepped closer, her gaze steady as she studied Luna with a quiet intensity. "But your energy—it's clouded. I could feel it from the path."

Luna blinked, momentarily caught off guard. "Who... are you?" she managed, her voice still shaky from the meditation's collapse.

The woman smiled faintly, her lips curving in a way that was both kind and knowing. "Althea," she said simply. "We haven't met. I moved to Everwood a few years ago." She hesitated, her gaze searching Luna's face before continuing. "I ran into Miriam this morning. She thought I might be able to help."

Luna frowned, her gaze dropping to the ground. "Help?" she echoed, her voice tinged with skepticism. "I don't think anyone can help me right now."

Althea crouched beside her, her movements fluid and unhurried, as though she had all the time in the world. "I wasn't sure if I should come," she admitted softly. "Uncertainty surrounds those who are caught between paths. You've been standing at a crossroads, undecided whether to move forward or turn back to the life you left behind. But now..." Her tone shifted, steady and assured. "Now, I see you've chosen your path."

Luna tensed, her jaw tightening. "And how do you know all this?"

Althea's smile didn't falter. "Because I've been where you are," she said softly. "Frustrated. Lost. Reaching for something that always seems just out of grasp. But the truth is, the answers you seek can't come to you until you're ready to receive them."

She paused, her expression reflective, as though weighing her next words carefully. Slowly, she lifted her hand and rested her palm gently on Luna's hesitating forehead. Althea inhaled deeply, her eyes fluttering closed as she seemed to attune herself to Luna's essence.

"You have great potential, Luna. That, I am certain of," she said, her tone tinged with quiet awe. "I've never encountered such energy in someone unpracticed. Quite honestly, it's stronger than many who have been practicing for years."

Her hand lowered as she glanced up at the old oak, a soft chuckle escaping her lips. "Now I see why Margaret was so adamant that I come live here," she added, a smile playing at her lips as if she were letting Luna in on a long-kept secret.

Luna's eyes lit up at the sound of her mothers name. "You knew my mother?"

"Oh yes. Your Mother..." Althea paused again, as if searching herself and making connections of truths out of half truths. "I was speaking at a conference in St. Louis when I met her for the first time. She was very convincing to get me to come here to share my story. She didn't need to be as convincing to make me stay though. This place, it's energy, it felt right."

Luna smiled, realizing it didn't take long for her to stop thinking about leaving too, despite the pain this place brought.

Luna's chest tightened, her breath hitching. The calm she had fought for felt further away than ever. "I thought I was ready," she said, her voice barely above a whisper. "But maybe... maybe I'm not."

Althea reached out, her hand hovering just above Luna's. "You're closer than you think," she said. "But you're holding on too tightly to what you believe the answers should be. Let go, Luna. Your essence will guide you when you're ready to listen."

The words hung in the air, their weight both comforting and challenging. Luna stared at Althea, her mind racing with questions she couldn't yet form into words.

"What was your speech about? The one my mother came to see?" Luna asked, her voice quieter now, though the curiosity in her tone mirrored the rhythm of her mother's wisdom.

"Chakras," Althea explained briefly, a soft smile touching her lips. "The energy centers of the body and how they connect us to... well, everything."

Luna nodded faintly, the weight of the morning pressing down on her. Her shoulders sagged slightly, and she ran a hand through her hair, her movements slower now, as though her body were catching up with the emotional strain of the day.

Althea studied her for a moment, then spoke gently. "Yours are blocked."

Luna blinked, caught off guard by the certainty in Althea's voice. "Blocked?" she echoed.

Althea nodded. "Your energy isn't flowing the way it should. The body holds onto pain, grief, resistance—whether we realize it or not. And when energy can't move freely, it affects everything. Your clarity. Your emotions. Even your body." She hesitated before adding, "I can help you, if you're open to it."

Luna exhaled slowly, uncertain yet drawn in by the quiet conviction in Althea's words. "How?"

"Not now," Althea said, shaking her head slightly. "First, you need to quiet your mind. Sit with what you've learned today. Let your thoughts settle, then find a way to let it go." Her gaze softened, but there was something firm beneath it. "When you're ready, come find me. There's work to be done."

Her tone held no urgency, only quiet assurance, as if she knew Luna's path would lead her there in time. With that, Althea turned and walked away, her presence lingering like the faint scent of the herbs she carried, a whisper of calm left in her wake.

Luna nearly jumped to her feet, tempted to declare she is ready now, but she knew it to be a lie.

Still seated at the base of the oak tree, her thoughts a tangled mess of frustration, curiosity, and a faint, fragile hope. Her mother's teachings, Althea's words, the geometric symbol—all of it swirled together, forming a puzzle she wasn't sure she was ready to solve. She turned to give thanks to Althea, only to see she was already gone.

She couldn't rest now, but she understood what Althea had meant. There was only one place, one person that could help her rest her mind from these puzzles. Recalling his little joke. '*Maybe next time you can come find me.*'

The path to Ezra's studio curved gently through the trees, their leaves tinged with the first hues of autumn—golden yellows, fiery oranges, and deep russets. A soft breeze stirred the branches, sending a rustle of leaves overhead that created a soothing cadence, like a quiet hymn to the changing season. Luna walked slowly, her thoughts a jumble of questions and doubts. Yet, with every step closer to Ezra's space, her mind grew quieter, the tension that had gripped her chest beginning to ease.

The studio stood at the edge of the main road, not far from the path leading to her cabin, its simple wooden frame bathed in the warm glow of the setting sun. The open door revealed a space alive with color: canvases leaning against the walls, jars of paint arranged in chaotic harmony on the worktable, and the faint scent of turpentine wafting through the air.

Ezra was there, standing before a large canvas, his hand moving with measured grace as he added a streak of deep blue to the swirling forms already taking shape. His dark curls fell slightly into his eyes, and his sleeves were rolled up, revealing forearms streaked with paint.

He didn't notice her at first, lost in the rhythm of his work.

Luna hesitated at the doorway, her heart quickening as she watched him. The sunlight caught the faint sheen of sweat on his brow, the strong lines of his profile illuminated by the golden light. For a moment, she forgot why she had come. All she could think about was the ease with which he moved, the quiet power of his presence.

"Hi Ezra," she said softly, her voice carrying just enough to draw his attention.

He froze for a fraction of a second, his brush hovering above the canvas. Then he turned, his eyes lighting up as they met hers. "Luna!" he said, his voice a mix of surprise and warmth. A smile spread across his face, wide and unguarded. "You found me."

"If I'm not mistaken, that is what you asked for," she said, a faint smile tugging at her lips.

He quickly covered the canvas, giving Luna his full attention, and hiding his unfinished work from her prying eyes. He set the brush down carefully, wiping his hands on a rag as he crossed the room to meet her. "And here I thought I'd have to wait a lifetime for that," he teased, his grin softening into something more sincere. "Come in."

She stepped inside, the vibrant energy of the studio enveloping her like a warm embrace. The walls seemed alive with Ezra's creations—Beautiful landscapes of the rolling hills nearby, children of the community playing and living life. A stark contrast from the abstract work of her mother. "It's beautiful," she said, her voice hushed as she took it all in.

Ezra's gaze lingered on her, his smile small but genuine. "I'm glad you think so," he said. "But it's not half as beautiful as seeing you here."

Luna glanced at him, her cheeks flushing slightly. She busied herself by examining a nearby canvas, its fiery reds and oranges of a beautiful sunset. "You've been busy," she said, her tone light, though her heart raced at his words.

"It keeps me sane," he admitted, leaning against the edge of the work-table. "There's something about the way paint moves on a canvas—it's like finding order in chaos. Or maybe it's the other way around."

She turned to face him, her arms crossed loosely over her chest. "Do you ever feel like it's more than that? Like what you're painting isn't just... yours?"

Ezra tilted his head, considering her question. "Sometimes," he said. "There are moments when it feels like the painting is guiding me, not the other way around. Like it's already there, waiting to be found."

His words struck a chord deep within her, echoing her mother's teachings about connection and rhythm. For the first time in days, though, she didn't want to dwell on the mysteries. She wanted to lose herself in this moment, in the way Ezra's presence seemed to steady her.

"Do you always talk like that, or is it just when I'm around?" she asked, her tone teasing but her eyes warm.

Ezra chuckled, the sound low and rich. "You bring it out of me, I suppose."

They fell into an easy silence, the air between them charged but comfortable. Luna let herself relax, the tension in her shoulders softening as she leaned against the edge of the worktable.

"Can I offer you a glass of wine?" Ezra offered, glancing over to an open bottle and a glass he had been sipping on.

Luna hadn't had a glass since the night her aunt called her with the news. "That sounds wonderful. Thank you." Luna accepted.

Ezra retrieved another glass from a nearby cabinet and began to pour. The deep red of the wine, reminiscent of shades in the sunset painting behind him. Luna sat on the stool opposite Ezra and raised her glass, offering a symbolic toast before they sipped.

They sat in silence for a moment, stared into each others eyes. Luna's nerves finally breaking the silence. "What are you painting?" she asked after a moment, her voice soft.

Ezra paused, glancing at her with a faint smile, then at the covered canvas. "It's not quite ready, but like all my work, it's something I find to be breathtaking and need to capture for the world." He said.

Luna arched an eyebrow at his cryptic response but chose not to press further. She swirled the wine in her glass, watching the deep red hues catch the light before taking a slow sip. The flavor was rich and grounding, a perfect complement to the serene energy of Ezra's studio.

"I'd expect nothing less from you," she said lightly, her tone carrying an undertone of curiosity. "You've always had an eye for beauty."

Ezra smiled at her words, the kind of smile that didn't just reach his lips but softened the intensity in his eyes. "Beauty's everywhere, Luna," he said, his voice gentle. "But it's not often that it walks through my door."

The air between them seemed to shift, charged with a quiet intensity. Luna felt her cheeks flush again, and she turned her gaze to the painting of the sunset behind him, her fingers playing with the stem of her glass.

"You always did have a way with words," she said, attempting to keep her tone light, though her heart raced in her chest, and her cheeks flush with heat.

Ezra leaned forward slightly, his expression thoughtful. "And you've always had a way of making me want to say them," he admitted, his voice steady but quieter now. His gaze held hers for a moment longer than she expected, and Luna felt her heart flutter.

She broke the moment with a soft laugh, shaking her head. "Careful, Ezra. You're going to make me think I'm special or something."

His grin widened, the teasing spark returning to his eyes. "That's the thing, Luna. You are and always have been."

The sincerity in his voice left her momentarily speechless, her usual defenses faltering in the warmth of his words. She took another sip of her wine, hoping it would steady her, and set the glass down on the worktable beside her.

"So," she said, tilting her head with a playful smirk. "How is it that a guy like you is still single?"

Ezra let out a short laugh, leaning back in his chair. "A guy like me?"

"You know, ridiculously talented, annoyingly charming," she said, quirking a brow. "And yet, no one's managed to lock you down?"

He shook his head, swirling the wine in his glass. "Haven't found the right person, I guess." His voice was casual, but there was something else beneath it—something unspoken. "I've had relationships, but nothing that stuck. Nothing that felt... real."

Luna nodded, tracing the rim of her glass with her finger. "Yeah. Same."

For a moment, the weight of unspoken things hung between them—past disappointments, missed connections, the quiet ache of wanting something more.

Ezra studied her, his gaze thoughtful. "Guess that means we're both still waiting."

Luna's lips parted slightly, but no words came. She wasn't sure she trusted what might slip out if she answered. Instead, she let the silence settle, warm and expectant, stretching between them like a thread waiting to be pulled.

They fell into an easy rhythm after that, their conversation meandering between lighthearted banter and comfortable silences. Ezra poured them another glass of wine, and Luna let herself relax in a way she hadn't in weeks. The weight of her mother's journals, the unanswered questions, and the lingering tension with her father all seemed to fade, replaced by the simplicity of sharing this moment with him.

"Maybe I was wrong," Ezra said suddenly, his voice thoughtful as he studied her. "I said you hadn't changed much, but... I can see it now. You're different."

Luna tilted her head, her brows knitting together. "What do you mean?"

"You carry yourself differently," he said. "There's a quiet strength in you now—like you've been through the fire and come out the other side."

His words settled over her, warm and unsettling all at once. She looked down at her glass, her fingers tracing its rim. "I don't feel strong anymore," she admitted softly. "Most days, I feel like I'm barely holding it together."

"That's the thing about strength," Ezra said, his tone gentle but firm. "It doesn't always look the way we expect it to. Sometimes it's just getting through the day, even when you don't think you can."

Luna met his gaze, the sincerity in his eyes making her chest tighten. She wanted to argue, to dismiss his words as overly generous, but a part of her wanted to believe him.

"Maybe," she said finally, her voice barely above a whisper.

They sat in silence for a while after that, the warmth of the wine and the quiet hum of the studio filling the space between them. As the last rays of sunlight faded from the windows, Luna felt something shift within her—a small but significant step toward understanding, not just of the mysteries surrounding her, but of herself. Or perhaps, it was just the wine...

The bottle sat nearly empty on the worktable, its deep red reflecting the soft glow of the lanterns Ezra had lit as night fell. The warm light cast flickering shadows across the studio walls, holding the space in a soft glow, as if time had slowed to a whisper. Luna felt the effects of the wine in the warmth spreading through her chest and the easy laughter that flowed between them. Ezra's stories, his teasing remarks, and his thoughtful observations had drawn her out of herself, easing the weight she carried.

A comfortable silence settled between them, the quiet hum of the night pressing in around the studio. Luna traced the rim of her glass with a fingertip, exhaling softly.

"I should get going," she said at last. "If I stay any longer, I'll probably fall asleep right here."

Ezra smiled, a touch of mischief in his eyes. "Wouldn't be the worst thing in the world. The couch is pretty comfortable."

She rolled her eyes, rising from her seat. "Thanks, but I think my bed might be a bit more accommodating."

He stood as well, reaching for his jacket draped over the back of a chair. "At least let me walk you back," he offered, his tone casual but his expression earnest. "It's late, and the forest can get dark."

Luna hesitated for a moment, then nodded. "Alright," she said, her voice softer now. "If you insist."

The air outside was crisp, the night sky glittering with stars that seemed impossibly bright against the inky darkness. They walked side by side along the dirt path, their footsteps soft on the earth. Their conversation rose and fell with an effortless rhythm—sometimes playful, sometimes thoughtful—woven together by a quiet sense of ease.

"You've really made this place your own," Luna said, glancing at him. "The studio, your beautiful paintings—you've built a whole world for yourself here."

Ezra shrugged, his hands tucked into his pockets. "It's a good place for that. Happiness isn't found in things, Luna. It is in the memories and experiences made in the present moment that joy finds you. The community, the quiet... it gives me space to breathe and create... joy."

Luna felt the warmth rise to her cheeks, stirred by the way he looked at her. She turned her gaze back to the path, but the small smile tugging at her lips was impossible to hide.

As they approached the cabin, the warm glow spilling from the window illuminated the porch steps, casting long, golden beams across the forest floor. The soft hum of crickets and the occasional rustle of leaves filled the air, but between them, there was only the quiet rhythm of their footsteps and the unspoken weight of the moment.

They paused at the door, the space between them charged with an energy that felt both fragile and undeniable. Ezra stepped closer, his presence steady and reassuring, a quiet strength that made Luna's breath catch.

"I'm glad you came tonight," he said, his voice low and filled with something that felt like hope. "I've missed this—missed you."

Luna's heart fluttered, her chest tightening with a mixture of nervousness and exhilaration. "I'm glad I came too," she admitted, her voice barely above a whisper. "I really needed tonight, to get out of my head, to feel..." She trailed off, searching for the right words. "To feel like myself again."

Their eyes met, and for a moment, the world seemed to hold its breath. Ezra leaned in slowly, his movements deliberate, his intent clear. He gave her the chance to pull away, to turn from this moment if she wasn't ready. She didn't.

When their lips met, the kiss was soft and unhurried, a delicate melding of emotions that had lingered between them. It wasn't just an expression of the present—it was a quiet promise, a tether to the past and a spark of something new.

When they pulled apart, the air between them felt charged with an unspoken understanding. Luna hesitated, her hand brushing the door handle, her gaze lingering on his. She didn't need to speak the invitation—it was there in her eyes, in the way her lips parted as if forming words she couldn't quite say.

Ezra smiled, a warmth radiating from him that seemed to chase away the chill of the night. His voice was soft but firm, his choice in her clear. "Take your time, Luna Zephyr," he said. "We have a lifetime for this."

The words drifted around her like soft evening light, soothing and thrilling all at once. She nodded, a small, genuine smile curving her lips as she turned to the door. "Goodnight, Ezra."

"Goodnight, Luna," he replied, stepping back as she slipped inside, the door closing gently behind her.

Leaning against the wooden frame, Luna let out a long breath, her heart racing as the quiet of the cabin embraced her. The weight she carried didn't vanish, but it felt lighter, easier to bear. Tomorrow no longer loomed—it shimmered with possibility.

EIGHT

REST, REPLENISH, REJOICE

Luna woke with the dawn, the pale morning light filtering through the cabin's curtains and casting soft shadows across the wooden floor. She hadn't slept much, but somehow still felt... rested. The events of the previous evening replayed in her mind—Ezra's easy laughter, the warmth of his gaze, the soft press of his lips against hers. A faint smile tugged at her lips as she stretched beneath the quilt, the memories settling over her like a comforting embrace.

Her mother's journals rested on the bedside table, their presence no longer a source of pressure but of quiet encouragement. Today, she would begin to take the steps her mother had envisioned. She swung her legs over the edge of the bed, her bare feet meeting the cool wood. There was a spark within her now, a renewed sense of purpose that had been absent for far too long.

As she sat down for breakfast, the clarity sharpened. Between bites of toast and fresh berries left by Miriam—along with a much-needed cup of coffee—Luna began searching for moving services, making arrangements to pack up the remnants of her old life. She didn't know where she was going yet, but she knew with certainty that apartment would never be home again.

After finishing breakfast, Luna set out to find Althea. The healer's presence had lingered in her mind since their encounter beneath the oak tree, the promise of understanding and clarity drawing her forward.

She found her near the community garden, crouched among the herbs with the same serene focus that seemed to define her. The healer's hands moved with practiced care, gathering sprigs of lavender and rosemary as though each stem held a secret.

"Good morning," Luna called softly, not wanting to startle her.

Althea glanced up, a small smile curving her lips. "Luna," she said warmly, rising to her feet. "You're here earlier than I expected."

"Sorry, I can come back later if you're busy. I just didn't want to waste any more time," Luna admitted, her voice steady but laced with anticipation. "I'm ready to start... whatever it is you think I need."

Althea's smile deepened, her dark eyes gleaming with quiet approval. "No, it is a good time. I see you found your rest" she said simply. "Follow me."

She led Luna to a small clearing at the forest's edge, just beside her cabin, its boundary marked by a ring of smooth stones. The air here felt different—lighter, charged with a subtle energy that raised the hairs on Luna's arms. Althea gestured for her to sit on the soft grass, then took a seat across from her

"Before we begin," Althea said, her tone calm but firm, "you need to understand the foundation of what we'll be working on. The body has seven primary chakras—energy centers that govern different aspects of our physical, emotional, and spiritual well-being. When these centers are open and balanced, energy flows freely. When they're blocked, it can manifest as fear, anger, doubt, or even physical ailments."

Luna nodded, leaning forward slightly. "And mine... they're blocked?"

"Yes," Althea said without hesitation. "Not all of them, but enough that it's keeping you from connecting with your true self. The good news is, blocks aren't permanent. With focus and practice, they can be freed."

She reached into a small pouch at her side, pulling out seven smooth stones, each a different color, and arranged them in a line between them. "These represent the chakras," she said, pointing to each one in turn. "Root, Sacral, Solar Plexus, Heart, Throat, Third Eye, and Crown. Each one corresponds to a specific part of you—your grounding, your creativity, your willpower, your love, your truth, your intuition, and your connection to the universe."

Althea picked up the red stone, holding it between her fingers. "We'll start with the root chakra," she said. "It's the foundation of everything—your sense of safety, security, and belonging. When it's blocked, you'll feel disconnected, unstable, like you're always running but never arriving."

Luna swallowed, the description hitting uncomfortably close to home. "How do I unblock it?"

"By reconnecting with the earth," Althea said simply. "Close your eyes, Luna. Breathe deeply. Feel the ground beneath you, solid and unyielding. Let it hold you."

Luna obeyed, her breaths slowing as her attention shifted to the sensation of the earth beneath her. Althea's voice was a gentle current, guiding her deeper into herself. "Imagine roots growing from your body, strong and unbreakable, anchoring you to the ground. Feel them winding through the soil, seeking the core of the earth."

As Luna visualized the roots, a warmth began to bloom at the base of her spine, subtle at first but growing with each breath. The sensation spread outward, like the slow awakening of a fire, steady and grounding. The warmth carried with it a faint vibration, a low hum that seemed to resonate in harmony with the rhythm of her breath. It was as though the earth itself had answered her call, its energy rising to meet her.

She saw flashes in her mind's eye: a deep crimson glow, pulsing in time with her heartbeat. The roots of a tree burrowing deeper, intertwining with ancient stones, rivers of molten orange glowing beneath the surface. She felt the weight of the earth cradling her, not as a burden, but as a solid foundation, unshakable and eternal.

The warmth at her base intensified, becoming a gentle current flowing upward through her body. The hum turned into a song, low and melodic, carrying whispers of something she couldn't quite name—strength, stability, belonging. Luna couldn't recall the last time she wasn't running. But now, she was still—rooted, and deeply, profoundly connected.

"That's it," Althea murmured, her voice a soft echo. "Let the energy flow freely, grounding you, stabilizing you. Let it remind you that you belong here, in this moment, in this life."

Althea fell silent, allowing the healing to take its course. The silence was not empty but alive, filled with the subtle pulse of the earth's energy and Luna's steady breath. Minutes stretched into what felt like hours as Luna remained still, her focus unwavering, her sense of self expanding with every passing second.

When she opened her eyes, the world around her had transformed.

Althea sat in front of her, hands raised, palms facing Luna, her fingers dancing through the air. Luna glanced around—the shifting colors of the forest shimmered with new vibrancy. The golden sunlight filtering through the leaves felt brighter, warmer. The birdsong, layered and complex, carried each note distinctly, yet somehow wove into a larger, harmonious melody. The very air felt alive, humming with an energy that hadn't been there before—or perhaps she had simply never noticed it.

Luna tilted her head, confusion etching across her face as she noticed the sun, now much higher in the sky.

"It's okay, Luna. Yes, it has been three hours." Althea said gently, as if plucking the words directly from Luna's thoughts. "Time is a funny thing. You will see."

"Was that you moving that energy through me?" Luna asked, looking down at her hands.

"No, not exactly. I was merely helping the energy find you. Our bodies are highly sophisticated. I only needed to guide the energy in—your body knew where it was needed."

Luna nodded politely. She understood the words, but struggled to accept their truth.

Althea smiled, her expression serene. "You did very well," she said. "That was the first step. The other chakras will take more time, believe it or not, but you've made wonderful progress."

Luna exhaled slowly, her heart swelling with a sense of accomplishment. At last, she felt the potential her mother had spoken of—not as a distant ideal, but as something real, something within reach.

"What's next?" she asked, her voice steady.

Althea's gaze softened, her smile widening slightly. "We continue," she said simply. "One step at a time."

Luna stretched her legs carefully as she rose from the soft grass, the tingling warmth at the base of her spine still resonating through her body. The sensation felt both foreign and familiar, as though she were waking up a part of herself that had been dormant for years. She glanced at Althea, whose serene expression seemed to mirror the calm settling over her.

"Come," Althea said, motioning toward the cabin. "Let's enjoy a tea together."

Inside, the space was filled with the scent of dried herbs and warm wood. Althea moved with quiet ease, preparing tea as Luna settled at the table. A small plate of berries, figs, and sliced peaches sat between them, the colors rich and inviting. Luna hadn't realized how hungry she was until she picked up a berry, the tart sweetness grounding her further to the present moment.

"Thank you," Luna said, her voice quieter now, but not from fatigue—she felt lighter, more present. "I didn't realize how disconnected I'd been."

Althea poured the tea, her dark eyes gleaming with quiet understanding. "Most of us don't," she said. "The world encourages us to look outward, to seek answers in things and achievements. But the truth is, the answers are already within us. We just have to clear the path to hear them."

Luna let the warmth of the tea settle in her hands, the steam curling in delicate ribbons. As she sipped, her mind wandered. The energy she had felt earlier wasn't just physical—it was alive, moving within her. She remembered something from a physics lecture, how everything, when broken down to its core, is energy. Even solid matter wasn't truly solid—at the atomic level, it was mostly empty space, held together by forces unseen.

Her fingers twitched as she glanced down at her hands, the questions began to form.

She hesitated before speaking, thoughtful. "Althea, if everything is energy at its base—the air, the trees, even us—then are we working with it in the same way? Is that what this is?"

Althea's gaze flickered with approval, a knowing smile curving her lips. "It's not so different," she said. "What science calls energy, we've known for centuries as prana, chi, or life force. The principles are the same: everything vibrates, everything resonates. Energy is ever present—never created, never destroyed, only transmuted. When you align with those vibrations, you step into harmony with the universe."

Luna let the idea settle, her thoughts drifting back to her college lectures on quantum mechanics. She remembered reading about how particles could be connected across vast distances—entangled. That their state wasn't fixed until measured.

"So... are you saying our energy works kind of like," she began, still piecing it together. "Like how quantum entanglement connects particles—except here, it's not just physics, but something... deeper?"

Althea nodded, her expression thoughtful. "Exactly. The universe mirrors us, Luna. Just as those particles are connected, so are we—to everything. And just as measurement collapses a quantum state, our own awareness can shift our reality. When you clear your inner energy, you change what you attract and what you perceive."

Luna's breath curled in surprise. "So... it's like everything exists as a potential until it's observed. But here, the observation isn't external—it's internal."

Althea's smile deepened. "Now you're beginning to understand."

Luna turned to face Althea, her heart racing not from fear or anxiety, but from the sheer magnitude of what she was beginning to understand.

"What if I can't do it?" she asked softly. "What if I'm too... broken?"

Althea reached out, placing a hand gently on Luna's shoulder. Her touch was warm, steady. "You're not broken, Luna," she said firmly. "You're becoming. And that's the most powerful thing you can be."

The words settled over her like a balm, soothing the last remnants of doubt. Luna nodded, her resolve strengthening. "One step at a time," she echoed, a faint smile tugging at her lips.

Althea's laughter was soft but vibrant, like the chime of a bell. "Exactly."

Luna straightened her posture. "I'm ready for the next step. My Sacral Chakra."

Althea chuckled softly, a spark of approval in her eyes. "You're eager, and that's good. But each step must be taken in its own time." She took a deep breath, looking out the window. "Look outside—the sun has traveled the sky. When you are deeply connected, your energy feels replenished, feeding off the infinite, but your body still needs nourishment. That's enough for today."

Luna blinked, surprised. A part of her was reluctant to stop, but she understood.

"Rest, replenish, rejoice in your success of the day," Althea continued. "Embrace the new bliss in your heart, your new eyes for life. Let it resonate and take hold."

Luna heard the tiredness in her words. She had not considered the effects of this work on Althea.

She nodded, rising to her feet, the hum of energy in her body guiding her movements. A sudden wave of gratitude swelled in her chest—so powerful she had the urge to embrace Althea, to hold onto the moment, to let her teacher know just how deeply this had affected her.

Instead, she placed a hand over her heart, offering a small but meaningful gesture of appreciation.

"Thank you, Althea," she said, her voice warm with sincerity.

Althea inclined her head, her expression serene. "The work is yours, Luna. I'm only here to help you remember how the energy flows."

As Luna walked back toward the cabin, her eyes recognized the vivid color of the forest, as if for the first time; the sun now low in the sky, painting a sunset that only nature could capture, although it reminded her of the beauty from Ezra's brush. She felt a profound sense of possibility. The energy she had unlocked wasn't just a sensation; it was a doorway to a new way of being. She was beginning to see herself not as broken, but as becoming.

Her mother's voice echoed in her mind once more: "To create is to connect." Luna began to understand that the creation her mother spoke of wasn't just in the magic of art—it was the magic of life itself.

The cabin's kitchen was modest but functional, its wooden counters and aged stove carrying a charm that reminded Luna of simpler times. She stood at the counter, slicing vegetables with practiced ease, the rhythmic motion grounding her. The hum of energy from her work with Althea still resonated faintly, but now it blended with the anticipation of the evening ahead.

Rest, replenish, rejoice. Althea's words repeated in her mind, a gentle reminder to savor this moment of calm and connection. Luna could feel the shift in herself—something deeper than she could articulate. Her chest no longer carried the weight of tension, and the constant undercurrent of unease had quieted. Rooted. Present. It wasn't a feeling she'd known in a very long time, but now it anchored her—gentle, real, and full of quiet promise.

Ezra had been surprised but pleased when she'd appeared at his studio door earlier, inviting him over for dinner. His easy grin and playful acceptance had steadied the energy within her, reminding her of the quiet strength she had begun to associate with him.

Now, standing in the kitchen, she found herself stirring a sauce with more enthusiasm than expertise, her lips curving into a smile at the thought of him. A month ago, she would have approached this task with the same calculated precision she applied to quarterly reports—efficient, structured, and utterly devoid of feeling. Now? The counters were a disaster, a smear of flour dusted her sleeve, and somehow, a wooden spoon had ended up on the floor.

She wasn't entirely sure if she was making dinner or orchestrating a small kitchen catastrophe, but for once, she didn't care.

Ezra had a way of grounding her, his presence a steady reassurance that made her want to embrace the mess—both in the kitchen and in herself.

The sound of footsteps on the porch pulled her from her thoughts. She wiped her hands on a towel and opened the door to find Ezra standing there, a bottle of wine in one hand and a loaf of fresh bread in the other.

"Wine and bread—classic," Luna teased, stepping aside to let him in.

Ezra chuckled, his dark curls catching the faint glow of the porch light. "I figured I'd bring something to balance out your undoubtedly superior culinary skills," he quipped, his voice warm.

Luna rolled her eyes with a smile, closing the door behind him. "You give me too much credit. It's just pasta."

Ezra stepped into the warm glow of the kitchen, setting the wine and bread on the counter.

"Pasta made by you," he said with exaggerated reverence. "That makes it special." He took in the sights and smells before flashing her a teasing grin. "And I see you cook with as much passion as I paint," he mused, bending to pick up the wooden spoon.

Luna smirked, wiping her hands on a dish towel. "Only when I'm passionate about the guest," she shot back.

Ezra's grin deepened, his gaze lingering on her for just a second longer than usual. Something in the air between them shifted—comfortable, but charged with something unspoken.

Luna turned back to the stove, but her mind lingered on the moment. This place, this person, had changed her. Once, she had lived in a world of control and calculated moves, where mistakes—whether in business or the kitchen—felt like failures. But now, standing here, flour-covered and unbothered, she realized something had shifted. She was allowing herself to be present, to feel, to simply... be.

She shot a glance at Ezra, who was watching her with quiet amusement.

"Don't just stand there looking pretty," she said, arching a brow as she reached for the wooden spoon. "Make yourself useful."

Ezra laughed, the sound rich and unguarded, as he opened the cabinet and retrieved two glasses. He poured the wine, his movements unhurried, and joined her at the counter.

"What can I do?" he asked, his tone playful but sincere.

Luna glanced at him, her lips curving into a smirk. "You can stir the sauce without burning it, while I finish the salad." She said, nodding toward the simmering pot on the stove in front of her.

As he stepped closer, she caught a faint whiff of his cologne, warm and woodsy, blending seamlessly with the scent of garlic and herbs. Their hands brushed briefly as he reached for another spoon, the contact sending a gentle ripple through her—a spark of energy she had forgotten long ago.

They worked side by side, the silence between them broken only by easy conversation and shared laughter. Luna noticed how effortlessly they moved together, like two pieces of a puzzle slipping into place. She felt herself relax in his company, the energy flowing through her settling into something steady and warm.

When the food was ready, they set the table near the window, its view of the darkening forest framed by the soft glow of the cabin's lanterns. Ezra picked up the two glasses of wine, setting one in front of her before lifting his own.

"To new beginnings," he said, his voice steady but laced with meaning.

Luna hesitated, the weight of his words settling over her. She felt the unspoken promise in them, the hope that came with shedding the burdens of the past. Finally, she smiled, lifting her own glass. "To new beginnings," she echoed, the toast resonating deeply within her.

They clinked glasses, the sound crisp and clear in the quiet cabin. As they ate, Luna felt a warmth that went beyond the food and wine—a sense of belonging that had eluded her for so long.

After dinner, they worked together to clear the table, their movements unspoken yet perfectly in sync. When the dishes were done, they lingered by the counter, the space between them charged with possibility.

"Thank you for this," Ezra said softly, his gaze steady. "It's been a while since I've had a meal that didn't involve reheating something out of a can."

Luna laughed, the sound light and genuine. "You're welcome," she said, her voice softening. "I needed this too."

The quiet of the cabin wrapped around them, broken only by the faint sounds of the forest outside. Ezra reached out, his fingers brushing hers in a tentative gesture. Her breath faltered, the flutter in her chest echoing the openness she now felt at her core.

He exhaled, his thumb tracing a slow circle against her skin before he finally spoke. "I should go," he murmured, though he made no move to step away.

Luna's lips parted, caught between the weight of the moment and the lingering warmth of his touch. *You don't have to*, she wanted to say, but the words stayed trapped behind the steady rhythm of her heart.

Ezra hesitated. He had always been the one to push forward first, to move quickly, to mistake urgency for meaning. But this was different. She was different. He didn't want to rush this—didn't want to risk turning something real into just another fleeting moment.

Still, walking away wasn't easy. His fingers curled slightly, as if resisting the urge to pull her closer. But instead, he took a slow step back, his reluctance evident.

"Goodnight, Luna," he said, his voice softer now, almost reverent.

Luna watched him, her pulse thrumming with something unresolved. And then she moved.

"Oh, wait—you forgot," she said, stepping toward him.

Ezra blinked, brow furrowing in confusion. "Forgot what?"

Her fingers curled around the fabric of his collar, a hesitation lingering in the space between them. Then, with quiet resolve, she lifted herself onto her toes, pressing her lips to his in a kiss that was both delicate and charged.

It was a quiet declaration, her way of stepping into the connection that had been growing between them.

When she pulled back, her feet landing solidly on the ground again, she smiled up at him. "Goodnight, Ezra."

Ezra's grin widened, his eyes warm with understanding. "Goodnight, Luna."

As the door closed behind him, Luna leaned against it, her heart racing. The cabin's quiet seemed fuller now, the weight she carried feeling lighter, as though the evening had offered her not just connection, but a promise of what could be.

The cabin grew quiet once more. Luna leaned against the counter, a contented smile playing on her lips, the warmth of the evening settling into her bones. *Rest, replenish, rejoice.*

She had done just that. She felt steady, present—rooted in herself. But more than that, warmth radiated from deep within her, spreading outward like a current of golden light, filling every corner of her being.

The quiet hum of joy rising in her chest wasn't fleeting or fragile; it was vast, unwavering. She felt open in a way she never had before, as if she was back in meditation and something sacred had unlocked—a connection not just to herself, but to the world, to the unseen threads that bound her to life itself.

NINE

AWAKENING THE UNKNOWN

The morning dawned with a quiet stillness, the kind that seemed to hold its breath before something significant. Luna woke early, her body still humming with the warmth of her work the day before. Her heart, still full following her evening with Ezra, made her feel steady. Yet, the clarity she'd found after unblocking her root chakras was accompanied by a deep curiosity—and a growing respect for the power within her.

After breakfast, she stepped outside her cabin, intending to take a short walk to clear her mind before meeting Althea. The forest trail was alive with the sound of birdsong and the occasional rustle of leaves, the cool morning breeze brushing her skin. She hadn't gone far when she spotted Althea approaching from the opposite direction, her pace purposeful but unhurried.

"Good morning," Althea greeted, her serene smile catching the sunlight filtering through the canopy.

"And what a beautiful morning it is," Luna replied, a hint of surprise and bliss in her voice. "I was just heading to your cottage."

Althea nodded but didn't stop walking, motioning for Luna to follow her. "There's been a change of plans. Today's work will take us somewhere else—my shop, just outside of Eureka Springs."

Luna blinked, quickening her steps to match Althea's. "Your shop?"

"It's a space better suited for what we need to accomplish today. More privacy, and the resources I keep there will help us go deeper," Althea said, her tone calm but resolute.

The certainty in Althea's voice left little room for argument, but Luna's curiosity flared. She followed her mentor to the main road, where a compact, well-worn car was parked. Althea gestured for Luna to get in.

"Walking away feels... strange," Luna murmured, glancing back toward Everwood, an unexplainable discomfort settling in her chest—something she couldn't quite name.

Althea smiled faintly. "You'll return soon enough. For now, trust that this journey requires a step away from everything familiar."

The drive was quiet at first, the engine's hum blending with the crunch of gravel beneath the tires. Luna stared out the window, her gaze tracing the rolling hills and dense forest that flanked the road.

"Your energy yesterday revealed much," Althea said finally, her hands steady on the wheel. "It's rare to see such intensity, especially for someone unpracticed. It's both a gift and a responsibility."

Luna turned to her, the weight of the words pressing on her chest. "A responsibility?" she echoed, the word settling uneasily within her. "What does that mean?"

Althea's lips curved into a faint smile, her eyes momentarily flicking toward Luna. "It means your energy doesn't exist in isolation. It's part of a greater rhythm, a force that connects you to everything around you. When it's untapped and untrained, it's wild—unpredictable. But when it's directed..." She paused, choosing her words carefully. "It can create profound change, it can heal, it can create. That's what we're working toward."

Luna swallowed, the weight of Althea's explanation settling over her. A quiet tension coiled in her chest—an unspoken understanding that she was on the edge of something irreversible.

"And if we don't? If it stays untapped?" she asked, her voice quieter now, as if speaking the question aloud would solidify the truth she already sensed.

Althea's voice softened, yet it held an edge of urgency. "Then the potential remains unrealized, and you risk sending ripples of chaos into the world that will manifest as chaos in your life and others."

She held Luna's gaze, steady and unwavering. "But I don't believe you came here just for clarity. You came to understand—to see what your mother was trying to show you. Let's uncover it."

Her words resonated deep within Luna, stirring something that had been waiting to surface. This was why she was here. This was what her mother had been leading her toward. A quiet resolve settled over her, giving her the courage to continue into the unknown.

When they arrived, Luna stared at the small stone building tucked into the clearing. Ivy wove its way up the walls, framing a hand-carved wooden sign above the door that read Haven of Harmony.

"This place feels... sacred," Luna murmured as she stepped out of the car.

"It is," Althea said simply, unlocking the door. "This is where I do my most focused work. And it's where we'll align the rest of your chakras."

Inside, the air carried the faint scent of lavender and sage, grounding and calming. Shelves lined the walls, holding jars of herbs, oils, and tinctures, while a wide work table occupied the center of the room. In one corner, a low sitting area offered a space for reflection.

"What are you making?" Luna asked, watching as Althea began measuring herbs into a clay pot.

"A special tea," Althea replied, her hands steady. "It will nourish us during the meditation. This process may take hours. I don't want hunger or thirst to disrupt the flow."

The words sent a shiver through Luna. She sat down at the low table, her gaze fixed on Althea. "I trust you," she said finally, her voice barely above a whisper.

Althea met her eyes, her own gaze steady and reassuring. "Good," she said softly. "Because this will take all of you, Luna. And the answers you're seeking will come when you trust and let go."

Althea poured boiling water into the clay pot, the steam rising in fragrant tendrils. "We'll work through the chakras together, in a shared meditation. It's a practice I've only attempted a handful of times, and never with someone whose energy is quite like yours." She paused, her gaze softening as she lifted the tea to her nose. "Mmm, I love this smell."

Luna took a deep breath, her curiosity mingling with unease. "How does a shared meditation work?"

Althea handed her a small clay cup, the tea's earthy aroma grounding

Luna as she held it. "We'll begin by discussing each chakra in turn. I'll guide you through the theory and purpose of each, but the healing will require your willingness to release, to open yourself fully. When we meditate, our energies will align, allowing me to help you navigate any blocks that we discover. You may see or feel things in meditation. It is important that you be the observer of these things. Don't judge, or engage, just see them for what they are."

Luna sipped the tea, its warmth spreading through her chest. "Mmm... It tastes as good as it smells. So, what happens if we can't unblock them?"

Althea's smile was faint but reassuring. "Healing isn't always immediate, Luna. Some blocks take time, revisiting, patience. But every step, no matter how small, brings you closer to alignment."

A silence fell between them, broken only by the gentle clink of Althea setting her own cup on the table. "I must caution you, again," she said, her tone turning serious. "This is unfamiliar ground, even for me. Your energy flows in ways I don't fully understand, and while I believe we'll find balance, I can't promise how the process will unfold."

Luna's heart raced at the weight of Althea's words, but rather than fear, she felt something else—a pull, a readiness that defied her uncertainty.

She exhaled slowly, then gave a subtle nod. "Okay," she said, steady and sure. "I'm ready to follow."

Althea inclined her head, her expression a mix of gratitude and quiet determination. "Good," she said. "Then let's begin."

They moved to a corner of the shop where a thick rug and a circle of candles had been arranged. Althea gestured for Luna to sit, as Althea lit the array of candles, the flickering light casting a warm glow across the space.

Althea handed Luna a blanket and sat across from Luna, the chakra stones glinting faintly in the candlelight. Her expression was serene yet focused, a blend of teacher and guide. "We will be going on an inner journey Luna, but our bodies will be subject to the lack of movement, you may want to cover yourself some, you will appreciate it when we open our eyes again." Luna nodded with understanding.

She picked up the orange stone first, holding it between her fingers.

"The Sacral Chakra," she began, her tone warm yet serious, "is the seat of creativity, emotion, and pleasure. It governs your ability to connect with others, to feel passion, and to express yourself fully."

Luna swallowed, the weight of the words pressing against memories she'd tried to suppress. "And what happens when it's blocked?"

Althea's gaze softened, a flicker of understanding passing through her eyes. "When blocked, it can manifest as guilt, fear of change, or a disconnection from your own desires. Creativity and emotional balance suffer, and you might feel unworthy of joy."

Luna's jaw tightened, her mind flashing to the years she had spent numbing herself, pushing her emotions aside in favor of structure and control. "I think I know what that feels like."

Althea smiled with understanding before moving to the next energy center.

"The solar plexus chakra," Althea continued, holding a small yellow stone. "is your power center. It governs your sense of self, your confidence, and your ability to take action. When balanced, it allows you to move through life with purpose and clarity. When blocked, it can leave you feeling powerless, doubting your abilities."

Luna listened intently, nodding as Althea set the stone down and picked up the green one. "The heart chakra is unique," Althea said, her tone softening. "It bridges the physical and spiritual realms, connecting the lower chakras to the higher ones. It governs love, compassion, and forgiveness—but it's more than that." She paused, meeting Luna's gaze. "The heart has its own set of neurons, separate from the brain. It can sense, remember, and even think in its own way. Some believe the heart is the truest center of intelligence."

Luna blinked, her curiosity piqued. "I've heard of the gut having neurons, but the heart? I didn't know that."

Althea smiled faintly, the glow of the candles reflecting in her dark eyes. "It's true. The heart communicates with the brain constantly, sending more signals upward than it receives. And its electromagnetic field— It extends at least six feet from the body, though in your case..." She trailed off, her gaze flickering with quiet awe. "I suspect it's much farther."

Luna's lips parted, a soft inhale betraying her wonder. "So when people talk about feeling energy or connection with others—"

"They're often responding to the heart's magnetic field," Althea finished. "It's why emotions can fill a room, why we can sense someone's presence before they speak. The heart isn't just an organ, Luna. It's a guide, a source of wisdom, energy and connection."

She placed the green stone back in the line and picked up the blue one. "The throat chakra governs your ability to speak your truth, to communicate authentically. When balanced, it allows you to express yourself freely. When blocked, it can stifle your voice, leaving you feeling unheard or misunderstood."

The indigo stone followed, its deep hue catching the light as Althea held it up. "The third eye chakra," she began, her voice calm and measured, "is your intuition, your ability to perceive beyond the physical. It's where insight and foresight converge, the center of your inner vision. When this chakra is balanced, it opens you to possibility, clarity, and a deep connection to your intuition. But when it's blocked, it can leave you feeling lost, disconnected from your inner knowing, and blind to the patterns unfolding around you."

She paused, her dark eyes meeting Luna's. "The third eye is often associated with the pineal gland, a small but powerful part of the brain. It sits deep within, and its role is fascinating—it helps regulate our circadian rhythms, sensing light even when our eyes are closed. It's almost as though it's built to perceive what we cannot see."

Luna frowned slightly, her fingers brushing her forehead as she listened. "The pressure..." she murmured, her voice trailing off.

Althea tilted her head, her expression encouraging. "You felt it, did you? A sensation behind your forehead?"

Luna nodded slowly, the memory resurfacing. "It was subtle at first, but it grew stronger during meditation. I didn't know what it was. It was like... something trying to push through."

"That was your third eye stirring," Althea explained gently. "The energy there was waking up, reaching for balance. It's no coincidence that you've been experiencing shifts in perception—colors sharper, sounds clearer.

These aren't just sensory changes; they're signs that your third eye is beginning to open."

Luna blinked, her thoughts racing as she tried to process the connection. The idea felt both intriguing and daunting, a glimpse into something far greater than she'd allowed herself to consider.

Finally, she lifted the violet stone. "The crown chakra is your connection to the universe, to the divine. It's where we transcend the self, recognizing our oneness with all things. When balanced, it brings a sense of peace and purpose. When blocked, it can leave you feeling isolated, adrift."

Luna absorbed the information, her mind swirling with connections. The concept of energy centers wasn't entirely new to her, but Althea's depth of understanding, combined with the tangible warmth she felt during their work, made it feel undeniable.

Althea leaned forward slightly, her eyes shimmering with quiet intensity, her tone deliberate and measured. "We'll begin with the heart chakra. It's the gateway to connection—the bridge that joins our inner selves and allows us to remain open to the world around us. To align the energy within you, we must first create coherence—between your heart and your brain, and between your heart and mine."

Luna's brow furrowed slightly, her curiosity piqued but tinged with hesitation. "How do we do that?"

"Through rhythm," Althea said simply, her words carrying a quiet power. "The heart and brain each vibrate at their own frequencies, their own patterns. When we synchronize them, we achieve coherence—a state where the heart's intelligence and the brain's logic become one. It's not just calming, Luna—it's transformative. This is the foundation of your true self, the rhythm that connects you to all that is."

The soft light filtering into the room seemed to shift, taking on a warmer hue as Althea's expression softened. Her voice dropped to a near-whisper, her words like a secret shared only with Luna. "Once we've achieved coherence individually, I'll attune my heart to yours. Our energies will align, flowing together like two rivers merging into one. The depth of that connection can take you places within yourself you've never been before."

Luna's breath stalled, tangled in the gravity of Althea's words settling over her with a sense of impossibility. "And if it doesn't work?" she asked, her voice barely audible.

Althea's faint smile was unwavering, her eyes steady with certainty. "Have confidence Luna, It will work," she said, her voice firm but kind. "Because it's not about hoping—it's about knowing. Your heart already understands, even if your mind still hesitates. Trust it, Luna. It's always been leading you."

She reached for the green stone, its polished surface gleaming like an emerald caught in the sun. Placing it carefully between them, Althea gestured to the steaming tea beside Luna. "Drink your tea," she said softly, her voice steady. "Feel the warmth of it, the way it anchors you to this moment. Pay attention to your breath—let your exhale stretch just a little longer than your inhale. Notice the space between us, the subtle hum of energy. We're already connected, sitting here in each other's magnetic field. Recognize it, if you can—the way our energies interact, like two ripples spreading across the surface of a still pond. Through the intersecting points, I will harmonize and connect."

The air between them seemed to shift, growing heavier, almost electric. Althea's gaze never left Luna's, her presence grounding yet charged with possibility.

"When you're ready, we'll begin," she said, her voice soft but resolute.

Luna took a final slow sip to finish the herbal tea, letting its warmth settle deep in her chest. She set the cup aside with quiet intention, inhaling deeply. A moment of hesitation flickered through her, but then—she let it go.

Her eyes met Althea's, steady now. "I'm ready."

She closed her eyes, focusing on her breath as Althea had instructed. Her first inhale was shallow, uneven, but she consciously extended her exhale, allowing it to stretch a moment longer. With each deliberate cycle, her shoulders softened, the tension slowly unraveling.

The soft crackle of the candle's flame punctuated the silence, its subtle flicker casting shifting patterns of light and shadow on the walls. Luna's awareness sharpened, tuning into the faint hum of energy that seemed to pulse not in the physical space, but within her. It wasn't static—it was alive, a gentle vibration that echoed through her body and beyond, like a song she had only just begun to hear.

Her perception expanded, and as she sank deeper into the moment, she felt Althea's presence differently. It was no longer just the proximity of another person—it was a tangible field of warmth and gravity, like a glowing sphere brushing against the edges of her awareness. The space between them seemed to resonate within her, a connection forming that transcended the physical.

"Very good," Althea murmured, her voice flowing like a soothing current. "You're beginning to feel it. Let that awareness deepen. The ripples between us are already interacting."

Luna's mind instinctively reached to analyze the sensation, to rationalize it into something familiar, but she caught herself. Exhaling slowly, she let the urge to think drift away, surrendering to the rhythm of her breath. It anchored her, each inhale and exhale syncing with the energy radiating from Althea.

"Now, focus on your heart," Althea said, her tone steady yet reverent. "Breathe as though you are breathing into your heart. Where your attention goes, energy flows. Feel its rhythm, Luna. It's not just yours—it's the rhythm of life itself, a bridge between your being and the universe."

Luna shifted her focus inward, becoming acutely aware of the steady thrum of her heartbeat. She imagined it as a pulse radiating outward, sending gentle waves across an unseen pond. Each wave carried warmth, spreading through her chest and filling her with a profound sense of peace. As she breathed into her heart, the sensation deepened, transforming into a gentle but radiant bliss that seemed to expand with every exhale.

Behind her forehead and above her right eye, she became aware of a faint pressure, an awakening energy glowing softly in her mind's eye. It was a luminous presence, subtle yet unmistakable, growing brighter as her breath steadied.

"Feel the connection between your heart and your mind," Althea continued, her voice quiet but filled with reverence. "Let their frequencies harmonize. See them not as separate, but as partners in a shared rhythm, moving together as one."

The light within Luna's mind began to take form, a realization dawning that the radiance was not her own—it was Althea, her presence merging with Luna's awareness. A euphoric surge of energy rippled through her, extending beyond her physical self. The sensation was overwhelming, a bliss so profound it brought tears streaming down her cheeks, the emotion spilling freely as the connection deepened.

She envisioned two streams flowing side by side, their waters merging into a single, powerful current. The imagery brought a sense of clarity that was almost visceral, her breath slowing until it seemed to dissolve entirely. Her heartbeat softened, steadying into a calm, powerful rhythm before fading into a stillness that wasn't empty but brimming with life.

In the stillness, Luna felt the coherence Althea had described—a seamless union of heart and mind, body and spirit. Everything within her aligned, moving in a rhythm so harmonious it was as if she had always known it, buried beneath the noise of her thoughts.

"Now, let your heart extend outward," Althea's voice echoed—not aloud, but within Luna's consciousness, carried as a thought that didn't feel separate from her own. "Feel its field expanding beyond your body. Allow it to meet mine in the shared space between us."

Luna hesitated, uncertain how to reach beyond herself. But as she focused, breathing deeply into the warmth in her chest, she began to sense it—a presence brushing against her awareness like the first touch of sunlight after a storm. It was faint, yet insistent, pulsing gently in time with her own energy. The rhythm between them overlapped, weaving together until the distinction between her and Althea blurred.

Althea's breath caught.

She had guided many through this process before, but never had she felt a presence so expansive, so immediate. Most took time to reach this depth of connection—Luna stepped into it as if she had always belonged there. The energy between them surged, not delicate, but vast, as if touching something greater than the two of them.

"*I can feel it*," Luna thought, her words not spoken but carried on the energy connecting them. The realization startled her, yet it felt entirely natural, like finding a door she hadn't known existed but had been searching for all along.

"Yes," came Althea's response, pushing aside her own astonishment as seamlessly as a breeze. "*Let it deepen. Our hearts are aligning—see it, feel it. Trust in the rhythm between us.*"

The silence thickened, becoming almost tangible, brimming with a vibrancy that transcended sound. Luna felt her awareness expand, stretching outward into a vast, luminous space. It was as if she were no longer in her body but floating within a shared current of light. Their connection became a single thread weaving through an infinite tapestry, the strands glowing with colors she couldn't name.

Althea steadied herself. If Luna could do this now, without training—what would she be capable of when she fully understood her gift?

"*Time is different here,*" Althea's thought-voice resonated. "*It flows, yet it is still. Let go of its measure.*"

Luna's inner vision filled with radiant fractals of light, their shapes shifting endlessly, yet each pattern felt connected to the next, as if part of a vast, living tapestry. The movements weren't random—they unfolded with purpose, each shift revealing something new. And then she understood.

Every turn, every flicker of light was a memory, an emotion relived and seen from a new angle. A different perspective. The pain she once clung to no longer felt sharp, but fluid—its edges softened by understanding. Love, once distant, stretched across time, weaving itself into the present. Longing became something weightless, neither absence nor ache, just an awareness of what had been and what would always be.

It was all happening at once, layered and infinite, as if time itself was merely a different way of looking at the same truth. She wasn't *trapped* in the past or *reaching* for the future—she was simply *seeing* it from another dimension, another vantage point. And in that, there was no resistance. No need to change or control. Just a quiet, undeniable knowing.

Their communication was wordless, a deep exchange of emotion and understanding. Luna felt the guiding presence of Althea as they moved through the flow of energy together. It was not teaching, but a shared knowing, an experience of being led while also leading, their energies entwined in perfect balance.

The love emanating from Luna's heart grew boundless, reaching beyond herself and Althea, extending outward into the vast web of life. She saw herself not as an individual, but as part of an endless whole. The sensation was overwhelming—a bliss so profound that the river of tears flowing down her face felt as natural as breath, an uncontainable expression of the love weaving through her.

The energy surged, cresting into something infinite—so immense it felt as though the universe itself trembled with it. And then, like a great tide retreating from the shore, it began to ease.

A deep, resonant stillness settled over her, not an ending but a gentle continuation. The connection remained, no longer blazing but steady, a quiet hum of existence that neither faded nor pressed forward.

Time unraveled.

She floated in that space, weightless, timeless, the rhythm of her breath indistinguishable from the pulse of the universe itself. Whether moments or eternities passed, she didn't know. It simply was.

The meditative silence dissolved into a still, almost breathless atmosphere. A gentle hum of energy pulsed within her, radiating outward, as if the very air around her vibrated in quiet harmony. Bliss coursed through her as she became present in her body again—not a fleeting rush, but a deep, resonant peace that filled every fiber of her being. She felt boundless yet grounded, her senses heightened to the warmth of the space, the soft whisper of existence itself.

Luna's eyes fluttered open, the world around her feeling altered yet eerily the same. She blinked, disoriented by the extinguished candles, their melted wax hardened in irregular pools. The faint light of morning peeked through the window, and for a fleeting moment, everything seemed ordinary—until her gaze landed on the clock.

"It's only been an hour," Luna murmured with surprise, her voice still tinged with the tranquility of their meditation.

Across from her, Althea sat unmoving, her gaze fixed on the candles as if seeing them for the first time. The flicker of confusion on her usually composed face was brief, but unmistakable. When she finally stirred, it was with measured, deliberate movement—like someone recalibrating their senses after stepping onto unfamiliar ground.

"Perhaps," Althea said at last, her voice softer than before. "Though... the candles." She reached out, running a finger along the hardened wax trails. "I don't recall them being so low when I lit them."

Luna shifted, wincing as stiffness pulsed through her muscles. "Why am I so sore?" she asked, rolling her shoulders.

Althea's fingers pressed lightly to her chest, her breath slow and deep, though her steady demeanor was at odds with the glint of something unreadable in her eyes. Wonder? Uncertainty?

"Meditative states can have interesting effects on the motionless body," she said carefully, though there was a weight to her words, as if she was considering them even as she spoke. She exhaled, smoothing a hand over her skirt before rising with deliberate caution, testing her footing like someone confirming the ground beneath them was still solid.

She turned toward the door, hesitating just a fraction before speaking again. "Let's step outside," she said, finally meeting Luna's gaze. "Fresh air might clear the fog."

Luna followed, the weight of the world feeling both heavier and lighter at once—as if something had been added to her, yet something else had been lifted.

The crisp morning air kissed her skin as they stepped onto the porch. The forest stretched before them, golden light filtering through the trees, illuminating the world with a clarity she had never noticed before. The rustling leaves, the distant song of birds, the way the earth exhaled with the breeze—it all felt alive in a way she hadn't understood until now.

She turned to Althea, a knowing warmth passing between them. The connection remained—not as an overwhelming surge, but as a steady undercurrent, something deep and unshakable.

Luna inhaled slowly, savoring the taste of the air, the sensation of simply existing in this moment. She had changed. Not in a dramatic, earth-shattering way, but in ways that truly mattered.

Her stomach growled, breaking the silence.

Althea chuckled, the moment shifting back into something grounded and real. "Come, Luna. Let's head back to Everwood, and I'll make us a replenishing meal."

The drive back felt longer than it should have, the road winding through shadows that clung to the car like echoes of something unseen. Luna's body ached as though she had run a marathon, each movement a reminder of how far she had gone in the meditation.

She exhaled, her fingers brushing absently against the seatbelt. *How long had they really been gone?*

"Do you think..." Luna hesitated, searching for the right words. "Do you think we were gone longer than an hour?"

Althea didn't answer immediately. The pause stretched—a beat too long—before she finally spoke. "Time moves differently in deep meditation," she said, her voice even but thoughtful. "But... what we experienced was far beyond what I expected. I think it may be playing tricks on our minds." Her hands remained steady on the wheel, yet something had shifted—an undertone of awe, maybe even uncertainty, threading through her words. "I wish we had brought our phones. Just to be sure."

Luna frowned, glancing out at the darkened treetops. *That shouldn't matter. An hour was an hour.* And yet, the unease creeping along her spine wouldn't settle.

As the car rounded the final bend and Everwood came into view, Luna's stomach tightened. The faint glow of activity near the community center caught her eye. People were gathered outside, their gestures animated, their voices just out of reach. Even at a distance, something about their energy felt... off.

Althea pulled into a parking space near the main path, her movements controlled but deliberate. She exhaled and turned to Luna, her dark eyes steady. "Quite a lot of commotion for a Wednesday morning," she murmured. "Something must be wrong."

She rested a hand briefly over Luna's. "Whatever happens next, remember to breathe. Trust yourself."

Before Luna could respond, she heard the crunch of hurried footsteps on the gravel. She turned, her breath catching as Ezra appeared, his face a mixture of relief and frustration.

"There you are," Ezra said, his voice hoarse with exhaustion. "Where have you been?"

Luna frowned, a flicker of unease tightening her chest. "What do you mean? We've only been gone a couple of hours."

Ezra stepped closer, his expression a mix of relief and frustration. "A couple of hours? Are you insane? Try two days, Luna. *Two days*, and no one knew where you were. Your car was here, but you weren't. People thought..." He stopped himself, exhaling sharply. "I thought something had happened to you."

Luna opened her mouth, but no words came. *Two days*. The number sent a jolt through her, but... it made sense now, didn't it? The way her body ached as if she'd been sitting still for an eternity, the melted candles, the strange fluidity of time in the meditation. Somewhere deep inside, she knew. But knowing didn't make hearing it any less shocking.

"Ezra, I didn't mean to—"

"Didn't mean to *what*?" he interrupted, his frustration bubbling to the surface. "Disappear without telling anyone? Do you have any idea what it's been like here? Something strange has been happening. People have been feeling... things. Intense emotions out of nowhere. Fear, anxiety, bliss, love... And then *you* disappear! Damn it, Luna. You had me so—"

Luna flinched at the sharpness in his tone, her old instincts kicking in before she could stop them. The walls she had perfected over years of corporate battles rose instinctively—ready to defend, ready to deflect.

Luna's throat tightened, guilt mingling with defensiveness. "Sorry Ezra, but I'm not accountable to you," she said, her voice sharper than she intended. "I don't need to check in every time I leave."

His expression faltered, hurt flickering in his eyes, but he held his ground. "Well, excuse me for caring," he muttered, rubbing a hand over

his jaw. "I've been worried sick, Luna. We all have. And on top of that—"
He exhaled sharply, his frustration battling against something deeper.

"People here felt something—something powerful." His voice dropped
slightly, the edge of accusation giving way to uncertainty. "Rumors have
been spreading. Speculating that you may have had something to do with
it, or at least your disappearance did."

His gaze searched hers, a silent question lingering beneath his words.
"Are they wrong?"

Althea stepped forward, her voice calm but firm. "Ezra," she said gently,
placing a hand on his arm. "This isn't the time for blame. I understand
your concern, truly. I took Luna to my shop to guide her through a
meditation—one that was meant to help her connect more deeply with
her energy. But I didn't anticipate the extent of her awakening, or the
time that would pass. To Luna and I, it has only felt like a couple hours."

She met his gaze, unwavering, reading the confusion in his eyes. "It
wasn't intentional, Ezra, but what happened is significant—not just for
Luna, but for the community."

Ezra hesitated, his eyes shifting between Althea and Luna. "And how
are we supposed to explain that to everyone else?" He asked, his tone
quieter but still laced with tension.

After a moment of consideration.

"We don't—at least not yet," Althea said. "Luna needs time to process
this, and so does the community. Rushing to explain something we barely
comprehend will only create more fear."

Luna swallowed hard, her mind racing. She hadn't meant for this to
happen, hadn't realized how deeply her actions would ripple. But as Ezra's
words sank in, a flicker of something else stirred beneath the guilt—an
understanding that this journey wasn't hers alone.

"I didn't mean for any of this," she said softly, her voice breaking. "But
I can't ignore it now. I have to see this through."

Ezra's shoulders relaxed slightly, though his concern remained etched
on his face. "Then let me be part of that, Luna. You don't have to do this
alone."

She almost bristled, but then she saw it—the raw worry behind his words. He wasn't doubting her, wasn't trying to hold her back. He just didn't want to lose her.

Her breath steadied as she took him in. "I know," she said gently. "And I won't."

Ezra exhaled, running a hand through his hair before nodding. "I'll talk to the others," he said, his voice quieter now, as if choosing his words carefully. "I'll let them know you two had been on a retreat, something planned. I'll do what I can to steer them away from... tying this to everything else that's happening."

Althea studied him for a moment, then inclined her head. "That would help."

The tension between them eased, though something still hung in the air—not fully resolved, but no longer pressing.

As Ezra stepped back, Althea placed a steadying hand on Luna's shoulder. "Let's get you settled," she said, her voice low. "This isn't the end of the conversation, but it doesn't have to happen now."

Luna allowed herself to be led toward her cabin, her mind swirling with questions and emotions. She glanced back at Ezra, who lingered by the car, his expression unreadable.

The air between them was thick with unspoken words, but for now, the silence would have to be enough.

TEN

ONE STEP AT A TIME

Althea guided Luna by the arm and led her up the path to Luna's cabin. Neither spoke, the weight of the lost two days pressing down on them like an unseen force. Luna's body felt heavy, her limbs aching from their prolonged stillness during the meditation. The soreness was a strange contrast to the intangible hum of energy that still buzzed faintly within her, as though her body and spirit were at odds.

Luna tried to open her door but winced as a sharp pang shot through her leg. Althea was at her side in an instant, steadying her as she stepped out.

"I've got you," Althea said gently, her voice a calm anchor.

"I'm fine," Luna mumbled, her cheeks flushing with embarrassment. She stumbled again as they reached the cabin door, muttering an apology as she gripped the frame for support.

"You've been through something extraordinary, Luna," Althea replied, brushing off the apology as she unlocked the door. Her own movements were slower than usual, deliberate, as though she too felt the toll of the meditation.

Inside, the cabin was cool and still, the faint scent of cedar lingering in the air. Luna sank into a chair near the small dining table, her legs folding beneath her as though they could no longer bear her weight. Her head fell into her hands, and for a moment, she simply breathed, the quiet of the room amplifying the chaos in her mind.

On the table beside her sat her phone—untouched since before the meditation. She hesitated before reaching for it, already sensing what she would find.

The screen lit up with a flood of missed calls and messages from Ezra, and Miriam. Each notification was a stark reminder of the world she had unintentionally left behind.

Her stomach tightened as she scrolled through the messages.

Miriam: *Are you okay? Please let me know when you get this.*

Ezra: *Call me, Luna.*

Miriam: *Luna, people are worried. Where are you?*

Ezra: *Where the hell are you?*

A lump formed in her throat, guilt settling deep in her chest. They had worried. They had feared for her. And she—lost in the boundless expanse of meditation—hadn't even realized.

She exhaled, ready to set the phone down, but before she could, it vibrated in her hand.

A new message.

Miriam: *I just talked to Ezra. I'm so glad to know you're okay. Come see me when you're feeling better. I love you.*

Luna swallowed hard, her fingers tightening around the device. Even now, after everything, Miriam's first response was love. No anger, no accusations—just relief.

Althea set her bag aside and moved toward the kitchen without a word. She opened the refrigerator, her gaze settling on a jar of rich, golden broth from an earlier meal. A small, satisfied nod—this would save time. With practiced ease, she set it on the counter before turning to gather the rest of the ingredients—a few vegetables, a bundle of herbs, a loaf of bread. The rhythmic chop of a knife against the wooden cutting board was the only sound in the room, grounding them both in its simplicity.

The aroma of herbs and simmering broth soon filled the cabin, weaving through the air like a soothing balm. Althea worked methodically, her back to Luna, who remained at the table, the phone still clutched in her hand, Miriam's latest message glowing softly on the screen.

Her fingers hovered over the screen as if she might reply, but instead, she exhaled and finally set the phone down, the weight of what she was capable of pressing down on her.

"How could I have caused this?" Her voice broke the silence, soft and strained, as though the question had been wrenched from the depths of her chest. She didn't lift her head, her words muffled by her hands. "Ezra said the community felt... everything. How could I do that without even realizing?"

Althea paused, her knife hovering over the cutting board. She turned slowly, her dark eyes calm yet piercing as they settled on Luna. "You didn't *cause* anything, Luna," she said firmly, her tone laced with reassurance. "You amplified. There's a difference."

Luna looked up, her face pale and drawn. "What does that even mean? How do I amplify something I don't even understand?"

Althea set the knife down and walked to the table, pulling out a chair across from Luna. She rested her hands lightly on the surface, her gaze steady but contemplative.

"Think of it like this," she said slowly, choosing her words with care. "Your energy is... different. Strong, untapped, and incredibly unique. When it awakened, it must have rippled outward, affecting the energy of those around you."

She paused, studying Luna, turning the thought over in her mind. *Did Luna cause it? Or did she simply reveal what was already there?*

"I don't think it created emotions out of nowhere—not without your intent," she said slowly, the words settling into place even as she spoke them. "But maybe... maybe it stirred what was already there, brought things to the surface in a way that couldn't be ignored."

Althea exhaled, tapping her fingers lightly against the table as she considered. The explanation felt right—not something she *knew*, but something that *resonated*.

"With every emotion you processed in deep meditation, that energy would have extended through the full reach of your heart's magnetic field. Anyone within it—especially those already resonating at a similar emotional frequency—might have felt their own emotions amplify. When two waves align in rhythm, they merge into a single, stronger wave. That could explain why different people experienced different things. It wasn't you forcing anything on them; it was their own emotions responding to the shift you were creating."

Luna swallowed, her chest tightening as the shifting fractals of emotion and memory resurfaced in her mind—each one unfolding, revealing, *pulling* at something deep inside her. The weight of it pressed against her ribs, heavy with understanding.

"But I didn't mean to," she whispered, her voice trembling. "I didn't want to hurt anyone."

"You didn't." Althea reached across the table, her fingers wrapping warmly over Luna's hand. "This journey you're on now—it's bigger than any single intention. It's about discovery, understanding, and alignment. And sometimes, that means things will unfold in ways you don't anticipate. That doesn't mean you're reckless, or act with malice."

Luna let out a slow breath, Althea's words settling over her like a fragile thread of comfort, though the guilt still lingered. She nodded slowly, her fingers tightening around the edge of the table as she tried to make sense of it all.

"So, if I can affect people this deeply without meaning to..." she hesitated, her voice quieter now, almost afraid of the answer. "What happens when I do?"

Althea's gaze held hers, steady and unwavering. She didn't answer right away, as if weighing the gravity of her next words.

"This is why your gift is a responsibility," she said finally, her voice low but firm. "The mind—your will—is a powerful thing, Luna. If you learn to harness the full strength of your energy field with intent, the possibilities will stretch beyond what we understand today."

She exhaled, her fingers tracing slow, thoughtful patterns against the table's surface. "That's why you must always act with kindness, with love. The heart is just as strong as the mind, and if they aren't aligned, power—true power—can become dangerous."

Her expression darkened slightly, just enough for Luna to catch it. "A mind that leads without the heart will create ripples just as deep, but not in the way you'd want," she warned.

The weight of Althea's words sank into Luna's chest, heavier than before. This wasn't just about what she could do. It was about what she chose to do. Luna nodded with understanding.

Althea gave her hand a final reassuring squeeze before standing and returning to the stove. "Eat," she said, ladling the steaming soup into two bowls. "Your body needs to recover before your mind can process any of this."

Luna accepted the bowl with a quiet "thank you," the warmth of it spreading through her hands. As she sipped the broth, the simple act of nourishment began to ease the tension in her chest.

The warm, herbal scent of the soup filled the cabin as Luna and Althea ate in a contemplative silence. The weight of what had happened lingered in the air, a presence neither could ignore. Luna's spoon moved mechanically, the rich broth warming her, though it did little to soothe the storm of thoughts in her mind.

The remains of their simple meal sat on the table, the air in the cabin heavy with the aftereffects of their conversation. Althea stood, her movements deliberate but marked with exhaustion. She gathered her shawl from the back of the chair and draped it over her shoulders, her dark eyes meeting Luna's as she approached.

"I'm going to leave you to rest now," Althea said, her voice steady yet gentle. She placed a hand on Luna's shoulder, the touch grounding. "Take the day to process everything. Don't rush yourself. Rest if you can. The answers will come, but not if you try to force them."

Luna nodded, her eyes clouded with lingering doubt. "Althea..." she began, her voice faltering. "What if I don't find the answers? What if I never figure out what all this means?"

Althea's lips curved into a faint, reassuring smile. "The answers are already within you, Luna. They always have been. But sometimes, they need stillness to surface." Her hand lingered for a moment before she stepped back, her presence calm and resolute. "I'll check on you tomorrow."

With that, Althea moved to the door, the wooden floor creaking softly beneath her steps. She paused, glancing back one last time. "Remember," she said, her tone firm but kind, "you're not alone in this. Trust the rhythm. It will guide you."

The door closed behind her with a quiet click, leaving Luna to process in the stillness of the cabin. The faint scent of herbs and broth lingered in the air, a comforting reminder of Althea's presence. Yet, as the silence deepened, Luna felt the weight of her thoughts pressing down on her chest.

She sank onto the edge of the small bed, her hands gripping the blanket beneath her. The day's events replayed in her mind—the overwhelming meditation, the confrontation with Ezra, the strange, shared emotions that rippled through the community. Every piece of it felt tangled, an unyielding knot she couldn't unravel.

I have got to find Elias. I need answers now more than ever. She thought as her heart thumped with concern.

Her thoughts drifted back to Ezra. She could still see the hurt in his eyes, the way his voice had wavered between frustration and care. She replayed her sharp words, each one cutting into her chest with fresh regret. He wasn't trying to control her—he was trying to protect her, to understand. And she had pushed him away.

"Why do I always do this?" she muttered to herself, her voice tinged with frustration. She pressed her palms to her temples, trying to quiet the self-recriminating thoughts.

But amid the guilt, a flicker of resolve began to grow. Ezra had been there for her, through her return to Everwood and all the uncertainty that came with it. He didn't deserve to be left in the dark, especially not after everything he had done to support her.

Luna exhaled slowly, lowering her hands. "I have to make this right," she whispered. Her gaze drifted to the window, where the sunlight filtered through the trees, casting dappled patterns on the wooden floor. The forest seemed alive with possibility, urging her to take the next step.

She rose from the chair, her movements steady despite the heaviness in her chest. Ezra deserved more than her silence and defensiveness. He deserved an explanation—maybe not the whole story, not yet, but enough to bridge the gap she had created.

Grabbing her sweater, Luna steeled herself. The path ahead felt uncertain, but one thing was clear: she couldn't leave things unresolved. Not with Ezra. Not with herself.

Luna stepped outside the cabin, the crisp afternoon air brushing against her skin. The light filtering through the trees had shifted, casting golden streaks across the forest floor. Each step felt purposeful as she made her way toward the heart of Everwood, where she hoped to find Ezra.

The distant hum of voices reached her ears as she neared the community's central clearing. Instinctively, she slowed her pace, staying close to the edge of the main path, where the canopy above cast shadows thick enough to conceal her.

A small group of community members stood in a loose circle near the open-air gathering hall, their tones hushed but animated. Luna recognized Eleanor among them, her sharp gestures and furrowed brow a telltale sign of her discontent.

"I'm telling you, something's changed," Eleanor said, her voice low but firm. "I've lived here for decades, and I've never felt anything like it. That wave of... fear—it wasn't mine. I know it wasn't mine."

Another woman, younger, shook her head. "Maybe it was fear for you, but for me? It was pure bliss. I felt weightless, like the universe itself was cradling me in its arms. It was delightful." Her voice trembled slightly, her hands clasped together as though reliving the experience.

A man with a heavyset frame and weathered hands crossed his arms, his expression skeptical. "Bliss? Fear? What about paranoia? That's what I felt—like I was being watched, judged. I couldn't shake it for hours."

Eleanor's eyes narrowed. "And none of you think it's strange that we all felt something, but none of it was the same? This wasn't natural. It came from somewhere—or someone."

Luna's chest tightened as the weight of their words settled over her. Her pulse quickening as she leaned against a tree for support.

"It couldn't have been one of us," the younger woman said, her tone uncertain. "Could it?"

Eleanor's lips pressed into a thin line, her gaze scanning the group. "We need answers," she said firmly. "If we don't find them, this will only get worse."

Luna's heart pounded as the conversation continued. Every word felt like a thread pulling tighter around her, binding her to something she wasn't ready to confront. She clenched her fists at her sides, torn between stepping forward and retreating into the safety of the shadows.

"Luna," a familiar voice called softly behind her.

She turned sharply, startled to find Ezra standing a few feet away, his expression a mix of concern and quiet reproach.

"You're eavesdropping," he said, though his tone lacked accusation.

Luna opened her mouth to respond, but the words caught in her throat. Ezra stepped closer, his presence steady and grounding.

"Come on," he said gently, nodding toward the path. "Let's talk somewhere else."

Luna hesitated, her gaze flicking back toward the group before nodding silently and following him. Her steps were heavy, the weight of the overheard conversation pressing on her as they walked in the opposite direction.

Ezra opened the door to his studio, the familiar scent of turpentine and paint filling the air. The light streaming through the large windows cast a warm glow on the scattered canvases and brushes. For a moment, Luna hesitated at the threshold, her gaze sweeping over the room.

"Come in," Ezra said softly, stepping aside to let her enter.

Luna moved past him, the warmth of the studio a sharp contrast to the chill she felt in her chest. She perched on a stool near the corner, her arms crossed as though bracing herself. Ezra remained by the door for a moment before walking to the table where his brushes were neatly arranged.

"This is the safest place I know," he said, his tone even. "Figured it'd be a good spot for an honest conversation."

Luna didn't respond immediately, her gaze fixed on the covered painting he had been working on, partly considering her next words.

"You think I should tell them," she said finally, her voice flat but laced with tension.

Ezra turned to face her, his expression calm but resolute. "I don't just think it, Luna—I know it. They deserve to know the truth. What happened wasn't ordinary, and people are scared. You heard them back there. They're looking for answers, and if you stay silent, the fear will only grow."

Luna's jaw tightened, her fingers curling into the fabric of her sweater. "And what am I supposed to say, Ezra? That I sat in meditation and accidentally unleashed a wave of emotions across the community? That I don't even understand how it happened?" Her voice rose, her frustration spilling over. "What if I make it worse? What if they reject me, make me leave?"

Ezra held her gaze, his steady presence unwavering. "I don't know exactly what happened, but I do know you, Luna. And I trust that whatever this was, it wasn't meant to harm anyone."

His voice softened, though the weight of his words remained. "They won't make you leave. Most will understand, eventually. But what they won't stand for is dishonesty."

Luna pushed back from the table, pacing as her thoughts spiraled. "I didn't ask for this, Ezra," she said, her voice cracking. "I came here to figure out my own mess, not to fix the community's."

Ezra watched her, patient but unyielding. "I know," he said quietly, stepping closer but keeping his distance. "And I'm not asking you to fix anything. But hiding won't help. You can't run from this. Especially if you intend to see it through."

The words hit their mark, stopping her mid-step. Her shoulders slumped, the anger draining just enough for exhaustion to take its place. She turned, her gaze searching his. "Do you really think they'll believe me? That they'll understand?"

Ezra hesitated, then shook his head. "The people who matter will. And the rest? They'll follow in time."

He held her gaze, his voice steady. "Trust me. But more than that—trust yourself. You're going to see this through, and when you do, there won't be any denying your words."

A heavy silence stretched between them, settling over her like an unshakable weight. Luna's breath came in shallow bursts, doubt pressing against her ribs.

"I need time," she said finally, her voice barely above a whisper.

Ezra nodded, his expression softening. "I get that. Take a couple of days, Luna. Process this, figure out how you want to approach it. But don't wait too long."

He exhaled, his voice quiet but firm. "This community—these people—they're part of you, whether you like it or not. Holding back from them will only make it harder to earn their trust."

Luna's lips pressed into a thin line, her thoughts tangled between resistance and reluctant understanding. Finally, she nodded.

"I see how important this is to you. And I know you're right." She exhaled, the weight of it settling over her. "I'll figure it out—as fast as I can."

Ezra stepped closer, his hand brushing her arm briefly, a gesture of quiet support. "I'm here, you know. Whatever you decide, I'm with you."

"I know, Ezra, and... I'm sorry for the way I reacted. You deserved better than that. I won't worry you like that again."

For a moment, the tension in the room eased, the quiet hum of the studio offering a fragile sense of calm. Luna let out a slow breath, her shoulders relaxing slightly.

Ezra gave her a faint smile, stepping back to give her space. "Thank you, Luna. You'll figure it out," he said, his voice steady with conviction.

But he didn't step away completely. Instead, he turned, walking toward the easel where a canvas stood, partially covered by a sheet. He hesitated only briefly before pulling it away.

The painting caught her breath.

It was them—not just now, but then. Two teenagers, wild and free, running through the grass at the base of Pyramid Hill, their laughter almost tangible in the brushstrokes. And above them, at the summit, sat their older selves, side by side, looking out over the landscape.

Looking back.

Luna swallowed hard, her fingers tightening around her sleeves. "You finished it," she murmured.

Ezra let out a small breath, rubbing the back of his neck. "Not quite. But I worked on it while you were gone. I guess..." He exhaled, his voice softer now. "I needed to distract myself."

Luna stepped closer, tracing the edges of the painting with her eyes.

Her past, her present. The place she had run from, the place she had returned to.

And Ezra.

The weight on her chest hadn't fully lifted, but it felt a little lighter. She turned to him, eyes filled with something unspoken.

"It's beautiful," she said, her voice quiet but full of meaning.

Ezra's gaze met hers, steady and sure. "So are you."

Luna looked away, a small, almost reluctant smile ghosting her lips. Her fingers itched to reach out—to trace the brushstrokes, to hold onto something tangible in a moment that felt too big to grasp.

Ezra leaned against the worktable, watching her, giving her space to process. He rubbed the back of his neck, a faint smile playing at his lips. "Look," he began, his tone lighter, "I know this has been... a lot. For both of us. But maybe it'd help to get out of here for a bit. A change of scenery."

Luna tilted her head, curiosity flickering in her eyes. "What do you mean?"

"There's a small church in Eureka Springs. Maybe you'd like to go with me tomorrow?" His voice was warm, inviting. "It's not what you'd expect—no fire and brimstone, no heavy dogma. It's more about community, reflection... a different kind of connection. I think you might find it interesting."

He smirked slightly. "Plus, the drive there is beautiful this time of year. The leaves are just starting to change."

Luna hesitated, her gaze dropping as she turned the idea over in her mind. "I don't know, Ezra. I'm not really... the church type."

He chuckled softly, shaking his head. "Neither am I, if I'm being honest. But it's not about religion—it's about stepping outside your head for a while. Letting yourself breathe. And maybe... finding some clarity."

She looked up at him, searching his face, finding only patience there. Then, after a moment, she exhaled and nodded. "Alright. Tomorrow it is."

Ezra's smile widened, relief flickering across his face. "Good. I think you'll like it."

As Luna turned to leave, the air between them felt lighter, though the weight of the day still clung to her like the scent of paint in the studio.

She paused at the door, glancing back at Ezra.

"Thanks... for not giving up on me."

His expression softened further, his voice low but steady. "Never crossed my mind."

The walk back to her cabin was quiet, the fading light of the evening casting long shadows across the forest path. Luna's thoughts churned with a mix of emotions—guilt from her argument with Ezra, the rawness of the community's unease, and the uncertain road ahead.

She stopped for a moment, turning her gaze toward the horizon. The setting sun bathed the trees in hues of gold and amber, the shadows stretching like fingers across the ground. A faint but determined smile tugged at her lips.

"One step at a time," she murmured to herself, her voice barely audible over the whisper of the wind.

The cabin door creaked as she stepped inside, the familiar scent of wood and earth embracing her like an old memory. Despite the uncertainty that lingered, there was a flicker of something else—hope.

ELEVEN

RIPPLES OF AWAKENING

The morning air was crisp and cool as Luna and Ezra set out for Eureka Springs, the sun casting a warm glow over the hills. The drive was quiet at first, but not uncomfortable as Luna had feared. She found herself watching the world blur past the car window, her mind turning over the events of the past few days. Beside her, Ezra hummed softly to the music, his hands steady on the wheel. There was something grounding about that.

"What's this church like?" Luna asked, breaking the silence.

Ezra glanced at her, a faint smile curving his lips. "It's different," he said. "Small, welcoming. Like I said, the pastor talks more about connection and compassion than fire and brimstone."

"Sounds refreshing."

Ezra nodded. "It is. You might even like it."

The winding road led them through lush forests and open fields, eventually giving way to the quaint streets of Eureka Springs.

"Althea's shop is just up that road," Luna said as they passed, her thoughts suddenly shifting to the previous day—the magic, the fallout. The consequences. She still didn't fully understand what had happened, only that it had reached further than she ever imagined.

The town seemed to emerge from the hills, its charming Victorian buildings nestled along steep, winding streets.

"Welcome to Eureka," Ezra said, his voice warm with familiarity.

The church itself was modest, a small white chapel with stained-glass windows that caught the morning light in dazzling hues. Luna hesitated at the steps, her fingers brushing against the journal tucked in her bag.

A flicker of unease rose in her chest—not fear, exactly, but uncertainty. Would her recent experiences align with the spirituality of this place?

"You okay?" Ezra asked, his voice gentle.

Luna nodded, steadying her breath. "Yeah. Just a little worried I might burst into flames," she quipped, thinking back to her corporate days.

Ezra chuckled, opening the door for her. "If you do, I'll have to reconsider my life choices."

Inside, the sanctuary was bathed in soft light, the wooden pews polished to a warm sheen. A handful of people mingled quietly, their voices blending with the faint strains of an organ. Ezra led her to a seat near the back, his presence reassuring.

The service began with a hymn, the congregation's voices rising in a harmonious swell. Luna closed her eyes, letting the music wash over her. It wasn't so different from the meditative hum she'd felt with Althea—a rhythm that resonated beyond words.

The pastor, a kind-faced man in his sixties, spoke of love as the ultimate force of creation. Not as an abstract concept, but as a tangible energy connecting all living things. His words stirred something deep within Luna, echoing the teachings her mother had left behind.

"Love is what calls us to one another," the pastor said, his voice steady. "It is not just a feeling, but an action—a choice we make in every moment. It lifts us when we fall, carries us when we can't walk alone, and reminds us that we are never truly separate. When we allow love to lead, we move closer to the divine, closer to the purpose placed in our hearts."

Luna's eyes prickled with tears. She felt Ezra's hand brush hers—a quiet, anchoring gesture. The words were new, yet they carried the same weight as what she had been discovering.

After the service, they lingered outside the chapel, the scent of blooming flowers mingling with the crisp air. Ezra leaned against the railing, his hands tucked into his pockets.

"Wasn't so bad, was it?" he teased, his tone light.

Luna smiled, her gaze drifting over the rolling hills in the distance. "It was... unexpected," she admitted. "But in a good way. What the pastor said—it felt familiar. Like it connected to what I've been understanding."

Ezra nodded, his expression thoughtful. "I believe all paths lead to the same truth. People just find different ways to explain it."

"I think Mom felt the same," Luna said softly, her fingers brushing the edge of her journal. "That everything is connected."

"I'd say she was right," Ezra said, his voice steady. "And you're starting to see it too."

Luna's chest tightened, a mix of emotion and clarity stirring inside her. "I think I am."

Ezra tilted his head, his gaze thoughtful. "Explain everything you've learned and experienced while meditating with Althea—" he paused, then added, "and please, in a way I'd truly understand."

His tone was almost casual, but something about it caught Luna off guard. She hesitated, searching for words that refused to take shape.

She tried anyway. "I—I don't know if I could even explain it to myself." She shook her head, frustration flickering in her voice. "I'm sorry, Ezra. I would if I could, but I think... you'd have to experience it to really know what I saw."

Ezra's lips curled into the faintest smirk. "Exactly."

Luna blinked. "Wait... you set me up?"

Ezra shrugged. "A little." He leaned back against the stone railing, arms crossed. "That's the challenge all religions have faced—trying to explain the unexplainable. They had to take something infinite, something beyond words, and fit it into pages. And on top of that, people thousands of years later would have to try to make sense of it."

He raised an eyebrow, as if to let the absurdity of the task settle in. "Doesn't make them wrong—just misunderstood. They're all trying to point at the same thing, but the way they explain it depends on the time and place they were written. If you find the right perspective, you'll find the right answers."

Luna exhaled, Ezra's words settling over her like a quiet realization. Her experience had already shown her the truth of what he was saying—she just hadn't put it into words yet.

She let a small, knowing smile slip through. "Handsome and smart. I've got it good."

Ezra chuckled, shaking his head. "I'm just saying... you're not the first person to struggle with this. And you won't be the last."

Ezra barely had time to react before she closed the space between them, grasping the collar of his jacket and pulling him into her. The world faded around them as their lips met—a kiss filled with gratitude, understanding, and something deeper that had been growing between them for longer than either had admitted.

Ezra responded instantly, one hand cupping the side of her face, the other pressing against the small of her back, drawing her in. The tension, the unspoken words, the weight of everything they had been through—it all melted away in that moment, replaced by the electric certainty of now.

When they finally pulled apart, Luna's breath was unsteady, but her smile was firm.

Ezra's thumb traced a slow, absentminded path along her jaw, his voice lower now. "Well, I asked for an explanation I'd understand... and I think you just made a damn good point."

Luna laughed, the sound light, free. "As they say, actions speak louder than words."

As they walked through town, the colorful shops and cafés bustled with life. The search for Elias loomed in the back of Luna's mind, but for now, she allowed herself to be present—to take in the beauty of the moment.

Eureka Springs thrived with vibrant energy: eclectic storefronts displayed handmade crafts, the soft melody of a street performer's guitar drifted through the air, and the rich aroma of baked goods wafted from nearby cafés. Luna drew in a slow breath, letting the warmth of the scene settle over her, the weight of her journey beginning to ease.

They stopped at a small café with colorful awnings, drawn in by the inviting scent of freshly brewed coffee. Luna ordered a lavender latte, the floral notes easing the tension in her chest, while Ezra opted for his usual black coffee. They found a seat near the window, sunlight streaming in as they watched the ebb and flow of the street outside.

Their light conversation lulled, and Luna's attention shifted to a television mounted in the corner. A news segment played, the headline scrolling beneath images of serene landscapes and uneasy faces:

"Regional Emotional Wave Unexplained."

A tremor danced on her exhale, her fingers tightening around her cup. "Ezra, look."

They both turned to the screen as the anchor described widespread reports of intense, unexplainable emotions that had swept through the region two days prior. Locals spoke of overwhelming feelings—love, fear, sorrow—that had consumed them for hours with no apparent cause.

Luna's voice dropped to a whisper. "Althea's shop... It's just up the road. This was me."

Ezra's jaw tightened, his eyes narrowing. "Um, you think?" His voice was hushed, his gaze flicking around the café. He subtly motioned for her to lower her voice.

Before they could process the revelation, a pair of volunteers approached their table. Dressed in matching polo shirts with the initials W.I. embroidered on the chest, they carried clipboards and wore practiced, friendly smiles.

"Good morning," one of them greeted, their voice upbeat yet professional. "We noticed you watching the news. We're actually conducting a survey about the unusual experiences reported in this area. Do you have a moment to answer a few questions?"

Ezra offered a polite but cautious smile. "Um, sure," he said, glancing briefly at Luna. She nodded, though her grip on her latte tightened.

The volunteer began asking questions: Had they felt any inexplicable emotions? If so, when and where? How intense were the sensations?

Ezra answered carefully, offering just enough to seem helpful without revealing anything useful. "I did feel a sense of bliss that felt out of place the other day, but I thought it was just from being on vacation," he offered. When asked for his name, he hesitated only a fraction before saying, "Ben." His tone was casual, effortless.

"And where were you at the time?"

"Oh, we are staying at the KOA, just outside town," Ezra replied smoothly. It was in the opposite direction of Althea's shop and Ever-wood—a safe enough misdirection.

Luna remained silent, her unease growing, but Ezra kept his expression neutral, his focus shifting to the clipboard in the volunteer's hands. As the survey wrapped up, his eyes caught a small line of text at the bottom of the page...

Data collected by Westfield Industries for ongoing research into paranormal phenomena.

Ezra's expression didn't change, but his tone took on a subtle edge. "Westfield Industries?" he asked casually. "What kind of research are you conducting?"

The volunteer hesitated, their smile faltering slightly—not out of secrecy, but uncertainty. "It's not our research exactly," they admitted. "We're just helping collect information. A lot of us—" they gestured toward the other volunteers in matching shirts, "—felt something we can't explain. It was... powerful, like a touch from God, or something bigger than us."

They shifted, as if searching for the right words. "When we saw the ad looking for volunteers to help gather stories, it felt important, you know? Like maybe they can help figure out why it happened."

Ezra nodded thoughtfully, then gave a half-smirk. "Probably something totally normal—solar flares, gas leak, or maybe aliens finally making contact." His tone was light, dismissive, like he wasn't taking any of it seriously.

The volunteer chuckled, shaking their head. "I doubt it was a gas leak, but who knows."

"Well," Ezra said smoothly, "good luck with your research."

The volunteers thanked them and moved on, their cheerful demeanor intact.

As soon as they were out of earshot, Luna leaned in, her voice low. "They're tracking it. They know something happened. Something's not right."

Ezra's expression darkened, his brow furrowing. "This isn't just about us anymore."

Luna's heart raced. "We can't tell the community," she said firmly. "Not yet. They're already unsettled, and this... it would only make things worse."

Ezra hesitated, his conflict evident. "I don't like keeping things from them," he admitted. "But you're right—they don't need more to worry about right now. And we certainly don't want people coming to Everwood asking questions." He sighed, his voice softening. "Until we have more answers, we keep this between us."

Relief washed over Luna, though the weight of secrecy settled uneasily alongside it. "Thank you," she murmured.

Ezra reached across the table, his hand brushing hers in quiet reassurance. "We'll figure this out, Luna. Together."

As they left the café, the bright afternoon sun felt out of sync with the uncertainty now hanging over them. The town's charm remained, yet Luna could feel the ripple of her awakening in every breath of the cool autumn air.

The hum of the truck's engine filled the silence as Ezra and Luna made their way back to Everwood. Luna sat quietly, her thoughts churning. The revelation that her meditation had reached far beyond the community unsettled her. She stared out the window, watching the rolling hills blur into streaks of green, her fingers absentmindedly tracing the smooth leather surface of her mothers journal resting in her lap.

"I'm having a hard time comprehending that I affected so many people at such distances. It feels like a crazy dream." Her voice was barely audible over the sound of the tires on the pavement.

Ezra glanced at her briefly, his expression thoughtful. "Whatever it is, Luna, we'll figure it out. You were meant to be here, and your mom knew it."

She nodded, but her mind was already shifting to another pressing question: *Where can I meditate without unintentionally impacting others?*

As they passed a bend in the road, something caught Luna's eye—a flyer stapled to a power pole, its bold colors standing out against the backdrop of green.

She barely registered it at first, her thoughts too tangled to focus. But then, another pole came into view—the same flyer.

Luna sat up straighter, her pulse quickening. A symbol caught her eye—intricate and geometric, familiar in a way that sent a jolt through her.

She had seen it before. In her mother's journal.

"History they didn't teach you," she read aloud, her voice tight with urgency.

Ezra glanced at her. "What was that?"

"Stop the car." Luna's voice sharpened. "Go back. I need to see something."

Ezra didn't hesitate. He slowed the car, turned around at the next opportunity, and pulled up beside the power pole.

Luna stepped out, her heart hammering. She approached the flyer, her eyes scanning the text.

The symbol was unmistakable now—its lines and curves nearly identical to the ones in her mother's journal.

Her breath caught as she read aloud, "Guest Speaker: Elias Morgenstern."

Ezra joined her, his brow furrowing. "What are the chances this is a coincidence?"

Luna turned to him, her eyes filled with a mix of disbelief and determination. "Elias Morgenstern," she repeated, the name rolling off her tongue as if testing its weight. "I don't believe in coincidences."

Ezra's lips quirked into a faint smile. "Neither do I. I stopped believing in them the day you came back into my life."

Luna's gaze returned to the flyer, her excitement dimming slightly as she noticed the date at the bottom.

"It was last weekend," she said softly, disappointment creeping in.

Ezra placed a steadying hand on her shoulder. "At least now we have a last name," he said. "That's more than we had before."

Luna nodded, determination tightening in her chest. "Then we start with this. If Elias is connected to my mother's work, he might be the key to understanding all of this."

Ezra's grip on her shoulder tightened briefly, a quiet reassurance.

"We'll find him, Luna."

As they got back into the car, the sun dipped lower in the sky, casting long shadows across the road ahead. Luna clutched the journal in her lap, her mind already racing with plans. Elias Morgenstern might have been a missed opportunity today, but she wouldn't let that stop her. The path to understanding her mother's legacy—and her own awakening—had just become a little clearer.

Ezra's attention remained on the road as he continued the last 10 minute drive back home, while Luna scrolled through her phone, her fingers tapping quickly against the screen. "Elias Morgenstern," she murmured, her search results narrowing with each keystroke.

Ezra glanced over. "Any luck?"

Luna's brow furrowed in concentration as she skimmed an academic webpage. "He's a professor," she said finally, her tone both relieved and curious. "University of Arkansas, Fayetteville. That's only about an hour south of us."

Ezra nodded, his hands steady on the wheel. "So, what's the plan?"

Luna sat back, her mind already mapping out the steps she'd need to take. "I'll go to the university Monday," she said decisively. "Find him, see if he'll talk to me. If he's connected to my mother's work, I need to know how."

Ezra's jaw tightened slightly. "We'll go, then. I'll drive you."

Luna turned to him, her expression firm. "Thank you Ezra, but I need to do this on my own."

A beat of silence passed before Ezra spoke, his voice calm but edged with concern. "Luna, this isn't just some casual meeting. You don't know what you're walking into."

"I'm not a child," Luna replied, her tone sharper than intended. "I've navigated far more dangerous situations than meeting a professor."

Ezra sighed, his grip on the steering wheel tightening. "It's not about doubting your abilities. It's about... everything that's been happening. The meditation, the emotions spreading through the community, those survey people—it's a lot, Luna. And it's not just you anymore. If something goes wrong—"

"Nothing's going to go wrong," Luna interrupted, her voice rising. "I'm perfectly capable of handling myself. I've done it my entire life."

Ezra pulled the car over to the side of the road, cutting the engine. He turned to her, his gaze steady but intense. "This isn't about your capability," he said firmly. "It's about having someone in your corner, someone to rely on if things don't go as planned. I can't just sit back and not be there, not when I..." He paused, exhaling heavily. "Not when I care about you, Luna. You literally just promised me that you wouldn't make me worry again..."

Luna's defensiveness faltered, his words cutting through her frustration. She looked away, her fingers tightening around her phone. "You're right Ezra. I'm not used to this," she admitted softly. "Having someone... care like that. I've spent so long relying on myself, I didn't see it that way."

Ezra's voice softened, the tension easing slightly. "I'm not asking you to give up your independence," he said. "I respect it. But caring about someone means wanting to be there for them, even if they don't need you to fix anything."

Luna's eyes met his, the vulnerability in her gaze mirrored by his own. She nodded slowly, the weight of his sincerity settling over her. "You're right... you're right," she said finally. "You can come. But when we get there, I need to speak to Elias alone. I need him to know this is my journey."

Ezra's lips curved into a faint smile, relief softening his features. "Fair enough," he said. "I'll stay out of the way. Just... let me be close by."

Luna managed a small smile of her own, the tension between them dissipating. "Thank you," she said quietly, reaching over and placing her hand on his.

As they resumed their drive, the evening sun dipped lower on the horizon, its warm light painting the road ahead. Luna felt a mix of apprehension and determination. The journey to Elias still felt like the beginning, but with Ezra by her side, she knew she wouldn't face it alone.

TWELVE

THE WEIGHT OF FORGIVENESS

Sunday had passed in quiet rhythms—turning pages, tending soil, and learning how to walk without rushing toward the future. Luna had spent the morning combing through her mother's journals, searching for more mentions of Elias, but the writings were scattered, cryptic at best. The afternoon had been spent in Miriam's garden, the sun-warmed earth beneath her fingers grounding her in the simplicity of the moment. And as evening settled, Althea had guided her through walking meditation along the wooded trails, teaching her to feel each step fully—to exist only in the now.

Now, as twilight deepened, the evening air carried the earthy scent of pine and the distant crackle of a fire, wrapping the quiet world in a tranquil embrace. Barefoot on her cabin porch, Luna stood grounded in the cool wood beneath her feet, gazing into the infinite twilight. Thoughts of Elias and the journey ahead swirled in her mind, but the soft hum of her awakening resonated in her chest, tethering her to the present.

A sudden flicker—not a thought, but an impression. A familiar presence brushed against her awareness, stirring something deep within her before her senses could catch up.

A moment later, the rustling of leaves confirmed what she already knew.

Emerging from the tree line, her father stepped forward, his broad shoulders weighed down by unspoken words. The flickering cabin light caught the lines of age and regret on his face, softening the sharp angles that time had not erased.

"Dad?" Luna said softly, surprise mingling with curiosity.

He stopped at the base of the steps, hands deep in his jacket pockets. "Evening, Luna. I—uh, ran into Althea. Actually, I went seeking advice." He corrected himself, shifting his weight. "I hear I have you to thank for the horror of hurt I felt the other day," he added, a thin layer of humor masking the vulnerability in his voice. "Don't worry, your secret is safe with me."

Luna's chest tightened. The ripples of her meditation had reached him, too. She met his gaze, a flicker of understanding passing between them. "It wasn't just you," she said quietly. "I felt it too." A beat passed before she added, "And I really am sorry."

He climbed the steps, each movement deliberate, as though carrying the weight of years. "I know," he said softly. "And I think... I needed to feel it. To understand what I put you through back then. I never truly faced it."

Luna felt her breath catch as he came to stand before her, his eyes shimmering with unshed tears. "Luna," he began, his voice breaking, "I was blind. Blind to your pain, to what it did to you... to us. I let my fear, my pride, and my trust in the wrong people cloud everything. I can't change the past, but if I could—" His voice faltered, and he swallowed hard. "I'd do anything to make it right."

The raw sincerity of his words breached Luna's defenses. Her journey had taught her that pain, though excruciating, was often the soil from which growth emerged. She stepped closer, her hands trembling slightly as she reached for his.

"I wouldn't change the past," she said softly, her voice steady despite the tears glistening in her eyes. "Pain shaped me. Made me stronger. If Mom were here, she'd remind us that pain and tranquility are two sides of the same coin—different degrees of the same essence. We can't become without the pain of experience."

Her lips curved into a small, tear-streaked smile. With a nudge to his shoulder, she said, "I forgive you, Dad."

His eyes widened, glistening with emotion as a single tear traced its way down his cheek.

Luna stepped forward, her movements steady yet tender, each step carrying the weight of their unspoken years. She wrapped her arms around him, the embrace fragile in its tenderness but fortified by the deep well of forgiveness within her.

She had felt this before—the effortless pulse of energy, the way emotions rippled outward like waves on a still lake. But this time was different. This time, she wasn't just an observer, an amplifier of what already existed—she was the source, the guide.

Althea had told her this was possible. That intent could shape the current, that her will could direct what she shared. Now, she wasn't just hearing those words—she was proving them true.

"Let me show you," she whispered, her voice trembling yet resolute.

Closing her eyes, Luna inhaled deeply, centering herself in the quiet hum of her heart. She didn't force or direct the energy—she simply allowed it to exist, surrendering to the flow of infinite love and bliss that emanated from deep within. It radiated outward like a gentle wave, an invisible light reaching into the spaces words could not touch.

Her father froze, his breath catching as the sensation enveloped him—a warmth that bypassed thought and reached directly into his soul. It didn't erase the past, but it softened its edges, turning pain into something that could be held without cutting. The weight he had carried for years seemed to melt in the quiet radiance of her embrace.

A slow exhale escaped him—not just a breath, but a release, as though he had been unknowingly waiting for this moment his entire life. His shoulders trembled, not with sorrow, but with something deeper, fuller, freer. And then, from deep within, a soft, astonished laugh broke free—a sound not of grief, but of something lighter. Something whole.

Luna didn't push or try to control. She simply let it flow, allowing love to do what words never could.

Her father pulled back just enough to meet her gaze, his eyes shimmering—not with sadness, but with something brighter. "Luna..." he breathed, shaking his head slightly as though grasping for the right words. His grip on her shoulders tightened—not in desperation, but in reverence, as though grounding himself in this moment.

He let out a quiet, unsteady breath, his voice thick but steady. "Thank you. You don't know what you've just given me."

She tightened her embrace, her tears mingling with his as she rested her cheek against his shoulder.

"I do know what I gave you," she murmured, her voice soft but unwavering. "And you deserve it."

The bliss lingered for a moment longer, a radiant afterglow that softened into tranquility. As the energy ebbed, it didn't leave emptiness—it left peace.

They stood in the embrace of the evening, the air around them quiet, as though the world had paused to honor their reconciliation.

Her father finally pulled back, his hands resting gently on her shoulders as he searched her face. His eyes, though red with tears, held a clarity that hadn't been there before.

"What you just did..." he began, his voice trembling. "That wasn't just forgiveness, was it?"

Luna met his gaze, her own eyes shimmering with understanding. "It was real unconditional love," she said simply. "It's always been here, Dad. We just had to find it again."

A small, trembling smile broke through his grief, and he nodded. "You're extraordinary," he said, his voice low with reverence.

Luna shook her head gently, not in denial, but in wonder. "This is extraordinary," she murmured. "Not just me—all of it. Love, light... the way it moves through us. It's not about control, but trust. It isn't something we give alone; it has to be received, felt, resonated into being." She met his eyes, her voice steady with quiet understanding. "We all have it, Dad. I just learned to follow it."

The quiet enveloped them again, but this time, it felt lighter. Together, they stood under the canopy of twilight—father and daughter, no longer bound by shared pain, but by a love that had always been waiting for them.

When they finally stepped apart, her father's eyes, though rimmed with tears, held something new—something bright and open.

"Thank you," he said, his voice raw with emotion.

Luna smiled gently, her hand brushing his arm. "Thank you, Dad. Tonight, you taught me something important—a lesson in control and connection. I needed that, and I need you."

As he descended the porch steps and disappeared into the night, Luna felt an unexpected lightness. Not just from the act of forgiving—but from finally allowing herself to receive forgiveness, too.

Tomorrow, she would search for Elias.

But tonight, she had reclaimed something just as vital: the healing bond of family.

THIRTEEN

THE BURDEN OF TRUTH

T he first blush of dawn painted the sky in soft hues of pink and orange as Luna stepped out of her cabin. The crisp morning air carried the scent of dew-kissed grass and fresh pine, filling her lungs with quiet vitality. Her father's embrace from the night before lingered in her mind, a vivid memory of connection and healing. It had been the first time she had consciously wielded her gift—not by accident, but with purpose. That realization carried both a quiet clarity and the weight of responsibility.

Standing on the porch, wrapped in the stillness of the morning, Luna felt a pull deep in her chest. She had hidden her truth for too long. At first, it hadn't been intentional—she was still discovering what it all meant—but now, with each passing day, it felt more like avoidance. *Ezra is right.* The community deserved to know. These people, who had trusted her, whose lives had already been affected by her awakening, deserved her honesty.

A moment of clarity struck. Now was the time. She couldn't leave for Fayetteville without addressing what had happened. Pulling her phone from her pocket, she typed out a quick message to Ezra, asking him to help spread the word: "*You were right. I need to speak with the community before we leave. Please let whoever is available know to gather in the hall.*"

Wrapping herself in a light shawl, Luna stepped onto the cool earth, the firmness beneath her feet steadying the resolve forming in her heart. Her steps carried her through the clearing toward the heart of the community, her eyes scanning the quiet cabins and the garden glistening with morning dew.

The first stirrings of life greeted Luna along the way.

Althea crouched by her herb garden, her hands tending the delicate leaves with practiced care. The scent of fresh basil and rosemary filled the air. She looked up as Luna approached, her dark eyes scanning Luna's expression—not with surprise, but with knowing.

"Good morning, Althea," Luna said, her voice steady but carrying the weight of her intent. "I'm gathering the community at the hall—I need to speak with everyone."

Althea studied her for a beat, then nodded, a slow, approving gesture. "I see," she said, her voice laced with quiet understanding. "You've found some answers." A hint of pride softened the edges of her tone. "I'll be there."

Luna continued toward the hall, inviting those she passed to join the gathering.

As she neared Miriam's cabin, the door creaked open and her aunt stepped onto the porch, a steaming mug in hand. When Miriam saw her, that familiar flicker of concern passed across her face—subtler now, but unmistakable.

"Luna," Miriam breathed, her voice warm with unspoken emotions. Without hesitation, she set her mug aside and descended the steps, closing the distance between them in an instant. She wrapped Luna in a firm, affectionate embrace, holding her as though anchoring herself in the moment.

"Please don't make a habit out of disappearing, I'm still recovering from the fright you gave me." Miriam murmured, pulling back just enough to search Luna's face.

Luna smiled softly, her heart swelling at the genuine love in her aunt's eyes. "I know," she said. "I'm sorry for that."

Miriam squeezed her shoulders before releasing her, eyes scanning her as if making sure she was truly standing before her. "You're alright?"

"I am," Luna reassured her. "And I need you to join me at the gathering hall. There's something I need to share with everyone."

Miriam studied her for a moment, then nodded. "Of course," she said, a reassuring smile breaking through. "I'll be there."

By the time Luna reached the hall, she was surprised to see how quickly word had spread. People were already filtering in, their expressions ranging from curiosity to concern, whispers threading through the morning air like ripples on water.

"I swear, I woke up in tears and I didn't even know why," someone murmured.

"You weren't the only one," another voice replied. "I felt... everything. All at once."

"I heard Miriam and Ezra checked in on her, but no one's said a word about what happened," a woman near the doorway whispered.

Luna paused just outside, listening as fragments of conversations drifted past her.

"Could this be what Eleanor was warning us about?"

"If it is, then why does it feel... different?"

"I just need to know I'm not losing my mind."

Luna swallowed, her pulse quickening. Their words carried more than speculation—they carried a longing for answers, for reassurance.

As she stepped into the hall, the low hum of voices continued, but something shifted. A figure approached—a man she didn't know well but had seen around the community. His expression was tight, his voice uncertain.

"Is this about the heartbreak I felt?" he asked, his voice barely above a whisper.

Luna met his gaze, seeing the raw vulnerability there. Without a word, she placed a steady hand on his shoulder and nodded.

His inhale stuttered slightly, but he nodded in return, stepping back to join the others.

The murmurs quieted as Luna walked to the center of the room. The hall, bathed in the soft glow of the morning sun, had always been a place for gathering—a space where truth, celebration, and challenge had been met together. Today, it would serve as the place where she would finally speak her own truth.

The faces around her blurred slightly, but she felt the collective energy—their focus, their trust, and their fears.

She raised her hand, and silence fell.

Placing a hand over her heart, she let its steady rhythm anchor her.

"Thank you all for coming this morning," she began, her voice soft but resolute. "I've been hesitant to speak openly about what's been happening—to me, to this community—but I've realized that I can't keep this to myself any longer. You deserve to know the truth."

The ripple of unease was almost tangible, but Luna pushed through it. "A few days ago, I began meditating to understand what my mother wanted me to find—what she believed was so important for me to uncover. What Althea and I found in that meditation wasn't just a personal experience. It... shifted something within me. I've discovered a connection to an energy I didn't fully understand, and during that meditation, it expanded beyond me—into this community. The emotions you felt—love, fear, sadness, joy—they weren't mine, but they were amplified by my energy. I didn't intend for it to happen, but I can't deny what's real anymore. This is real. And it's bigger than me."

The silence broke into scattered murmurs, their reactions as varied as Luna expected. Some nodded, their faces thoughtful, while others looked skeptical, their arms crossed defensively. Eleanor stepped forward, her sharp gaze fixed on Luna. "And we're just supposed to take your word for this?" she asked, her tone laced with doubt. "How do we know this isn't some... misguided explanation for what's been happening? What proof do you have?"

Luna met Eleanor's eyes, her own gaze unwavering. "I don't have proof," she admitted. "All I have is my truth—and my trust in the people here. I may have been away for a long time, but I'm starting to understand what my mother saw in this place, what she left behind for me to find. This is a journey I'm still uncovering. Ezra and I are heading out today to seek answers, but I didn't want to leave without being honest with all of you."

A man near the back of the hall, his expression thoughtful, raised his hand. "I don't understand everything you're saying, Luna, but I felt something. It wasn't fear—it was love, pure and overwhelming. It felt like... hope and understanding."

Others began to speak up. A woman near the front nodded. "I felt it too—like joy was spilling out of me, and I didn't know where it came from."

But not everyone shared their sentiment. "I felt fear," another voice cut in. "It wasn't hope. It was like my worst memories were dredged up and forced to the surface."

The room filled with a mix of agreement and dissent, the tension palpable. Luna's chest tightened, but she stood firm. "I can't take away the pain some of you felt, and I won't dismiss it," she said. "But I want to make something clear—this isn't about control or harm. It's about connection. This energy isn't mine alone. It's in all of us. We're all connected, like threads in a web. What affects one of us ripples through the rest."

The murmurs softened, the crowd's focus sharpening as Luna closed her eyes briefly, centering herself. When she opened them, she spoke from a place of pure intention.

"I can't give you the kind of proof you're asking for," she admitted, her voice steady. "But I can offer you this—an experience. A moment of connection. If you'll allow me, I'd like to share what I've learned, to show you that this isn't something to fear. Maybe it won't be enough for everyone, but for now, it's the only proof I have."

She placed her hand over her heart, letting the warmth of her energy rise within her. Closing her eyes, she focused on the love and unity she had found. The vibration within her body grew, spreading outward like a gentle wave, soft yet powerful, brushing against the edges of each person in the room.

A collective stillness fell. Some closed their eyes, their features softening as warmth washed over them. Others stood rigid, their skepticism holding them apart from the experience, but even they felt a faint ripple of peace.

When Luna opened her eyes, the room was hushed. She exhaled slowly, her voice quiet but steady. "Thank you for listening. I don't have all the answers, but I'll keep searching—for myself and for all of us."

A murmur rippled through the crowd, soft at first, then growing into hushed conversations. Some people exchanged uncertain glances, processing her words, while others stepped forward with quiet words of gratitude. A few, like Miriam, approached with warmth, their expressions filled with encouragement. Others lingered at the edges of the hall, reluctant to leave, whispering amongst themselves.

Eleanor remained at the back, her arms crossed, her skepticism unshaken. She didn't speak, but the way her gaze lingered on Luna suggested she was weighing something deeper than mere doubt.

Luna didn't focus on those who still questioned. Instead, she turned to Miriam, who placed a reassuring hand on her arm, then to Ezra, whose quiet smile reminded her she wasn't alone.

As the last of the community members began filtering out, a few lingered, their expressions softer now, touched by something deeper. An older woman approached first, her eyes glistening with emotion.

"I don't have the words for what I felt," she murmured, placing a gentle hand over her heart. "But it was love. And it was beautiful. Thank you for sharing it with us."

Luna swallowed past the lump in her throat, offering a quiet, heartfelt nod.

Another man stepped forward, his brow furrowed, but his voice steady. "I don't know if I understand everything yet, but at least now we know what happened. That means something. Thank you for not leaving us in the dark."

Luna met his gaze and squeezed his arm lightly in gratitude.

As she stepped out into the morning light, the weight on her chest felt lighter. She didn't know what lay ahead, but she felt ready to face it—one step at a time.

The last of the community members disappeared into their daily tasks, leaving Luna standing at the edge of the hall, the sunlight catching the edges of her hair like a soft halo. She exhaled deeply, letting the moment settle over her.

The sound of approaching footsteps drew her attention, and she turned to see Ezra coming toward her, his expression warm and full of pride.

"You did it," he said, his voice low but filled with admiration. "You trusted them. You trusted yourself."

Luna's lips curved into a faint, grateful smile. "It wasn't easy."

"And yet, you made it look like it was," Ezra replied, closing the distance between them. He wrapped her in a warm embrace, his arms strong and steady around her. The world seemed to pause for a moment, the silence between them comfortable and profound.

Ezra stiffened slightly as a wave of emotion washed over him, an extraordinary sensation of love and peace flooding his senses. It wasn't just the warmth of her body against his—it was something deeper, something alive and vibrant, resonating from within her. His breath came short, his grip tightening as the energy seemed to pulse through him, filling every corner of his being with a love so pure it was almost overwhelming.

Luna pulled back slightly, her brow furrowing as she looked up at him. "Are you okay?"

Ezra nodded, his voice barely above a whisper. "I've never felt anything like that before. It's... incredible." He searched her eyes, his own glistening with unspoken emotion. "You don't just carry this gift, Luna. You are the gift."

Her cheeks flushed, and she looked down for a moment, her voice soft. "I don't know what it all means yet, but... thank you. For believing in me; for helping me find my way."

"Always," Ezra said firmly, his hand brushing hers as they parted. "Now, let's get ready, and have a quick breakfast. We've got a journey ahead of us."

Luna nodded, a quiet determination sparking in her chest. She watched as Ezra walked away, his steps purposeful but lighter than before. The vibrations of her gift still hummed faintly within her, a reminder of the power she now understood she carried—not just for herself, but for those who walked beside her.

Back at her cabin, Luna stood for a moment at the steps, gazing out at the awakening community. She whispered a silent promise to herself and to them: *I'll find answers, not just for myself but for the balance of this place, this family.*

Luna felt ready—ready to face Elias, ready to uncover the truth, and ready to step further into the light her mother had always believed in.

FOURTEEN

THREADS OF CONNECTION

T he car hummed steadily as Ezra navigated the winding roads through the lush Ozark hills. Sunlight filtered through the dense canopy, dappling the pavement in shifting golden patches. The crisp morning air flowed through the open windows, carrying the earthy scent of dew-drenched leaves and wildflowers.

Luna leaned back in her seat, scrolling through her phone, her thoughts tangled between anticipation and nerves.

Ezra glanced over, his lips curving into a faint smirk. "You're quiet again. Not having second thoughts, are you?"

Luna shook her head, mirroring his smirk. "Not second thoughts. Just... a lot on my mind."

Ezra tapped his fingers against the steering wheel. "Want to talk about it, or should I just keep playing chauffeur and let you brood?"

A chuckle escaped her, light but genuine. "A little of both, maybe."

The road curled around rolling hills, revealing misty valleys and meadows bursting with wildflowers. Luna's gaze drifted across the vibrant landscape. "It's beautiful out here," she murmured, the steady rhythm of the drive soothing her restless energy.

"Perfect day for a drive," Ezra agreed, his voice calm, grounding.

Luna returned her attention to her phone, skimming articles and profiles. "He's a professor of metaphysics," she read aloud. "Elias Morgenstern. Respected, but unconventional."

Ezra raised an eyebrow. "Unconventional how?"

She scrolled further, pausing on a headline: "Bridging Ancient Wisdom and Quantum Physics: The Philosophy of Elias Morgenstern." She read aloud, "'Morgenstern's work explores the intersection of ancient teachings and modern science, drawing connections between Hermetic principles, quantum mechanics, and the untapped potential of human consciousness.'"

Ezra let out a low whistle. "Sounds like someone your mom would've gotten along with."

Luna's fingers hesitated over the screen, a tightness settling in her chest. "Yeah," she said softly. "It sounds like he's been following a similar path. His lectures tie together ancient symbols, metaphysical concepts, and scientific discoveries in ways most people don't even think about."

Ezra's grip on the wheel tightened slightly. "Do you think he'll talk to you? Some of these deep thinkers aren't exactly approachable."

"I don't know," she admitted. "But if my mother trusted him, I have to try."

Ezra nodded, eyes never leaving the road. "We'll figure it out when we get there. One step at a time, right?"

Luna smiled faintly, his words echoing their earlier conversation. "Right."

They fell into a companionable silence, the gentle hum of the tires blending with the rustling trees. A hawk soared overhead, its shadow sweeping across the road before disappearing into the sky.

Ezra shot her a sideways glance, his tone laced with amusement. "Ever think about how wild this all is? A week ago, you were in a city, running meetings and making deals. Now you're chasing ancient secrets in the Ozarks."

Luna let out a soft laugh. "Yeah, it's surreal. But... it feels right. Like I'm exactly where I'm supposed to be."

Ezra's smirk widened. "Good. Because I have a feeling you're on the verge of something big."

A warmth spread through her chest, gratitude for his steady presence anchoring her. "Thanks, Ezra. For being here. For coming along."

"Always," he said simply.

Another beat of silence, then Luna sighed, her voice thoughtful. "It's strange. I keep trying to recall what I experienced in meditation, but it's like trying to grasp mist—just out of reach, shifting between memory and something deeper." She shook her head, frustrated. "It's maddening."

Ezra cast her a knowing glance. "Maybe it's not meant to make sense all at once. Give it time."

Ahead, the university skyline emerged from the hills, academic buildings nestled against the autumn-drenched landscape. Luna's pulse quickened, the weight of the moment settling over her.

"We're almost there," Ezra murmured.

Luna exhaled, steadying herself. "Yeah. Almost."

The car's hum softened as they neared campus, the road ahead stretching like a bridge between the past and the unknown future. She inhaled deeply, bracing herself for what came next.

The sprawling campus of the University of Arkansas buzzed with life as Luna and Ezra stepped out of the car. Students milled about in small groups, their laughter and conversations blending with the rustling of leaves in the gentle breeze. Luna adjusted the strap of her bag on her shoulder, her eyes scanning the rows of brick buildings and the towering oaks that lined the walkways.

"Impressive place," Ezra remarked, his tone light as he stuffed his hands into his jacket pockets.

Luna nodded, her nerves simmering just beneath the surface. "Let's find the philosophy department."

Navigating the campus proved easy enough, thanks to the clearly marked signs and helpful students who pointed them in the right direction. The philosophy department was housed in an ivy-covered building with grand wooden doors. As they stepped inside, the scent of aged books and polished wood greeted them, lending the space an academic weight that Luna found both comforting and daunting.

They located Elias Morgenstern's office near the end of a quiet corridor. The door bore his name in neat, engraved lettering, but what caught Luna's eye was the intricate symbol etched just below it. She inhaled sharply.

"This..." she murmured, tracing the symbol with her fingertips. "It's the same as in my mother's journal."

Ezra leaned closer, his brow furrowing. "That's not a coincidence. This is your guy, for sure."

Luna's attention shifted to a nearby bulletin board. Among the flyers and announcements was a small schedule that listed Elias's lectures. Her eyes landed on today's date: *Philosophy of History – Room 204, 10:00 AM.*

She glanced at her watch. 10:05 AM.

"He's giving a lecture right now," she said, her voice tinged with excitement and nerves.

Ezra tilted his head toward the staircase. "Let's go."

The lecture hall was easy to find, its doors slightly ajar. The faint murmur of a deep, resonant voice spilled into the hallway, pulling Luna forward as though the sound itself had a magnetic force. She exchanged a glance with Ezra before they slipped inside, taking seats at the very back. The room was dimly lit, the glow of the projector casting shadows against the rows of students hunched over notebooks. The scent of old wood and faint chalk dust filled the air, mingling with the quiet rustle of papers.

Luna's gaze was immediately drawn to the man at the podium. Elias Morgenstern stood tall and poised, his presence commanding yet unpretentious. His silver-streaked hair caught the light in a way that made him seem almost ethereal, his angular features etched with years of wisdom and inquiry. He gestured subtly as he spoke, his fingers drawing invisible connections in the air. The room, though packed, felt wrapped in a hushed reverence, as though the walls themselves leaned in to listen.

"History," Elias intoned, his voice deep and measured, "is not merely a record of past events. It is a living narrative, shaped by the perspectives and choices of those who record it. It is not static—it breathes, shifts, and reshapes itself with every retelling. It is both a teacher and a mirror, reflecting not only what has been but what is, and what could be."

Luna shivered, the weight of his words settling over her like a tangible presence. The cadence of his voice felt familiar, almost unnervingly so, echoing the philosophies her mother had written about in her journals. It was as though Elias wasn't simply speaking—he was weaving truths into the very air around them, pulling at threads she had always sensed but never fully grasped.

Elias paused, glancing down at his notes before lifting his gaze to the audience. For a moment, his expression softened, his sharp eyes scanning the room with a subtle intensity. Then, something shifted. His posture stiffened almost imperceptibly, his brow furrowing as though he had caught a faint scent in the air or a whisper just out of earshot. His eyes narrowed, sweeping the rows of students as if searching for someone.

Luna felt her pulse quicken. The air seemed to hum with a quiet tension, the kind that precedes a revelation. She leaned toward Ezra, her voice barely above a whisper. "Is he...?"

Ezra's gaze flicked to Elias, his jaw tightening. "I think he's looking for someone," he whispered. "Let's hope it's not us."

For a fleeting moment, Elias's eyes darted toward the back of the hall, his gaze grazing over Luna and Ezra. His expression faltered—just for a heartbeat—as though recognition flickered through his mind but failed to fully ignite. Luna held her breath, her heart pounding so loudly she was certain it would betray her. Then, just as suddenly as the moment had come, it was gone. Elias's face smoothed into a thoughtful smile, his demeanor returning to its calm, scholarly elegance.

"History invites us to question," he continued, his voice steady once more. "To challenge not only what we've been told but what we've told ourselves. In doing so, we become co-authors of the narrative, not passive recipients."

The energy in the room remained charged, as though an unseen thread now connected them all. Luna felt it in her chest, an almost magnetic pull toward the man at the podium. Her mother's voice echoed faintly in her mind: *Trust in him, but remain discerning.* The words felt heavier now, as though they carried not just a message but a warning.

She and Ezra sat in rapt attention, absorbing every word as Elias seamlessly wove together philosophy, science, and something more—something unspoken yet deeply felt. Time slipped by unnoticed, his voice pulling them into a realm of understanding just beyond their grasp.

Midway through the lecture, Elias paused, his eyes sweeping across the crowd before shifting the image on the projector. A familiar map of

Mesopotamia filled the screen, centered on the ancient civilization of Sumer.

"Sumer," Elias said, his voice calm but brimming with intent. "Historians call it the cradle of civilization, the first great society on Earth—dating back around six thousand years." He allowed the image to linger before clicking to the next slide.

The screen filled with images of ancient ruins, with intricately carved stone pillars standing in silent defiance of conventional history. "But then we found this," Elias continued, his tone shifting subtly, tinged with curiosity and challenge. "Göbekli Tepe, carbon-dated to be at least eleven thousand years ago—far older than Sumer, completely upending what we thought we knew."

He paused again, letting the significance sink in before moving to a new set of images—ancient megalithic structures, obscure carvings, and ruins hidden deep in jungles and beneath oceans. "These are just fragments—glimpses of civilizations lost to time. Civilizations that may have thrived thirty thousand years ago or more. Our ancestors were far more advanced than we've been led to believe."

The room was utterly still, tension coiling with every new slide. "The truth is," Elias said, his voice dipping to a near whisper, "we haven't yet found the first civilization. We've merely scratched the surface. There's so much more beneath the sands, beneath the oceans, waiting for us to discover—waiting to rewrite our entire history."

Luna's pulse quickened as the images burned into her mind, stirring something deep within her—something almost familiar.

As the lecture drew to a close, Elias stepped back from the podium, his hands clasped in front of him. "What we call history is just the beginning of the story. The deeper truths... lie buried beneath our feet."

Students shuffled their papers, filing out in murmured conversation, breaking the spell of the room. Ezra touched Luna's arm lightly, his voice low. "You okay?"

Luna blinked, as if waking from a vivid daydream. The images Elias had shown lingered in her mind, whispering fragments of meaning she couldn't yet grasp. Her pulse thrummed with a strange resonance—like she was standing on the edge of something long buried, just waiting to be unearthed.

She nodded slowly, her voice soft but certain. "Yeah... I'm okay." A small, almost knowing smile touched her lips. "I'm ready."

"You've got this," he murmured, his tone calm but encouraging. "I'll wait outside."

Luna nodded, swallowing the lump in her throat as she watched Elias collect his notes. A quiet urgency stirred within her—this was her moment, and she couldn't let it slip away.

As the last of the students filtered out, she descended the lecture hall stairs, her heart pounding with every step. Elias, lost in thought, shuffled his papers at the podium, his silver-streaked hair catching the light. His movements were slow, almost absentminded, as if his mind were elsewhere—somewhere far beyond the room they stood in.

Then, as if pulled by an unseen force, he lifted his head.

Their eyes met, and a flicker of something unreadable passed through his expression. His piercing blue gaze bore into her—not just seeing her, but searching, confirming. A quiet intensity settled in his features, his focus sharpening as if he were trying to reconcile what he felt with what he saw.

For a long moment, he simply stared, leaving Luna unnerved.

Then, understanding dawned. His expression shifted—not just recognition, but something deeper, something unspoken.

A slow, knowing smile spread across his face.

"You must be Margaret's daughter," he murmured, his voice rich and steady, yet carrying the weight of realization. "Luna. Right?"

Luna froze, a shiver running through her as her mother's name rolled off his tongue with effortless familiarity. So, this was him. The Elias she'd been searching for. But before she could process that relief, another thought hit her—he knew who she was.

Her lips parted, surprise flickering across her face. "You... know me?"

Elias nodded, stepping around the podium with an urgency that caught her off guard. He gestured toward the side exit, his tone quiet but firm. "I knew your mother. And during my lecture just now, I felt something—a presence I haven't encountered in... too long. You're not Margaret, but you feel like her. So, logically, you must be Luna. Let's talk in my office."

Luna hesitated, glancing toward the main entrance where Ezra waited outside. A knot of guilt tightened in her chest. She should tell him... shouldn't she? She pulled her phone from her pocket, fumbling with it, her fingers hovering over the screen.

Before she could finish, Elias turned, his sharp gaze catching hers. "You have a presence like your mother, but stronger," he said, a wistful smile crossing his face. "For a moment, I thought you were sitting in the front row. Just like her. She was right about your potential—I can see that clearly now."

Distracted by his words, Luna slipped her phone back into her pocket without further thought and followed Elias through the side exit. Her mind raced with questions. "You can sense people's presence?" She asked, a note of fascination in her voice.

Elias chuckled softly. "I wish. No, I'm not that fortunate. I could only ever sense Margaret's presence... and now yours, it seems," he said, glancing at her as they walked. His voice lowered slightly, his expression turning thoughtful. "That was your mother's doing—a gift she left behind, perhaps."

The quiet hallways of the philosophy department stretched before them, the soft hum of fluorescent lights overhead the only sound. As they walked, Elias's measured steps seemed purposeful, each one carrying him deeper into his thoughts. Luna tried to keep pace, her heart pounding with a mix of apprehension and curiosity.

They stopped at a modest wooden door, the brass handle worn smooth from years of use. Elias pushed it open, revealing a space that felt more like a scholar's sanctuary than a professor's office.

The room was dimly lit, the glow from a single desk lamp casting golden light across shelves that stretched to the ceiling. Every inch of the walls was lined with books—leather-bound tomes with faded titles, scrolls stored in delicate cases, and journals stacked in precarious piles. Artifacts from various cultures filled the room: polished stones glinting under the light, ancient figurines carved with meticulous detail, and intricate metalwork that looked almost alive.

At the center of it all was a large desk, cluttered with diagrams, charts, and open books, their pages brimming with arcane symbols and notes written in a precise hand. The air felt charged, almost humming with a quiet energy that seemed to resonate with Luna's own.

"Have a seat," Elias said, motioning toward a chair by the desk as he moved to close the door behind them. "I'm eager to learn what brought you here."

Luna sat carefully, her fingers brushing against the armrests of the chair as her gaze darted around the room. The weight of her decision to follow Elias lingered in her mind, but the pull of his presence—and the threads connecting him to her mother—was impossible to ignore.

She settled in, her gaze wandering over the eclectic collection in Elias's office—the walls lined with books, symbols scrawled on parchment, and artifacts from cultures she couldn't immediately place. She traced the edges of her mother's journal before pulling it from her bag.

Luna set the journal on the desk between them, the weight of it heavier now than it had ever felt. "My mother's journals mentioned you," she said, watching his expression closely. "She believed you held answers. I was hoping they were meant for me, and by the sounds of it, I was right."

Elias leaned back, his sharp eyes studying her as though piecing together a puzzle. A quiet chuckle escaped him. "Answers for you?" He shook his head, amusement flickering in his gaze. "Margaret was always the one I went to for answers."

He tapped his fingers against the chair's armrest, his voice turning more introspective. "We studied together in college—philosophy, metaphysics, the Hermetic principles. But it wasn't just academic curiosity. We pushed each other beyond the limits of what we thought was possible. Whenever one of us hit a wall, the other seemed to have the missing piece." He exhaled, a small, knowing smile crossing his lips. "Margaret was one of the most brilliant minds I've ever met. Her ability to seemingly tap into unseen knowledge always astonished me, but even she had moments of doubt. We both did. It's why we worked so well together."

Luna's heart sank. "You helped her when she was stuck?"

Elias nodded. "More times than I can count. And she did the same for me. We were constantly unraveling ideas that felt just out of reach."

Her grip on the journal tightened. The realization settled heavily in her chest.

The message wasn't for me after all.

Her mother had left Elias's name as a reminder to herself—to seek guidance, to work through something she couldn't grasp alone. *Was this trip a mistake?* Had she chased a ghost, only to find she was never meant to in the first place?

But then, a familiar thought surfaced, steadying her pulse.

There are no coincidences.

She straightened, shifting her focus. Maybe the message was for both of them. Maybe this was where she was meant to be after all.

Elias studied her carefully, his brow furrowing. "You look disappointed. Did I say something wrong?" His gaze flickered toward the journal. "What question did you come here to answer, and why not ask Margaret?"

The air between them seemed to thrum with unspoken meaning, the weight of her mother's presence lingering in the space she left behind.

She lowered her gaze, her fingers curling against the armrest of the chair as a lump formed in her throat. "My mother—" she began, her voice faltering. She swallowed hard, forcing the words past the ache in her chest. "She passed away this past week."

Elias stilled, his expression shifting as her words registered. He turned his gaze toward the window, his jaw tightening as if bracing against the weight of loss. The sunlight streaming in seemed to grow softer, muted, as a heavy silence filled the room.

"I'm sorry," he said finally, his voice low and laced with genuine sorrow. "Margaret was... remarkable. The world is dimmer without her light."

Luna nodded slowly, her head still bowed as her heart ached with the memories of her mother.

Elias's gaze returned to her, a newfound intensity in his eyes. "And now you're here," he murmured, almost to himself. "You've taken up the path she always spoke of. The journey she was so certain would one day be yours."

Luna shifted, caught off guard by his certainty. "She spoke of my journey?"

Elias exhaled sharply, his expression unreadable. "Well, you know your mother—she spoke in cryptic ways. It was less about your journey and more about hers, and how it would inevitably shape yours." He leaned forward, the weight of understanding settling between them.

After a brief pause, he let out a soft, almost disbelieving chuckle. "Honestly, I'm a bit surprised that your path led back to me." His fingers drummed lightly against the desk, his expression turning reflective.

He leaned back, folding his hands together. "A year after we graduated, Margaret saw what she called an impasse—a fork in the road." His voice softened, though the weight of memory pressed against it. "She told me that if she chose one path, it would separate the two of us forever. But it was a path she had to take... because it was the only way a much more important journey would unfold as it was meant to... your journey."

Emotion cinched her breath tight. "She knew she had to leave you?"

Elias nodded, his gaze distant, as though reliving the moment. "She didn't want to, but she knew it was necessary. At the time, I fought her on it—I didn't understand how she could make that kind of decision based on a future that hadn't even happened yet." His jaw tensed for a fraction of a second before he let out a quiet sigh. "But you know how it was with your mother. Once she saw something—really saw it—it was impossible to change her mind."

Luna swallowed, her heart pounding in her chest. "So, you let her go."

Elias's lips quirked into a sad smile. He hesitated for a moment, studying her carefully, as though sensing an unspoken assumption. "Your mother and I... we weren't intimate," he clarified gently. "But our connection ran deep—deeper than most could comprehend. We loved each other in a way that didn't fit into conventional definitions. That kind of closeness... it wasn't always easy for others to accept or understand. I think that's why I always felt like a secret in her life."

His gaze met Luna's again, sharper now, as if ensuring she understood. "She never asked for permission to go. She only asked for understanding."

A shadow of something unreadable flickered across his face. "And if I had fought harder, if I had convinced her to stay... you may not be sitting here right now."

He exhaled slowly, his expression shifting, softened by something distant. "For a while after she left, she sent me letters. Pictures, too." His fingers traced idle patterns along the desk. "She wanted me to know how she was doing, how you were growing." He shook his head with a quiet chuckle, though there was no humor in it. "But life kept moving. She had you, I had my work. Eventually, the letters stopped."

The weight of his words settled over Luna like a quiet storm, her mother's foresight suddenly feeling more immense than she had ever realized. Margaret hadn't just made choices for herself—she had made them for Luna.

Luna's grip on the journal tightened. "She gave up everything for me."

Elias shook his head, his voice gentle but firm. "No. She chose everything for you. There's a difference."

Luna stared at him, absorbing the gravity of what he was saying. Her entire life—every moment that led her here—had been woven together by choices her mother made long before Luna ever had a say in them.

Her pulse quickened. "And now I have to figure out where to go from here."

Elias studied her carefully, his expression unreadable. "That's the question, isn't it?" He gestured to the journal. "You're following her path, but maybe the real question is... are you ready to step off of it and forge your own?"

The thought unsettled her in a way she couldn't yet name. But deep down, she knew—this was why her mother had sent her here. Not just to find answers.

Elias leaned forward, his voice quieter now, almost reverent. "So tell me, Luna—what is it you're truly seeking? What led you to find me?"

Luna hesitated before speaking. His words caught her off guard, but by now, she was used to the enigmatic puzzles her mother had left for her to unravel. Her fingers brushing the edge of the journal. "Understanding," she said. "Of what my mother believed, of what I'm experiencing. I feel like I'm being pulled toward something bigger, but I don't know what it is—or why. My Mothers journals don't make sense to me. I have a hard time understanding what she wants."

Elias leaned back in his chair, his eyes narrowing slightly as he considered her. "Before we dive into the specifics, there's something you should know about those journals," he said, his tone soft but deliberate. "They weren't written to be a guide for you—they were a guide for her. Margaret's mind worked in ways most people couldn't follow. The journals were her way of mapping her thoughts, connecting ideas only she could see." His gaze locked onto hers. "It's no wonder they feel like a puzzle. They were never meant to be read with ease."

Luna frowned, her grip tightening on the journal. "So... I'm not supposed to understand them?"

Elias chuckled softly. "Perhaps not, or at least, not right away. But here's the thing—you don't need to solve the whole puzzle at once. You just need the next piece. Eventually, you'll find that the journal runs out of pieces... yet the puzzle remains." His voice softened, carrying an almost fatherly warmth. "You'll hear what you need to hear when the time is right. Let's start with something simple—or at least something that might *sound* simple."

He stood, gesturing toward a nearby bookshelf filled with worn volumes. "Your mother understood the world through Hermetic principles—ancient teachings passed down from lips to ears for thousands of years. These principles, which formed the foundation of esoteric knowledge in ancient Egypt and Greece, were once hidden from the masses, taught only to initiates. Over time, much of that knowledge was lost... only to be rediscovered through modern science."

He paused, watching her reaction carefully. "Margaret helped me see this connection—the bridge between what ancient sages knew and what modern physicists are now uncovering. It changed the course of my academic career. While my colleagues focused on established theories, I began digging into the unconventional history most scholars dismissed."

Elias leaned forward, his eyes intent. "You see, Hermetic teachings tell us that everything vibrates. Nothing is truly solid. The illusion of physical matter comes from energy vibrating at different frequencies—the *Principle of Vibration*. Modern science is finally catching up. What the ancients described as the fabric of existence, we now know as the quantum field. Even in a vacuum, where we think there's 'nothing,' there's still energy—always moving, always alive."

Luna's breath quickened, her mind racing to keep up with the depth of what he was saying. Elias smiled, sensing her curiosity.

"The universe, according to Hermetic teachings, operates through vibration, polarity, and rhythm. These principles align perfectly with quantum discoveries like *quantum entanglement*—how two particles once connected remain linked no matter the distance. The universe isn't just a collection of separate objects—it's a vast, interconnected web of energy."

Luna blinked, leaning in. "I remember studying quantum physics. I loved the double-slit experiment, but... I always saw it as an experiment, something to observe—not something practical or usable. My mother believed it could be?"

Elias nodded, his eyes lighting with recognition. "Not in the traditional sense, but she saw it as a metaphor—proof that reality is shaped not just by observation, but by intention, *the principle of mentalism*. Understanding these principles wasn't just academic for her; it was a way to engage with the unseen forces around us. If I remember correctly, she believed your journey would take you far beyond mere observation."

Luna nearly objected to the idea, but something deep inside wouldn't let her. A quiet, unspoken part of her had already begun to believe it.

"Let's talk a little bit more about entanglement. Our current science points to a singular event, The Big Bang...I won't insult your intelligence with those details, but what I mean to point out is that prior to that event, everything was one. If quantum entanglement holds true, then all matter in the universe is still connected." Elias holds his thought once more, looking for understanding, providing an opportunity for questions. "I remember reading about an experiment where they split a photon and separated it. Both would react to the stimulation imposed on one at the same time, despite the distance between them." Luna recalled.

Elias smiled, his eyes lighting with recognition. "Exactly. The experiment with the split photon is one of the clearest demonstrations of quantum entanglement. What happens to one particle instantly affects the other, no matter how far apart they are. Einstein called it 'spooky action at a distance.'" He paused, giving her a moment to process. "It's a perfect example of how everything remains connected, even when it seems separate."

Luna nodded, her pulse quickening as the dots began to connect in her mind. "I remember being fascinated by it, but I never thought of it as... practical. I always saw it as something theoretical."

"Well, what if I told you it's not so different from the technology we use every day, better yet, the technology we will use tomorrow?" Elias leaned forward, his eyes sparkling with curiosity. "Pull out your phone. What's the last thing you searched for?"

Luna hesitated, her fingers curling around her phone. "I... looked you up," she admitted, her voice tinged with nervousness. "We were driving here—well, I wasn't driving. Ezra was."

Elias chuckled, holding up a hand to ease her embarrassment. "Relax, Luna. What you were searching for isn't the point. Think about how effortlessly you accessed that information. We've created technology that stores data on physical material—data that can be requested and received in an instant. Information, traveling invisibly through space, encoded and decoded in what feels like the blink of an eye. And when we perfect quantum computing, well... I can't even fathom the possibilities. We take it for granted, but it's remarkable."

He paused for emphasis, his gaze steady. "Now think about the principle of Correspondence. 'As above, so below.' What exists on this physical plane reflects something higher. The ability to encode and retrieve information exists on other planes too—planes your mother understood better than most."

Luna's eyes widened as the concept began to take shape. She felt the spark of understanding, a connection between her mother's teachings and the world she lived in.

"Have you heard of Akashic Records?" Elias asked.

"I'm sorry, no." A clear response.

"The Akashic records are a compilation of all universal events, thoughts, words, emotions and feelings ever to have occurred in the past, present, or future in terms of all entities and life forms, not just human. Within them is a storehouse or archive of information about your soul's journey across time and space, containing the "record" of your soul's thoughts, deeds, experiences, and traumas in this lifetime and all past lifetimes. According to Theosophist philosophy, the Akashic records don't pass judgement or label actions as good or bad; rather, they simply state what has been. Call them what you will, according to the principle of correspondence, and our human ability to record history; both your mother and I believe it to be real."

Elias paused, his eyes narrowing in thought. "It's curious, though... why does this seem new to you? Why hadn't Margaret taught you all of this herself?"

Luna's throat tightened. She lowered her gaze, her fingers tracing absent patterns on the journal's cover. "She might've tried," she admitted softly. "When I was younger, she talked about things like energy and vibration, but I wasn't ready to hear it. We... had a falling out when I was a teenager. I wanted a normal life—a career, independence. So, I left to create my own path. For a while, we barely spoke."

Elias leaned back, digesting her words with a slow nod. His expression softened, and after a pause, he said, "Margaret always trusted life to unfold as it should. She always trusted in the bigger picture—more than anyone I've ever known. If she let you go, it's because she believed you needed to live that life first... so it would lead you here, now."

Luna looked up, her heart tightening at the unexpected reassurance. There was something in his voice that rang true—a deeper knowing she couldn't ignore.

"Your mother believed deeply in the concept of the Akashic Records—a universal library of knowledge encoded within all things, including our very DNA," Elias continued, his tone both gentle and profound. "Science now backs up this potential, estimating that one gram of human DNA can hold more than 215 petabytes of information."

He leaned forward again, his eyes locked onto hers. "Margaret believed that you, Luna, would one day unlock the ability to access this encoded knowledge—not through technology or machinery, but through the awakened potential of your own consciousness. She thought you carried the key to unlocking something humanity has forgotten since the last time Earth was exposed to powerful universal energies."

Luna felt a chill run down her spine. "She thought I could decode... history?"

"Not just history," Elias clarified, his voice steady but electric with possibility. "The past, the present... maybe even glimpses of the future. The story of humanity, of the cosmos. It's all written within us. And right now, the world is shifting—cycles of energy from beyond our planet are activating dormant aspects of our DNA." He tilted his head slightly, his eyes searching hers. "You've felt this, haven't you?"

Luna nodded slowly, her mind flashing back to the intense meditations and the surge of power that rippled through the community.

Elias's gaze softened. "You're standing at a threshold, Luna. What lies beyond it is vast and profound, but it's not a path you'll walk alone."

"I know I am not alone. I keep getting that reminder. I have Someone." Luna says, a flash of Ezra's handsome face enters her mind's eye.

"Not just someone Luna, many will awaken with you, many are awakening now." His words give Luna hope.

The weight of his words settled over her, the enormity of her journey crystallizing in that moment. "My mother believed this knowledge could change the world?" she asked quietly.

Elias leaned forward, his expression earnest. "And so do I."

Luna clutched her mother's journal tightly, her mind racing as the pieces of the puzzle began to shift and align in unexpected ways. She wasn't just following her mother's legacy—she was stepping into something much larger, something she hadn't fully grasped until now.

"I have more to share," Elias said, gathering his lecture notes and glancing at the clock. "But I also have another lecture hall of students probably wondering where I am. Can you come back tomorrow?"

Luna blinked, caught off guard by the question. "Tomorrow?" Her voice wavered slightly as her mind scrambled to process everything. Could she? Should she? Staying meant committing to something she wasn't sure she understood yet. Did she have what she needed—clothes, supplies—or even the mental capacity to take in more?

Her thoughts whirled, but deep down, she already knew the answer. Of course she could. Of course she had to. This was the path her mother had set her on, and if Elias had more to reveal, there was no choice but to listen.

"Yes," she said, her voice steadier now. "I'll come back tomorrow."

Elias smiled warmly. "Good. Trust yourself, Luna. You're on the right path."

As she turned toward the door, her heart beat a little faster, the weight of the day catching up with her. Tomorrow felt like both an eternity away and the next step she couldn't avoid. She would be back—ready or not.

The crisp afternoon air greeted Luna as she stepped out of the philosophy building, her mind still swirling with Elias's revelations. She spotted Ezra leaning casually against a lamppost near the entrance, his arms crossed. His expression softened when he saw her, but a flicker of concern remained in his eyes.

"There you are," Ezra said, pushing off the post where he had been waiting, his tone carrying equal parts relief and frustration. He met her halfway, his shoulders tense. "I thought we agreed I'd stay close by. You disappeared without a word... again."

Luna hesitated, her fingers tightening around the strap of her bag. "I know," she admitted softly, guilt flashing across her face. "I was going to text, but..." Her voice faltered. "There is no but. I should have let you know."

Ezra's expression remained stern, but the sharp edge in his eyes softened slightly. He studied her face for a long moment, his brow furrowed as if weighing whether to press the matter further. Finally, he let out a long exhale, running a hand through his hair. "Alright," he said, his voice quieter now. "As long as you're safe."

A faint smile flickered on Luna's lips, though it didn't quite reach her eyes. "I am. I promise." She gestured toward a nearby bench shaded by a towering oak. "But we need to talk. There's... a lot to unpack."

Ezra followed her, the tension still lingering between them as they sat. The quiet hum of campus life surrounded them: the faint rustle of leaves, the distant murmur of voices, the rhythmic squeak of a bicycle wheel passing by.

Luna's hands rested in her lap, fingers fiddling with the strap of her bag as she began. "I barely scratched the surface with Elias, but what I learned... it's big, Ezra. Bigger than I expected." Her words tumbled out quickly, her thoughts racing to keep up.

She recounted her conversation with Elias, her voice wavering with both awe and trepidation. She described his teachings on energy and vibration, the interconnectedness of all things, and how the universe's intricate design reflected the principles her mother had always believed in.

When she reached the part about the Akashic Records—her mother's belief in her potential to unlock them—her voice grew quieter, more uncertain. "It's like... everything she worked for, everything she believed, is leading to this," she said, her gaze distant. "And now it's on me to figure it out."

Ezra listened intently, his hand resting on the bench between them. He didn't interrupt, but his eyes reflected the weight of her words. When she finally stopped, her breath catching, he leaned forward slightly. "That's... a lot," he said, his voice steady but laced with concern. "But it sounds like Elias knows what he's talking about. And if anyone can help you make sense of this, it's him."

Luna nodded, though her shoulders sagged under the burden of it all. "One meeting with him isn't enough. There's so much more I need to understand."

Ezra's gaze swept the campus, as though seeking an answer in the world around them. Then he looked back at her, his expression resolute.

"Then we'll make time. Let's find a place to stay nearby for a few days."

The quickness of his response caught Luna off guard. She blinked at him, her lips parting. "You're okay with that? I thought you might..."

"Luna," Ezra interrupted gently, his tone firm but kind. "I told you I'm here. If staying longer means you get the answers you need, then that's what we'll do."

A wave of gratitude washed over her, momentarily easing the tightness in her chest. "Thank you, Ezra. I mean it."

He smiled, the tension in his face easing for the first time. "Let's find somewhere to stay."

Together, they pulled out their phones, scrolling through options in the area. Luna's mind drifted as they searched, her thoughts returning to Elias's words about energy and connection. Even something as mundane as looking for a hotel seemed to hum with an underlying rhythm.

"How about this?" Ezra asked, showing her his screen. The photo depicted a charming inn with ivy climbing its brick façade. "It's close to campus, and it looks quiet enough to get some rest."

Luna glanced at the image, nodding. "It's perfect."

Ezra booked the room, and as they stood to leave, he placed a hand on her shoulder, grounding her. "We've got this," he said, his voice steady.

Luna smiled, his words wrapped around her like a comforting embrace. "Yeah. We do."

The fading sunlight bathed Fayetteville in golden hues as they approached the inn. Its quaint charm felt almost magical, with soft lanterns glowing at the entrance and a faint breeze carrying the scent of nearby jasmine. Just down the street, a charming restaurant caught Luna's eye, its outdoor seating illuminated by twinkling string lights.

"That place looks nice," she said, nodding toward it. "What do you think? Check in and then grab dinner?"

Ezra followed her gaze, his lips curving into an easy smile. "Sounds like a plan."

After settling into their room—a small but cozy space with lavender-scented linens and old-fashioned charm—they returned to the restaurant. The patio buzzed with quiet energy, the low hum of conversation blending with the soft strumming of a musician's guitar in the corner.

Luna sipped her wine as they waited for their meal, her gaze drifting to the people around them. A couple laughed softly over their drinks. An older man, alone at a table, savored his meal with an expression of contentment. The musician's melody wove through it all, a subtle thread connecting the scene.

"It's funny," Luna said, breaking the silence. "Elias talked about quantum entanglement today. How particles, once connected, remain connected no matter how far apart they are." She glanced at Ezra, her voice turning thoughtful. "I think people are like that too. Even when we're apart, we leave marks on each other—energetic imprints. We're never really separate."

Ezra leaned back, studying her with quiet admiration. "So, you're saying... we're all connected? Like pieces of the same whole?"

She nodded, her lips curving into a small smile. "Exactly. Every interaction creates a ripple. Every thought, every action—it's all connected. We're co-creating reality without even realizing it." Her eyes flickered with growing clarity. "Now that I have this perception, it's like I can't unsee it. It's faint, but it's everywhere—woven into everything." She glanced around, almost as if watching those unseen connections unfold before her.

Ezra's gaze softened, and he reached across the table to take her hand. "Sounds like your mom's wisdom is starting to make sense after all."

Luna laughed gently, her heart swelling with warmth. "It is. I just needed someone like Elias to help me see it from a different angle."

Their conversation flowed easily as the evening deepened, stars emerging in the indigo sky above them. By the time they returned to the inn, Luna felt lighter, as though some invisible weight had lifted.

That night, she lay still but restless, her mother's journal in hand—reading, reflecting, and bracing herself for the truths that might lie ahead.

FIFTEEN

FRACTALS OF TRUTH

The morning sun streamed through the thin curtains of the inn, casting a warm glow on the simple but cozy room. Luna stood by the small desk, carefully packing her notebook and her mother's journal into her bag. Each turn of the pages the night before had revealed her mother's quiet urgency, the threads of her research now looping together in ways Luna could barely comprehend.

Ezra leaned against the doorway, his coffee steaming in his hand. "Morning," he said. "Ready for round two with the professor?"

Luna stretched, her mind already racing ahead. "More than ready. I feel like I've barely scratched the surface of what he has to share."

Ezra nodded, setting his cup down. "I figured as much. The way you tossed and turned all night." He chuckled.

As they shared a quick breakfast, the comfort of their companionship steadied her. Before long, it was time to leave.

"I'll be fine," Luna reassured him as they stood by the door. "You don't have to worry so much."

Ezra chuckled softly, his hands resting lightly on her shoulders. "It's not worry—it's care. Big difference."

Luna's cheeks warmed, and she squeezed his hand before stepping outside. "I'll call when I'm done." She said, planting a kiss on his cheek before leaving.

The campus was already alive with activity as Luna made her way back to the philosophy department. The sunlight danced off the glass-paneled buildings, and a crisp breeze carried the faint rustle of papers and distant laughter.

When she reached Elias's office, the door was slightly ajar, and the familiar scent of old books and parchment greeted her. Elias looked up from his desk, his face brightening with recognition.

"Luna," he said warmly, standing to greet her. "Right on time. I trust you're ready to dive deeper?"

"Absolutely," she replied, taking the seat he gestured toward.

Elias packed up a few things into his briefcase in preparation for a later class, his expression turning thoughtful. "Where to begin? Hmm, yesterday, we touched on the interconnectedness of all things, the principle of vibration, and the vast potential encoded within us. Today, I want to take that understanding further, to explore how these truths are reflected on a cosmic scale."

Luna leaned forward, her pulse quickening.

Elias found his seat, leaned back, the soft light from the window catching the edges of his silver-streaked hair. "Let's begin with something fundamental yet profound: the rhythm that shapes our existence," he said, his voice steady and deliberate.

Luna's pen hovered over her notebook, ready to capture every word.

"Imagine the Earth, not as a static sphere, but as a dynamic entity, moving through the cosmos. Our solar system itself orbits the center of the galaxy, encountering regions of intense energy along its path. These shifts are not just astronomical; they impact everything—climate, ecosystems, even human consciousness."

Luna furrowed her brow. "This is why we have different ages, like the ice ages, or golden ages?"

"Exactly," Elias affirmed. "Ancient civilizations tracked these cycles, understanding that each age brings its own energy and we should adjust our way of living to match. Much like we adjust to the changing seasons. I am sure you have heard of the Age of Aquarius. It is said to herald a time of awakening—a shift from external authority to internal wisdom, from division to unity. Some say that is the energy we are flowing into now."

"What do you say?" Luna asked, reading his expression.

Elias huffed, "Well, I say the universe moves in rhythms far beyond our comprehension—like the solar system's 225-million-year journey around the galaxy."

"In other words, you don't know." Luna nodded as she read between the lines. Her thoughts drifted, beginning to make connections between this wisdom and her personal experience. She recalled the meditative surge she had experienced and its ripple effects on the community. "So, what is happening is a result of the energy we are moving into?"

Elias's gaze sharpened. "I can't say for certain. Every human has their own rhythm they follow. The ancients studied and understood these cycles and their own rhythms far better than we do now. They knew how to align themselves to the present energy they flowed through. It is my guess that your rhythm is naturally attuned to the coming age. Like a tuning fork vibrating in response to a resonant frequency" He paused. "We're entering a time of heightened energetic influence, a cycle that many believe could activate dormant possibilities in our DNA and reconnects us to aspects of our potential that have been lost for millennia."

Elias leaned back for a moment, his eyes distant as if tracing invisible lines in the air. "To understand how this energy works in us, it helps to look beyond the human body—to see how the earth itself mirrors those same patterns. Just as we are affected by these cycles, so is the planet."

Elias reached for a large, leather-bound book, opening it to a page filled with intricate illustrations of human energy centers and planetary maps. "Now, consider this. Just as your body has 7 major energy centers, so does the Earth. Its 7 major tectonic plates function like chakras, each one resonating with a specific energy. The earth also has its own meridians"

Luna leaned forward, captivated. "As above, so below..."

"Precisely," Elias said, his finger tracing a line on the map. "These are called ley lines—channels through which the planet's energy flows. Ancient structures like Stonehenge and the pyramids were built on central points, harnessing their power. The principle of correspondence—'as above, so below'—teaches us that the micro reflects the macro. The human body mirrors the Earth, the solar system, and even the universe."

Luna's mind buzzed with connections. "So, when the Earth shifts energetically, it affects us on a physical and spiritual level?"

Elias nodded. "And vice versa. When we heal ourselves, we contribute to the healing of the planet. The cycles of energy we spoke of earlier are affecting the earth's energy as well. As that happens, I suspect you will continue to experience a continued shift alongside it." Luna heard his words and shook her head slightly with concern for her ability to continue.

"These natural energy patterns aren't limited to ley lines; they exist at every level of reality, from the smallest particle to the vastest structure," Elias said, his voice growing more intent. "That's where fractals come in—the very structure of reality itself. Have you heard of fractals, Luna?"

"Yes," she said thoughtfully. "Fractals are mathematical patterns that repeat at different scales—self-similar structures. No matter how much you zoom in, the same pattern keeps appearing."

Elias nodded, a knowing smile tugging at his lips. "Exactly. Nature is filled with fractals—snowflakes, mountain ranges, even the veins in your body. They reveal something essential: nature operates through repeating patterns, scaling up and down infinitely. And if nature is a reflection of the universe's deeper structure, then fractals are a glimpse of something far more profound...."

Luna's mind flashed to the vision she had while connected with Althea—a strand of diamond-like pearls stretching into infinity, each one reflecting the others in a shimmer of light. "I saw something like that during my meditation," she said softly. "It was beautiful... like each piece held the whole inside it. I looked into one, and it felt like falling through it—like I flowed into the web and ended up right back where I began."

Elias's smile deepened. "What you experienced was a glimpse of what has been called Indra's Net—a concept from ancient Hindu philosophy. It describes the universe as a vast web of interconnected jewels, each reflecting every other jewel. It's a poetic precursor to what modern science calls string theory."

Luna's head swam with the magnitude of what he was saying, but the connections felt undeniable.

Luna leaned forward, her eyes locked onto Elias, the soft hum of the office's ancient energy filling the air. The faint rustling of leaves outside the window seemed to mirror the tremor of anticipation in her chest.

"I'll share something your mother believed," Elias began, his tone gentler now, his fingers tracing the edge of a worn leather-bound book on his desk. "She believed we had lived before—her and I—in an age far older than any recorded history. She spoke of a time when humanity was profoundly connected to the earth, to each other, and to the cosmos itself."

Luna's breath faltered under the weight of his words. "You and mom shared a past life?"

Elias nodded slowly, his gaze distant, as if peering through the veil of time. "Your mother was convinced of it, she said our souls carried fragments of knowledge from that age, knowledge meant to awaken in this lifetime. She would speak of it with such vivid detail that it felt less like memory and more like an echo reverberating through the fabric of our beings."

Luna's fingers tightened around the journal in her lap. "Do you believe it?" she asked, her voice barely above a whisper.

Elias hesitated, his expression thoughtful. "I've spent my life studying what lies beyond conventional understanding—symbols, cycles, lost civilizations, and the hidden architecture of existence. Yet, proof of past lives is... elusive." He paused, a wistful smile softening his features. "But the way your mother spoke of it—the clarity in her eyes, the conviction in her voice—it felt undeniably true. It's one of the reasons I devoted my career to uncovering such truths—to catch even a glimpse of what she saw."

Luna's pulse quickened, her curiosity blazing. "I think I'm starting to understand what you meant before—the depth of your unconventional love." She searched his eyes, watching as his chin dipped in a slight nod. "What did she say about that time? About the lives you lived?"

Elias leaned back, his hands resting lightly on the arms of his chair. "She spoke of a civilization that thrived in harmony with the natural and ethereal worlds. A society where the physical and spiritual were not separate but seamlessly intertwined. She believed we were builders, not just of structures, but of bridges—between realms, between knowledge and application, between humanity and the divine."

"Builders?" Luna's voice carried a note of wonder.

He nodded, his eyes alight with memory. "She told stories of constructing great pyramids, not as tombs or monuments, but as centers of energy, places where the earth's power lines converged. The construction wasn't done by brute force but by an intricate understanding of vibration, resonance, and harmony with the earth's natural frequencies. Everything was a cooperative effort—humans, the elements, even the stones themselves. It wasn't just work; it was a symphony of intention, every being attuned to a higher purpose."

Luna felt a shiver run down her spine. "That sounds... like heaven on earth, and almost too perfect to be real."

Elias smiled knowingly. "I imagine it was as close to heaven on earth as it could be. But not without its challenges. Even in that time, there were those who sought to dominate rather than harmonize, to control rather than understand. It was part of the cycle, your mother said—a lesson in balance that humanity would face again and again. Don't forget the principle of polarity. For perfect to exist, they must also be imperfect. Where there is good, there must be evil. It is due to the constant movement along polarities that life evolves."

"And she thought... I'm connected to all this?" Luna's voice trembled with the weight of the possibility.

"Well, Luna, we are all connected to it," Elias said firmly, leaning forward. "What Margaret believed was in you. That you were significant to this time, that you would be among the first to awaken, and she was very proud of that."

Luna swallowed hard, the enormity of his words settling over her like a heavy cloak. "But how. How did she know? I wasn't even born yet. Why me? What makes me different?" Too many questions crossed her mind to hold back.

Elias hesitated, his eyes narrowing slightly as if weighing his next words. For a brief moment, concern flickered across his face—a silent debate playing out behind his thoughtful expression. When he finally spoke, his voice was softer, more deliberate.

"If I tell you too much, I risk altering the path you're meant to walk," he admitted. "But then again... if you weren't meant to know these things, you wouldn't be here asking." He leaned back slightly, his fingers tapping a thoughtful rhythm on the edge of the desk. "It's not about being different, Luna. It's about a collective journey your soul has been on for ages."

He paused, his gaze locking onto hers. "Your mother saw that potential in you because she understood it deeply—she carried it herself. This is how she knew. Every experience, every step she took led her here... and every step you've taken has brought you to this exact moment."

The room fell into a reverent silence, Elias's words lingering in the golden light like whispered truths. The way he spoke of her mother—as if she had never truly left—stirred something deep within Luna. The realization struck her with quiet force: *we never actually die.* Death isn't the end, but a threshold—a milestone in the soul's greater journey. A warmth bloomed in her chest, tethering her to something far beyond her understanding, yet undeniably real.

"I don't know if I'm ready for this," she admitted softly.

Elias's smile was gentle, his voice steady. "None of us ever feel ready. But the path finds us regardless."

The profound stillness in the room mirrored the sense of stillness within Luna, as if the past and present were converging, folding into a singular, timeless moment. She had come seeking answers, but instead, she'd found a doorway—a doorway to a truth that had been waiting for her all along.

As the late afternoon light slanted through Elias's office windows, Luna sat across from him, her mind brimming with questions. The day had been heavy with revelations, yet one lingering thought surfaced as she reached for her mother's journal. Her fingers brushed over the familiar symbol sketched on the page.

"Elias," Luna began, her voice hesitant, "this symbol... I saw it in my mother's journal, and again when I first found your name. What does it mean?"

Elias leaned back, his sharp gaze falling on the drawing. A soft smile tugged at his lips, a mix of reverence and curiosity. "Ah, yes of course. I can't believe I overlooked this. The Squared Circle," he said. "It's an ancient alchemical symbol—a representation of the Philosopher's Stone. Alchemists believed it to be the key to transmuting base metals into gold, but it was always more than that. It signifies the interplay of the four elements: earth, water, air, and fire. Together, they create balance, a microcosm of the universe itself."

Luna traced the symbol with her finger, her brow furrowed. "So, it's about finding balance in nature, and using it to change the properties of matter. I assume through the manipulation of vibrations?"

"Very good. Yes," Elias said, leaning forward. "But alchemy wasn't just about transforming metals; it was about transforming the self. The Philosopher's Stone was believed to be both the elixir of life and a tool for spiritual enlightenment. Many sought it as a physical object, but your mother had a different theory."

Luna's eyes flicked up to meet his. "What theory?"

Elias's voice grew quieter, almost reverent. "She believed the Philosopher's Stone wasn't an object at all, but an internal human ability—an awakening of the highest potential within us. She saw the symbol not just as a guide for external alchemical processes, but as a roadmap for inner transformation. The circle represents the infinite, the square symbolizes the material world, and the triangle is the connection between the two—through the mind, body, and spirit, or the holy trinity to some, working in harmony."

Luna sat back, her pulse quickening. "An inner awakening to unlock hidden potential?"

"Exactly," Elias said, his tone charged with conviction. "Your mother believed this alignment could help humanity transcend its perceived limitations. She devoted her life to understanding these principles, but she didn't intend for you to follow her exact path. She knew you were meant to take what she learned and forge something entirely your own—something she couldn't see but trusted you would create. To her, the Philosopher's Stone wasn't about turning lead into gold; it was about transforming ignorance into understanding, fear into love, and separation into unity—on your terms, in your time."

Luna lowered her head, through her hands came the muffled words.

"Why didn't she just tell me all this when..."

"Remember Luna, we have our own rhythm we unfold too. Your mother knew that. She would not have interrupted that. Her gift was to see it, yours to live it"

Luna absorbed his words, the symbol taking on a deeper significance. "And you believe this too?"

Elias paused, a thoughtful look crossing his face. "I didn't always," he admitted. "But the more I learned, the more I saw how interconnected everything truly is. Your mother's insights weren't just theories; they were glimpses of a larger truth. Seeing you now, Luna, I'm certain she was right."

Luna felt a strange mixture of awe and responsibility settle over her. The weight of her mother's legacy loomed large, yet it felt oddly empowering. She held her journal tightly, the symbol now a guiding star in her evolving journey.

Elias leaned forward, his eyes bright with a mix of awe and intensity. "Luna, this isn't just a path that few walk—it's a path almost no one has walked in thousands of years. What you carry, what you're beginning to unfold, is something few have even glimpsed in fragments. Your mother believed it could change everything we think we know—about humanity, about history, about our very existence."

He paused, his breath hitching as he seemed to take in the gravity of his own words. "You're not just continuing her work. You are stepping into something far greater. Something ancient, something forgotten... until now. If even a fraction of what she believed is true, then you may hold the key to understanding a wisdom that's been lost for tens of thousands of years."

The air between them seemed to hum with unspoken energy, the magnitude of his words sinking deep into Luna's chest, and pulling tears of undefined emotions to her eyes.

"I can only imagine what it feels like for you," Elias said, his voice softening. "But being here, witnessing this... being part of it, even on the edges—I've waited my entire life for a moment like this, never believing it would come."

Luna heard the words, but was frozen by their meaning. She only offered a weighted nod.

Elias smiled, the pride and excitement unmistakable in his eyes. "I don't know what more I can tell you, I am a little concerned I have already said too much." Elias said finally, his voice tinged with both reverence and humility. "Your journey is unfolding exactly as it's meant to, Luna. My role, I think, was simply to offer you a map—not to chart the course for you."

Luna brushed the cover of her mother's journal resting on her lap. "You've given me more than I could have hoped for," she said softly. "A foundation. A direction. I feel... I feel like I can finally begin to understand. I just need to process all of this."

Elias's expression softened, his gaze steady. "That understanding will come in waves, sometimes as a whisper, sometimes as a storm. Trust in that process. And trust yourself, Luna."

Luna felt her chest tighten, her throat thick with emotion. "Thank you," she managed, her voice trembling slightly. "For believing in me. For teaching me."

Elias stood, walking around the desk to stand before her. He placed a gentle hand on her shoulder, his eyes bright with excitement. "It's not just belief, Luna. It's certainty. I see in you the very vision your mother described—an awakening, not just for yourself but for humanity. We're on the cusp of something profound, something that could change the world as we know it."

She met his gaze, her resolve deepening. "I don't know where this path will take me, but I'm willing to walk it. And I won't stop until I understand what my mother was trying to show me."

Elias's smile widened, his pride unmistakable. "I have no doubt you'll succeed. But remember, you're not alone. If ever you need guidance, or even just a steady voice, call me. I'll be there."

He reached into his pocket, retrieving a small, weathered business card, the corners slightly frayed. Handing it to her, he said, "My personal number. Day or night, Luna."

She took the card, her fingers brushing over the raised lettering.

"Thank you," she said again, her voice firmer this time. "I'll call if I need you."

The two stood in silence for a moment, the weight of their shared understanding settling between them. Finally, Elias extended his hand, a gesture filled with respect and quiet reverence. Luna hesitated, her eyes searching his face. In that instant, she saw not just a scholar but a man who had loved her mother in a way few could understand—a man who had waited decades for this moment of connection and clarity.

She smiled softly, stepping closer. Instead of taking his hand, she wrapped her arms around him, the embrace warm and genuine. At first, Elias froze, surprised by the unexpected gesture. Then, slowly, he relaxed, his arms folding around her in return.

As their hearts aligned in that brief, timeless moment, Luna focused inward, opening her heart center fully. A radiant wave of love and reassurance flowed outward—pure, unconditional, and deep. It was the same love Elias had once felt in the presence of Margaret, now magnified and renewed. The energy cradled every part of him, filling the empty spaces left behind by loss and longing.

Elias drew in a shaky breath, his shoulders trembling as tears welled in his eyes—tears of joy, of release, of profound gratitude.

He stepped back just slightly, his hands still resting on her shoulders, his eyes glistening. "Thank you, Luna," he whispered, his voice thick with emotion. "You are... more than I ever imagined."

Luna smiled through her own tears. "You deserved that," she said softly. "And you needed to know that what you gave my mother lives on—not just in me, but in everything she believed."

Elias wiped his eyes, a tremulous breath escaping him as he nodded. "Thank you, Luna. Until next time."

His voice, though steady, carried the weight of something rare—hope, renewed and unbreakable. He hadn't felt this in what seemed like lifetimes—the future no longer a forgotten dream, but an open door

"Until next time," Luna echoed, her heart now steady.

As she turned to leave, she felt a renewed sense of purpose. Elias had given her more than knowledge—he'd given her the confidence to move forward. And as she stepped out into the bright afternoon, she carried with her not just the legacy of her mother's vision but the growing conviction that she was exactly where she needed to be.

Sixteen

Under the Lantern Light

The golden midday light bathed the streets as Luna walked back to the inn, her heart still thrumming from her conversation with Elias. The air carried a crisp coolness of autumn. As she turned a corner, she spotted Ezra sitting on a bench outside the inn, just where he said he would be when she called, two small coffee cups in hand. He glanced up and smiled as she approached, his relaxed demeanor a comforting counterpoint to the whirlwind of emotions swirling within her.

"Hey, you," Ezra said, standing to greet her with a cup of coffee. "How'd it go?"

Luna smiled faintly, her eyes meeting his. "It was... intense. He shared so much, things I'm still trying to wrap my head around."

Ezra gestured toward the bench, and they both sat. "Give me the high-lights," he said gently. Luna recounted her conversation with Elias—the ancient cycles, past lives, the Philosopher's Stone, and her mother's profound belief in her potential. As she spoke, Ezra listened intently, his hand occasionally brushing hers in quiet reassurance.

When she finished, Ezra sat in silence for a moment, absorbing every-thing. His eyes narrowed in thought before he spoke. "It's more than just guidance, Luna. It sounds like Elias gave you a mirror—one that reflects the bigger picture of who you really are. And I think... you're starting to see it too."

Luna blinked, his words hitting deeper than she expected. "Maybe," she admitted, her voice soft. "But it's overwhelming. It feels like I'm standing at the edge of something infinite, unsure of where to begin." She shook her head, a faint, incredulous laugh escaping her lips. "I mean, I know what I'm searching for... sort of. It's just hard to put it into words."

Ezra's hand tightened gently around hers. "You don't have to have it all figured out right now. Sometimes, the first step is just giving yourself permission *not* to know. Trust that each step will lead you to the next. And when you need help figuring it out—well, that's what I'm here for."

Ezra paused, watching the weight of it all settle on her shoulders. "I had a feeling today might leave you overwhelmed, which is why I planned something to help clear your head."

Luna arched a brow, curiosity flickering across her face. "Oh? What did you have in mind?"

Ezra grinned. "Just trust me. Go freshen up, and we'll head out."

A short while later, Luna emerged from the inn, her face refreshed and her spirits lifted by Ezra's enthusiasm. He led her down a quiet street lined with quirky shops and colorful murals, their steps falling into an easy rhythm. They stopped first at a local artisan market, where they browsed handmade jewelry, pottery, and vibrant paintings. Luna found herself drawn to a delicate silver pendant shaped like a crescent moon, its surface etched with intricate patterns.

Ezra noticed her fascination and quietly purchased it when she wasn't looking. As they left the market, he presented the pendant to her with a playful flourish.

"For the moon that guides me," he said with a soft smile.

Luna's cheeks warmed as she accepted the gift, her fingers grazing his. "Thank you, Ezra. It's beautiful."

Their exploration continued, from a scenic overlook offering breathtaking views of the rolling hills to a cozy bookstore where they spent an hour lost among the shelves. As the evening approached, they found a quaint bistro tucked away in a quiet corner of town. They chose a table on the patio, the flickering candlelight casting a warm glow between them.

The conversation flowed effortlessly over dinner, their laughter blending with the soft hum of the bistro. It had been days since Luna felt this light, the weight of her journey momentarily eased by Ezra's presence.

As the meal came to an end, Luna leaned forward, her heart pounding with unspoken words. "Ezra," she began softly, her gaze steady, "I need to say something."

He set his glass down, his attention fully on her. "What is it?"

Luna hesitated for a moment, then drew a steady breath. "I've been so focused on this journey, on figuring out my mother's legacy, that I haven't stopped to appreciate what's right in front of me. You. You've been my anchor through all of this, and I—" She faltered, her voice thick with emotion. "I love you, Ezra. I love you for being here, for walking this path with me, for everything."

Ezra's expression softened, his eyes shining with a warmth that seemed to wrap around her like a quiet embrace. He reached across the table, taking her hands in his, his touch steady and grounding. "Luna," he began, his voice rich with emotion, "I've loved you since the moment I first saw you, and every day since—even when you weren't here. You are my compass in all of this, the reason any of this feels worth it. Being by your side... it's not just where I'm meant to be—it's where I want to be. Always. Wherever this journey leads, we'll face it together."

A tear slipped down Luna's cheek, and Ezra brushed it away with a tender touch. The world around them seemed to fade, the bustling restaurant reduced to a distant hum as they sat in their shared moment of truth.

"Thank you," Luna whispered, her heart swelling with a love that felt as vast as the journey ahead.

Ezra smiled, leaning closer. "Always."

As the stars began to twinkle above, they lingered in the soft glow of the evening, two souls intertwined, ready to face whatever lay ahead—together.

The bistro's soft hum faded behind them as Ezra guided Luna toward their next destination. The path wound gently upward, and soon they stood at the entrance of a botanical garden illuminated by hundreds of soft, glowing lanterns. The air was fragrant with the scent of blooming flowers and fresh earth, and the quiet rustle of leaves in the evening breeze added a soothing backdrop.

"I remembered you always loved gardens," Ezra said, his voice low and steady. "Thought this would be a good way to end the day."

Luna smiled, her fingers brushing against his. "You thought right."

They entered the garden, their footsteps muffled by the soft gravel path. Lanterns cast a gentle light on vibrant blooms and delicate vines that wove around wrought-iron arches. The garden felt like a sanctuary, a world apart from the complexities of Luna's journey.

They strolled through winding paths, pausing occasionally to admire the intricate beauty of the flora. A fountain bubbled softly in the center of a clearing, its surface reflecting the lantern light like a mirror to the stars above. Luna felt the day's weight ease further with each step, her mind quieting as the tranquility of the garden enveloped her.

Ezra led her to a secluded bench beneath a sprawling oak tree. They sat side by side, the silence between them filled with unspoken under-standing. Luna tilted her head back, her eyes tracing the constellations peeking through the canopy.

"Do you ever think," she began softly, "that moments like this are what we're meant to hold on to? The quiet ones, where everything feels... connected?"

Ezra turned to her, his gaze warm and steady. "I think these moments remind us why we keep going. They're the anchor points that keep us happy and fill us with purpose."

Luna rested her head on his shoulder, her heart swelling with grati-tude. "Thank you, Ezra. For all of this."

He placed a gentle kiss on her forehead. "You don't have to thank me. I'm just happy to be here—with you."

The soft sound of the fountain blended with the distant chirping of crickets, wrapping them in a blanket of peace. The peace was so com-plete, it startled her. It had been so long since her thoughts and emotions had moved in harmony.

As the night deepened, they lingered in the garden, savoring the still-ness. It wasn't just a date or an escape from the weight of her journey—it was a moment of renewal, a quiet affirmation of the path ahead.

When they finally made their way back to the inn, the world around them felt softer, almost suspended in time. What followed was qui-et, wordless—an intimacy born of trust and something deeper. Later, wrapped in Ezra's warmth, Luna slept deeply, the weight of the day softened by dreams of swirling symbols and the faint echo of her mother's voice.

By morning, the heaviness of the night before had lifted. The early sunlight stretched across the Ozark hills, casting everything in a golden glow. Refreshed and centered, Luna and Ezra began their drive back to the community, the hum of the car a comforting rhythm beneath the easy silence between them. Outside, autumn leaves danced on the breeze, the landscape rolling by in fiery bursts of red and gold.

Luna leaned her head against the window, her eyes catching the reflection of Ezra's profile. His hands rested confidently on the steering wheel, the faint shadow of stubble tracing his jawline. There was a softness in the way he occasionally glanced her way, a quiet warmth that spoke volumes without a single word.

Her lips curved into a small, private smile as she remembered the night before—the whispered confessions, the electricity in his touch, the way they'd melted into each other as though the universe had finally aligned their stars. The lingering traces of their intimacy shimmered in the space between them, a secret that only they shared.

"You're quiet," Ezra said, breaking the silence, his voice low and filled with affection. "Penny for your thoughts?"

Luna's smile deepened, her gaze flicking to him. "Just thinking about how everything feels... different," she admitted. "Like a weight's been lifted. And also..." She hesitated, her cheeks warming slightly. "How much I'm looking forward to being home."

Ezra's smile grew, his eyes softening as he looked at her. "I love hearing you call it home," he said, his voice warm and sincere. "It means everything to me that Everwood feels like that for you."

Luna's heart fluttered at his words, the depth of their connection settling over her like a warm blanket. She reached out, her fingers brushing his free hand on the console.

They drove on, the conversation flowing effortlessly as they recounted the highlights of their trip—the beauty of Fayetteville, the peaceful strolls through the botanical garden, and, of course, Elias's profound teachings.

But beneath the surface of their words was the quiet certainty that something fundamental between them had shifted, solidified.

As they neared the community, the familiar sights of winding dirt roads and dense trees came into view. Luna felt a sense of grounding, as though the energy of the place welcomed her back, ready to support her as she carried the weight of new knowledge and possibilities. "Nearly there. I hope you're ready for Miriam's questions. You know she's going to grill us about the trip." Ezra quipped.

Luna laughed, the sound bright and unguarded. "Let her," she said. "I think I'm ready for just about anything now."

The chapter of Fayetteville had closed, but Luna knew it was only the beginning of a much larger story. And this time, she didn't feel afraid—she felt prepared.

SEVENTEEN

FOUR POINTS CONVERGING

The afternoon sun towered above the tree line as Luna and Ezra pulled up the community's narrow gravel road. The soft hum of the car's engine quieted as Ezra parked, and Luna felt a gentle flutter in her chest, a mixture of anticipation and serenity. She could see the familiar figures of Miriam and a few others gathered near the main hall, their heads turning as the car came into view.

As Luna stepped out, Miriam's face lit up with a warm smile. "There she is," Miriam called, her voice carrying over the chatter of other curious community members. "And look at you—absolutely glowing! Must've been quite the trip." Her tone carried a playful lilt, and her eyes sparkled with curiosity.

Luna chuckled softly, her cheeks warming as Ezra joined her, slinging his bag over his shoulder. "It was enlightening," she replied, her voice steady but warm.

Miriam stepped closer, pulling Luna into a gentle embrace. "You feel different," she murmured, her voice soft. "Like you've shed a layer and found something deeper. I take it you found what you were looking for, as if there was any doubt."

Luna pulled back, her smile faint but genuine. "I did, Aunt Miriam. I feel different. It's hard to explain, but... something's shifted, another step closer."

The others gathered around, offering welcoming nods and curious glances. There was a subtle pause, a moment where Luna felt their collective energy attuning to hers, as though they could sense the changes within her. Her presence was a quiet ripple in a still pond, expanding outward and touching each of them in ways they couldn't quite articulate.

"Welcome back," one of the elders said warmly. "We've missed you. Something about the air feels different without you here," he chuckled.

As the group dispersed, Althea appeared at the edge of the clearing, her presence almost spectral in the golden morning light. She stood still, her dark eyes studying Luna with an expression that blended curiosity and quiet pride. She didn't approach immediately, letting the moment stretch between them.

Luna caught the look and gave Ezra a reassuring smile. "I'll catch up with you in a bit," she said, her fingers brushing lightly against his arm. With a subtle nod, she made her way toward Althea.

The two women walked in companionable silence, their footsteps muted by the dew-laden grass. The air carried a coolness that hinted at the coming change of season, the scent of earth and wood mingling around them. When they reached the shelter of a towering oak, its sprawling branches casting dappled shadows over them, Althea finally spoke.

"You've grown," she said, her voice low but brimming with quiet intensity. There was no mistaking the pride in her tone. "Your energy feels... fuller. More aligned. You're beginning to step into your own."

Luna rested her hand against the oak's ridged bark, grounding herself in its ancient steadiness, its energy wrapping around her like an old friend. "It's hard to describe," she said, her voice thoughtful. "Like I'm finally seeing the whole picture, but only through glimpses. The pieces are shifting into place, but... there's still so much more beneath the surface."

Althea moved closer, her presence warm and grounding, as if the energy she carried reached out to cradle Luna's uncertainty. She placed a gentle hand on Luna's shoulder, her touch firm yet comforting. "Understanding is never the last piece—it's a piece that reveals itself again and again," she said. "And it will come when it's meant to. Right now, what matters is that you've embraced the unknown. That takes courage—and trust."

Luna met Althea's gaze, the sincerity in the healer's dark eyes rooting her in the moment. "Elias said something," she began hesitantly, her voice tinged with curiosity and doubt. "He spoke of the philosopher's stone—not as an object, but as something within us. Something we can unlock. Do you know anything about it?"

For a moment, Althea was quiet, her eyes softening as she listened. Then, instead of answering directly, she stepped closer, her voice low but steady. "It's not about unlocking some grand secret, Luna. It's about embracing every part of who you are—the light, the shadow, and everything in between. Transformation isn't a destination; it's a constant unfolding. The philosopher's stone... it's the courage to face yourself fully. To trust your own becoming, even when it feels messy or unclear."

Luna's breath hitched at the unexpected depth of her words. "So, it's not something you find—it's something you live," she whispered, her pulse quickening. "Do you really think... I can do it?"

Althea's grip on her shoulder tightened, her voice steady and unwavering. "Luna, I believe you've already begun. Every moment you've faced your fears, every choice you've made to follow your heart—it's all been part of the process. Awakening the stone is not an event. It's a journey."

A shallow breath hovered, suspended Her emotions rising like a tide within her. "It feels so... immense. Like it's bigger than me."

"It is," Althea said simply, her tone carrying the weight of a truth long held. "The path reveals itself in layers. Sometimes you'll find clarity, and other times... only questions. Trust your instincts, Luna. They'll lead you where you're meant to be."

Luna exhaled, the tension in her shoulders easing as Althea's words settled over her like a balm. "Thank you," she whispered, her voice trembling with gratitude.

The wind stirred gently, rustling the leaves above them like a whisper of agreement. For a long moment, neither spoke, the connection between them speaking louder than any words could. Luna felt the weight of Althea's faith in her, and with it came a spark of confidence she hadn't known she needed.

As Althea turned to leave, she glanced back once, her expression serene but knowing. "Your strength is already guiding you, Luna. I can see it with every step you take."

Luna watched her continue down the path, the healer's words reverberating in her heart. She leaned against the oak, closing her eyes and
let the steady rhythm of its ancient presence steady her own. She felt
ready—not for answers, but for the journey to seek them.

Luna felt a renewed sense of purpose as she turned the other way,
heading back to the car to gather her things. The pieces were falling into
place, and though the road ahead was still shrouded in uncertainty, she
knew she was exactly where she needed to be.

The soft glow of dusk blanketed the community as Luna retreated to her
cabin. The quiet murmur of the evening—a gentle rustling of leaves, the
faint chirp of crickets—provided a soothing backdrop as she lit a small
candle on the wooden table by her bed. She arranged her mother's journal
alongside her notebook and pen, the well-worn leather cover catching
the flickering light.

With a deep breath, Luna settled onto the small, cozy rug that softened
the otherwise bare floor. She crossed her legs, her palms resting upward
on her knees, and closed her eyes. Slowly, she began to center herself,
letting her breath steady the flurry of thoughts swirling in her mind.

Elias's voice lingered in her thoughts, his words weaving with the
memories of her mother's teachings. "The Philosopher's Stone was believed to be both the elixir of life and a tool for spiritual enlightenment."

Luna exhaled slowly, centering herself. This time, she promised, she
wouldn't let her meditation go too deep. She wasn't ready for another
uncontrolled surge of energy—not yet. The memory of her previous
awakening was still fresh, a reminder of the power that lay within and
the responsibility it demanded.

Sinking onto the floor, she closed her eyes and drew in a steady breath,
her hands resting loosely on her knees. She imagined roots unfurling
from her body, plunging deep into the soil. The sensation was immediate—effortless. The grounding felt as natural as breathing, as though the

Earth itself reached back to meet her. Her thoughts faded like distant echoes, leaving only stillness and the gentle, rhythmic pulse of the Earth.

The beat of her heart seemed to merge with that pulse, a cadence older than time itself. Her breathing slowed. Luna's awareness expanded, her senses sharpening. She felt the cool weight of the air, the faint hum of energy beneath her, the soft vibrations of existence wrapping around her like a quiet current.

Her eyes fluttered open briefly, drawn to her mother's journal resting on the table. With a sudden urgency, she reached for it, her fingers tracing its worn cover. Flipping through its delicate pages, she stopped as if guided by an unseen force. Her gaze landed on a passage written in her mother's flowing hand:

"Seek not the truth solely in the stars, but in the soil beneath your feet. The stone we chase is the bridge—it is the center, the anchor, the awakening."

The words seemed to pulse on the page, their meaning unfurling like a hidden bloom. The philosopher's stone wasn't an object or a prize to be found—it was a process, an inner alchemy of transformation and unity. But as the passage resonated within her, another layer of its meaning whispered just beyond her reach, tugging at her intuition like an unanswered call.

She closed the journal, her hands lingering on its cover. "I think I'm starting to understand, Mom," she murmured, her voice soft with realization.

The stillness of the cabin felt stifling. Compelled by the pull of the night, Luna rose and stepped outside. The cool air wrapped around her, carrying the faint scent of pine and damp earth. She followed the winding path that led away from her cabin, her bare feet brushing against the dew-kissed ground.

The forest welcomed her in its quiet majesty. The trees, towering and ancient, stretched their limbs like sentinels watching over her journey. Shadows danced among the trunks, shifting with the breeze. Luna walked in meditation, the rhythm of her breath steadying her connection to the energy around her.

She found herself at the edge of a secluded clearing, the air thick with the scent of moss and wildflowers. An ancient oak stood at its heart, its sprawling roots winding into the earth like veins carrying life. Drawn to its presence, Luna settled against the oak, her back pressed to its sturdy trunk.

Closing her eyes, she slipped into meditation again, deeper this time. Her awareness sank through layers of existence—the hum of the Earth, the rhythm of her heartbeat, the faint vibration of energy threading through her.

Then the visions began.

Images flickered behind her closed eyes—glimpses of something ancient and vast. She saw four points converging into one, their geometry impossibly precise yet weathered by time. The points formed the outline of a structure etched into the earth, monumental and enduring. Its shape seemed both alien and familiar, as if it had always existed, hidden beneath the surface of her awareness.

She saw stone pathways snaking through dense forests, their destinations obscured by distance yet pulsing with an irresistible call. Symbols began to emerge—lines, spirals, and geometric patterns that seemed to hum with energy. She recognized some from her mother's journal, while others were entirely new, their meanings just out of reach but heavy with significance.

The visions deepened, and Luna felt herself drawn closer to the convergence of the four points. The earth beneath her seemed to vibrate in harmony with the images, her own energy syncing with the ancient rhythm. It was as if the Earth itself whispered its secrets, inviting her to listen, to feel, to remember.

The moment she opened her eyes, it stole her breath. The clearing around her seemed subtly transformed. The air shimmered faintly, as though her meditation had awakened an unseen vibrancy. The moonlight cast the clearing in an otherworldly glow, the shadows of the oak's branches stretching like ethereal fingers across the ground.

Her thoughts raced as she stood slowly, the weight of the visions still settling over her. "Four points meeting into one," she whispered to herself, the words trembling with both awe and anticipation. "Could that be the four elements? Or... something more?"

The fragmented images stayed with her as she retraced her steps through the glowing forest path, her connection to the Earth still humming softly in her chest. She knew the visions were a sign—a guidepost on her journey. But the meaning, the full truth of what she had seen, remained just out of reach.

As the cabin came into view, Luna's resolve solidified. She needed a space where she could go deeper—a sanctuary untouched by distraction or fear of herself. The path ahead was unfolding, and it required courage and trust.

Standing at the threshold of her cabin, Luna glanced back toward the forest, her heart alive with both wonder and purpose. "Whatever this is... I'm ready," she whispered, stepping inside.

Eighteen

A Call to Trust

The evening sky was painted in soft purples and oranges as the community gathered near the central clearing, lanterns casting a warm, flickering glow. Luna stood at the edge of the circle, her heart thumping, alive with purpose as she surveyed the scene. Two dozen familiar faces, from elders to young families, had come to listen. Among them, Althea stood quietly near the front, her serene presence a source of silent encouragement. Ezra lingered nearby, offering Luna a small, confident nod.

Throughout the day, Luna had felt the quiet pull of the moment ahead. The decision to gather them had come naturally, a sense of knowing she couldn't ignore. She hadn't rehearsed her words or crafted a speech. Instead, she had walked among the gardens, letting her thoughts settle like petals on still water. What she needed to say, she trusted, would rise when the time was right.

Now, as the murmurs of the crowd softened and all eyes turned to her, Luna stepped forward into the circle. Her movements carried a calm authority, the kind of presence she'd once relied on in corporate boardrooms. But this time it wasn't strategy or control. The energy within her wasn't a tool—it was a truth, alive and unshakable.

Luna took a deep, calming breath, the cool evening air filling her lungs. The clearing was alive with an expectant energy, lantern light flickering in the gentle breeze and casting shifting shadows across the gathered faces. She let her gaze sweep over them—men and women of all ages, her chosen family, her community. Each person carried a different expression: curiosity, concern, skepticism, and quiet hope.

The rhythmic chirp of crickets created a soft undercurrent, blending with the whisper of leaves rustling in the cool breeze. The moment felt electric, as though the very air held its breath. Luna placed a hand over her heart, grounding herself, and then stepped further into the center of the circle.

"You are my family," she began, her voice steady but soft, the weight of her words carrying through the stillness. "And I love you. Each of you is here for a reason. Nothing—" her stare held a few familiar faces, lingering just a moment longer—"happens by accident."

The pause stretched, and the gathering leaned in, her voice a magnet pulling them closer.

"Life is a journey, forged by our emotions, shaped by our choices. It's a rhythm—always moving, always shifting. And another shift... is coming... rather, it's already begun."

A ripple of unease moved through the crowd. A pair of whispers stirred briefly but quieted just as quickly. Luna let the weight of her words settle before continuing, her voice growing stronger.

"We are standing on the edge of great change. I can feel it—deeply. It's why we are here. It's why we chose this place, this community. Together, you've created a home, a sanctuary. But sanctuaries are not untouched by change. Change often brings resistance, even chaos. The pendulum is already swinging. Our role isn't to stop it—we couldn't if we tried. Our role is to understand it and move from within it."

The lanterns flickered, their flames bending as a soft breeze whispered through the clearing. Luna let her eyes meet Althea's briefly, the older woman's calm, contagious presence a quiet anchor.

"I'll need your help," she continued, her tone firm now. "Althea..." Her eyes found the healer again. "Please, guide those who wish to connect—to meditate and create coherence within themselves and with the Earth. More people are awakening, even now, but not everyone has the love and support we've built here. They'll need us."

Althea nodded without hesitation, stepping forward. "Of course," she said, her voice carrying both warmth and quiet conviction. "Anyone who wants to learn, I'll teach. We'll create a space for this together."

A soft murmur of interest rippled through the crowd. A few people stepped closer, their faces lit with curiosity and quiet determination.

"I'd like to join," someone said from the edge of the group, their voice resolute. "I want to learn how to feel that infinite love you showed me."

"Me too," added another, a spark of hope shining in their eyes.

Luna felt a surge of gratitude, the gentle threads of connection weaving through the group. She took a breath, centering herself before addressing the rest. "Thank you," she said, her voice steady but warm. "There will be many ways to contribute. This is just one."

Her gaze swept the circle. "For those of you with other skills, we'll need builders, planners, teachers... everyone has something to offer. Every effort will matter."

Several heads nodded. A voice called out, "I'll help." Others murmured in agreement. But amidst the flickers of support, a current of doubt moved as well. Luna felt it—the hesitations, the unspoken fears.

"You already know I'm in," Ezra's voice rang out, cutting through the moment like a rhythmic drumbeat. He stepped closer, his presence a warm reassurance.

Luna smiled faintly, gratitude shining in her eyes. "Thank you," she said softly before turning back to the group.

"There's more," she continued, her tone plunging into something quieter but no less urgent. "This place—this ground we walk on—it has a purpose. I don't fully understand it yet, but I feel it. There's something about this land, about us being here together. My mother..." Luna's breath snagged on the moment as her mind conjured the image of *The Shift*, the swirling spiral from the painting flickering in her memory. For a moment, she could almost see it shimmer, as if alive, pulsing with hidden meaning. "...My mother believed in it too. And I believe we're closer than ever to understanding why."

As her words settled over the group, Luna opened her hands, palms up, inviting questions or doubts. "I'm asking for your trust. I don't have all the answers, but together, I know we can find them."

The silence that followed was thick, vibrating with tension. Then, as expected, Eleanor stepped forward, her arms crossed, her sharp narrowed eyes cutting through the quiet.

"With all due respect, Luna," she began, her tone even but laced with skepticism, "what exactly are we preparing for? You talk about shifts and change, but you haven't given us any proof. People here have responsibilities—jobs, children, homes to care for. Not everyone can drop everything to chase visions. Why should we trust that this isn't just... imagination?"

A murmur rippled through the crowd. A few nodded in agreement, while others exchanged wary glances. Luna met Eleanor's gaze directly, her expression calm but steadfast.

"I understand your doubt," Luna replied, her voice unwavering and measured. "This path isn't one we can fully see yet, and I won't pretend to have all the answers. But I know what I've felt, what I've seen. Change doesn't wait for us to be ready. It happens regardless. I am not asking for people to give up their lives, but I am asking for is your trust—not in me, but in the work we're doing together. Trust the foundation you have built here. It serves a greater purpose."

Before Eleanor could respond, a new voice broke through the tension—calm, proud, and deliberate. "I believe her."

A tremor danced on her exhale as her father stepped into the light, his face open but solemn. For a moment, his gaze held hers, and in that shared silence, something unspoken passed between them—a bridge being built where there had only been distance before.

"Luna is right," he said, his voice commanding, yet layered with a quiet vulnerability. "And I've seen the change in her. I've felt it. We all have. Aren't the emotions she has shared proof enough?" His gaze swept over the crowd, his expression unyielding as he continued. "I trust her, and so should you."

His words carried the weight of years—of the pain that had lingered unspoken between them, of regrets left hanging in the air, and of a bond that had been tested but never broken. Luna's heart swelled, the rawness of his support washing over her. It wasn't just what he said; it was that he said it, in front of everyone, putting his faith in her above the doubts of the elder.

A ripple moved through the group, quiet murmurs of agreement blending with the crackle of the lanterns. Luna's eyes glistened as she met her father's encouraging eyes. This wasn't just a gesture—it was a reckoning, an unspoken apology, and an offering of trust that healed something deep within her.

Althea nodded, stepping forward to support his words. "The signs are there for those willing to see them. This isn't blind faith—it's preparation. It's growth."

Eleanor hesitated, her sharpness softening, though not entirely fading. She exhaled and took a step back, her arms still crossed. "I'll listen," she said quietly. "But I'm not convinced."

Luna barely heard her. Her father's words still echoed in her mind, filling a space that had long felt empty. She stood taller, the weight of his trust lifting her spirit.

The tension eased as murmurs filled the clearing, conversations buzzing with renewed purpose. A few stepped forward to offer quiet words of support, while others lingered in clusters, processing what they had heard. Slowly, a small group began to gather around Althea, their curiosity evident in the way they leaned in, eager to hear more.

Althea met their interest with a calm, open smile, gesturing for them to follow her toward a quieter spot beneath the old oak tree. "We'll start simple," Luna heard her say, Althea's voice fading gently as she led the group away.

Luna watched, a swell of gratitude rising in her chest. The seed she had planted was taking root faster than she'd dared hope.

As the energy shifted, the focus widening to different pockets of conversation, a few others spoke up with offers of help. "We're builders and craftsmen," one man said, his voice steady. "Whatever you need, just say the word. We'll make it happen."

Others nodded in agreement, their enthusiasm spreading through the group. The hum of collaboration filled the air, a steady current of shared purpose.

Luna felt a lightness she hadn't known she needed.

As the crowd began to disperse, Ezra approached her. His smile was warm, his gaze steady. "You did it," he said quietly. "You put yourself out there, and they're with you."

Luna let out a soft, relieved breath. "Not everyone."

Ezra's hand found hers, his grip soothed her beating heart. "Not yet. But give them time. Truth has a way of revealing itself."

Luna met his eyes, a faint smile curving her lips. "One step at a time," she murmured.

Ezra nodded. "One step at a time."

As they stood together in the soft fading light of the remaining lanterns, the clearing emptying around them, Luna felt the weight of her journey shift. It was still heavy, still uncertain, but now it was shared. And that made all the difference.

Nineteen

Awakening the Shift

T he morning light filtering through the high windows of the gathering hall cast muted reflections on the floor. Luna stood before her mother's painting, the swirling patterns almost seeming to pulse under the shifting light. Her breath quivered at the edge of wonder, as her fingers hovered just above the surface, the air between them charged with an almost magnetic pull. A hum—faint but insistent—vibrated beneath her skin, rising with each passing second. Her heart quickened, her senses sharpening. She could feel the power coiling there, waiting, watching.

Her pulse thudded in her ears, the space around her tightening like a held breath. If she touched it, something would happen—something irreversible. The knowing wasn't logical; it was primal, woven deep into her bones. *Did you leave me a message here, Mom?* she wondered, considering the possibilities and thinking back to what she'd learned from Elias.

"I can't do it here," she said softly, drawing her hand back, her voice barely more than a whisper. "It's too close to everyone... too risky."

Ezra stepped closer, his footsteps light on the wood floor. His expression was calm, resolute, but his eyes searched hers with quiet understanding. "Then we'll take it somewhere safe," he said, his voice a steady anchor in the swirling tension.

Luna nodded, her fingers brushing the edge of the painting's frame. "Wrap it up. I'll need time to prepare, and a place far enough from the community."

Ezra studied her, then gave a firm nod. "I know a spot," he said, his voice low but steady. "There's an old shelter north of here. It's tucked away along a remote trail, rarely used and far enough to avoid drawing attention. We'll have to hike to it, but it'll give you the privacy you need."

Relief flickered across Luna's face. "That sounds perfect."

Ezra set to work, carefully wrapping the painting in layers of cloth. His hands moved with practiced precision, each knot secure but gentle, as though he understood the significance of what he was handling. Once the painting was safely bundled, he hoisted it onto his back, testing the straps to ensure it wouldn't shift during their journey.

While Ezra prepared, Luna made her way to Althea, who stood near her table. Luna shared her thoughts in a hushed tone, her words deliberate. Althea listened closely, her gaze steady, before turning to her small cauldron. She reached for a trio of glass vials and sprinkled their contents—dried blue lotus, powdered damiana, and a pinch of crushed moonstone—into the warming water. The scent of sage and lavender mingled with something deeper, more mysterious, curling through the air in soft, hypnotic tendrils. This wasn't just a tea; it was an elixir, crafted with intention. The energy around them shifted, dense with purpose. Althea glanced up, her eyes warm but discerning, as if sensing the gravity of the moment.

When she was finished, Althea poured the elixir into a glass thermos. "This will help open your mind and steady your energy," she explained, handing it to Luna. "Take only small sips before you begin. Too much, and it will muddle your senses rather than sharpen them."

Luna accepted the thermos with a grateful nod but hesitated, her fingers tightening around its smooth surface. "Althea, I'm not entirely sure what I'll find... or even where this journey is taking me. But I *feel* the answers pulling me toward the painting. When I was with Elias, he talked about the Akashic records and how information is encoded into everything. Do you think it's possible my mom found a way to... embed something into the essence of the painting? Because it's starting to feel like that—like she left something hidden there for me to discover."

Althea's eyes softened as she studied Luna, her gaze drifting briefly toward the painting. "I've never heard of such a thing—encoding knowledge into a painting—but that doesn't mean it's impossible. If anyone could find a way, it would be your mother." She moved closer, her voice lowering as though sharing a secret. "I can feel her presence radiating from it—strong, protective, alive. Whatever she left behind, it's waiting for you. Trust yourself to find it, in your own time and in your own way."

A pause settled between them, thick with meaning. Then Althea added, "Let me come with you. I can help—if something happens, you won't be alone."

Luna's heart swelled at the offer, but she shook her head gently. "Thank you, Althea. Truly. But this... this is something I have to experience for myself. It's not just about understanding—it's about feeling, listening to what my mother left for me. I can sense her pull in the painting, calling me toward something I'm only beginning to grasp." She paused, her gaze softening as it swept toward the community outside. "Besides, they need you here. Your work is already beginning, and they'll look to you for guidance."

Althea smiled knowingly, her fingers tightening briefly on Luna's arm before releasing her. "You're right. I'll stay and help the others find their footing." Her voice dropped to a softer, more intimate tone. "But remember, you are never truly alone. If you need me—if anything feels beyond what you can carry—call for me. I'll find you."

Luna's chest tightened, a warmth blooming beneath her ribs. "I will," she promised, her voice steady. "Thank you—for everything."

Althea watched her for a beat longer, as if silently blessing her journey, then turned back to her herbs, her calm presence lingering even as Luna walked away.

Ezra enlisted the help of an old friend, James Wiley—a seasoned hunter and outdoorsman who knew the Ozarks like the back of his hand. Though James lived just beyond the edge of Everwood and mostly kept to himself, the community regarded him as one of their own—the kind of man you'd always want in your corner when things got rough. He arrived swiftly, his rugged pack slung over one shoulder, a well-worn cap casting shadow over his weathered face. As he approached, his sharp eyes immediately caught the covered painting, now fashioned into an improvised harness.

"That's not exactly standard hiking gear," James remarked, his voice carrying a gravelly mix of humor and curiosity.

Ezra chuckled, clapping him on the shoulder. "Yeah, not exactly 'pack light and enjoy the view.' But hey, it builds character, right?" His tone shifted, just enough to ground the moment. "Thanks for helping James. This is important. I wouldn't have called you otherwise."

James's eyes flicked to Luna as she hoisted her backpack into the back of the truck, her movements steady but deliberate. "Thanks for helping us out," she said, offering a small but sincere smile.

"Of course," James replied, his voice warm with easy confidence. "Anything for a little adventure." His eyes lingered on her for a moment, a spark of curiosity in them as he added, "Something tells me this isn't just a normal hike, though."

Luna's grip tightened briefly on the edge of the truck. "Not exactly," she admitted, her tone measured.

James nodded knowingly as he climbed into the driver's seat, his tone light but turning serious. "Well, let's make it a good one; I've got everything we'll need for a few days—food, tools, maps. Let's just hope your gear isn't as delicate as it looks."

Ezra chuckled faintly, the weight of the moment softening just a bit. "It's tougher than it seems."

James nodded and gestured toward his truck. Luna climbed into the back cab, tucking the wrapped painting securely beside her. Ezra slid into the passenger seat while James settled into the driver's seat, adjusting his cap.

He shot them a quick, easy grin. "So, secret mission to the middle of nowhere? I hope you brought snacks—this truck runs on coffee and limited conversation."

Luna smirked, leaning back in her seat. "Perfect. I'm fresh out of snacks but fully stocked on cryptic one-liners."

James chuckled as he cranked the engine, the truck rumbling to life. "We'll get along just fine, then."

They pulled onto the narrow dirt road, the surrounding trees leaning in like hushed companions as they left the clearing behind.

The journey to the shelter began with a drive through winding back-roads, the landscape shifting from open fields to dense woods. Before long, the road narrowed, and they had reached as far as the truck could take them. James parked in a small turnout, and they began their hike, the weight of their mission growing heavier with each step. Ezra led the way, the painting strapped firmly to his back, while James carried most of the food and water. Luna followed close behind, her eyes scanning the terrain, each footfall drawing her closer to the answers she sought.

After nearly an hour of slow, steady trekking, they reached the shelter—a modest wooden structure nestled in a grove of ancient trees. The air was crisp and still, humming with an almost sacred quiet. Ezra and James immediately set to work, unpacking supplies and preparing the space for an extended stay. Ezra glanced at Luna as he laid out bedding and organized food provisions. "We don't know how long this will take," he said calmly. "Better to be ready for a few days."

James nodded, checking the door and testing the sturdiness of the cabin's windows. "I'll take a short walk around the area to check it out, and collect some fire wood. The nights can get awfully cold out here this time of year."

As Ezra made further preparations at the cabin, Luna began preparations of her own. Her focus narrowing to the bundled painting leaning against the wall. She could feel its pull—a low hum in her chest, an ancient song, just out of reach. Her breath slowed as her senses sharpened, tuning into its energy. There was no hesitation in her this time, only the deep certainty that this was exactly where she needed to be. She turned her attention inward, her fingers brushing the edge of the thermos Althea had given her. She closed her eyes briefly, grounding herself, opened them again with renewed clarity. The soft orange glow of the setting sun filtered through the trees, casting long shadows that flickered like whispers across the painting's surface.

She sat in stillness, releasing herself from thoughts and expectations of what was to come. Her awareness expanded gently, attuned to the life around her—Ezra igniting a flame in the old fireplace; the distant whistle of a cardinal singing an evening lullaby; the rhythmic chirping of crickets joining the night's quiet symphony. She was present for it all, but unengaged, existing only as an observer in the moment called *now*—until that moment softened into dusk.

"I'm ready," she said finally, her voice clear and resolute despite the weight of the moment.

Ezra's eyes met hers, his expression calm but watchful. "We'll be right here," he promised. "James and I will take turns keeping watch."

Luna nodded and turned toward the painting, her pulse steady but thrumming with anticipation. There was no time to waste. The sun dipped lower behind the trees, the day's light barely a whisper in the sky. Luna steadied herself, preparing for whatever lay beyond the threshold of her awareness.

Luna lifted the thermos to her lips, taking a few slow sips. The earthy, slightly bitter taste settling into her chest, spreading a comforting heat through her body. Setting the cup aside, Luna shifted into a meditative position before the painting, her gaze lingering on the swirling spiral.

Closing her eyes, she centered herself. She felt the solid earth beneath her, the faint hum of the world around—crickets chirping, the distant rustle of leaves in the breeze, the faint crackle of the fire. Her breathing deepened as her awareness anchored into the present moment. It's *time.*

When she opened her eyes again, the painting seemed to come alive. The spiral shifted subtly, its colors deepening into luminous hues of indigo and gold, the strokes shimmering like liquid light. It pulsed, slow and steady, like a heartbeat. Her own breath seemed to sync with its rhythm, the world narrowing to the mesmerizing flow of the pattern's motion.

Compelled, Luna reached forward, her fingertips trembling as they brushed the surface of the canvas.

A shock of energy erupted from the painting, racing through her fingertips and up her arm. It wasn't painful, but it was overwhelming—a torrent of light and vibration that surged into her core. The cabin dissolved around her, replaced by a kaleidoscope of fractal light. She felt herself being pulled, her consciousness stretching and unraveling as though it was threading through a cosmic loom. The sound of rushing wind roared in her ears, mingled with the faint hum of chanting voices.

When her vision returned, she was no longer in the cabin. She stood in a vast open field, the air alive with a sense of ancient purpose. Rolling hills stretched out before her, crowned by a sky that swirled with stars, their light weaving patterns that seemed almost intentional. Each breath she took filled her lungs with an intoxicating mix of cool earth and fragrant blossoms, the sensory details so vivid they felt hyperreal.

Beside her stood a man with an aura of quiet authority. His tall, broad frame radiated strength, and his features—foreign, yet oddly familiar—carried an ageless wisdom. Luna felt an inexplicable pull toward him, as though she had known him for lifetimes. Standing near him was a woman whose energy was unmistakable: Elias. Or rather, someone whose essence mirrored his. They moved together with an unspoken harmony, their connection etched in every gesture and glance.

Luna's breath caught as a wave of recognition rippled through her. Her mother's thoughts and emotions began to bleed into her own, seamless and undeniable. She wasn't just observing this memory—she was *living* it. Her mother's past life surged through her, a male form with the weight of leadership, reverence, and profound purpose.

The scene shifted suddenly, the air around her vibrating with energy. Luna watched in awe as four great points converged toward a single pinnacle—a small pyramid under construction. The harmony of the people was palpable, their movements synchronized with an almost musical rhythm. The very air hummed with their collective intention, a resonance that seemed to connect them with the cosmos itself.

She stepped closer, her senses drinking in every detail. Craftsmen worked with tools that seemed impossibly simple, yet with a fluidity that defied explanation. Massive stones softened under the vibrations of their commands, molded as though they were clay, before being placed with perfect precision. Luna felt the resonance within herself, the deep hum of creation vibrating in her chest. It was a harmony born not of force but of alignment—an art of shaping matter through will and sound.

The memory surged again, pulling her deeper. She found herself speaking, her lips forming words in a deep, resonant voice not her own. It was her mother's voice—his voice, the sounds foreign but understood. "*Nearly completed. Our people will have its connection soon, and we can continue...*" The words carried weight, a solemn finality. As they echoed into the air, the vision began to blur.

The stars swirled faster, the ground beneath her feet dissolving into light. She felt herself being pulled back, her body resisting the sudden, jarring motion. The fractals shattered into darkness, the hum turning into a deafening silence.

With a sharp gasp, Luna's eyes flickered open—only to collapse backward as her connection to the present snapped violently into place. Her torso hit the floor, the back of her head bouncing off the hardwood with a dull thud. The room swam around her, the faint glow of the painting flickering before her vision dimmed completely.

Ezra's heart thundered in his chest as he crouched beside Luna, gently cradling her head in his lap. Her breathing was shallow, each rise and fall of her chest a fragile reassurance. "Luna! Wake up!" His voice cracked, panic creeping into every syllable. He brushed her hair back from her face, lightly tapping her cheek. Nothing. Not even a flicker.

Behind him, James moved with purpose, crossing the room in a few strides before kneeling beside them. "She's out cold," James said, his voice low but steady. His weathered hands hovered near her wrist, checking her pulse. "It's faint, but she's stable. What happened?"

"She touched the painting," Ezra rasped, his eyes fixed on Luna's serene, unmoving face. "One moment she was fine, and the next—she just... collapsed."

James's gaze flicked to The Shift, its colors still shimmering faintly, as if the energy had not yet settled. Whatever had happened, he could feel it—an unsettling hum lingering in the air, just beyond reach. He rested a firm hand on Ezra's shoulder, grounding him. "We don't have time to figure it out here. Call Althea."

Ezra fumbled with his phone, his trembling hands making the device feel foreign and uncooperative. He found Althea's number and pressed it, the ringing in his ear somehow louder than his frantic heartbeat.

"Ezra," came Althea's calm voice. "What's happened?"

"It's Luna," he choked out. "She drank the tea, meditated with the painting, and then she just collapsed. She's unconscious—unresponsive. What do I do?"

The line was silent for a beat, and Ezra gripped the phone tighter, fear constricting his throat.

"Get her home immediately," Althea instructed, her tone calm but resolute. "Do not delay. Wrap her warmly, and bring her to me. Her body needs grounding, and I need to see her in person to guide her back fully."

"We're on our way," Ezra said, his voice steadier now, fueled by her direction.

James was already moving, extinguishing the fire with efficient precision. He gathered their supplies, leaving the food and water behind and secured the painting with the makeshift harness on his back. "I've got this," James said, adjusting the straps and glancing at Luna. "Focus on her."

Ezra scooped Luna into his arms, her body limp but warm against his chest. He clung to her as if letting go wasn't an option. "We're not stopping," he said through clenched teeth. "Not until she's safe."

The forest seemed alive in its stillness, the weight of the moment amplifying every sound. The hard crunch of boots on dirt, the rustle of leaves overhead, and Ezra's labored breaths created a rhythm of urgency. The path ahead was bathed in the pale glow of the full moon, silver light weaving through the trees in ghostly strands. Where shadows grew thick and uncertain, James swept his flashlight across the trail, its beam cutting through the darkness with quiet precision.

James led the way, his steady pace never faltering. "Watch your footing," he called over his shoulder, his voice rising above the sounds of their passage.

Ezra barely registered the words, his focus entirely on Luna. He glanced down at her every few steps, searching her face for any sign of movement. Her expression was peaceful, almost too peaceful, as though she was caught in a dream she couldn't escape.

A low breeze rustled the treetops, carrying with it an unplaceable tension. Ezra's mind raced. *Why didn't I stop her? Why didn't I stay closer?* The weight of his guilt threatened to crush him, but he pushed it aside. There wasn't time for doubt—only action.

When they reached the truck, Ezra, breathless and sweating, carefully slid into the center seat, keeping Luna cradled against him. Her legs rested on the passenger seat, and his arms wrapped securely around her. His chest rose and fell in ragged rhythm, and he paused just long enough to wipe the sweat from his brow before gently brushing his hand over her cheek. Her skin felt cool, too cool, and his thumb moved in slow circles, a quiet attempt to wake her.

"Stay with me," he murmured, his voice strained but steady. "We're almost home."

James stowed the gear into the truck bed, then placed the wrapped painting carefully in the rear cab, securing it tightly. He glanced over at Ezra and Luna, his jaw tightening before climbing into the driver's seat. The engine rumbled to life, and without a word, James steered them onto the narrow dirt road, the trees blurring into shadows as the sun dipped lower behind the hills.

The soft hum of the engine and the occasional jostle of the truck on the uneven road filled the cab. Ezra kept his eyes on Luna, his fingers never leaving her cheek, watching for any flicker of response. His whispered reassurances mingled with the rhythm of the tires crunching over gravel. "We're almost there," he repeated, his voice steady despite the tightness in his throat.

Through the dense forest, faint flickers of light broke through the trees—small, fleeting glimpses of Everwood nestled in the darkness. As they pulled up to Althea's home, the porch light was already on, casting a warm glow across the front steps. Althea stood in the doorway, her calm composure betrayed only by the urgency in her eyes.

James cut the engine, and Ezra wasted no time. He slid out of the truck with Luna still in his arms, her body limp but breathing. Althea motioned him inside without a word, her hands already reaching for her herbs and tools as she guided him to a prepared cot.

"Set her down gently," Althea instructed, her voice firm yet soothing. Ezra obeyed, his movements careful as he laid Luna down. Her stillness felt unnatural, and the sight of her like this tightened something deep in his chest.

Althea crouched beside Luna, her hands hovering above her form as she closed her eyes. "Her energy is still tethered, but it's fragile," she murmured, more to herself than to Ezra. "She's in between—neither here nor entirely gone. I'll try to guide her back."

Ezra lingered, his hands flexing and curling at his sides, his need to do something at odds with his helplessness. "Will she be okay?"

Althea opened her eyes briefly, meeting his gaze. "You've done what you needed to do. Let me handle the rest."

Ezra hesitated, his jaw tightening, but finally stepped back. He didn't leave the room, though, his eyes never straying from Luna as Althea began her work. Murmured mantras filled the space, mingling with the scent of burning herbs and the faint hum of energy that seemed to emanate from Althea herself.

Ezra leaned against the wall, his chest rising and falling with deep breaths. *Come back to me, Luna. Please.*

TWENTY

THE ARCHITECT OF DESTINY

T he cabin held its breath, steeped in a hush that wrapped around Luna's unmoving form. Her body lay still—abandoned, breath shallow but steady—while her consciousness drifted far beyond the veil of the material world. She was no longer tethered to time or space, pulled instead into the boundless expanse of the Akashic Records, a realm alive with infinite possibilities and timeless truths.

Luna stood at the edge of a vast, glowing field, where shimmering threads of light wove an intricate tapestry of existence. Each thread pulsed with its own unique rhythm, containing the essence of lives lived and the echoes of events both ancient and yet to come. As she stepped forward, the threads parted, forming a path that seemed to hum with recognition.

She looked down at her arms, legs, torso—her entire being composed of the same luminous threads of woven matter. And as her gaze settled on herself, the threads began to unravel, only to reweave in response to her awareness. It was the act of seeing that gave her shape. In that moment, she understood: she was both the observer and the observed, her existence manifesting through the very expectation and will of her consciousness.

Her bare feet moved over a surface woven into existence before her eyes—neither solid nor liquid nor air, but a foundation of swirling colors and patterns. The patterns shimmered and danced, their meanings elusive yet profoundly familiar. Under any other circumstances, she knew terror would seize her—how could it not, faced with the surreal unknown? Yet fear was an impossibility here, held at bay by something greater, something ancient and vast. A soft echo drifted through the luminous air—not a voice, but an essence of thought, calm and steady, carrying understanding without words.

"You've come far, Luna."

She turned to find a figure woven into existence before her, the presence both foreign and achingly familiar. Her mother's past life emerged from the infinite, a cloud of possibilities coalescing into the form of a man with a commanding yet gentle aura. His piercing eyes held centuries of wisdom, and his essence resonated like a deep chord within her soul.

"Who are you?" Luna asked, the understanding of her own question arriving as soon as the words were spoken.

"I am the part of your mother that walked this earth long before your time," the figure replied. At the mention of her mother, the form wavered—unraveling in a delicate weave of light before momentarily reshaping into the woman Luna had known, her soft eyes filled with warmth and knowing. The image held for only a breath, then dissolved again, reforming into the man from the past.

"Mom." A pulsing light of love traversed the threads of her existence with the simple word.

"And you, Luna, are the bridge between what was and what will be."

Then the threads of light wove a new tapestry around them, pulling reality into tangible form.

The scene shifted, and Luna found herself standing in a grand hall filled with intricate carvings and towering stone pillars. Though unfamiliar, the energy of the place felt like home. Her mother's past life gestured toward the walls, where vivid depictions of elemental forces merged into a single radiant symbol—a circle within a square, within a triangle, within another circle.

"The Philosopher's Stone," the figure said reverently. "It is not merely a thing to be found, but a state to be realized. It is the union of opposites, the alchemy of spirit and matter, the awakening of human potential."

As Luna watched, the symbol shifted and blossomed into overlapping circles, forming a flower-like pattern.

"The flower of life," the voice said through the veil of existence. "Hidden within it lies the foundation of all creation. Study this symbol, Luna. It is the most powerful of all, representing the interconnectedness of life throughout the universe."

Drawn by the carvings, Luna reached out and brushed the cool stone with her fingertips. A surge of understanding coursed through her, and she became the observer of ancient civilizations where harmony with the earth was unbroken, where physical and ethereal realms intertwined seamlessly.

"They understood the balance," the figure said, his voice resonant—each word rippling through the very fabric of the space around them. "But that balance was lost. And now, there are forces working to keep it hidden, to suppress the awakening that must come."

His form began to shift, its edges blurring and reshaping, flickering through countless faces and forms—some human, some celestial, and some far beyond either. Some looked ancient and wise; others glowed with a radiant energy that defied earthly comprehension.

"The cycles are already in motion," the figure continued, his voice unwavering as the shifting stilled. "And your awakening—it isn't about a human experiencing the spiritual. It's the other way around. You are a spirit, Luna... having a momentary human experience."

The figure's form shimmered again, cycling through its many iterations, its eyes holding hers with steady purpose. "Do you see?" the figure asked, morphing from an ancient healer into a luminous being of light, then briefly into a creature with wings like shimmering crystal. "These are all me." The figure's voice deepened, and at last, it settled into the form she knew best—her mother, gazing at her with quiet strength and infinite love.

"You have been here before, long before you were given this name. You know this journey; you designed it. Remember, Luna... you are the one who set this pendulum in motion, and your true essence has always been guiding you. Trust that guidance."

A jolt of frustration cracked through her composure. "But I don't have all the answers," she said, her voice trembling. "Take me to my higher self... let me speak to her. She'll know what to do."

The figure smiled gently, the warmth in her mother's eyes returning for a fleeting moment. "Luna, this space—the one we stand in—is a fractal of my own essence. It was embedded into the painting I created, a private place where I could leave pieces of myself for you. But it has its limits. You are a visitor here, and only you can walk this path."

Her voice softened, her form shimmering like silk woven from light. "You cannot bring anyone else into this space. But hear me, child: You are already your higher self. One day, you will have a clearer understanding of that truth."

The air seemed to hum with energy as her words settled deep into Luna's core, filling her with a strange blend of peace and purpose.

The hall dissolved, its luminous weave loosening into a shifting new reality. Luna found herself amidst a sprawling city—its golden spires reaching toward a sky filled with unfamiliar constellations. Yet, even in its grandeur, a shadow loomed. She turned, her gaze drawn to figures cloaked in darkness, their forms shifting like smoke. Greed emanated from them, a suffocating force.

"Westfield Industries," her mother said with a heavy cautionary tone. "They do not yet understand the full scope of what they pursue, but their interference threatens the delicate balance. Your mission to reunify the past and future is at risk."

A chill coursed through Luna as the vision shifted again. This time, she saw her own community—their faces glowing with hope, their energies weaving together like threads of a greater purpose. Yet, within this unity, conflict simmered: Eleanor standing apart, her skepticism a fracture among the group; strangers approaching with unclear intentions; and a shadowed figure watching from the edges of light.

Through the distant tapestry, a faint shimmer caught Luna's eye. Her will pushed aside all distractions to focus on the shape: four points converging into one, forming a pyramid that still stood, though time had altered its faces. It's not a hill....

"These visions," Luna whispered, her voice trembling, "are they what's to come?"

"Possibilities," the figure corrected gently. "This time is delicate, receptive to the will and the observer. The power of collective intent can harness this incoming energy for great good—or great destruction. You must be vigilant, Luna. Become the observer shaping the path. Trust yourself, for the designer holds the secrets you need."

The glowing threads of the Akashic realm returned, and in the center of the tapestry appeared a radiant stone, its surface reflecting all colors imaginable. It pulsed gently, a heartbeat in tune with her own.

"Let this be your guide to creation," the figure said softly. "The philosopher's stone is not an end but a beginning. Through it, you will unify the earthly elements and bridge the masculine, feminine, and divine energies. Apply the fifth element—aether—to create from above."

Luna reached out, her hand trembling, and her fingers grazed the stone's surface. Instantly, the threads around her flared brightly, a torrent of energy surging through her. Ancient knowledge settled into her soul as her vision began to blur.

Before everything dissolved into darkness, her mother spoke once more, her voice a fading melody.

"The stone now lies within. You are stronger than you know, Luna. Trust the journey, and trust those who walk it with you."

As the threads of the Akashic Records unraveled, Luna felt herself spiraling toward an empty void. Yet the warmth of the stone's energy lingered, fading into the threads of her being, a quiet reminder of the path she was destined to walk.

The hall unraveled completely, the woven threads dissolving into an endless void. The vision her mother had left behind—a memory carefully encoded into the fabric of the painting—had reached its limit, like a recording fading to black.

Luna remained adrift, suspended in darkness. The warmth of her mother's presence had vanished. It was gone—like a flame snuffed out mid-breath—leaving only an empty void. She tried to summon the golden threads, to call back the essence of herself she had touched moments ago, but there was nothing.

The darkness pressed around her, dense and absolute, swallowing even the memory of light. Her presence quivered, the vast emptiness stretching infinitely in all directions. For the first time, she was utterly alone.

Her voice trembled in the void. "Mom? Are you still there?"

Only silence answered.

Luna closed her eyes, if they even existed—not to escape the darkness, but to find the light within herself. It had to be there. It had to be.

TWENTY-ONE

GUIDED BY SHADOWS

The golden hues of late afternoon blanketed the clearing as the sound of tires crunching on gravel broke the tranquil rhythm of Everwood. A sleek black SUV rolled to a stop just outside the main circle, its glossy surface catching the sun and casting sharp reflections across the earthy paths.

Ezra stood near the garden, a rake in hand, motionless. He wasn't tending the soil so much as grounding himself, the motion a quiet remedy for his frayed thoughts. All day, a strange energy had stirred in his chest—an unease he couldn't quite place. Still, his thoughts were mostly on Luna, who hadn't stirred since the vision.

The driver's door of the SUV opened. A tall man stepped out—clean-shaven, striking, his clothes crisp in a way that didn't belong here, and yet, somehow, he wore them like armor that he no longer needed. There was a quiet reverence in the way he moved, taking in the landscape as though recognizing something sacred.

Ezra narrowed his eyes slightly, his grip tightening instinctively on the rake before loosening it again. Old habits.

A few community members drifted closer, their curiosity piqued. The stranger met their glances with warmth, his voice even and full of awe.

"Afternoon," he said, taking a step toward them, his smile disarming. "My name's Caleb. I know I probably look like I took a wrong turn, but... I don't think I did."

Miriam was among the first to respond, her instinctual compassion overriding any reservations. "What brings you out this way, Caleb?" she asked, her tone open.

Caleb laughed, sheepishly at first, then with surprising vulnerability. "I wish I could give you a solid answer. All I know is that something's been pulling me here. I've been having these... flashes. Dreams. A feeling that something important was waiting for me, but I didn't know what until I passed the road leading in here. The moment I saw it—I just knew."

There was a pause, and then murmurs of recognition passed through the small crowd.

"I think I've felt that," someone whispered.

Ezra remained at the edge, quiet.

Caleb's smile softened. "Sorry, I don't mean to sound dramatic. I've just never experienced anything like this before. I was on my way to Eureka Springs, but... my GPS glitched, I took a wrong exit, and found myself here. It's like the road led me, not the other way around."

His sincerity seemed to ripple through the group. He wasn't forceful, not a performer—if anything, he appeared humbled by his own bewilderment.

Miriam stepped forward, offering her hand. "You're not the first person to find your way here under strange circumstances. If something brought you here... maybe you're meant to be here."

Caleb's posture eased. "That would mean more than you know."

Within minutes, Caleb's presence stirred conversation, not suspicion. His ability to speak about intuition and inner shifts struck chords in many who had been uncertain about Luna's path forward. He listened more than he spoke, asked thoughtful questions, and recounted moments from his own journey with an honesty that resonated.

Even Eleanor, normally skeptical of outsiders, seemed drawn in by Caleb's quiet conviction.

"And what are you hoping to find here?" she asked, watching him closely.

Caleb took a breath. "Understanding, I guess. I've been trying to piece things together on my own, but something about this place... it feels like a missing piece. I'm not here to take anything. I just want to learn."

Ezra, still listening, watched Caleb's interactions closely. Nothing about the man's words raised red flags, but something tugged at the edge of his awareness—something he couldn't name. A flicker of doubt, like a shadow glimpsed just beyond the trees.

He dismissed it.

Miriam gently touched Caleb's arm. "Luna, someone we care about deeply, had a powerful experience yesterday. She hasn't regained consciousness since. Some of us believe it's part of a larger transformation, but it's been... hard to watch. You've had visions. Maybe you can offer some insight."

Caleb's face shifted, concern lining his features. "Of course. I'd be honored to help, even if it's just to sit and offer support."

Inside the cabin, Althea looked up as they entered. She was seated by Luna's side, her hands lightly resting over Luna's. The air was heavy with the scent of herbs and oil, the atmosphere still and sacred.

"Althea," Miriam said softly, "this is Caleb. He's had experiences like Luna's... we thought he might be able to lend his energy."

Althea's eyes moved to Caleb slowly. "You felt drawn here?"

He nodded, humbly. "I didn't even know why until I saw her. It's... strange to say out loud, but it feels like something I've been heading toward without knowing it."

Althea gave a small nod, her voice quiet. "Sit, then. See what arises."

Caleb knelt beside the bed, carefully, as if afraid to disturb something delicate. He didn't touch Luna, only bowed his head slightly, closing his eyes. A hush fell over the room. His breathing slowed. His presence, for all its polished exterior, settled into a calm rhythm that surprised Ezra even from outside.

After a long pause, Caleb opened his eyes, thoughtful. "May I ask... what was she doing when this happened?"

Miriam, still standing near the window, glanced toward a cloth-covered canvas leaning in the corner. "She was trying to connect with her mother... through this." She walked to it slowly, hands gentle as she lifted the edge of the cloth and pulled it away, revealing the swirling, luminous painting beneath. "It was the last piece her mother painted before she passed."

Caleb turned his head, his gaze landing on the newly revealed canvas.

His breath caught slightly. "Through the painting?" he echoed, stepping closer. The reverence in his voice was unmistakable. "That's... I mean, I know it doesn't help the situation right now, but... I'm grateful to hear that. I've been questioning whether what I've experienced is real or just me losing my grip. Hearing this... I know it's real."

Miriam didn't take her eyes off the painting. "It's more than just a painting," she said quietly. "There's something in it. Something alive. Not everyone sees it. But Luna did.."

Althea studied him in silence, then gave a faint nod. "You're not the only one seeking clarity. That's often where transformation begins."

Caleb stood slowly. "Thank you for letting me be here."

Althea's voice softened. "Sometimes being present is the most important thing."

As they exited, Ezra stood watching the cabin from the garden's edge, the rake now leaned forgotten against the fence. Caleb's integration into Everwood felt... easy. Too easy?

Ezra shook the thought from his head. He had no reason to doubt the man. And right now, Luna was the only one that mattered.

Later that evening, Ezra stood in Althea's cabin, his voice trembling with barely contained desperation. "I've tried to meditate on my own, but I can't get past the fear. It's like it's blocking me. I need your help. I need to find her," he pleaded, his eyes searching Althea's for answers.

Althea placed a steadying hand on his shoulder. "We'll try," she said softly, her tone calm but resolute. "But to reach her, you'll need to quiet that fear."

The evening sun dipped below the horizon, casting long shadows over the community. In Althea's cabin, a faint aroma of sage and lavender lingered, the herbs smoldering gently in a small clay bowl. Ezra sat cross-legged on a woven mat, his hands resting on his knees, palms upward. His jaw tightened with a mix of determination and frustration.

Althea regarded him calmly, her serene expression a counterbalance to his storm. "Close your eyes, Ezra," she said softly, her voice steady and grounding. "Let the tension go. You cannot force this. Breathe and focus on the love that binds you to Luna."

Ezra exhaled slowly, closing his eyes. "It's just... she's out there somewhere, and I feel so helpless," he murmured.

Althea placed a reassuring hand on his arm. "I understand. But Luna is on a journey that reaches beyond the stars. To connect with her, you must trust the bond you share. Focus on your love for her, not your fear of losing her."

Ezra nodded, inhaling deeply. He began to concentrate, his breathing steadying as the world around him faded into a quiet hum.

At first, there was only darkness behind Ezra's closed eyes, a vast and empty void. But as he followed Althea's guiding voice into a deep state of relaxed presence, faint impressions began to form—soft flickers of light like distant stars, shimmering just beyond reach. He could feel her presence, a familiar feeling, faint and in the distance.

"Luna," he whispered, the name carrying a weight of longing.

For a fleeting moment, he felt her presence—distant and diffuse, like a shadow caught between worlds. She was adrift in the vastness, her form barely visible, blending into the darkness.

Ezra's breath hitched as he reached for her, his heart clenching with the aching distance between them. He could feel her searching for the thread that connected her to the world she had left behind.

But as quickly as the vision came, it flickered and blurred, slipping away like grains of sand through his fingers.

"Luna!" Ezra called out, his voice trembling with desperation as it echoed through the room.

There was no response, only the faint hum of the universe echoing in his ears.

Ezra's breathing faltered, and he opened his eyes, frustration etched into his features. "I saw her, or felt her rather, but it was like trying to hold onto smoke. She's searching for a way out"

Althea nodded slowly, her gaze steady. "You've touched her essence,

Ezra. That's no small feat. And now you should know that she is safe, present in that place. Luna is traveling deeper into a realm beyond our comprehension, a place where even the strongest bonds may not fully reach. Your love connects you, but it may not bring her back yet. This is her journey. She is strong and will find her way Ezra. We will keep her safe while she does."

Ezra clenched his fists, his voice low and pained. "I just want to help her, Althea. I need her to know she's not alone."

Althea's expression softened. "She knows, Ezra. Even in the depths of her journey, she feels the love that surrounds her. Keep meditating. Strengthen the connection. When the time is right, she will return. Until then, you must trust."

Ezra nodded. "I'll keep trying," he said quietly. "I won't give up. Thank you for this, Althea."

The room fell silent, the soft flicker of the candlelight casting gentle shadows on the walls. Though Luna remained beyond their reach, Ezra felt the first stirrings of hope that their connection would guide her home.

TWENTY-TWO

THE PRESENCE OF ABSENCE

Days had passed, and Ezra had become a fixture at Luna's side—spending hours each day in silent meditation, his breaths synced to rhythms he no longer tried to explain. Morning, noon, and late into the night, he entered the stillness, reaching, listening, trying to feel her presence beyond the veil. Sometimes, there were glimmers—a hum in the quiet, a faint warmth curling around the edges of his consciousness—but she never came closer. The void remained just that: wide, waiting, and painfully silent.

"Luna," he whispered into the aether, his voice laced with exhaustion and a hint of desperation. "Please come back."

Outside those sessions, the world moved on around him, though he barely noticed it—until Caleb.

There was nothing obvious to point to, nothing sinister or sharp. On the surface, Caleb had woven himself into the fabric of Everwood with ease. He helped where help was needed, listened when others spoke, and carried himself with the humble reverence of someone who had found exactly what he was seeking.

And yet, Ezra couldn't shake the feeling that something wasn't adding up.

It wasn't in Caleb's words, which were thoughtful and often echoed Luna's philosophies. Nor in his actions, which never once crossed a boundary or raised alarms. It was in the spaces between—the long pauses when no one else was looking, the way his eyes sometimes lingered on the covered painting, his questions about Luna that seemed more studied than spontaneous.

Ezra tried not to fixate on it. He told himself the tension was born of fear—his own fear of failing to bring Luna back. Still, it remained.

Late one afternoon, Ezra passed the meditation circle and saw Caleb seated with a small group of younger members, listening intently as they described their early dreams and energetic shifts. Caleb's posture was relaxed, his responses encouraging but never condescending. He shared stories of his own journey—moments of loss, strange synchronicities, emotional upheaval—and the others responded with open admiration. They liked him.

So did Ezra, in moments. That was part of the problem.

That evening, as the sun slipped below the trees and the shadows stretched long across the clearing, Ezra found himself walking the edge of the forest. He wasn't even sure what he was doing there until he saw Caleb seated alone by the firepit, poking gently at the embers with a stick.

Ezra hesitated, then approached.

Caleb looked up, offering a small nod. "Evening."

Ezra didn't respond immediately. He stepped closer, letting the silence settle between them before speaking.

"You seem to be fitting in," Ezra said at last.

Caleb smiled faintly, the firelight reflecting off his eyes. "I'm trying. It's... different here. Peaceful in a way I didn't expect. But also intense. There's a lot happening, even when it's quiet."

Ezra folded his arms. "What brought you here? I mean really?"

Caleb met his gaze, unflinching. "Like I have said before. I don't fully know. It started with dreams, and then turned into emotions i could not explain. Then visions. The sense that something was waiting. I'm not here with answers Ezra—I'm here with questions."

Ezra's jaw flexed. "You always seem to say the right thing."

A quiet laugh. "That's not a gift, I promise. Just a lifetime of second-guessing myself before I speak."

Ezra didn't smile. "You spend a lot of time talking about Luna. Watching her."

Caleb's expression softened. "Of course I do. She's at the heart of something powerful. And I don't mean that in a mystical, elevated way.

I mean it's personal. I recognize something in her—like we're navigating the same current. She's just... ahead of me."

Ezra stared at the fire, the flickering light unable to warm the tangle inside him—distrust, jealousy, something harder to name. The words slipped out before he could catch them.

"You don't think it's dangerous? This current?"

As soon as he said it, he felt the weight of it—like he'd revealed more than he meant, without fully understanding why.

"I think it's transformation," Caleb said, his voice even. "And yeah, it's always dangerous. But also necessary. We're not here to stay the same, Ezra."

Ezra turned toward him fully, his voice steadier now. "Then tell me this: what are your intentions with her?"

Caleb's brows rose slightly. He took a breath, not defensive but deliberate. "To support her. To learn from her. If I can help her, I will. But if you're asking if I'm here to take her from you—no. I'm not."

Ezra narrowed his eyes. "You think I'm just being protective."

"I think," Caleb said gently, "you're afraid. I can see it, and I don't blame you. She's the axis everything is turning around right now. That's a lot to carry. I see it in you—the weight, the ache. And maybe, when you look at me, you see something else that could spin it all further."

Ezra didn't reply. His fists were clenched, but he wasn't sure why anymore.

Caleb added, "You don't need to trust me, Ezra. But I hope you'll keep your focus where it matters. On her. Not me."

Ezra watched him for a long moment, then nodded once and turned away, his steps carrying him into the trees, toward the foot of Pyramid Hill.

The trail rose before him in the waning light, soft leaves rustling underfoot. He climbed slowly, letting the movement calm his nerves. The wind shifted through the trees, brushing past him like a whisper, and in that quiet, he could almost hear Luna's voice.

He reached the summit and stood at its edge, his breath heavy in the cooling air. The valley stretched below, the shapes of Everwood cloaked in shadows and moonlight. He sat down on the familiar spot him and Luna often found themselves.

He didn't know if Caleb was telling the truth. He didn't know if Luna would come back. But in that moment, with the sky above him and the earth beneath, he realized what he could do: stay present. Stay grounded.

Ezra sat in the hush of the mount, watching the last light of day spill across the horizon. Caleb's words echoed softly in the stillness—*You're afraid... and I don't blame you.* Ezra hadn't wanted to admit it at the time, but maybe Caleb had seen something true. Maybe his suspicion wasn't rooted in anything Caleb had done, but in his own fear—fear of what Luna was going through, fear that he couldn't protect her, couldn't guide her back.

Maybe I've been watching him too closely, Ezra thought, because I'm terrified of what I can't see.

For days now, he had been convinced that Caleb was hiding something, that his presence in the community was more than coincidence. But here, away from the noise and tension of the others, certainty slipped from his grasp like sand through his fingers. Was he truly seeing Caleb for who he was, or was his judgment clouded by fear—fear of losing Luna, fear of what he couldn't control?

Ezra paused at the base of the hill, drawing a deep breath to center himself, just as Althea had taught him. The pyramid-shaped rise jutted from the earth like an ancient sentinel, its angular form strikingly out of place amid the rolling landscape. He'd walked this path a dozen times before but had never really looked at it. Now, curiosity stirred within him as he traced its sharp lines with his gaze, a question forming unbidden in his mind: What are you hiding, old hill?

He closed his eyes, imagining Luna beside him, the way she had been so many times before in moments like this—calm, steady, her presence like a balm to his restless thoughts. His breath caught in his throat as he spoke softly into the stillness.

"I wish you were here," he said, his voice barely a whisper. "Your simple presence is the foundation of my clarity."

His eyes opened, the soft light of dusk casting long shadows across the hill. "I miss you," he admitted, his voice thick with emotion. "More than I ever thought possible. And I've learned to rely on you, maybe too much. Without you, I feel... lost."

Ezra ran a hand through his hair, frustration flaring briefly before the calm returned. "I wish I'd never lost you to the painting," he said quietly, his eyes drifting to the horizon.

The words hung in the air, their meaning sinking in like a sudden weight. He straightened, his pulse quickening as the realization struck him. The painting. She's not gone. She's there. Trapped. Waiting.

Ezra's pulse quickened. Without hesitation, he pivoted and hurried back toward the community, his focus narrowing to a single goal. This wasn't a theory—it was something deeper, something he knew with every fiber of his being.

Twenty-Three

Where the Silence Ends

By the time he reached Althea's cabin, the sky had darkened to a deep indigo, stars just beginning to blink into view. Althea stood on the porch, her arms crossed lightly, but her eyes betrayed a quiet worry that never left her since Luna fell into this state. She had done everything she could to sustain her, yet the longer Luna remained unresponsive, the more fragile her body became. It was a race against time—a balance she feared she could not hold much longer. Her expression softened as Ezra approached, his urgency unmistakable. She straightened, sensing the shift in him.

"I need the painting," Ezra said, his voice steady but urgent. He glanced past her to where Luna lay on the cot, her face serene but distant, like a dream she couldn't wake from. His chest tightened as he stepped closer, kneeling beside her.

He leaned in, brushing a gentle kiss against her forehead. "I'll find you," he whispered. "I promise."

Althea studied him, arms folded, worry etched into her otherwise calm demeanor. For days, she had watched Luna drift into a near-stillness—not lifeless, but suspended. Her pulse was barely a whisper, her breath a thread so faint it felt like the room itself paused to listen. It was as if she had entered a place beyond time, where the body answered to ancient rhythms no doctor could touch. Though Althea's voice stayed steady, the weight in her eyes deepened. She didn't know how long Luna could remain in that delicate space—but looking at Ezra now, grounded and unflinching, she felt the smallest flicker of faith.

The universe was moving, revealing its plan in quiet, deliberate strokes.

She gave a slow nod, her lips curving into the faintest smile of recognition.

"Be careful," she said, her voice steady but layered with meaning. "The bond between you is strong. Trust it."

Ezra rose and moved to the painting, his hands steady but reverent as he lifted it from its resting place. He could feel its energy thrumming beneath his fingers, a quiet hum that seemed to vibrate in time with his heartbeat. He wrapped it carefully in cloth, his grip firm but gentle, as though cradling something fragile yet immensely powerful.

"I'll bring her back," he said softly, more to himself than anyone else.

Althea watched him, her expression unreadable but knowing. "Follow what guides you," she said simply.

Ezra cradled the painting against his chest, careful with every step as he carried it through the darkening paths. The cool night air whispered through the trees, brushing his skin like a faint reminder of what lay ahead. His cabin's light glowed in the distance—a beacon of safety and solitude. Inside, Ezra moved with purpose. He cleared a space near the center of the room and set up one of his old easels, adjusting its height before placing the painting carefully on it. His fingertips brushed the edge of the frame, and for a moment, the air seemed to hum around him.

He couldn't tell if the sensation in his chest was the painting's energy or pure adrenaline, his heart racing with anticipation. But the certainty in his bones told him something big was coming—something that would demand all his focus and strength. Rushing wouldn't help. He knew that. A slow heart was a strong heart.

He took a deep breath, crossing the room to retrieve the candles Althea had given him. One by one, he lit them, their warm glow filling the space and bringing with it a sense of calm. Ezra settled onto the floor in front of the painting, his body tense at first, his mind swirling with possibilities. He closed his eyes, grounding himself the way Luna had taught him.

Follow the breath. In... slow and steady. Out... even slower.

At first, his thoughts resisted, pulling him back to the uncertainty, the fear, the urgency of finding Luna. He forced his focus to return to the breath. His body began to soften with each exhale, the energy inside him shifting, transforming.

Minutes passed, or perhaps longer—time felt irrelevant now. His breathing deepened, his heartbeat slowing to a steady rhythm. The tension in his chest released like a coiled spring unwinding. Calm washed over him, clearer than it had been in days. He sank deeper into the stillness, his mind opening, reaching for that familiar, unbreakable thread that connected him to Luna.

"Guide me to her," he whispered, the words almost a prayer.

The air seemed to thicken around him, the room falling into a profound, vibrating silence.

He was ready.

Ezra drifted deeper, his breath steady, his awareness expanding beyond the limits of his body. The gentle hum of the room fell away, the sensation of touch dissolving until there was nothing—no weight, no edges, no boundaries. His body no longer felt like something he inhabited but rather a distant memory, a fading echo left behind.

The candlelight vanished, swallowed by an endless void. It wasn't darkness—it was nothingness. But there was no fear. Ezra had been here before, in the stillness where love had no edges, only presence.

His mind's eye awakened, a soft pulse in the center of the void. He focused, anchoring himself to the vision of the painting. Though he couldn't see it in the traditional sense, he knew it was there, just beyond the veil of his awareness.

I'm coming, Luna.

He felt himself moving—not physically, but in that space of expanded consciousness—drifting toward the energy of the painting. The image sharpened in his mind: the swirling spiral, luminous and alive. He ventured closer, drawn by its magnetic pull. Its rhythm echoed in his mind, slow and steady, like a heartbeat calling him forward.

In the void, the painting seemed to breathe, its colors whispering in vibrant waves. Ezra focused on the center of the spiral, allowing its motion to guide him, its pull growing stronger with every moment. His awareness tunneled toward it, the outside world fading completely.

The closer he came, the more he could feel her. Not a physical presence, but something far deeper—a resonance, a frequency that was unmistakably hers. It pulsed in harmony with his own being, a thread of connection too powerful to deny.

Luna.

The spiral expanded, wrapping around him, its energy coursing through his consciousness like a current of light. He ventured further, deeper into the spiral's center, his focus unwavering. Time dissolved, leaving only the pulse of that connection—strong, unbreakable.

In the distance, faint at first but growing stronger, he felt it: a spark, a flicker of Luna's presence. His heart surged with recognition, his awareness leaning toward her like a moth to a flame.

"I'm here," he called, his voice carrying across the vast emptiness. "I'm with you."

The void seemed to ripple in response, the spiral tightening, its motion growing faster—no longer a gentle pull but something else entirely. Ezra stilled, his awareness sharpening as an undeniable knowing gripped him.

Stop.

It wasn't a voice, but the message was clear, reverberating through his being. The spiral was no longer a path forward; it was a threshold—a boundary not to be crossed. His breath locked tight in his chest, but he didn't panic.

He slowed his focus, drawing his awareness inward, retreating from the pull of the spiral. His heart, steady and unwavering, became his new center. He no longer needed to search.

From this still place, he focused on her—on Luna—not where she was or what surrounded her, but on the truth of who she was. His love for her filled the void like light spreading across a darkened room, warm and encompassing. He held onto every detail: the sound of her laugh, the way her eyes softened in moments of quiet, her courage in the face of the unknown.

He surrendered fully to the love that pulsed between them, trusting that it would reach her. Not with force, not with urgency, but with gentle certainty.

"I'm here," he whispered, his voice a beacon. "I'll always be here."

The spiral slowed, its rhythm softening, the warning fading into stillness. In that stillness, Ezra felt her presence grow stronger—like the
whisper of a breeze brushing past his consciousness, faint but unmistakable.

In the infinite stillness of the void crafted by her mother, Luna drifted
weightlessly. There was no up or down, no boundaries—only a vast
emptiness that stretched endlessly in all directions. Time unraveled,
losing all meaning. She tried to anchor herself, to observe her own form,
but found nothing—no hands, no body, only the faintest whisper of her
existence.

She was an echo, a fragment unmoored from reality—and in the nothingness where even her body no longer belonged to her, she had never
felt so free.

The silence pressed in, heavy and all-consuming, its presence more
suffocating than the darkness. In a moment of acceptance, she wondered
if this was how she would remain—suspended forever in the void, forgotten by the world she had once known.

Then, from the heart of the emptiness, something shifted.

A single thread of light pierced the darkness, thin but radiant, weaving
through the vast expanse like liquid gold. Its glow pulsed gently, and with
every pulse, a warmth spread outward, cutting through the cold void. The
thread moved with purpose, winding toward her. Its light wasn't blinding;
it was familiar.

It was home.

Luna stilled, her awareness locking onto the thread as it reached her.
The moment it touched her essence, a wave of love—pure and overwhelming—washed over her. It filled the cracks where emptiness had
taken root, warming her from the inside out.

Ezra.

The thread wrapped around her, weaving into her essence. Piece by
piece, she began to reassemble—not in the way a body reforms but in the

way memories resurface after being lost in darkness. Her identity took shape once more.

Sensations returned like whispers—first the faint brush of air, then the weight of her physical form. The warmth of the thread never left her, weaving her back into the world she had almost forgotten.

In the distant reality where her body lay, her lips trembled, and a single tear traced down her cheek. Her heart, dormant for so long, now pulsed with a steady rhythm, radiating love outward.

The light grew stronger, the thread pulling her upward, faster and faster, until—

A surge of energy burst through.

Her eyes flew open, wild and wide, her chest heaving as she gasped for air. It was as if she had been dragged from the depths of an endless sea, her lungs greedy for the breath of life. The world was too bright, too loud.

Her heart pounded in her chest, and for one disorienting moment, she could still feel the golden thread tethered to her soul, its energy humming in rhythm with her breath.

Althea staggered back slightly, overwhelmed by the force of Luna's awakening. "You've returned," she whispered, her voice trembling with awe.

Simultaneously, Ezra emerged from his meditation, a sharp jolt of certainty coursing through him. He didn't need confirmation; he knew Luna was back. Without hesitation, he sprinted barefoot toward Althea's cabin, his heart pounding in rhythm with his feet hitting the ground.

Bursting through the door, Ezra found Luna sitting up, her chest rising and falling in deep, steady breaths. Her eyes blinked against the soft glow of the lantern light, adjusting to the world that seemed almost too solid, too vivid after the vast darkness she had left behind. For a heartbeat, they just stared at each other, no words needed—only the silent exchange of recognition, relief, and something deeper.

Ezra dropped to his knees beside her, his hands gently cradling hers, his grip firm but trembling. "I found you," he whispered, his voice thick with emotion. "I knew I'd find you."

Luna's gaze softened, her fingers curling around his. "You pulled me back," she said, her voice raw and full of awe. "I could feel you... guiding me home. Thank you, Ezra."

The weight of her words settled between them. Despite the days of rest her body had endured, exhaustion clung to her like a shadow, but it was different now—less heavy, almost purposeful.

Ezra brushed a loose strand of hair from her face, his thumb lingering at her temple. "You don't have to say anything," he murmured. "You're safe now."

Luna leaned into his touch, her breath steadying as the edges of reality began to sharpen once more. "Safe," she repeated, the word wrapping around her like a warm blanket.

Ezra scooped Luna into his arms, her body light and fragile against his chest. He cradled her with care, his heart steady but overflowing with emotion. For days, he had watched over her, waiting, hoping. Now, holding her like this, he felt the world align again.

"Thank you, Althea," Ezra said, his voice low but full of gratitude. His eyes met hers, and in that shared glance, a quiet understanding passed between them—a promise of continued care and vigilance.

Althea nodded softly. "Take her home, Ezra. She'll need time, but she's strong."

He stepped out into the cool night, the air crisp and fresh around them. The stars blinked above, silent witnesses to their return. His boots made soft thuds on the dirt path, the familiar rhythm grounding him as he carried her toward his cabin.

Inside, he gently laid Luna down on his bed, tucking a blanket around her. She stirred, her fingers curling faintly in his shirt, refusing to let go. Ezra slipped onto the bed beside her, wrapping an arm around her waist and pulling her close.

"I'm right here, and nothing's going to take you from me again." he whispered, his breath warm against her hair. "I've got you."

Luna's body relaxing into his. Her breathing slowed into an even rhythm, her presence grounding him as much as his did her. Ezra rested his head beside hers, holding her through the night, the weight of everything fading into the quiet hum of their shared heartbeat.

Twenty-Four

A Stolen Legacy

The soft clink of a plate on the nightstand stirred Luna from sleep. The warm scent of toasted bread and fresh herbs filled the air, mingling with the soft light filtering through the cabin's windows. She blinked slowly, the weight of exhaustion replaced with a lightness she hadn't felt in days.

"Morning," Ezra said quietly, nudging the plate closer with a gentle smile. "Figured you could use something more substantial than the tea and oils Althea's been brushing on your lips these past few days.

Luna sat up, the blanket slipping from her shoulders. She accepted the plate, her fingers brushing his. "Thank you," she murmured, her voice still soft from sleep.

The first bite was almost jarring—warm, rich, grounding. She hadn't realized how empty she felt until now. The bread was soft, the eggs perfectly seasoned, and as she ate, strength seeped back into her limbs. She savored those first few bites, letting the warmth of it settle deep inside her.

Ezra sat beside her, watching as color returned to her cheeks. "You look better already," he said. "Take your time. There's no rush."

But Luna barely heard him. Her body had other plans. Before she knew it, the plate was nearly empty. She blinked down at it, as if surprised by her own hunger.

Ezra chuckled. "Well, that didn't last long. Can I get you some more?"

Luna wiped her lips with the back of her hand, glancing at the empty plate as if it had betrayed her. "Guess I was hungrier than I thought," she said with a sheepish grin—then let out a tiny, surprised hiccup.

She placed a hand on her stomach and laughed. "Okay, maybe I ate a little too fast. I'm good, thank you. Any more and I might float away."

Ezra smirked. "I'll let you believe whichever makes you feel better."

She laughed, setting the plate aside and stretching her fingers as a quiet energy settled into her. "I feel... ready. Really ready," she said. "There's much to be done."

A spark of resolve lit in her eyes, and Ezra nodded with a smile, happy to see how quickly she bounced back.

After a cup of coffee, Luna stepped outside for a walk down the clearing in front of the gathering hall, Ezra by her side. The fresh morning air filled her lungs, the sensation painting a glowing smile across her lips. The sun cast a soft golden light across the landscape, and the hum of the waking world seemed to rise in rhythm with her steady pulse. The familiar sounds of birdsong and rustling leaves wrapped around her like an old friend's embrace.

A voice called out as she strolled toward the heart of the clearing.

"You look great, Luna!" came Miriam's voice, filled with unmistakable warmth.

Before Luna could reply, Miriam was already closing the space between them, arms flung wide. She enveloped Luna in a tight hug, holding on for a few extra seconds like someone who had been holding her breath and could finally exhale.

"I've missed you so much," Miriam said softly, her voice thick with emotion. "You scared the life out of us."

Luna melted into her aunt's embrace, the connection grounding her more than she realized she'd needed. "I'm okay," she whispered, her voice catching. "I'm really okay."

Miriam pulled back slightly, hands on Luna's shoulders, eyes searching her face. "I know you are. I can see it in your eyes." She smiled, brushing a strand of hair from Luna's cheek. "It's like something settled in you. Like you've found something we haven't even named yet."

Luna nodded, her expression gentle. "It felt that way. Like I went somewhere... beyond."

Miriam smiled through her lingering worry, her voice lightening. "You won't believe who showed up while you were... away. Caleb. Just as you said would happen—another awakened soul found us. And he's—Luna, he's amazing. Articulate, grounded, thoughtful. He's already helped with one of the younger members who's been struggling with dream interpretation. He just... fits. The whole community's buzzing."

Ezra shifted slightly beside Luna, but said nothing.

Luna tilted her head. "Caleb?"

Miriam nodded enthusiastically. "You'll meet him soon, if you haven't already. He came right after you collapsed. Said he was pulled here by visions, just like you. I swear, it was like watching your words come to life."

A strange ripple moved through Luna's chest, not quite doubt but something quieter. She smiled anyway. "I'd like to talk to him."

"You will," Miriam said, squeezing her arm.

The three of them—Luna, Ezra, and Miriam—began walking slowly toward the gathering hall, the sun warming their faces as the soft crunch of gravel echoed beneath their feet.

After a few quiet steps, Luna turned slightly toward Ezra, her voice low, just above a whisper. "Why didn't you tell me about Caleb?"

Ezra glanced ahead, then down at the path. His answer came with careful calm. "I was too focused on you. Everything else faded out."

Luna held his gaze for a second longer, reading something unspoken in the tight line of his jaw, the faint hesitation in his step. But she didn't press him. Not yet.

As they drew nearer to the hall, voices and movement began to ripple outward. One by one, members of the community emerged—some stepping from cabins, others appearing from the nearby path or garden, their faces lighting up at the sight of Luna.

A small group began to gather around her, drawn as much by their curiosity as by their affection. They closed the space gently, naturally—some standing close, others lingering near the edges of the clearing, listening quietly, their expressions a tapestry of relief, wonder, and quiet reverence.

"You had us worried," Althea said, stepping closer, her voice warm but tinged with maternal care. "But I knew you'd come back stronger."

"I feel stronger," Luna said softly, her eyes sweeping over the group. "Stronger and clearer than ever before."

The hum of quiet conversation faded as the growing crowd stilled, their attention centering on her. The anticipation in the air was palpable, every gaze turned toward Luna, waiting for her next words, her next step.

Near the edge of the crowd stood Caleb, his posture as casual as ever, but his expression... wrong. Too still. Too practiced. His usual charm flickered like a candle in the wind, and when Luna's eyes found his, something fractured in her.

It hit her all at once—an unrelenting surge of images flooding her senses: files exchanged in dim-lit corners, hushed voices behind mirrored glass, the sterile hum of surveillance rooms, and Caleb—calm, collected—shaking hands beneath the gleaming Westfield Industries logo. It wasn't foggy or symbolic. It was clear, sharp, true. Her breath locked tight in her chest. The earth itself seemed to draw inward beneath her feet.

Her steps forward were slow but unwavering. The crowd parted before her like water cut by a blade. The energy around her changed—shifted—turned electric. Ezra followed in her wake, instinctively falling into step beside her.

She stopped a few feet from Caleb, the space between them suddenly charged like a drawn bowstring.

"You're a spy."

The words weren't shouted. They didn't need to be. Her voice cut through the murmurs like thunder in a chapel.

Gasps. A ripple of disbelief rolled through the gathering. Miriam's hand flew to her mouth. Others recoiled, glancing toward Caleb with widening eyes.

Caleb's mask cracked—just for a flicker. A twitch in his jaw. A tightening of his throat. Then came the charm, resurrected in a heartbeat.

"Luna, I think you're confused—"

"Don't insult me," she snapped. Her voice was steel now. "I saw it. Everything. Westfield. The labs. Your meetings. You've been reporting on us this entire time."

Ezra surged beside her, his voice finally unbound. "I knew something was off with you. I knew it!"

Caleb's posture stiffened. "I didn't hurt anyone," he said quickly. "All I've done is observe. Share insight. That's not betrayal, that's—"

"Deception," Luna said, stepping forward again, her voice low but searing. "You wormed your way into this community. Played the part. Earned our trust. You stood over my unconscious body while plotting with people who see us as experiments."

"I was trying to help!" Caleb's voice cracked slightly now, rising. "They're not the enemy. They want to understand. That's all they've ever—"

"No," she said, eyes burning now. "They want to dissect us. To own what they don't understand. And you... you handed them the key."

Ezra took a step forward, fists clenched. "You used her. All of us."

Caleb turned, scanning the crowd. No friendly faces now. Only shock. Betrayal. Fury. Even the ones who had once sung his praises now stood frozen, disillusioned.

"I didn't want it to go this way," he muttered, the air draining from him.

"Then you should've chosen differently," Luna replied, cold and resolute. "This isn't just a place—it's a sanctuary. You came as a seeker, but you were always a thief."

She looked deep into Caleb's eyes. Her final words were quiet but commanding. "You're done here. Go."

Caleb stood frozen. Eyes darting. Mouth slightly open. Then—just a slight nod. Resigned. Exposed. He turned and walked, alone, toward the wooded path. Every step he took landed like a stone tossed into silence.

Not a soul moved to stop him. Not a voice rose in protest. Just the rustle of leaves, the breath of the forest, and the weight of truth settling heavy in the clearing.

Luna took a few deep breaths to still the fury surging in her chest. Around her, the energy shifted—the community's anger blooming like wildfire. But Eleanor wasted no time.

"Do you see what's happening?" Her voice rose. "This stranger comes here, spies on us, and why? Because we drew attention to ourselves.

Because we put faith in visions and shifts."

Her eyes locked on Luna, laced with doubt. "We've lived in peace for years. Now we're being watched. Are we ready for the risk?"

Whispers of agreement surfaced. "She has a point," someone muttered. "It used to be quiet here."

"What if more people come, like Caleb?" another asked, fear creeping into their voice.

Luna stepped forward, calm but unyielding. "Caleb didn't succeed because we stood together."

"And yet he came at all," Eleanor snapped. "We've opened a door we may not be able to close."

"Enough." Silas's voice cut through the growing tension. He stepped beside Luna, his presence grounding the moment.

"What more does my daughter have to do to prove herself?" His voice rang out across the clearing. "She's risked herself for us. If you can't see that, you're not paying attention."

He looked to Eleanor. "Yes, it was quieter before. But we can't hide from the world. Caleb's arrival was a warning—not to shut down, but to be vigilant and united."

Heads began to nod. The crowd leaned in. His words struck something real.

"I trust her," Silas declared. "With my life. It's time we prepare for what's coming—together."

The weight of his words settled over them, turning murmurs of doubt into murmurs of agreement.

Eleanor held her stance, but her pride was already cracking. "And when the next stranger comes? When Westfield sends more than spies?" Her tone faltered.

"Eleanor," Miriam said softly. "Luna's strength is what brought the truth to light. This isn't abandoning what we built. It's growing with what's already changing."

Luna stepped forward again, her voice softer now but no less powerful. "You want to know what I saw?" She looked out at the faces gathered before her. "Inside that painting—my mother's final work—I wasn't just unconscious. I was somewhere else. Held in a space beyond time, sur-rounded by light that pulsed like breath. She was there. Not as a memory, but as a presence. She showed me pieces of what came before us—what lies ahead."

The crowd fell silent. Even Eleanor leaned in slightly, curiosity soften-ing her posture.

"I saw circles carved into stone, figures gathered beneath stars, their voices lifting into something beyond sound. They weren't praying. They were remembering. Aligning. Holding the Earth's pulse."

Luna's gaze rose to the distant ridge.

"That energy... that place... it led me to Pyramid Hill."

A few in the crowd gasped softly.

"It's not just a hill," Luna said. "It's a marker. An ancient one. Built by those same souls who understood what we're only beginning to glimpse. It's a gateway—subtle, quiet, but alive."

She looked down briefly, then raised her eyes again with renewed cer-tainty. "I used to think my mother's painting was a message meant only for me. But I see now—it was a key. A reminder that our connection to this land, to each other, is not new. It's ancient. Waiting to be remembered."

Her voice steadied. "The shift is coming. And our choices matter. This place—Everwood—it's not just where we hide. It's where we stand. Together."

A charged silence followed.

Then a voice: "The hill's been here my whole life. I thought it was just a hill. But now..."

More murmurs. Heads turned. Nods of agreement. Excitement bloomed.

Althea stepped forward. "Luna has my full support. Let's move forward together—not divided by fear."

The crowd held their place, hushed, yet steady. No one followed—but no one turned away. They stood together, not in confusion, but in quiet conviction. Something had changed. Not just in Luna, but in all of them.

As Luna and Ezra began walking—hand in hand toward the distant rise of Pyramid Hill—those left behind remained rooted, not as bystanders, but as stewards. The air held reverence. The shift she had spoken of was no longer abstract; it had begun.

One by one, heads bowed—not in submission, but in acknowledgment. Whatever lay ahead, they would meet it—not as individuals, but as a people reawakened.

Ezra leaned closer. "They're with you."

Luna nodded. "I know."

But as they walked toward his cabin, guilt nipped at Ezra's resolve. "I should've done something sooner," he muttered. "I knew he wasn't right."

"You weren't wrong," Luna said. "And you trusted your instincts. That's growth, Ezra."

He gave a faint smile. "You think so?"

"I know so."

They reached the cabin, the soft afternoon light filtering through the trees. For a moment, the golden glow made everything feel safe—until Luna stepped inside and froze.

The easel was empty.

"No," she gasped. "No, no, no."

Ezra stormed in behind her, his eyes scanning the room like a hawk. "Where the hell is it?"

Then he saw it—the scuff marks on the floor, the absence screaming louder than any alarm. "Caleb," he snarled. "That bastard took it."

He spun and kicked a chair across the room, the wooden legs splintering against the wall. "I should've locked it down. I should've seen this coming."

"Ezra—" Luna started, but he was already moving.

"He can't have gone far," Ezra growled, reaching for his keys. "I'm sorry, Luna. I'll track him down and bring it back."

Luna's voice was quiet, tense. "It's not your fault, Ezra." She reached for his arm. "Don't bother. He's long gone by now. You won't find him."

"I should've gotten rid of him the moment he arrived," he said, clutching his fists in rage.

"You couldn't have known," she said, staring at the empty space. "But we'll get it back."

Ezra turned to her, anger giving way to focus. "You're damn right we will."

A heavy silence fell. But within it, something powerful stirred—resolve.

"We start tomorrow," Luna said. "We'll track him down, and get it back."

Ezra nodded. "Together."

And together, they stood—unshaken. Ready.

TWENTY-FIVE

THE TIPPING POINT

L una stood at the base of Pyramid Hill, her boots sinking slightly into the damp earth. The air was rich with the scent of moss and wildflowers, the hush of the evening settling around her like a held breath.

She let her gaze drift upward, tracing the sharp lines of the hill's peak. How much of its truth had been buried?

Closing her eyes, she let her awareness stretch outward. A flicker of something ancient pressed at the edges of her consciousness—not quite memory, not quite vision. A whisper of the past.

For a moment, she could almost see it. The pyramid as it once was. Smooth, sunlit stone rising above the valley, its carvings alive with shifting energy. She caught the impression of movement—figures working in perfect harmony, their actions guided by a rhythm older than time.

The flicker of vision faded, leaving only the quiet, unyielding hill before her.

Luna exhaled. *Not yet.*

Her pulse beat steady as she placed a hand against the cool earth. "We'll get to you soon," she murmured. "But first, I need to get the painting back."

She turned, stepping away from the hill, toward the clearing and made her way back to the Ezra's cabin.

Ezra hunched over his laptop, its screen casting a faint glow across his face as he scrolled through pages of documents. The table in front of him was a mess—scattered notes, printouts, and half-empty coffee cups. Luna approached, sensing the tension in his posture.

"Ezra?" she prompted.

He barely looked up. "You need to see this."

Luna stepped beside him, her eyes flicking to the screen. A Westfield Industries shareholder transcript was open, a highlighted section catching her attention.

A whistleblower came forward, exposing how Westfield had been conducting secret excavations at ancient sites—only to destroy artifacts before anyone else could study them.

Luna's stomach twisted. "Destroying them? Why would they do that?"

Ezra clicked to another file, frustration lacing his movements. "Because if people knew what they were finding, the world would start asking questions. Westfield doesn't want to share their discoveries—they want to control them."

He scrolled further, revealing a tangled web of corporations funneling millions into these projects, each connection deliberately obscured. "They're not doing this alone. Other companies—private investors—are backing them. It's a network. Whatever they're after... it's not just about money or history. They're looking for something powerful."

Luna clenched her jaw, her pulse quickening. "Then we need to find it before they do."

Ezra nodded, determination etched into his features. "Whatever it is, we'll find it first. And we'll make sure they can't use it."

Her eyes flicked back to the screen as Ezra navigated to another document. "And look at this," he said, pulling up a corporate photo. Caleb stood among a group of Westfield employees, his polished demeanor unmistakable.

Luna's jaw clenched. "I'm sure he's reported back by now," she said, her voice a simmering edge of frustration. She slammed her fist on the table, the sharp sound echoing in the quiet room. Closing her eyes, she drew a deep breath, her body trembling slightly as she reined in her emotions.

"They won't stop, will they?" she said finally, her voice quieter but no less determined.

Ezra shook his head, his expression grim. "Not unless we give them a reason to."

Luna leaned back, her mind racing. "Then we need to act," she said firmly. "If Westfield is digging up history, and tracking energetic phenomena, they'll eventually uncover the pyramid here and destroy our home in the process of uncovering it. They don't understand the power they're after—it's greed, nothing more. We need to make it clear their effort isn't worth the reward here. I'll find a way to see them clearly, uncover their secrets, and confront them."

Ezra raised an eyebrow. "How do you plan to do that?"

"First, we need to find out where Caleb has taken the painting," Luna said, her voice steady but laced with determination. "I'm tied to it in a way no one else can be. I believe the essence she left within it is something only I can access—something meant for me alone." Her gaze sharpened. "But if I'm wrong, and someone else manages to unlock even a fragment of that essence... it could be dangerous. I can't take that risk."

She inhaled deeply, grounding herself in the presence of the moment, feeling the threads of the aethereal weaving into her resolve. "I'll track it through meditation and seek guidance from my higher self—the designer of my path. The answers are there; I just need clarity to see them."

Ezra nodded, his confidence in her plan growing. "How can I help?"

"Continue your investigation," Luna said. "Look into the other locations they're targeting. We might find others like me awakening there. We may be able to rely on each other if we need help."

That evening, Luna retreated to her cabin, her thoughts turning to Elias. She lit a small candle, the flame casting flickering shadows on the walls, and opened her journal. Tucked between the pages, where she had placed it for safekeeping, was Elias's weathered business card.

With a steadying breath, she dialed his number. After a few rings, his familiar voice answered. "Hello?"

"Elias," she began, a mix of excitement and urgency threading through her voice.

"Luna," he said warmly, his tone a grounding presence. "Wasn't expecting your call so soon. What's going on?"

"I know, I'm sorry. Things are moving fast—and I've made some progress. It turns out Mom discovered how to encode a fractal of her Akashic record into her painting."

There was a pause. "Are you serious?" Elias's voice crackled through the phone, thick with astonishment. "That's incredible!"

"Almost as incredible as being trapped inside it for three days," Luna said with a chuckle, her tone light despite the gravity of her experience.

"Trapped?" Elias's fascination grew. "Were you in her memories?"

"I was," Luna confirmed, her voice softening. "But that's a story for another day." She paused, her tone shifting back to the matter at hand. "I need your advice. While I was gone, Westfield sent someone into our community. They took the painting. And they're after something much bigger. Their misunderstanding of the energy they're chasing could seriously disrupt the balance. We've uncovered parts of their plan, but they seem to be after ancient sites—like they're looking for something. I thought you might know what that could be."

"Westfield Industries?" Elias's voice grew serious, the weight of her words hanging heavy in the silence. "I may be able to do more than just speculate. I'm familiar with the company—I knew the founder, Herold Westfield. An... old acquaintance," he said carefully. "If they're involved, you're right to be worried. But I might have someone who can help you."

Luna leaned in, her heart quickening. "Who?"

"A colleague of mine, Dr. Beth Marin," Elias explained. "I introduced her to Herold back in college. She's brilliant—deeply familiar with Westfield's operations. If they're up to no good, either she doesn't know or she's fighting from the inside to stop them. She's a good person, Luna. If anyone would be willing to help, it's her."

A spark of hope ignited within Luna. "Thank you, Elias. This means everything."

"I'll reach out to her and get you in touch," he promised. "But Luna, be cautious. If Westfield is involved, then it's Herold pulling the strings. He plays a long game, and he's ruthless. Protect your people. Trust your instincts—you're stronger than you know."

"I will," Luna said, her voice steady with resolve. "I'll trust my instincts—and I won't let Westfield catch us off guard."

As the call ended, Luna let out a long breath, the weight on her chest easing just slightly. She stepped outside, the night air cool against her skin, carrying with it the scent of pine and earth. Looking toward the horizon, she felt a renewed sense of purpose.

The path ahead would demand unity, trust, and unwavering strength. But she wasn't alone. Together, they would face whatever lay beyond the shadows.

Luna slept deeply that night, the kind of sleep that heals fractures unseen. When she woke, the sky was just beginning to lighten, the promise of a new day stretching across the horizon. The morning sun filtered through the trees, casting dappled patterns of light on the soft earth as Luna made her way toward the grove. Each step was deliberate, her presence grounded by a growing sense of purpose. The events of recent days had shifted something deep within her. The weight she carried was no longer burdensome; it was the steady pull of destiny.

Ezra walked beside her, his brow furrowed with concern. "You're sure about this?" he asked, his voice low yet steady.

"I have to be," Luna replied, her tone calm but resolute. "The painting holds more than just my mother's legacy—it might be the key to it all, and I need to understand it before Westfield finds a way to exploit its power." She paused, glancing at him with softened eyes. "I trust myself to do this."

Ezra's gaze lingered on her, his faith evident. "Then I'll stay close," he said after a moment. "If anything feels off, you call for me, alright?"

She nodded, her expression grateful but determined. "I will."

As they approached the grove, its ancient oaks rose like guardians, their towering branches forming a natural sanctuary. This spot had always felt special, the deep roots of the trees drawing forth wisdom from the earth. But today, the air carried a distinct charge, the energy almost humming with anticipation.

Luna knelt at the grove's center, the cool moss cushioning her as she unpacked her satchel. She drew out a bundle of sage, a small bowl, and a thin shard of amethyst—tools Althea had given her to purify the air and channel her connection.

Ezra struck a match, lighting the sage and placing it in the small bowl beside Luna. Its fragrant smoke curled upward in delicate spirals, weaving into the grove's ancient energy. He crouched beside her for a moment longer, his concern evident. "I'll give you space," he said. "But I'll be right here, at the edge of the grove, if you need me."

Luna met his gaze, her smile brief but reassuring. "Thank you, Ezra. That's all I need."

With a quiet nod, Ezra stepped back, positioning himself under the canopy of a nearby oak. His watchful presence lingered, steady yet unobtrusive.

Luna lifted the smoldering sage, guiding the smoke in slow, deliberate arcs around her body. With each pass, she whispered silent intentions—protection, clarity, connection—letting the sacred scent wrap the space in peace. Once the circle felt complete, she returned the sage to the bowl, exhaled deeply, and closed her eyes.

The rhythmic symphony of the forest enveloped her. The rustle of leaves above became a gentle cascade of whispers, the birds' chirps softened into melodic echoes, and the wind's caress wove a steady, low hum, like a heartbeat thrumming beneath the surface of the earth. Her hands formed a mudra, the tips of her fingers pressing together lightly, an anchor in the sea of infinite possibility.

She inhaled deeply, the coolness of the air filling her lungs, and with each exhale, the physical world began to recede. The warmth of the moss beneath her faded into a faint vibration that hummed in harmony with her body. Time stretched and unraveled, and the edges of reality blurred until the grove seemed to dissolve, replaced by an expanse of luminous darkness—a void alive with the subtle shimmer of unseen forces.

In this stillness, threads of golden light began to emerge, delicate and infinite, their glow weaving an intricate tapestry that pulsed faintly with life. Luna gasped, but the sound never came as she became aware of their presence: the Akashic Records, ancient and eternal, spinning stories within the fabric of existence itself. The threads hummed with energy, each one a living memory. Unlike the dark void of the painting's fragmented record—cold and disorienting—this space was vast yet full of light, inviting her deeper with each pulse of connection. She focused on the one resonating most strongly, a strand glimmering with her mother's essence, its rhythm familiar and warm, like a lullaby from long ago.

The void pulsed. A thread of golden light guided her forward, pulling her toward something familiar—something waiting.

As Luna reached out with her mind, the painting responded, its vibrant energy rippling outward like concentric waves on still water. Fragments of her mother's voice whispered through her consciousness—softer than a breeze yet resonant with unshakable clarity.

"*Be the observer,*" her mother's voice urged, her words imprinted like a kiss on Luna's soul. "*Through you, the path will unfold.*"

A shimmer of light fractured the vision, and suddenly, Luna was no longer drifting—she was seeing.

The warmth of the golden thread vanished, replaced by the sterile cold of a Westfield Industries lab. Shadows loomed over the painting, now locked away in a featureless room of steel and glass. Caleb stood before a faceless figure, his posture rigid as he reported. Luna's stomach churned as she felt the violation of the painting's energy, its brilliance dimmed but not extinguished.

Her mother's voice cut through the vision, steady but urgent.

"*Protect the balance, Luna. Seek what lies beneath, and you will find the strength to counter them in the Angel City.*"

The words echoed with a clear understanding as the threads of the vision began to unravel. The golden glow dimmed, the connection thinning, but the message remained clear. Before she could retrieve the painting, she had to understand the wisdom hidden beneath the pyramid.

The world of the grove slowly reassembled itself around her. The earth beneath her felt warm again, grounding her in the present moment. She could hear the wind threading through the oaks and the faint call of a distant bird.

Luna gasped as her awareness snapped back into her body, her chest rising in a sharp breath. The world felt disjointed for a heartbeat—the hum of the grove distant, the cool earth beneath her hands the only anchor to the present. Her pulse thrummed in her ears, her breath uneven as she pressed her palms into the mossy ground.

Nearby, Ezra's head snapped toward her, his instincts on high alert. He crossed the grove in quick strides, dropping to a crouch beside her. "Luna," he said, his voice taut with both worry and curiosity. His eyes searched her face, catching the faint sheen of sweat on her brow and the distant look in her eyes. "Are you okay? What happened in there?"

Luna blinked slowly, taking a few steadying breaths. The echoes of the vision still pulsed within her, but clarity returned with each exhale. "I'm fine," she said, though her voice trembled slightly. Meeting Ezra's gaze, her expression sharpened with purpose. "I saw enough. Westfield has the painting... and I know where to start."

Ezra's jaw tightened, his commitment unwavering. "Where do we go?"

Luna inhaled deeply, gathering her thoughts. "The painting is in Los Angeles, but if I go now, I'll lose. We need to uncover the secrets of the pyramid first. It's not just a relic—it's a shield, a source of protection against what Westfield seeks to disrupt." She met his gaze, her eyes steady. "I'll need your help."

Ezra didn't hesitate. "You've got it," he said, his voice firm. "Whatever it takes."

The grove seemed to pulse in agreement, its ancient energy a silent witness to their shared conviction. Together, they would uncover the truth and protect the delicate balance the world now depended on.

TWENTY-SIX

BENEATH THE CANOPY, BENEATH THE EARTH

L una stood beneath the golden light of the late afternoon, the wind carrying whispers of secrets buried deep within the Hill. She closed her eyes, tuning into the rhythm of the earth beneath her feet, a connection that was quickly becoming second nature. Her meditation had unlocked something—a faint pulse of energy resonating with her own, as if the land itself was calling to her.

The vision came swiftly, sharper than before. In her mind's eye, the dense greenery of the northern hillside peeled back like the pages of an ancient book. There, beneath layers of thick moss and earth, was an arched entrance carved into the rock, almost imperceptible but unmistakably ancient. Symbols etched into the stone shimmered faintly, glowing with a soft golden light. The patterns weren't random; they were purposeful—familiar. The Flower of Life stared back at her from the peak of the arch, its sacred geometry pulsing with life.

Her breath caught as the energy surged, the entrance before her no longer just a doorway but a living threshold, pulsing with eternal life. It called to her, ancient and steady, filling her with awe rather than fear. Her heart swelled, each beat resonating in harmony with the hum of the vision. Gradually, the light dimmed, and the vision dissolved into the warm glow of twilight. Luna stood rooted, her chest rising and falling in slow, deliberate breaths, the weight of the experience settling over her like a quiet promise.

Luna stood for a moment longer, the last traces of the vision humming in her mind. Then, with deliberate steps, she turned and began her walk back to the cabin. The air was cool and crisp, carrying with it the scent of pine and damp earth. The world around her seemed to pulse with life—the rustle of leaves in the breeze, the distant chatter of birds hidden among the branches, the soft crunch of her footsteps on the well-worn path.

A flash of movement caught her attention—a small bird weaving through the air, its wings catching the golden light of late afternoon. Luna paused, following its path with her eyes, marveling at its effortless grace.

Life is everywhere, she thought, the corners of her lips curling into a faint smile.

Luna slowed her steps, turning her focus inward. A warm pulse of energy hummed beneath her skin, deep and familiar—like roots anchoring her to the land. As she breathed, the energy spiraled upward, expanding, aligning, flowing freely.

By the time she reached the cabin, she felt alive—as if the land itself had whispered its secrets into her bones. She spotted Ezra through the open doorway, hunched over his laptop, papers scattered across the table as he poured over his notes. His brow was furrowed in deep concentration.

Luna stepped inside, the gentle hum of her meditation still vibrating within her. The warmth of love and life flowed through her like an overflowing cup, radiant and steady. She leaned into Ezra's side, resting her head lightly against his shoulder as he scanned the text on the screen. His focus was intense, but her touch softened his expression. Without hesitation, she pressed a gentle kiss to his forehead, her lips brushing his skin like a promise.

Ezra looked up, startled for a second, his eyes softening as they met hers. "You're glowing," he said, his voice barely above a whisper, caught between awe and affection.

"I feel like I am," Luna said with a smile that lit her entire face, her eyes clear and filled with certainty. "I saw it, Ezra. I found the way in."

Ezra turned toward her, his hand instinctively resting on hers. His expression shifted from curiosity to quiet focus. "What did you see?" he asked, his voice steady but edged with urgency.

Luna held his gaze, her conviction unwavering. "An entrance. Hidden in the northern hillside. It's the way in—it's how we'll reach the pyramid. But it's more than just a door. It's a point of balance, a place that demands respect. We can't disturb its harmony."

Ezra nodded, his trust in her unwavering. "Then we'll do it carefully. Step by step."

Ezra hesitated for a moment, then said, "We'll need someone who knows these woods better than anyone. James can help us find the entrance without disturbing the land."

Luna considered his words before nodding. "He's the right person. We'll need his expertise if we're going to approach this without causing harm."

That evening, Ezra met James at the edge of the community garden, laying out what they needed. James's sharp gaze flicked toward the northern tree line, then back to Ezra. He crossed his arms, his mouth curling into a smirk.

"You two don't do anything normal, do you?" James said with a dry chuckle. "Last time, you ended up dragging her out like a sack of potatoes. What's next? Fighting ghosts?"

Ezra grinned despite the tension in the air.

James clapped him on the shoulder, a sly grin spreading across his face. "I caught bits and pieces, but you know me—I stay out of the drama. Tell me everything back at your cabin, and make it worth the drink you owe me. Who knows? I might even consider helping."

Ezra nodded, smirking. "As if you'd ever say no."

James snorted. "Don't ruin my image."

That night, as the forest settled into its usual hum of nocturnal life, Luna drifted into sleep, the warmth of the day fading into an otherworldly dream.

In the dream, she stood at the heart of a vast and endless plain. The ground beneath her shifted and swirled like liquid light. Four elements emerged, vivid and alive. Water flowed with silken grace to her left, its rhythm calm but unyielding. Fire crackled to her right, burning fiercely, its heat a relentless pulse of creation and destruction.

Opposite each other, Earth and Air formed another axis. The ground cracked and re-formed under her feet, rising into mighty cliffs, while the wind whipped around her, carrying whispers from unseen places. The elements crossed at perfect angles, like North meeting South, East meeting West—two sets of opposing forces locked in harmony.

At their intersection, something incredible happened. The dimensional planes folded inward, rising into the sky. The elements merged at the crossing point, and from that unity, a structure formed—a pyramid, shimmering with golden light, its peak touching the heavens. It pulsed with ancient energy, a bridge between the elements and something far greater.

Luna's heart swelled with a profound sense of knowing. This wasn't just a symbol; it was a gateway.

She reached toward the pyramid's base, but the dream dissolved around her, its glowing image seared into her mind as she awoke with a start. The memory remained vivid, accompanied by a deep sense of satisfaction and certainty—she was exactly where she was meant to be.

The morning sun barely pierced through the dense canopy as Luna, Ezra, and James set off from the clearing. The air was thick with the earthy scent of moss and damp leaves, and their footsteps crunched softly against the forest floor. James led the way, his machete slicing through the occasional vine or bramble that blocked their path. Luna walked in the center, her eyes distant yet focused, following the faint tug of her intuition. Ezra brought up the rear, ever-watchful, his hand resting on the hilt of the hunting knife strapped to his belt.

The forest hugged the steep northern hillside, the ground narrowing into a dense, uneven path. To their left, the hillside rose sharply, its surface blanketed with tangled roots and moss-covered boulders. On the right, the terrain dropped off steeply, the trees thinning just enough to reveal glimpses of the distant valley below. The air was thick with the scent of damp earth and pine, the canopy above filtering only slivers of sunlight.

They moved slowly, clearing their path as they went, each step deliberate on the narrow, flat ground. Nearly an hour passed, but they couldn't have traveled more than half a mile. James led the way, his machete slicing through stubborn vines and low-hanging branches.

"James, how often do you come out this far?" Ezra asked, breaking the silence.

James chuckled, his voice a gravelly mix of humor and nostalgia. "Not often," he admitted. "This part of the woods is thick as a thief's alibi. Even the deer tend to skirt around it. But back in my younger days, I used to scout places like this for fun. You'd be surprised what you find in the untouched corners of the world."

"Like what?" Luna asked, her voice soft but curious.

"Once, I stumbled across an old homestead," James said, pausing to cut through a stubborn vine. "Cabin was long gone, but the foundation was still there, half-buried in the earth. Found a rusted horseshoe and an old whiskey flask. It was like stepping back in time." He glanced over his shoulder, his eyes glinting with the memory. "Places like this? They hold stories. You just have to look and listen."

They pressed on, the thick foliage closing in tighter around them. The path grew more difficult, the forest seeming to resist their presence. Vines wrapped around tree trunks like forgotten sentries, while low-hanging branches clawed at their clothing. Luna's steps slowed as a growing sense of tension settled in her chest—not fear, but an intuitive nudge.

She stopped, closing her eyes and drawing in a deep breath, allowing the sound of the forest to recede. The thread she had been following felt faint but present, calling her back into alignment. Her pulse steadied, and clarity returned.

"What is it?" Ezra asked, his voice laced with concern.

"We're too far," Luna murmured. She turned back the way they'd come, retracing her steps about ten meters before stopping again. Her breathing slowed, and the familiar hum of the Akashic Records began to resonate within her mind. The fabric of reality shifted, threads of light weaving and unweaving as the dense woods before her seemed to dissolve.

In its place stood a grand arched entrance, carved into the hillside and partially shrouded in vines. At its peak, the Flower of Life glowed faintly, its interlocking circles pulsing with ancient energy. The stonework was weathered but intact, the patterns etched into its surface seemingly alive with the rhythm of the earth.

Luna gasped, her voice barely above a whisper. "Here. It's here."

Ezra and James exchanged glances, their eyes scanning the dense wall of greenery before them. "Luna, there's nothing there," Ezra said cautiously.

"I can see it," Luna insisted, her tone firm yet awestruck. "The entrance—it's hidden beneath the growth, but it's real. The Flower of Life marks the way."

With a slow, deliberate breath, Luna brushed her head to the left, her eyes fluttering closed. The vision dissolved like mist in the morning sun, the vibrant images folding back into the depths of her mind. When she opened her eyes again, the unyielding wall of forest stood silently before her, grounded and real.

She exhaled, steadying herself as the lingering hum of the vision faded from her body. Ezra noticed the shift and took a step closer, his eyes scanning her face for reassurance. "You good?" he asked, his voice low but steady.

Luna nodded, a calm certainty settling into her expression. "I'm fine. Just... following the thread."

James swung his machete with practiced precision, hacking through the dense undergrowth until the stubborn vines gave way to bare ground. He paused, wiping his brow, his eyes scanning the exposed earth. Something caught his attention—a shape that didn't belong in the wild chaos of roots and soil.

Frowning, he crouched down, using the machete to scrape away layers of dirt and moss. Bit by bit, the object revealed itself—a stone edge, rough and weathered, jutting slightly from the earth. At first, it could have been mistaken for an ordinary rock, but its shape was too deliberate, too clean.

"Ezra," James called, his voice low but urgent. "Come take a look at this."

Luna stepped closer, her breath catching as she saw it—a small but unmistakable section of stonework emerging from the hillside like a long-buried secret.

"Well, I'll be," James muttered, stepping back and wiping the sweat from his brow. "She's right." Brushing the dirt from the exposed stone protruding from the earth. "Nature doesn't make 90 degree angles. There's something here."

Ezra crouched beside him, running his fingers along the barely visible outline of stone. "How are we going to uncover this? It's completely buried."

Luna knelt beside them, her hand resting lightly on the exposed stone. "Carefully," she said. "We won't rush this. We'll work with the land, not against it."

James nodded, his respect for Luna's vision evident. "I'll mark the spot and clear a path back to the main trail. We'll need more hands to do this right."

As they worked their way back through the forest, cutting a clearer path for the others, Luna felt a deep sense of resolve. The entrance was real, and the way forward had been revealed. Together, they would uncover the secrets buried beneath Pyramid Hill—one careful step at a time.

By the time they reached the clearing, the weight of their discovery hung heavy in the air, but so too did a renewed sense of purpose. The community would need to rally once more, but Luna knew they were ready. The entrance was only the beginning.

TWENTY-SEVEN

PREPARING THE WAY

T he sun hung high, casting warm light over the clearing as the community began to gather, their conversations a low hum of curiosity and apprehension. The events of the past days—the discovery of the hidden structure and the presence of Westfield Industries—had left them on edge. Yet, there was a quiet hopefulness in the air, a recognition of something greater taking shape.

Luna stepped into the center of the group, her calm yet resolute presence commanding attention. She waited for the murmurs to fade, then began, her voice steady.

"Thank you for coming," she said, meeting the eyes of those before her. "We've confirmed that Pyramid Hill is not just a hill. Beneath the earth lies a structure—a legacy of the past—and we've found its entrance."

James stepped forward, his weathered hands resting on his hips. "I've seen it myself," he said, his voice carrying the weight of experience. "Stonework buried deep under the soil, thick with roots and time. It's not natural—no way. But uncovering it won't be easy." He glanced around the group, his gaze steady. "Nature's had centuries to claim this place. We'll need careful hands to bring it back into the light."

A ripple of murmurs passed through the crowd, a mixture of awe and trepidation.

A young woman with braided hair raised her hand. "If it's that old, shouldn't we call in experts? Archaeologists or preservationists who know how to handle something like this?"

Luna nodded, her expression thoughtful. "It's a fair question," she acknowledged. "But bringing in outside experts would mean turning this place into a dig site. It would draw attention—not just from academics, but from corporations like Westfield Industries. Please know that this—this is not a relic. It is not a thing of the past to uncover and admire. This is a tool, used thousands of years ago to help the people of this very land. A tool that I am being called back to, so it can be used once again. If Westfield finds out what's here, they'll stop at nothing to take it and abuse its power. What's buried isn't just an artifact. It's wisdom, energy, and purpose—something that must be revealed with care, not greed."

The murmurs grew louder, unease creeping through the group. Miriam stepped forward, her voice tinged with concern. "And you're sure we can do this ourselves? Without damaging it?"

Luna nodded firmly. "We won't dig up the entire hill. Our goal is to uncover the entrance—a small, precise path to reach it. Once I'm inside, the work becomes mine to carry. What lies beyond isn't something we need shovels for—it's something I've been called to connect with."

James chimed in, his tone practical yet reassuring. "It's not impossible. We'll clear the immediate area around the entrance. No bulldozers, no heavy machinery—just careful hands and patience. I'll lead the effort, but it's going to take time. We'll need volunteers who understand this isn't about speed or brute force."

A moment of silence passed before a middle-aged man stepped forward, his weathered face resolute. "Count me in," he said.

"Me too," added a younger woman, nodding with quiet resolve as she stepped forward.

"I'll help," Miriam said, her voice carrying quiet determination.

One by one, hands rose, voices joining in agreement.

Eleanor, who had been standing silently at the edge of the group, finally spoke. "And what happens if the entrance isn't stable? If it collapses while you're inside?" Her voice was steady, but her concern was clear.

Luna met her gaze with quiet strength. "Thank you for your concern, Eleanor. I won't ignore the risks, and we'll take every precaution. But I trust that the path ahead is meant to be walked. I'll move carefully and remain aware of every step. Sometimes, the only way forward is to meet the unknown head-on."

The crowd was silent for a moment, the weight of her words settling over them.

Althea stepped forward, her presence soothing as she placed a hand on Eleanor's arm. "Luna has shown courage and wisdom at every turn," she said. "Let's support her in this. Trust the journey she's leading us on."

The murmurs shifted, growing into quiet affirmations.

"We're with you," said an elder, his voice firm.

"Let's get to work," another chimed in, the resolve spreading like a ripple through the group.

Luna offered a small, grateful smile. "Thank you," she said. "We'll start tomorrow. James will organize the effort, and I'll work closely with him to ensure we move with care and intention. This isn't just a restoration—it's a step toward rediscovering the balance and connection we've been seeking."

The group began to disperse, their energy focused on preparing for the task ahead.

As the clearing emptied, Ezra approached Luna, his expression calm but his eyes betraying a flicker of worry.

"You're really planning on going inside alone?" he asked with quiet concern.

Luna turned to him, her gaze steady. "I am," she said. "This is where the path is leading me. I can feel it."

Ezra hesitated, his hand brushing against hers. "It's not the work I'm worried about. It's you. Going in there alone... we don't know what's waiting for you."

Luna placed her hand on his arm, her touch grounding. "I know you are worried. I can feel it a mile away." Luna said, rising on her toes to embrace his lips with hers. "Trust the path with me. I have guides showing me the way." Luna could feel his internal struggle to believe over his growing fear of potential loss.

She placed her hand firmly on his chest, just over his heart. "Let me try and show you what I see," she whispered. Closing her eyes, Luna focused her energy, drawing from the deep well of calm and clarity within her.

A warm current surged through her arm, flowing like an electric tide to her fingertips. The sensation built slowly, a subtle hum growing into a powerful pulse. She felt the energy transfer from her hand to Ezra's chest, a steady stream of light and warmth, like the sun breaking through storm clouds.

But even as the warmth settled, Ezra's lungs froze mid-breath, his heart still resonating with the lingering echo of the love Luna had shared. It pulsed gently, comforting yet unfamiliar—like sunlight through a mist. His brow furrowed, his mind struggling to grasp something just beyond his understanding.

Luna withdrew her hand, her eyes meeting his with calm assurance. "You felt the love," she said softly. "But the message... it hasn't reached you yet. It will, in time—when you're ready. Not with words, but with knowing."

Ezra blinked, his lips parting as if to respond, but no words came. The meaning slipped away, elusive and incomplete, leaving him grounded in feeling yet untethered by certainty.

Ezra's jaw tightened. "I want to believe, Luna," he admitted, his voice low. "But this... this is bigger than us. I can't shake the fear of what might happen."

Luna nodded, her expression serene yet knowing. She placed her hand on his cheek, a voice, a silent whisper in a cloud of thought. **"The words of wisdom are spoken to ears ready to understand them,"** Luna smiled with empathy. "Your heart is still learning to listen. That's okay. You're here with me, and that's...perfect."

Ezra closed his eyes, leaning into her touch. "I just don't want to lose you," he said quietly.

"You won't," Luna assured him. "This journey isn't meant to separate us. It's meant to strengthen us. One day you will recognize how impossible it is for us to lose each other. I promise"

She took his hand in hers, their fingers intertwining. "Walk with me, Ezra. Even if you can't see what I see yet, trust that I'll guide us where we need to be."

Ezra exhaled deeply, nodding. "Always," he said, his voice steady now. "I'll walk with you, no matter what... I'd just maybe like to know where we're walking to."

Luna chuckled, and bounced her hip into his. "I need to see Althea. You've shown me something, and I need to do something about it." Luna said with a mysterious undertone.

Luna and Ezra walked side by side through the quiet forest path, the late afternoon sun casting soft rays through the canopy above. The sound of their footsteps mingled with the rustle of leaves and the distant song of a bird. Despite the comforting serenity, Luna's thoughts churned. She carried the weight of the community's trust, their expectations pressing against her resolve.

As they neared Althea's cabin, Luna could feel the quiet power of the elder woman's presence even before stepping inside. Althea greeted them at the threshold, her serene expression lighting with curiosity.

"You've come with purpose," Althea said, motioning them inside.

Luna nodded, her gaze steady. "The community has placed their trust in me, but the path ahead isn't just mine to walk. I need your help. While the excavation continues, I want to prepare them—to teach them how to connect with the wisdom that awaits. Morning and evening meditations, and I want to be there to answer any questions they have, provide the guidance that will prepare them to accept what is to come."

Althea folded her hands, her lips curving into a soft smile. "Guiding them to readiness," she said thoughtfully. "It's a wise step."

"They'll begin to understand when they're ready," Luna replied, her voice calm but introspective. "This wisdom isn't something I can force on them, but every effect has its cause. Perhaps I can guide them to find the wisdom within themselves."

Althea nodded in approval. "The sessions will give them time to reflect, to develop and ask their questions and explore these ideas for themselves. We'll guide them gently."

That evening, they spread the word of a morning gathering to begin at 8 am, before any work to begin excavating is started.

TWENTY-EIGHT

HANDS IN THE EARTH, EYES ON THE STARS

T he soft glow of dawn broke through the forest canopy, casting a golden hue over the clearing where the community had gathered. Voices murmured in quiet excitement, a hum of anticipation filling the cool morning air. The scent of dew and earth mingled with the cleansing smoke of sage as Althea moved gracefully around the space, her bundle crackling softly as wisps of smoke spiraled upward.

The group stood close, eyes bright with curiosity and purpose, drawn together by the promise of discovery. The air seemed to vibrate gently, charged with the energy of what lay ahead—the uncovering of the hidden entrance.

Luna stood before them, calm and centered, her presence a steady anchor in the growing buzz. She waited a moment for the crowd to settle, her voice steady and soothing when she spoke. "These sessions are our chance to draw strength from one another, to ground ourselves for the work ahead. In the evenings, I will be here again—to recover, to release the strain of the day, and to listen to what the silence may reveal. I hope you'll continue to join me—not just to seek answers, but to feel the purpose within yourselves and the connection we share on this journey."

Luna watched as more members came into the shared space. Smiles grew across faces as they gave morning greetings to their friends and families.

Some sat cross-legged on the ground, mimicking the appearance of Luna and Althea, Others found themselves more comfortable in chairs.

Althea led the group through a series of deep, steady breaths, her melodic voice guiding them inward. "Feel the earth beneath you, the sky above you, the breath that connects them both. Let each exhale carry away tension, and each inhale bring you closer to stillness."

As Althea's voice flowed like a gentle river, guiding the group into the stillness of the present moment, Luna closed her eyes and turned inward. She focused on the steady rhythm of her heart, letting it become a conduit for her intentions. With each exhale, she sent waves of warmth and light outward, invisible ripples that spread through the shared energy of the group. The faint hum of the earth beneath them seemed to respond, amplifying her resolve. She envisioned golden threads weaving between their hearts, connecting them as one, their collective strength growing with every breath. The air grew charged, subtle but electric, as Luna channeled her intentions—strength to face the unknown, energy to sustain them, and resolve to hold their purpose steady. Each ripple she sent forth felt like a soft vibration through the space, touching each soul with a gentle yet unwavering embrace of love and support.

Luna witnessed peace and calmness settle over their faces as one by one, the group opened their eyes. The faint morning light filtering through the canopy above seemed to shimmer softly, as though the forest itself had absorbed their shared energy. Some members stretched slowly, their movements languid and unhurried, while others simply sat, basking in the lingering warmth of the meditation.

Althea's voice broke the gentle silence, soothing and steady. "Carry this stillness with you today. Let it anchor you, even when the winds of uncertainty blow."

Luna's gaze swept across the group, and she felt a swell of gratitude rise within her. Miriam, seated closest to her, exhaled deeply, her hands resting on her knees as she met Luna's eyes with a small, appreciative nod. Others exchanged quiet murmurs or soft smiles, their spirits visibly lighter, as though a weight had been lifted from the collective.

She couldn't help but feel the subtle pulse of their interconnected energy, like embers glowing brighter after being fanned. This moment, she realized, wasn't just about preparation—it was about unity, a shared strength that could hold them together through whatever trials lay ahead.

Before the group began to disperse, Luna stood, her voice warm but resolute. "What we're building here is more than a practice. It's a bond, a foundation for everything we hope to achieve. Trust in each other, and trust in what you felt today." Her words hung in the stillness, carrying a quiet power that seemed to deepen the peace in their faces.

James approached Luna as the crowd began to rise from their seats, mingling and enjoying the snacks and coffee Miriam had graciously prepared. He gave her a nod of appreciation, his voice low but earnest. "Thanks, Luna. I didn't need much motivation to start the day—I'm too excited about what we might find—but during the meditation, I felt something. Something different. Hard to put into words."

Luna smiled, her gaze warm with understanding. "You don't have to put it into words. Some things aren't meant to be explained—just felt. Trust it, James. Follow it."

James hesitated briefly, then returned her smile, his usual stoicism softening. Luna opened her arms, pulling him into an expansive hug, their shared energy grounding them both for what lay ahead.

The first morning of excavation dawned with a quiet but palpable sense of purpose. The hillside stretched steeply before them, shrouded in thick vegetation that had grown unchecked for millennia. Massive trees stood sentinel at the base, their roots snaking up the incline like ancient tendrils clutching the earth. Moss-draped branches hung low, casting dappled shadows over the dense underbrush, which rose waist-high in places, tangled with thorny vines and stubborn brambles.

James stood at the edge of the site, surveying the daunting task before them. His machete glinted in the morning light as he gave a low whistle, shaking his head. "This isn't just a bit of clearing. We're carving through centuries," he muttered, driving the tip of his spade into the soil with a deliberate thrust. The sound of metal scraping against the compact earth echoed, breaking the morning stillness and signaling the start of their effort.

The group began their work, attacking the layers of growth that blanketed the hillside. Axes and machetes swung methodically, felling smaller trees and cutting away dense tangles of vines that refused to yield without a fight. The rich, dark soil beneath the vegetation was thick with roots, some as thick as a man's arm, twisting and burrowing deep into the ground. Volunteers used saws and pruners to sever them, their hands aching with the effort.

Near the lower end of the hill, where the vegetation was most overgrown, Ezra wiped sweat from his brow as he worked alongside two others to uproot a massive stump, its gnarled base clinging stubbornly to the earth. "This thing's older than any of us," he said, grunting with exertion. "Feels like it doesn't want to give up its place."

Meanwhile, further up the incline, where the hill grew steeper, the vegetation thinned. Luna had described the archway in her vision as being at the upper end, where trees hadn't had the chance to grow tall. With fewer obstacles above, James and a few others cleared smaller brush and loose dirt, their movements quicker but no less careful.

It was there, midmorning, that James called out, his voice cutting through the rustle of work. "Hey! Everyone—get up here!"

The team gathered, their tools in hand, sweat streaking their faces and dirt caking their gloves. James knelt by an exposed section of stone at the upper hillside, its surface slick with moss and lichen. With careful strokes of a brush, he cleared away the organic layer, revealing intricate carvings beneath. The Flower of Life symbol began to emerge, its geometric patterns seemingly burned into the structure of the stone, faint but distinctive.

The group froze in collective awe, the weight of history pressing down on them like a tangible force. Luna stepped forward, her breath catching as her fingers grazed the stone. The energy was unmistakable—a pulse, subtle but alive, radiating through her hand and into her chest. She closed her eyes briefly, grounding herself in the connection.

"It's here," James said, his voice hushed, almost reverent. "Exactly like you said, Luna."

Luna opened her eyes, her gaze steady and filled with conviction. "This place has been waiting for us," she said softly. "The entrance is ready to reveal itself—but it needs us to uncover it fully."

The group exchanged glances, their fatigue momentarily forgotten as determination surged through them. With renewed focus, they returned to their work, clearing the area around the exposed stone. Every strike of their tools, every shove of a spade felt purposeful now, as if they were not merely unearthing rock and soil but uncovering a truth buried beneath the weight of time.

By late afternoon, they had exposed more of the arched structure. What had first seemed like a simple stone threshold now hinted at something more—its form too precise, too deliberate to be natural. The surface was impossibly smooth, unmarked except for a single, delicate carving at the top center—the Flower of Life. No tool marks, no seams, no indication of how it had been shaped. Just a perfect, rounded formation emerging from the hillside. As the golden light filtered through the canopy above, dust motes swirled in the air, the team exchanging quiet glances as a hushed sense of realization settled over them.

"We're not just uncovering history," Ezra said quietly, his gaze fixed on the exposed carvings. His voice held a reverence that resonated through the group. "We're laying the foundation for what comes next—for the future. This isn't just about what's buried here. It's about what we do with it."

The clearing hummed with the sounds of rustling leaves and distant bird calls, the natural symphony blending with the steady rhythm of their labor. As they worked, Luna kept her focus on the entrance, her heart aligned with its energy, drawing strength from the land and radiating it to the people around her. She knew they were on the cusp of something extraordinary.

As the sun dipped below the horizon, painting the sky in hues of amber and violet, the team trudged back to the central clearing outside the gathering hall. Their movements were slow, muscles aching from the day's relentless work. The air carried the rich scent of freshly turned earth, crushed vegetation, and the lingering tang of sweat, mingling with the faint sweetness of wildflowers on the evening breeze.

Luna sat cross-legged near the center of the clearing, the soft glow of lanterns flickering around her, casting a warm halo as dusk settled in. Quiet murmurs passed between the group as they gathered, settling into a loose circle beneath the starlit sky. Their faces reflected a blend of exhaustion and quiet triumph—worn but resolute, driven by the promise of what lay just beyond the hidden entrance.

Luna closed her eyes, letting the stillness of the evening seep into her. She could feel the land beneath her, steady and alive, its energy humming softly like a heartbeat in the earth. She placed her hands palms-up on her knees and began to speak, her voice low and serene.

"Today was extraordinary," she said, her tone carrying both gratitude and reverence. "We didn't just clear the soil; we uncovered the beginning of something powerful—something that has been waiting for this moment. None of this would be possible without all of you. I feel the strength of your hands, your hearts, your dedication, and I am deeply, endlessly grateful."

She paused, letting her words settle into the quiet. The crackle of a distant fire punctuated the stillness, grounding the group further.

"Tonight, let's focus on healing," Luna continued, her voice a soothing thread that wove through the clearing. "Let's release the strain of the day and invite restoration into every part of us. Close your eyes. Breathe in the energy of this place—the earth, the sky, the stars above. Feel its rhythm, its balance. As you exhale, release your weariness, your tension. Trust that this land will hold it, transform it, and give it back as strength."

She extended her heart outward, her intentions radiating through the circle like a gentle wave. Gratitude flowed from her like a warm current, wrapping around each person, softening their muscles and quieting their minds. Luna's words dissolved into silence, leaving only the steady cadence of their collective breaths and the whispers of the night.

In that shared stillness, Luna felt the day's energy settle. The bonds between them, between the land and the sky, felt unbreakable. When she opened her eyes, she saw the same peace reflected in the faces of those around her. She knew they would rise with renewed strength, ready to face whatever came next.

As the group dispersed, some whispering quiet words of thanks, Luna lingered, her heart full. Beneath the stars, with the pulse of the land beneath her, she whispered a silent promise to the pyramid: *We're ready for you.*

TWENTY-NINE

THE THRESHOLD OF KNOWING

The days passed in a rhythmic cycle of meditation, excavation, and quiet revelations. As the community worked together, their efforts transcended mere labor; it became a shared awakening. The morning meditations set the tone for the day, each breath a tether connecting them to something unseen yet deeply familiar. The evening gatherings, filled with soft conversations and the murmurs of realization, became spaces of reflection—places where walls within them crumbled, making room for something new.

For many, the changes were subtle—a heightened awareness, a sense of connection that hadn't been there before. But for some, the shifts were profound.

Matthias, barely nineteen and still wide-eyed with curiosity, had begun to speak of sensations he couldn't quite explain. "I don't think I was here during meditation," he admitted one evening, his voice tinged with wonder. "I felt like I was part of something else. Like I was there, but... not."

Luna studied him carefully, recognizing the pattern. "Did it feel like a loss of self? Or was it more like an expansion of yourself?"

Matthias hesitated, then nodded. "An expansion. Like,... like I could see more, feel more. It wasn't scary, though. It felt—" he struggled for the words, his brows knitting together. "It felt true."

Luna smiled, resting a hand lightly on his shoulder. "That's great, Matthias. You're beginning to understand one of the oldest truths—that consciousness is not confined to the body. It stretches beyond, reaching into the greater whole. Some call it divine presence, others universal energy. It's the same force that sparks intuition, that stirs the air before a storm, that hums beneath the surface of the earth itself."

Matthias tilted his head, clearly still grappling with the concept. "Like when Paul said, 'To be absent from the body is to be present with the Lord'?"

A flicker of recognition crossed Luna's face. "Yes," she said, intrigued by his connection. "He spoke of it through his lens, through the language of his faith. Many spiritual traditions describe the same experience in different ways. The words change, but the truth remains the same."

Matthias absorbed this, a quiet awe settling over him. "So, that presence I felt—that was real?"

"As real as the ground beneath your feet," Luna affirmed. "And this is just the beginning."

Across the community, these small shifts wove themselves into the fabric of their days. Some, like Matthias, found language for their experiences in scripture. Others, like Stephen, an observant boy with a quiet intensity, simply listened, sensing more than he spoke. He had grown especially close to Luna, his small presence often shadowing hers as if drawn to the currents she carried.

One afternoon, as they sat beneath the great oak near the excavation site, Stephen fidgeted with a small twig, his expression unusually serious. He glanced up at Luna, his wide eyes filled with a mix of curiosity and something else—excitement, anticipation.

"I don't know why, but..." He hesitated, searching for the right words. "It feels like... like something really, really cool is about to happen."

Luna smiled knowingly. "You can feel it, can't you?"

Stephen nodded quickly, shifting his gaze toward Pyramid Hill. His voice dropped to a hushed whisper, as if sharing a secret too big to keep inside.

"It's like..." He scrunched his nose in thought, then his face lit up with understanding. "Like the night before Christmas, and I can't wait for Santa anymore."

Luna's smile widened. She reached over and ruffled his hair, her touch light and affectionate. "I know the feeling," she said. "I feel it too."

Stephen grinned, leaning into the warmth of her reassurance.

"But," Luna added, her voice playful but patient, "Christmas morning always comes at just the right time, doesn't it?"

Stephen sighed dramatically, kicking at the dirt with the toe of his boot. "Yeah... but waiting is so hard."

Luna laughed softly. "I know. But some things are worth the wait."

Stephen huffed but nodded, hugging his knees to his chest as he looked back toward Pyramid Hill. He didn't know how, but he knew—something big was coming.

Two weeks into the excavation, the earth had finally given way to what lay beneath.

The team had worked tirelessly, moving with an intuitive reverence for the land they had dedicated themselves to uncovering. They were not archaeologists—not in the way scholars might define it—but they were something else entirely. Craftsmen, builders, woodsmen, and foragers, all of them having great respect for the earth. They moved with care, knowing that what they unearthed was not just history, but something alive, something waiting.

And now, as the last layers of soil and debris were pulled away, the tunnel's entrance was revealed through a narrow passage, into a vast opening.

It wasn't grand. It wasn't adorned with intricate carvings or elaborate structures like the ruins of other ancient civilizations. Instead, it was... simple.

Perfect.

A tunnel, recessed ten or more meters into the hillside, round and smooth as if shaped by an impossible hand. No seams, no tool marks could be seen as they shined their lights on it—just a continuous, un-interrupted curve of polished stone, appearing as though it had formed naturally this way. As if the hill itself had grown around it.

James, who had led much of the work, ran his fingers along the entrance's interior. The tunnel was unlike anything he had ever seen. It wasn't just smooth—it was impossibly smooth. Not the way modern construction might create a synthetic finish, nor the way time and erosion might wear something down. This was something else.

Something beyond his understanding.

He stepped into the tunnel, his breath shallow, his calloused fingers brushing along the walls as he walked toward the end.

And then—nothing.

A dead end.

James froze, his heartbeat thrumming in his ears. The tunnel simply... stopped. What should have been a passage into something greater was met with an unbroken wall of stone.

No doorway. No markings. No handle or mechanism.

Just a seamless barrier.

Behind him, the others followed cautiously, their murmurs rising in uncertainty.

A weight settled over them.

Weeks of work. Countless hours. The belief that they were on the edge of something monumental—only to be met with this.

A wall.

The team exchanged uneasy glances, the spark of triumph in their eyes beginning to dim. Had Luna been wrong? Had the entrance been nothing more than an illusion?

A young woman named Laurel broke the silence. "James... what do we do now?"

James clenched his jaw, swallowing down the frustration creeping up his spine. He didn't have an answer. And that—more than anything—unnerved him.

He turned, nodding toward Gregory. "Go get Luna. Tell her we have a problem."

Gregory hesitated for only a second before he took off running, his footsteps fading as he rounded the corner of the narrow passage.

The rest of the team stood in silence, their hands still dirty and calloused from hard labor, the weight of disappointment settling over them like a heavy fog.

James' flashlight guided his gaze, staring at the smooth stone ahead, unwilling to give up so easily. With a quiet breath, he pulled the canteen from his belt and poured a slow trickle of water over the surface, hoping—praying—that something would reveal itself.

The water ran down the face of the stone in slow, shimmering streaks.

James exhaled slowly, pressing a hand against the stone. It was cold. Solid. Unyielding.

He turned back toward the others, frustration pressing against his ribs. Had they uncovered nothing but a tomb with no key?

Then, the trickle of water glistened in the glare of his flashlight.

At first, it was nothing. Just a sheen over the surface. But as James shifted his hand, the angle of the light changed.

A line.

So fine it was almost invisible. But it was there.

A perfect circle, as he followed it with the tip of the light.

Not carved. Not cracked. But perfectly sealed.

It wasn't long before an out of breath Luna arrived at the tunnel, in her shadow was young Stephen rushing to keep up.

Luna caught her breath, then lost it again somewhere between awe and disbelief. She had seen the entrance take shape over the last two weeks, had felt its presence growing stronger with every layer of earth removed. But standing before it now—fully revealed, impossibly smooth, and undeniably whole—was something else entirely.

She made her way through the cleared passage, the tunnel stretched before her, perfectly round, its walls a seamless continuation of the same single stone. Unnatural in its perfection.

Her jaw slackened, her mind racing to comprehend what her eyes beheld.

Then, her heart sank.

James stood at the tunnel's end, his hands resting against the wall of smooth, unbroken stone. "This is it," he said. "This is as far as it goes."

Luna felt the air shift. The weight of so many expectant gazes pressed against her back.

This wasn't right.

She had seen this entrance open. She had felt the way forward. But now, with her own eyes, all she saw was a dead end. For the first time, doubt took hold.

Was I wrong? Had we uncovered a false path? A decoy meant to deceive?

Her stomach twisted at the thought. The possibility hit her like a wave of cold water, numbing her limbs. The community had trusted her. James, who had helped lead the excavation. Ezra, who had never once questioned her intuition.

Had she led them to nothing?

James let out a slow breath and pressed a hand flat against the stone, his gaze shifting. A crease formed between his brows as he stepped back, running a palm over the surface. "There is some hope. Look,... a hairline seam. If you follow it, it is a circle. Could be a door." He traced it with his fingers. Then, hesitantly, "We could start breaking through. Chisels, sledgehammers—whatever it takes. If we can't find another way, we make one."

Luna shook her head slightly, still staring at the stone wall, something deep inside her resisting the idea. But her mind was in turmoil, tangled between logic and something far less tangible. "No... We can't do that, there must be another way," she paused. "I need a moment."

She turned away from the others, lowering herself onto her knees. Her hands rested on her thighs, fingers curling slightly as she closed her eyes. The others took a few respectful steps back.

Breathe.

She felt the cool, solid stone beneath her. The wind whistled past the entrance. The quiet rise and fall of breaths behind her. She reached for her heart center, grounding herself in the moment.

She let go of the fear of failure.

Let go of the idea that she had to force her way forward. She found the *Now*.

And then—the knowing followed.

Like a gift, a memory that had never been hers before but now arrived fully formed, settling into her mind with perfect clarity.

The entrance was sealed purposefully, not as a barrier, not as an obstacle, but as an act of protection.

The ones who had come before understood what was to come. They knew that humanity would stray, would lose its connection to the wisdom they once held so naturally. They had not hidden this place in greed or fear—but in reverence.

Until the right time.

Until those who were ready to understand returned.

Luna's breath quivered between the moment and the memory, her body thrumming with the realization.

Until now.

Luna rose slowly to her feet, turning back to the group. Their eyes followed her, waiting for an answer, waiting for her to lead them forward.

She stepped into acceptance of the moment, her destiny to become the path for many to follow.

The tunnel was still and silent, its depths cool and waiting. Luna placed her fingertips against the smooth surface where James had noticed the faint circular seam. The coldness of the stone met her skin, but beneath it—something more.

A hum.

Not audible at first, but felt. A resonance, like the soft strum of a distant chord.

Her breath slowed.

She traced the seam with her fingertips, following its impossible precision. As she moved, the energy beneath her touch shifted. It pulled her, guiding her hand—not with force, but with a current that felt as though it had been waiting for her touch, waiting for her to remember the way.

The pull deepened, her palm pressing fully against the stone.

And then, it began.

The hum that had been a whisper grew. Soft at first, but rising, like a tuning fork finding its perfect resonance.

A glow bloomed beneath her hand.

A deep orange light, like fire within crystal, seeping out from the stone itself.

The glow spread outward in delicate lines, forming a pattern within the circle. It was not random—it was the Flower of Life.

Luna inhaled sharply, her heart pounding as the pattern pulsed with energy.

Her fingers continued their path, not of her own will, but as if they had done this before, as if something ancient guided her movements.

At first, she did not understand what she was drawing.

Then, she saw it.

She was tracing the Tree of Life— aligning perfectly within the sacred geometry of the Flower.

The moment she completed the final connection, the hum became a tone—beautiful, unearthly, like the sound of heaven itself.

The group behind her felt it—not just heard it. It resonated in their bones, in their hearts, in their very breath.

The tunnel vibrated, the deep resonance shifting the air around them.

Luna stepped back, her pulse roaring in her ears.

The deep, celestial hum filled the tunnel, resonating through the stone and into the marrow of their being. The vibration pulsed outward, rippling through the air, carrying the weight of something ancient waking from its long slumber.

Then—movement.

The stone shuddered.

A whisper of shifting air.

It began to retract, sinking inward with slow, deliberate precision.

Not the grinding, grating sound of stone scraping against stone. No dust, no rough friction. It was smooth. Perfect. Effortless.

The sound was almost melodic—a deep, resonant glide, like the turning of a celestial gear, like the hush of silk drawn over polished metal.

The circle of stone, impossibly heavy yet moving as if weightless, retreated into the tunnel's thick wall. A flawless mechanism, operating with the grace of something made to move, despite the centuries—perhaps millennia—that had passed.

The soft hum deepened, the air shifting as the door began to roll.

A precise, measured rotation—no hesitation, no jarring movement—just a perfectly engineered motion, as if it had only been waiting for the right moment, the right touch.

A final hushed click echoed, subtle yet profound, as the door disappeared seamlessly into the hillside.

Then—silence.

A deep, still quiet.

And then—a breath.

A rush of cool, untouched air spilled from the darkness beyond, rolling over their skin like an exhale from another time. It carried a scent that did not belong to the world above—ancient cedar, rich and grounding, and something floral, something delicate yet powerful. A scent that whispered of sacred spaces and forgotten knowledge.

A gasp rippled through the group.

Mouths fell open.

Eyes widened in disbelief.

The entrance was open. It had been waiting for this moment.

And now—it was ready to answer.

The deep, celestial hum faded into stillness, and in its wake, silence.

A charged moment of awe held them all captive. The impossible door had moved as if it had only been waiting—for them, for this moment.

Then, footsteps. Rushing. Urgent.

Ezra.

His voice carried through the clearing before his form fully emerged. "Is it true? Are we in?"

His question was unnecessary. The answer was written on every face.

He slowed as he reached them, his breath labored from the run, a small backpack slung over his shoulder—the one Luna had prepared for this moment. He caught her eyes beneath the archway, his gaze flicking between her and the now-open entrance.

Luna stepped toward him without hesitation, wrapping her arms around him. Warm. Familiar. Safe.

"Yes, love," she whispered against his ear. "It's true. Today is the day."

Excitement rippled through the gathered community. This was their victory.

But James, ever the grounded voice of reason, was the first to break the celebration. His voice carried steady over the murmurs, bringing them back to the reality of what lay before them.

James' voice was steady. "So, are we going in?"

Luna did not hesitate. She turned toward the entrance, the cool air curling around her like an exhale from something ancient. The shadows inside stretched endlessly, waiting.

She knew.

She had always known.

"I am," she said, her voice carrying the weight of something final. "This path was sealed until the right one came to walk it. I go first—alone. I will return with what is meant to be known, so that others may follow."

Silence stretched across the gathering. No one spoke. No one argued.

Because the truth in her words was undeniable.

Ezra handed her the backpack, watching as she knelt and methodically checked its contents.

She moved with precision.

A small lantern. Extra flashlights. Rope. Her well-worn journal. The amethyst Althea had gifted her. A first-aid kit. A folded notebook and pencils for sketching. Her fingers brushed a talisman, its smooth edges cool beneath her touch—Miriam's quiet gift of protection.

The weight of each item grounded her.

The amethyst, steady and solid in her palm, sent a pulse of warmth through her fingertips—a quiet affirmation.

Closing her eyes, she inhaled deeply.

Letting the moment settle over her.

Letting herself listen.

The path was open.

The pyramid was calling.

She lifted her head and nodded, voice sure. "I can feel her... the path is clear."

Ezra knelt beside her, hesitation shadowing his face. "Are you sure I can't come with you?"

Luna met his eyes, feeling the weight of his concern, the quiet battle between his trust in her and his fear of what lay ahead.

She reached for his hand, her grip steady, reassuring. "You've always looked out for me," she said softly. "And I love you for it. But this—" she glanced toward the darkened passage, "—this is the surest thing I have ever known."

Ezra's lips pressed into a thin line, his fingers lingering in hers. "I'll be waiting," he said quietly. "Just... come back to me."

"I will," she said with confidence, knowing it was the truth—but also knowing she wouldn't return the same.

A rustle of movement stirred behind them.

Several members of the community stepped cautiously into the entrance tunnel, their lanterns casting flickering light along the smooth stone walls. Shadows danced across their faces—some filled with wonder, others with quiet apprehension. They gathered in a loose semi-circle, their unspoken question hanging in the air, a shared breath of anticipation, concern, and hope.

Little Stephen, eyes wide, standing beside his father Joseph.

James, his arms crossed, expression unreadable.

Miriam and Althea, their presence a steady, quiet force.

Even Eleanor, once skeptical, silent now—her gaze thoughtful, unreadable.

James, ever the pragmatist, was the first to speak. "You've got this, Luna." His tone was gruff but certain. "We'll hold things steady out here."

Luna gave a small nod of gratitude before turning to the others.

"This isn't just my journey," she said, her voice carrying clarity, strength. "The wisdom within this pyramid belongs to all of us. I go first because I've been called to do so, but everything I learn will guide us forward—together."

A ripple of understanding passed through the group.

They knew.

They had all felt the pull of this place now.

Luna turned back to the entrance. The cool air curled around her, brushing against her skin like an invitation.

She moved forward, pausing as she stepped through the circled entrance.

The stone frame hummed beneath her fingertips, thrumming with the quiet energy of something ancient, something aware.

She closed her eyes.

A silent prayer.

Guide me. Protect me. Reveal what I must remember.

A breath.

And then—she continued inside.

The light of her lantern cut through the darkness, her shadow stretching ahead of her as the murmurs of the community faded behind her.

The stillness inside was not empty.

It waited.

The pyramid's forgotten song had only just begun.

THIRTY

THROUGH THE EYE OF ETERNITY

L una's lantern cast flickering shadows on the smooth stone walls as she navigated the narrow, enclosed tunnel leading into the pyramid's depths. The air was cool and carried a faint mineral scent, a stark contrast to the warm, sunlit clearing she had just left. The passage was tight, her shoulders occasionally brushing against the cold stone, and the faint sound of her footsteps echoed in the stillness.

The walls bore little decoration, only the occasional set of faint carvings—symbols woven into simple but deliberate patterns, their meanings just out of reach. As Luna's light illuminated one such panel, she paused, running her fingers over the etched lines. It depicted a simple story of unity: a spiral flowing into a circle, then splitting into two paths that rejoined further along. The simplicity of the design carried a profound weight, it reminded her of the balance of masculine and feminine energies working together in creation.

The silence was broken by the faintest rustling sound—a soft, almost imperceptible shift in the air. Luna's heart quickened, but she pressed on, the tunnel gradually widening and branching off into a series of intersecting passages.

Luna stopped at the first fork, her breath catching as she surveyed the diverging tunnels. Each was identical in size and appearance, their darkened lengths vanishing into shadow. Her fingers tightened around the lantern as she closed her eyes and centered herself. The right path will not be chosen by sight, but by feeling, she reminded herself, Althea's teachings echoing in her mind.

A faint warmth spread through her chest, a pull that guided her to the tunnel on the left. She stepped forward, her trust in the unseen force steadying her.

The next fork came quicker than the first, and then another. At each, Luna paused, her breaths deep and measured, waiting for the subtle signals from within: a tingling sensation in her palms, a soft pressure behind her eyes, or the faintest whisper of an inner voice urging her onward. The labyrinth seemed alive, testing her intuition, drawing her deeper into its mysteries.

At one point, the path seemed to close in, the air growing heavier as the tunnel sloped downward. The flickering lantern light revealed nothing unusual, but Luna could feel a quiet resistance, as though the pyramid itself was testing her will. Luna questioned herself for a moment, running through the path she had taken, but it was only a momentary lapse in trust.

"Keep going," she whispered to herself, her voice steady but soft. "You were chosen for this." Luna steadied herself as she moved down the sloping stone floor.

The air grew colder, and the faint hum of distant vibrations began to echo through the stone. The sound was neither threatening nor welcoming; it simply was. Luna followed the faint vibration calling her forward, her steps careful but sure, her focus unwavering despite the slight tremor in her hands.

After what felt like a half hour of winding corridors and silent decisions, the tunnel began to widen. The vibrations grew stronger, their resonance vibrating in her chest like the strings of a finely tuned instrument. The flicker of her lantern caught on a broader expanse of stone, and she knew she was nearing something significant.

As she stepped forward, the narrow passage gave way to an immense chamber, its vastness swallowing her whole. The ceiling soared into a shadowed abyss, its height unknowable, while the walls curved outward in a perfect, endless expanse, cradling the room in a cosmic embrace. At the heart of the chamber stood a grand stone platform, its surface etched with spiraling symbols that shimmered faintly, their glow rising and falling in rhythm with the vibrations thrumming through the air.

Luna drew in a sharp breath as a wave of energy swept through her, its resonance threading through her veins and harmonizing with the beat of her heart. The frequency of the chamber wasn't just external—it reached inside her, amplifying something dormant and ancient, pulling her into the rhythm of the space. For a fleeting moment, she felt untethered, as though she had become part of the pyramid itself, her essence folding into its infinite pulse.

The faint beam of her lantern cast a delicate glow across the smooth stone floor, catching intricate carvings that wove together in impossible complexity. Geometric patterns, sharp yet fluid, seemed to shift when she looked too long, their lines whispering secrets just beyond comprehension. Beneath her feet, the Flower of Life revealed itself, its interlocking circles glowing softly, weaving her path toward the central platform.

Each step carried her deeper into the hum, her breaths steady yet weighted with reverence. The chamber seemed to breathe with her, its vibrations rising and falling in an ancient symphony that echoed within her bones. The platform loomed closer, its presence commanding, not with menace, but with an undeniable gravity that drew her forward. This was no mere stone; it was alive, its purpose waiting to be uncovered.

At the base of the platform, Luna extended her hand, her palm brushing the cool, flawless surface. The moment they touched, a gentle pulse of light rippled outward, cascading like a pebble dropped into still water. It enveloped her, a warm yet electric current that grounded her and simultaneously set her adrift. The pyramid seemed to acknowledge her presence, its energy merging with hers in a silent accord.

Luna closed her eyes, surrendering to the flow, allowing the vibrations to settle deep within her core. Time dissolved into the hum, the moment stretching into eternity. The chamber spoke—not with words, but with rhythm, with energy, with truths that had always been but never seen.

"This," she whispered, her voice a soft echo swallowed by the infinite song of the chamber, "is where it begins."

Luna eased herself onto the stone platform, its cool surface alive with a subtle, rhythmic pulse that seemed to mirror the cadence of her own heartbeat. The hum of the chamber grew, swelling like an ancient tide, resonating within her chest as though the pyramid itself was breathing in harmony with her. She sat cross-legged, her hands resting lightly on her knees, her breath steady and effortless. There was no need to close her eyes—no need to summon focus. The moment she let go, it began.

A soft light bloomed beneath her, rising like a delicate mist, weaving itself into a shimmering cocoon. It wrapped her in warmth, gentle and radiant, like the first light of dawn kissing the earth. The air around her shifted, thickening with a presence both intangible and alive, enfolding her as though the pyramid itself had opened its arms.

Shapes began to emerge, their geometry unfolding with liquid precision. Two pyramids formed around her, interlocking as they spun into existence. One reached skyward, its apex stretching toward the heavens, drawing her spirit into the vast expanse above. The other descended, its tip plunging deep into unseen roots, anchoring her to the timeless wisdom of the earth. Together, they wove a star tetrahedron, a celestial harmony bridging the earthly and the divine.

Within this sacred geometry, Luna felt herself suspended—cradled in the architecture of the cosmos. The tetrahedron shimmered with an iridescent glow, its edges humming a melody older than time itself. Each line, each vertex, pulsed with the quiet song of creation, vibrating softly against her skin like a tender caress. As she inhaled, the energy swelled, cascading over her in waves—a dance of light and rhythm that resonated with the core of her being.

Time unraveled, dissolving into a boundless void where the world outside the chamber ceased to matter. At each intersection of the pyramids, gentle pulses of light flared, opening doorways to dimensions she could sense but not yet see.

Her awareness stretched outward, beyond the confines of her physical form. The boundaries of her being softened, her edges dissolving into rivers of light that flowed effortlessly between worlds. She was not lost in this dissolution—she was whole, unified with something immeasurable and eternal. The sharp lines of the star tetrahedron blurred into fluid motion, a shimmering bridge that carried her between the realms of the seen and unseen, between what she was and what she could become.

It was a paradox, a stillness humming with motion, a harmony that wove the finite into the infinite. In this sacred space, Luna felt herself dissolving into the very fabric of the universe, her essence no longer separate but a thread in the eternal tapestry of life.

The light around her brightened, folding inward with elegant precision, as though the cosmos itself were drawing her into its core. This new realm shimmered like a dream given form, its crystalline ground reflecting the constellations above—a mirror of infinity beneath her feet.

In the distance, a figure began to take shape—radiant and fluid, shifting like light on water. It was both her and not her, familiar yet transcendent—the higher self that had quietly guided her from the beginning. A surge of belonging washed over Luna, warm and encompassing, like the return to a place she'd never been but had always known.

The light condensed, growing sharper, until it took on a clear and glowing form: a reflection of herself, but imbued with timeless serenity. Made of golden light, the figure stood as both a mirror and a promise—holding within it all the wisdom she was just beginning to touch.

"Welcome, Luna," it spoke, its voice resonating not in her ears but in the depths of her being, bypassing sound to become truth. "You have come far, but your journey is only just beginning."

Luna stepped forward, her heart steady despite the vastness of the moment. Her voice carried with it a quiet eagerness. "I'm ready."

The figure's light intensified, spilling warmth through every corner of her soul. "Yes, you are," its tone a blend of joy and certainty, "just as we had hoped. Now, let us unlock the wisdom that lies within. Together, we will awaken what has long been dormant."

In a wave of brilliance, Luna was drawn deeper into the heart of the realm, where knowledge stretched out like a shimmering sea. The luminous figure extended its hand, and the crystalline ground beneath her dissolved into a boundless cosmic expanse. With a single step, she was swept into the flow of existence itself, her awareness expanding to encompass both the infinitesimal and the infinite.

Stars blazed in every direction, their light pulsing with ancient wisdom that seemed to sing through her very being. She hurtled through galaxies, their spiraling arms cradling worlds teeming with life and possibility. Each planet she passed offered glimpses of herself—different forms, different lives, all woven together by a single golden thread of consciousness. She was everything and nothing, a traveler across lifetimes, carried by the rhythm of a universe that had always known her.

Flashes of memory surged through her—brilliant as starbursts, vast as galaxies. She saw herself in countless forms: a radiant being gliding across crystalline plains, her touch dissolving fear and weaving peace into the air; a healer beneath emerald skies, her hands channeling the symphony of renewal through fields of glowing life. In another breath, she stood as a warrior cloaked in celestial shadow, her blade forged from starlight, holding the line between chaos and sanctuary. And beyond all these lives, she was a builder—shaping civilizations from the dust of stars, forging harmony with others like her, the architects of sacred order. In each life, her path never wavered—drawn always to the frequency of harmony, to the quiet power of light against the rising dark. She was not just one thing. She was all of them, woven together by the golden thread of consciousness that stretched through time, guiding her ever forward.

None of it was coincidence. None of it was without purpose.

The visions coalesced, each thread of memory weaving into the tapestry of her soul. Clarity washed over her: good and evil were not opposing forces, but two poles of the same coin, necessary and inseparable. Each played its role in the continuation of all within The All. Luna saw herself not as a warrior of light alone, but as a harmonizer of frequencies—a force attuned to counter the dominance of evil's path, restoring equilibrium where chaos sought to tip the scales.

Her breath deepened as the truth settled within her: she had always existed within the rhythm of balance. Across lifetimes, she had been drawn to the frequency of harmony, standing as a quiet but unwavering force against the tides of darkness. The choices she had made, the lives she had lived, were not accidents. Each had led her here, to this moment of reckoning, to embrace her role not as a conqueror, but as a custodian of the delicate dance that sustains creation.

The journey began to shift, its trajectory drawing her inward. From the sweeping grandeur of galaxies spinning in their eternal dance, she descended into the boundless depths of the microcosm. The threads of the aether coiled and wove themselves into intricate patterns, resolving into the elegant spirals of the double helix. Luna's vision narrowed, honing in on the DNA's luminous vibration, its delicate strands pulsating with a rhythm that mirrored the heartbeat of the universe.

The spirals twisted and flowed in a perpetual dance, expanding and contracting with liquid grace. Threads of radiant light emerged, filaments reaching outward to bridge unseen voids. These glowing tendrils carried the wisdom of eons—ancient codes etched into the fabric of existence, dormant no longer. They hummed with awakening, a song of renewal that reverberated through every cell of her being.

Luna felt the resonance of this transformation coursing through her, a fusion of mind, body, and spirit that dissolved all boundaries. Her awareness shifted inward still, settling within the symphony of her own form. She became acutely aware of herself as an orchestra of energy, every atom singing in harmony with the cosmos. The left and right hemispheres of her brain no longer stood in contrast; their duality softened, flowing seamlessly into a single river of thought and intuition.

Sparks of light cascaded along her spine, each ripple rising in a deliberate wave, igniting dormant pathways one by one. The energy ascended in a spiraling current, coiling upward like a serpent made of light. It paused momentarily in places that felt profound—luminous wells of vitality stirring to life—before surging outward, awakening something deep and timeless within her. It was as though her essence was aligning, layer by layer, with the pulse of the universe, unlocking a power that had always been waiting to rise.

The light continued their ascent, their rhythm quickening yet steady, as though climbing an ancient ladder etched into her very being. At last, they converged at the center of her mind, where light and awareness intertwined in a radiant burst—a nexus where perception expanded beyond its limits and consciousness unfolded into infinity.

Her heart echoed the rhythm, its steady beat infused with a newfound clarity. Each pulse resonated with unity, a harmonious bridge between her physical self and the vast, aethereal essence she now embodied.

She felt her DNA shifting, its tightly coiled codes unraveling to reveal latent potentials long buried in the depths of her being. The masculine energy of her higher self's will guided this unfolding with quiet determination, steady and sure. Within her, the feminine energy rose in response, weaving creation into existence with fluid grace. Together, they danced in perfect harmony—masculine will igniting possibility, feminine energy shaping and giving it life.

Her awareness expanded again, spiraling outward and inward in perfect harmony. A new sense stirred deep within her core, ancient yet unfamiliar, awakening with a brilliance that transcended her understanding. She became a vessel, a transceiver for the universe's boundless flow of information. Thoughts and emotions rippled through her consciousness, their energy emanating from hearts and minds spread across immeasurable distances. She felt the collective hopes, fears, and dreams of existence, their threads weaving an intricate tapestry that pulsed with life. And though she perceived herself as distinct—her essence held apart—she could also sense a higher unity, a boundless oneness from which all things were born and to which all would return.

In the infinite expanse of this awareness, Luna felt the cosmic pendulum swing, its arc steady and inevitable. The law of cause and effect resonated within her, its rhythm unshakable—but something deeper stirred beyond the surface of understanding.

She was both the seed and the soil, the spark and the flame, she was not bound to the lower cycles of causation.

Her higher self's voice rose again, a melody that vibrated through her very cells, each word a golden thread weaving into the fabric of her becoming.

"You are both the cause and the effect, Luna. But the awakened do not drift in the currents of fate—they rise above, learning to sail by the winds of higher law. Trust the rhythm, trust the flow. Observe, and the static of possibility will quiet before you."

The figure's light flared softly, its tone deepening with quiet urgency. "The land beneath your feet is more than sacred—it is an anchor, a conduit for the energy you now carry. The pyramid does not merely contain wisdom—it amplifies what is within you, weaving it into the currents of time and space. It is a passage to the higher plane, where the awakened may step beyond the lower tides of causation and into mastery over them. Rule not as one bound to the cycles, but as one who understands their rhythm. Protect it, nurture it, and this place will hold the balance until the new age rises with the strength you will need."

The words resonated through her, a gentle command that stilled the storm of her thoughts. Luna's breath deepened, her spirit quiet yet alive with purpose. She opened her eyes—or had they ever truly closed?—and found herself standing in stillness. The star tetrahedron that had enveloped her spun slower and slower, its radiant edges softening until they faded like whispers into the ancient air of the chamber.

The silence that followed was profound. Her chest swelled with gratitude, her heart beating with a rhythm she could finally hear as her own. A sense of purpose coursed through her, vast and undeniable, as though the universe had turned its gaze upon her and whispered, *You are ready.*

The magnitude of what lay ahead stretched beyond anything she could fully comprehend. A flicker of uncertainty stirred—but her feet moved anyway, guided by the rhythm now thrumming within her. For the first time, Luna didn't feel separate from the flow of existence, but woven into it—a thread shimmering with intention in the grand design.

She drew a deep breath, her voice a quiet promise to herself and the infinite expanse beyond: "I am ready."

The moment Luna stepped across the threshold of the star tetrahedron, the pyramid breathed her in, and the world unfurled in a cascade of light and energy. The stones beneath her feet pulsed like ancient hearts, alive with the whispers of their creators, their silent stories radiating outward in waves that rippled through her very core. The walls shimmered with an otherworldly glow, and the etched symbols seemed to awaken, their meanings unraveling not in words, but in a flood of truths that resonated deeper than language.

Her breath suspended, her steps faltering as the weight of the moment pressed into her. The air felt charged, heavy with knowing, as if each particle carried the memory of creation itself. Beneath her fingers, the stone vibrated, alive with the rhythm of existence. In the space between breath and thought, truths she had once touched freely now returned like echoes through dense fog—still present, but no longer effortless.

Every sensation converged at once: the dense hum of life, the pulse of ancient wisdom, and the delicate threads of the universe unfurling within her. It was too much and yet not enough, as though the entire cosmos had been compressed into her being, begging her to see, to feel, to understand.

The sensation swelled—a force greater than gravity, greater than thought—an unbearable crescendo pressing down on her, suffocating, absolute. Luna collapsed to her knees, the weight of the infinite universe pinning her against the cold embrace of the stone. Every breath came shallow, her chest struggling to rise against the crushing force. Her heart pounded in her ears, each beat a drum echoing through the vast, endless depths of time.

She wanted to scream. To unleash the tidal wave of knowing that surged within her. But the sheer magnitude of it—the sheer enormity of everything—crushed the sound before it could form, sealing it within her throat like a secret too immense to bear. Her body trembled, her fingers splaying across the ground in search of something, anything, to hold onto. But there was nothing. The world around her swam, dissolving into cascading light and the deafening roar of creation itself.

"I can't... it's too much," she whispered, her voice barely a thread against the symphony of knowledge unraveling her from within. Her limbs quaked, her very essence seeming to fracture beneath the pressure. The weight of eternity bore down, and for a fleeting moment, she felt herself breaking.

Then—

A resonance. Soft but unwavering. A frequency steady and sure, cutting through the chaos like a beacon in a storm.

"Be the observer, Luna."

The voice of her higher self. Calm. Unshaken. A whisper carrying more power than the force that sought to undo her.

"Intent is the key. See only what you wish to see."

The words wove themselves into her core, anchoring her against the storm. She gasped, drawing breath—not just into her lungs, but into her being. The gravity crushing her did not relent, but something within her shifted. The energy that had once flattened her now began to stir, coiling in response. Not resistance. Not defiance.

Adaptation.

Luna's trembling ceased. Her spine straightened, not in opposition to the force, but in harmony with it. She was no longer drowning beneath its weight—she was moving with it, allowing it to pass through her instead of against her.

"Be the observer." she whispered it aloud, her voice steadier, a lifeline woven from the fabric of her own will. She pictured herself as the eye of the storm, unmoved by the winds raging around her. The force did not control her—she controlled her place within it.

She inhaled deeply, feeling the shift in her very atoms. Energy surged through her, no longer an unbearable flood, but a river she could direct. She lifted her gaze, her vision sharpening.

She saw.

And now, she understood.

Slowly, the cacophony began to dim, the threads of infinite knowledge softening into a harmonious hum. Luna willed her vision to narrow, focusing on a single glowing symbol, its gentle light pulsing beneath her hands like a heartbeat.

Unsteadily, she rose, her breath quieting as the storm ebbed within her. The luminous life of the walls called to her now—not with deafening insistence, but with a subtle, magnetic pull. The corridors stretched infinitely before her, their forks veiled in mystery, each one a choice laden with possibility. Yet now, she felt the quiet current of energy beneath her skin, leading her onward with a precision that silenced her doubt.

She paused at an intricately carved wall, its symbols softly glowing with a pale blue light. The air around it hummed, alive with an energy that felt like recognition.

As she reached out, the markings leapt to life, unraveling into a visual story not written in words, but in emotion, in knowing.

Visions unfurled before her—ancient civilizations, their hands shaping the earth, their minds shaping reality itself. Not merely in tune with the rhythm of the universe, but masters of its flow.

A single depiction caught her attention.

It was older than the rest, a lost tale buried within the stone itself—one that did not speak of harmony alone, but of something greater.

A time before the written word was needed. A time when knowledge was not learned, but remembered. When humans walked fully awake, their minds the living key to transformation itself.

Luna's heart quickened.

She had spent so much time experiencing the ancients through visions—glimpses of their lives woven into her meditations, echoes of memories she could not explain. She had thought she understood them, believed they had simply lived in harmony with the universe in ways humanity had forgotten.

But this story was different.

They were not merely aligned.

They were alchemists of reality itself.

She traced the flowing lines of the carving, the soft pulse of energy beneath her fingertips carrying a lesson not spoken, but felt.

Change was not something that happened to them.

They became the change.

They had not been passive in the tides of cause and effect.

They had learned to move between forces, shifting their own state of being as easily as one moves from shadow into light.

To alter their own frequency, refining thought into will, and will into form.

Luna inhaled sharply, her entire being awakening to the truth carved in front of her. The secret had never been about finding something external. It was about knowing how to become something new.

She breathed the words, realization dawning like the rising sun. "They weren't just keepers of wisdom... They were the creators of it.

The walls responded, their glow intensifying. Not in confirmation. But in recognition. As though the pyramid itself knew—she understood now. Her steps felt lighter as she moved forward, her path now clearer than ever. She had not just uncovered history. She had uncovered what had always been inside her. And she would bring it back.

Luna emerged through the circular entrance into the tunnel at last, her steps heavy, as though the pyramid itself clung to her—unwilling to let her go. She crossed beneath the Flower of Life, the narrow passage framing her exit as sunlight poured down in warm cascades, blinding her for a moment. The air struck her skin like a blessing—fresh, alive—a stark contrast to the dense, electric stillness she had left behind. Her body felt fragile, as though it could barely contain the vastness swirling within her, but her spirit burned with purpose, flickering yet unbroken beneath the strain.

The clearing stretched before her, quieter now than when she had descended. Most of the crowd had dispersed, but a small group remained, their faces upturned toward her, their energy a grounding tether she desperately needed.

Her father was the first to step forward, his eyes wide with relief, his unspoken gratitude radiating like a steady flame. Althea stood close beside him, her serene gaze anchoring Luna as the weight of her transformation threatened to overwhelm her. Nearby, James, Miriam, Stephen, Joseph, and even Eleanor formed a loose circle, their expressions etched with awe, hope, and something deeper—an unspoken belief that whatever had happened inside the pyramid would change everything.

And then there was Ezra. He moved through the group with a quiet urgency, his presence cutting through the haze in her mind. His hands found her shoulders, gentle but firm, and his eyes searched hers with a depth that steadied her even as her knees threatened to buckle. His breath caught between disbelief and awe. Her eyes—the emerald green he knew so well—seemed different. They glowed with a new vibrancy, as though they weren't merely reflecting the light but emanating it from within, a subtle radiance that seemed to pulse in harmony with her breath.

"You're here," he said, his voice soft yet trembling, as though those two words carried all the weight of his fears and his relief.

Luna nodded, her breath ragged, her senses drowning in the tidal wave of emotions radiating from the group. Anticipation, concern, joy—they surged toward her like crashing waves, but with them came flashes of something deeper. She saw threads of their lives unfurling before her, moments etched into their very essence. James's childhood laughter echoed in her ears—a boy running through sunlit fields; Miriam's grief carved deep scars, a shadow of loss she carried silently; Stephen's growing curiosity for life pulsed like the steady beat of a drum.

Each fragment wove itself into her, pulling her apart with the sheer weight of their stories, their hopes, their humanity. This was different. The silent artifacts within the pyramid had overwhelmed her with knowledge, but they had been still, indifferent—echoes of the past. Here, the weight was alive. Willful. Every emotion, every thought directed at her collided in a chaotic storm, pressing against her mind with relentless force.

She steadied herself, forcing her voice to rise above the noise converging in her mind. "The path..." she began, the words thick in her throat.

"It's clearer now. But this… this is only the beginning."

The enormity of what she felt threatened to break her. Unlike the memories within the pyramid, these emotions did not simply exist—they reached for her, tangled with her, demanded her attention. She could feel them merging, flooding through her in ways she could not yet control. Her hands trembled as she gripped Ezra's arm for balance, struggling to separate herself from the tidal wave of feeling.

"The universe is open to me," she managed, her voice uneven, the words thick with awe and strain. "I see and feel it all… but it's… too much."

The group murmured softly, their voices weaving a tapestry of support, but the sounds only deepened the strain. Ezra stepped closer, his face creased with concern. "You're shaking," he said, his voice low, steady, like a hand reaching into chaos. "Let me help you. You need to rest."

Luna didn't argue. She leaned into Ezra, his strength steadying her as they began the slow walk back to her cabin. The group instinctively cleared a path, their gazes filled with a mix of awe and quiet under-standing. Relief and hope lingered in the air like a soft glow, but as she moved further away, the weight of their energy began to lift. Ezra's hand remained firm on her back, guiding her along the winding path.

"She's okay," Ezra assured them, his voice calm but resolute. "She just needs rest."

Luna glanced back briefly, catching a glimpse of their fading emo-tions—relief tempered with anticipation. Gratitude welled within her, but the storm inside her consciousness was still too much to bear. She turned away, focusing on each step forward.

As they approached the cabin, her strength faltered. The vastness of what now coursed through her stretched her spirit thin, her body trem-bling under its weight. The woman who had descended into the pyramid was forever changed—her essence expanded, her edges dissolved and reformed into something new. Yet this transformation came with a cost.

Every breath was a fragile thread, a delicate balance between surren-der and control. She would need time—time to quiet the storm, to learn how to carry the infinite without being consumed by it.

Ezra guided her inside, his steady presence grounding her as the earthy stillness of the cabin wrapped around them. In the dim light of the room, his eyes searched hers again, confirming what he had glimpsed when she emerged from the pyramid. Her eyes were indeed brighter, almost fluid, their emerald depths shimmering as though alive. The intricate patterns of her iris seemed to shift and flow, catching the light in mesmerizing ways.

He couldn't look away, his breath catching in his throat. "Luna," he whispered, awe and astonishment woven into his voice. "Your eyes... they're beautiful. I mean, they've always been beautiful, but now... they're extraordinary. You're extraordinary." His hand brushed lightly against her cheek. "I'm so proud of you—of your courage to walk this path, no matter how difficult it's been."

Luna smiled softly, her heart swelling with gratitude for his words, for his unwavering presence. But beneath her calm exterior, the storm of new sensations and visions raged on. She could see *everything* about him—his entire life, layer upon layer of experiences, choices, emotions. Even fragments of his past lives flickered in her mind's eye, weaving together a tapestry too intricate to process all at once.

Her hand slipped gently into his, squeezing it with affection. "Ezra... I love you. More than words can say. And I'm so grateful for you." She hesitated, her voice softening. "But right now, I need to be alone. I can see everything—your life, your past lives. It's... too much. I just need some time to adjust, to adapt to all of this."

Ezra's eyes filled with understanding, though a hint of sadness crossed his face. He leaned in, pressing a tender kiss to her forehead. "Of course. I'll be at my house if you need me."

He lingered for a moment longer, his hand slowly slipping from hers before he turned and left, closing the door quietly behind him.

Luna exhaled, sinking onto the floor as the stillness of the cabin wrapped around her like a cocoon. The path ahead was vast and uncertain, but she had survived the awakening. For now, she will rest. She needed to learn, to adapt, and to master the rhythm of her new abilities.

Stillness would be her sanctuary—a space to weave herself back together before the universe called on her once again.

THIRTY-ONE

THE ART OF OBSERVATION

The soft morning light filtered through the sheer curtains of Luna's cabin, casting delicate patterns across the room. She sat cross-legged on a woven mat in the center of the space, her back straight, her eyes open but unfocused, gazing beyond the limits of the physical world. For the past two days, she had retreated into quiet solitude, devoting herself to the delicate art of finding balance within the immense power now coursing through her.

The first day had been the hardest—a test of patience and precision. Luna had spent hours in deep focus, practicing the delicate art of becoming the observer. Each time she opened herself to the flow of the universe, it threatened to incapacitate her, a flood of raw energy and knowledge rushing toward her like a torrent. Her task was to see without drowning, to sharpen her attention on the hidden essence of what she desired to observe, while letting the rest fall away like mist. She began small—like focusing on the rhythmic dance of a single flame in an array of candles, she traced the life of a single leaf, following its thread back to the seed, to the soil, to the sky that nourished it. Slowly, she learned to contain the vastness, to filter the chaos into clarity, holding only what she needed in her mind's eye without the weight of everything else pressing in.

Every object in her cabin was alive, its presence humming with an energy she could feel as much as see. The floorboards beneath her feet, worn smooth by countless footsteps, creaked a gentle protest with each step she took. They had once been part of a majestic forest, their grain bearing witness to the passage of time and the changing seasons.

Towering trees, reaching for the sun, had been felled by the sharp bite of an axe, their trunks transformed into planks and placed with the skilled hands of a craftsman. Each knot and whorl in the grain told a story, a testament to the life they had once lived. As she walked, she felt the wind rustling through the leaves it once bore, the sunlight dappling the forest floor, and the birdsong filling the air. The floorboards, though now silent and still, held within them the echoes of a vibrant past, a connection to the natural world that time and human intervention had not entirely erased.

The mat beneath her pulsed with a subtle but undeniable energy, its intricate patterns and woven fibers a testament to the countless distant hands that had meticulously spun, dyed, and braided it into being. Each knot, each twist, held the echoes of lives lived and stories whispered, a tangible connection to generations long past. The very air of the room seemed to thrum with a vast, interconnected symphony of lives and choices, a boundless expanse where every thought, every action, every whispered word rippled outward, weaving itself into the grand, ever-evolving tapestry of existence.

She could almost see the threads of fate shimmering around her, each one a luminous strand representing a life lived, a decision made, a path chosen or forsaken. They intertwined and danced, sometimes clashing, sometimes harmonizing, but always moving forward, creating an intricate, breathtaking design that stretched beyond the confines of the room, beyond the boundaries of time itself.

The fabric of existence thrummed around her, like an endless symphony with no conductor, every note clamoring for her attention. Each vibration pressed against her mind, insistent and unrelenting. But slowly, she began to find harmony. By tuning her awareness like a musician adjusting the strings of a harp, she could isolate a single note, a single story, amid the cosmic cacophony. The effort was immense, but it brought her a fragile sense of control.

Her fingers brushed the surface of an amethyst that rested in her lap, its cool, smooth texture grounding her like a steady anchor in a storm. The stone thrummed with the familiar energy of the pyramid, a resonance etched into its crystalline structure during her awakening. Luna exhaled deeply, her breath carrying away the tension that lingered in her chest, as the overwhelming flood of universal energy eased, retreating into a calm ebb.

She closed her eyes and smiled faintly. The rhythmic footsteps on the earth outside, the subtle shift of energy drawing near, informed her who had come even before the soft knock at the door broke the stillness.

"It's open, Althea," Luna said, her voice quiet yet certain.

The door creaked slowly, and Althea stepped inside, her serene energy wrapping around the room like a gentle breeze. She held a small bowl of herbs, their earthy aroma already mingling with the cabin's tranquil air. "Good morning, Luna," she said softly, her voice soothing, her presence a steady counterweight to the vastness within Luna.

Luna remained seated, her eyes closed as she continued to study the pulse of the aether. She could feel the currents of Althea's thoughts and emotions, flowing toward her like the clear waters of a spring. "You're here to check on me," Luna said, her fingers tracing the amethyst in her lap. "And to remind me to slow down."

Althea smiled faintly, setting the bowl on the nearby table. "You're learning fast," she said, her tone tinged with admiration. "But how are you truly feeling?"

Luna paused, her focus drifting inward. "Stronger," she admitted, though her voice held a quiet weariness. "But there's so much... it's all connected, and I feel it all. Every thread, every ripple. It's hard to know where I end and the universe begins."

Althea knelt beside her, her presence calm and unhurried. "That is a gift—and the challenge," she said. "But you're finding yourself. The balance will come. The universe flows through you, but you are its vessel, not its captive. Remember, you have the power to guide the flow."

She let Althea's words ripple through her like a soft breeze over still water. "*Guide the flow*," she murmured with the smoothness of an epiphany, the phrase lingering on her lips like a mantra. Her focus remained on the pulse of the aether, filling the empty space around her, each vibration weaving into the unseen fabric of life in the room.

Her thumb and forefinger began to move in gentle circles, a rhythmic gesture, like a conductor guiding the orchestra of forces around her. The air stirred in response, a soft breeze rising from nowhere. It swept lightly through the space, swirling gently before extinguishing the flames of the few candles she had lit on the table, leaving the room bathed in the dull morning light and a lingering warmth.

A glowing smile spread across Luna's face as she turned toward Althea, her voice steady and filled with warmth. "I love you, Althea... so brilliant..."

Luna opened her eyes, her gaze calm yet luminous. The emerald light in her eyes seemed to shimmer, glowing faintly like sunlight through polished crystal.

Althea gasped softly, her breath catching as she leaned in closer, awe flickering across her face. "Luna... your eyes," she whispered, her voice barely audible. "They're... radiant." She reached out gently, as though afraid the light might fade if she disturbed it. "It's like they carry the light of the earth itself."

Luna's glowing smile deepened, a quiet knowing settling into her expression. "They are not just reflecting light—they are entangled with it," she said softly, her voice like the hum of the aether itself. "It's the sparkle of connection, the quantum dance written into the essence of all things. When I see the truth in something, the light responds, as if the very particles remember me. It's not just light *touching* my eyes—it's light *answering.*"

Althea gasped, her eyes widening as she took in the profound beauty of Luna's words. "You're... connected to it all," she murmured, her voice filled with reverence.

"Entangled," Luna corrected gently. "Every fragment of life, every thread of existence, is linked in ways we have barely begun to understand. When I see the truth, I touch the spark within it—and it touches me back."

Althea's eyes softened, her awe blending with pride and deep affection. "I've always known there was something extraordinary in you. Now the world will see it too."

The enlightened moment was interrupted by the sound of footsteps approaching the door. Luna's awareness stirred, her heart swelled with the familiar energy announcing Ezra's presence before he appeared in the doorway. When he stepped inside, his expression was a blend of concern and quiet resolve, a steady force that anchored her amidst the tides of her new reality.

"Morning," he said, holding up a small tray with tea and a bowl of fresh berries. His voice was calm, understated, yet laced with care. "Thought you could use a break."

A faint smile softened Luna's face as she watched him place the tray beside her. His eyes lingered on her for a moment—taking in her quiet strength but also the weariness that clung to her like a shadow. Ezra lowered himself to the floor across from her, his gaze steady, but his brow furrowed slightly with concern.

"You've been carrying so much," he said, his voice low, his vulnerability breaking through. "I see it—the weight of it all. I don't think I need to tell you this, but I'm here for you," he added, his tone gentle but firm.

Her hand reached for his instinctively, their fingers intertwining in a quiet gesture of trust. "I know," she said, her voice barely above a whisper. "You've been my anchor, Ezra. I wouldn't have made it this far without you. But trust me, I'm doing well."

Ezra's grip tightened slightly, his touch grounding her in the moment. "I believe you, Luna. But trust me when I say I'll be here for you, and for whatever comes next," he said, his words carrying a quiet certainty that warmed her heart.

Luna felt his presence not just in the warmth of his touch but on a deeper, more subtle plane, where the echoes of his thoughts brushed gently against her mind like whispers carried on the wind. An image flickered to life within her—a vivid, unbidden vision: Ezra kneeling, a ring resting delicately in his hands, his heart radiating hope and quiet determination. The clarity of the moment startled her, the depth of his intention catching her breath, but as the image lingered, it softened into something natural, something inevitable. Her answer bloomed in her heart, resounding and certain—yes, always yes. Yet she held this knowing close, honoring the rhythm of life as it unfolded. It was Ezra's moment to create… his question to ask, and she would wait, letting him find the words in his own time. She closed her eyes and turned her head slightly, afraid her excitement would give her away.

Ezra gave her hand a final reassuring squeeze, his eyes warm but thoughtful. "I see you're still working out how to handle all this," he said gently. "Promise me you'll at least get out for some fresh air today."

Luna nodded with a faint smile. "I will."

Satisfied, Ezra rose to his feet. Althea followed with a warm smile, gathering her herbs before slipping quietly out the door.

Luna remained seated, her thoughts drifting between the present and the gentle future that seemed to hum in the air around her. She breathed deeply, allowing the stillness to settle in her chest.

For a while, Luna sat in the deep quiet of the room, her breath steady and measured. She let herself slip into the stillness, her mind returning to the pulse of the aether that filled the air like a hidden current beneath the surface of life. Althea's words echoed softly in her thoughts: *Guide the flow.*

It struck her then—everything was vibration, a frequency weaving through every particle of life. Her gift wasn't simply about observing; it was about tuning in, like a transceiver capable of interpreting the hidden waves surrounding her. The changes in her DNA had opened a door, allowing her to read the information carried in those waves. She just needed to tune into the right frequency.

Luna closed her eyes and shifted her focus inward, into the space behind her forehead—her third eye. A subtle tickle of pressure began to build there, warm and steady. She had grown comfortable with the clarity of this eye and the tingle it gave, but now she noticed something else. A second presence, a growing pressure just above her right eye, deeper than the surface tension of her third eye.

Curious, she concentrated on the new sensation, willing the energy to rotate slowly, clockwise. The pressure responded, spiraling in gentle turns. The world within her began to shift. Hues of light and tones of sound danced and changed, the hum of the aether bending and weaving in new ways. The layers of vibration separated and sharpened in her awareness, revealing hidden depths.

It was then she understood it—the seat of her internal tuner. Not a physical dial, but a center of energy she could guide with intention. She turned it delicately, each adjustment altering the textures of the frequencies around her. The sounds of life pulsed more clearly—the whisper of wind through leaves, the faint creak of the floor beneath her, the quiet hum of insects beyond the cabin.

And then she felt it. A flicker of something different, something almost foreign, yet somehow familiar. She leaned into it, her focus sharpening as she moved the wheel ever so slightly. Two voices—clear and distinct—emerged from the hum. They weren't from another world or some spiritual plane. These voices were human, grounded and real.

"...I just worry about you being so far from home, sweetie. College is stressful enough."

"It's okay, Dad. I'm doing fine, really. I promise."

Luna's breath caught as the realization dawned on her. This wasn't a natural frequency. It was a phone call—a conversation carried on waves of human-made energy. She wasn't just observing the hum of life; she had tapped into the vast network of signals humans had scattered across the world.

Her mind raced as she processed what this meant. The energy around her wasn't limited to natural life. The man-made frequencies, the endless data flowing through the air, could be observed and interpreted as well. She sat perfectly still, listening to the fading echoes of the conversation, a mix of awe and disbelief coursing through her. *I can hear it all,* she thought. *Not just life's song, but everything humanity has layered on top of it.*

Luna breathed deeply, her fingers still gently guiding the spiraling energy within her mind. The textures of the frequencies sharpened further, expanding into patterns of sound and light, each carrying hidden messages waiting to be heard.

A memory stirred—a teaching she had meditated on many times before: As *above, so below; as within, so without.* The phrase resonated with new clarity. Of course, it made sense. If humanity could build machines to tune a radio, plucking voices from invisible waves and bringing them to life, how could the infinite wisdom of the universe not have designed such a capability within its own creation?

Her newly awakened DNA was the key. It had unlocked the natural transceiver within her—a receiver embedded in the very structure of her being. The transformation had given her not just access to the energy around her, but the ability to decode it, to interpret the knowledge hidden within the waves. The hum of the aether wasn't just sound; it was information, rich with meaning, waiting to be heard.

The realization was both humbling and exhilarating. This ability had always been there, dormant, waiting for the right moment to awaken. Now it had, and the endless streams of data—the vibrations of life and beyond—lay open to her perception. She merely needed to listen.

Luna smiled to herself, a warmth blooming in her chest as she realized how quickly she was gaining control over this new ability. The images and sounds no longer rushed at her like an unstoppable torrent. She was guiding them, shaping her experience with growing precision.

Her fingers brushed lightly over her lap as if mimicking the turn of an invisible dial. "Okay," she said with a quiet chuckle, "I've found the tuner. Now... where's the volume knob?"

The joke was lighthearted, but the desire was real. She'd love to be able to adjust the intensity—or even turn it off entirely when needed. The constant hum of energy was exhilarating, but it left little room for quiet. Still, she knew this was progress, and progress was everything.

Later that afternoon, Luna did as promised, she stepped out on the small porch of her cabin, the breeze carrying the soft whispers of the forest. She closed her eyes and let herself simply exist—rooted in the earth beneath her feet, open to the vast sky above, and cradled by the delicate balance between the two.

The flow of energy thrummed around her, no longer an overwhelming torrent, but a steady, harmonious rhythm, each beat aligning with the pulse of her own heart. Luna had found her internal tuner and was learning to guide the frequency of information she received. Though she was still working on lowering its intensity—or even turning it off entirely—she had gained enough control to feel steady in the current. Every moment of focus brought her closer to understanding how to balance her heightened awareness with the limits of her physical form.

It was no longer an unwieldy storm but a river she was learning to navigate with intention and grace. Each wave of knowledge flowed past her, and she could choose what to reach for and what to let slip by. It was imperfect, but it was progress.

Her task was far from complete, but she knew she couldn't remain hidden away in the stillness of her cabin, no matter how much sanctuary it offered. The path ahead was clear: her gift had awakened not just for her own sake but for a greater purpose. The community was waiting for her—not just for guidance, but for the strength and clarity she now carried.

Her true journey—the one that mattered most—would only begin when she stepped back into the world and embraced what lay ahead.

Thirty-Two

The Gathering Storm

The gathering hall swelled with quiet anticipation as the community members entered, their footsteps softened against the worn wooden floor. Lantern light flickered gently, casting shifting patterns across the walls, as if the room itself breathed with their presence. The air held a pulse, a rhythm shared by every soul within it—a collective heartbeat that mirrored the one Luna had felt within the pyramid. Whispers of her journey, her connection to the ancient energy, had spread like ripples on still water. Today, they would finally hear from her.

Luna stood at the center of the room, her posture steady yet humble, the weight of countless lifetimes converging in this single moment. Her father stood close, his steady presence a quiet reassurance. Ezra, Althea, and James lingered nearby, their energies warm and grounding, like anchors holding her to the earth. She closed her eyes for a brief moment, inhaling deeply. The hum of the room washed over her—the emotions of the community weaving together into a symphony of curiosity, wonder, and a touch of apprehension.

As she opened her eyes, her gaze swept over the faces before her, a shallow breath hovered in suspense. In that instant, she saw them—not merely as a group, but as individual lives, each thread in the vast tapestry of existence. Each face carried a story, etched into the lines of their brows, the light in their eyes. She saw the struggles they had endured, the choices that had shaped them, the quiet courage it had taken to arrive here. Compassion bloomed within her, a wellspring of love that threatened to spill over.

A shimmer sparked in her eyes—subtle at first, then brightening with every connection made. The emerald light within her eyes seemed to ripple and shift, reflecting the deep resonance of each soul she looked upon.

The crowd gasped, a collective intake of breath filling the space. Some stared in awe, their eyes wide with wonder; others exchanged glances, their astonishment unspoken but palpable.

Luna said nothing, allowing the moment to settle, the hum of connection weaving silently between them all. She smiled gently, the glow in her eyes softening as her gaze lingered on each face in turn.

Luna swallowed against the surge of emotion, her hands trembling slightly as she folded them in front of her. She longed to tell them everything—to open the floodgates and share the vast, indescribable truths that now lived within her. But she remembered the wisdom etched in her mother's journal: *The lips of wisdom speak to the ears of understanding.* Not all truths were meant to be spoken at once. Some were seeds, meant to be planted gently and nurtured over time.

"Thank you all for coming," she began, her voice steady yet carrying an undercurrent of emotion that made her pause to breathe. "These past weeks have brought me closer to something profound—something far greater than myself. The pyramid's energy, the truths it holds... they are not mine alone. They belong to all of us. I stand here not apart from you, but as one thread in the same tapestry, bound by the same rhythm that connects us all."

Her voice softened as she spoke, her eyes drifting over the room. She could feel their questions without words, the quiet wonder, the tentative hope. Some, she knew, harbored fears of what her awakening meant—what it might demand of them. Yet beneath it all, she sensed their shared desire to understand, to belong, to find their place in the unfolding story.

Luna's eyes swept over the gathered faces, the shimmering light within them soft and steady. Her lips curved into a gentle smile, her voice tender and unhurried as she spoke. "I know some of you may feel uncertain. Perhaps you wonder if I can see your secrets, your regrets, your mistakes." She paused, her gaze warm and steady. "The truth is... I do see everything.

Every choice, every decision—but with each one, I also see every moment that led to it. I see the path that brought you here, the intentions, the struggles, the lessons. And with that comes an understanding so clear, so complete, that there is no room for shame or regret. Everything has purpose. Every step, even those that felt like missteps, were a part of the journey that shaped you."

Her tone softened, carrying the weight of compassion. "Let me reassure you—I do not seek to peer into what you guard closely. My gift is not a tool for judgment, nor is it a burden I carry lightly. It is not my place to uncover what you do not wish to share. We all walk our own paths, paths shaped by the choices we've made, the lessons we've endured."

As she paused, the flood of emotions from the crowd hit her all at once—a surge of raw, unfiltered thoughts and feelings crashing into her like a tidal wave. Joy, grief, fear, love, hope—all tangled together, each demanding her attention. Her lungs seized, shallow and strained—knees threatening to buckle beneath the weight. Her heart raced, the sheer intensity pulling her toward the brink of collapse.

But then, something ancient stirred within her—a hidden wisdom, deep and instinctual, woven into the very threads of her being. From the center of her chest, it unfurled like a magnetic bloom, expanding in luminous waves. A soft pulse, invisible yet radiant, arced outward from her heart, casting shimmering ribbons of energy into the air.

They danced like auroras—fluid, ethereal, alive—bending and refracting the emotional deluge around her. Each wave of intensity met the shield and scattered into light, their force redirected, their impact softened. The air shimmered with colorless hues, like wind catching sunlight, as the magic cocooned her—not a wall, but a flow, an ancient rhythm echoing the Earth's own magnetic field—its shield against the sun's fire, allowing life to thrive beneath its invisible grace.

Here, within the quiet eye of the storm, Luna stood untouched. Connected, but not consumed. Protected, not closed. The flood became a current, and she—its guide.

The torrent eased, the overwhelming intensity melting into a gentle hum, like distant music carried on the breeze.

It wasn't a volume knob after all, but something far more sacred—a gift she hadn't known she possessed. This magnetic current was a guardian of balance, allowing her to remain open while protecting her essence. It filtered the flow, sifting through the chaos and grounding her in the calm at her core.

Ezra had rushed to her side at the first signs of trouble, his hand reaching for her arm in steady support. But Luna's newfound protection held, and she quickly regained her composure. With a deep breath, she steadied herself and offered him a reassuring smile and a nod of gratitude.

His eyes lingered on hers, noticing the shimmer and sparkle had faded, returning to the rich emerald hue life had given her. A calm settled over him. It wasn't disappointment—it was relief. She had found control, and in that control, she had reclaimed a piece of herself.

With renewed steadiness, her gaze swept across the room, catching the subtle nods of understanding, the quiet exhale of relief as her prior words found their mark.

"To understand where we are going," she said, her tone shifting into something more reflective, "we must first understand where we have been." She stepped toward the wooden podium at her side, her hand resting lightly on the rolled sketches she had prepared over the past few days. "What we uncovered beneath Pyramid Hill is more than an ancient structure. It is a record—a message from those who lived on this land long before us."

With careful hands, she unrolled the sketches, revealing intricate drawings of the symbols and carvings she had seen within the pyramid. The community leaned forward as one, their curiosity pulling them closer. Eyes widened, fascination illuminating their faces as they took in the mysterious designs, each line and curve rich with meaning and history.

"These symbols tell the story of a people who walked this land before the last great ice age," she explained, her voice reverent, almost sacred. "People our history books know nothing about. They were deeply attuned to the earth and the stars, understanding the balance of the elements, the rhythm of the seasons, and the harmony that binds all living things. They lived not in dominion over nature but in rhythm with it."

She paused, letting her words linger in the air like the final note of a song. "Their knowledge wasn't lost. It was hidden, waiting—waiting for a time when the heavens and the earth would align once again, when power would flow freely, and when the hearts of people would be ready to uncover it. To learn from it. To protect it from those who would seek to exploit it."

A hush fell over the room, the weight of her message pressing gently on each listener like the turning of an unseen tide.

"That time is approaching," Luna said, her voice stronger, resolute. "And you are the ones it has been waiting for."

Her words carried through the hall like wind threading through tall grass, subtle yet impossible to ignore, stirring something deep within the hearts of those gathered. "Life is a delicate dance of opposing forces," she continued, her tone steady yet fervent. "Progress is not born from stasis, but from the constant shifting of light and shadow, creation and destruction. The future will hold uncertainty, and we will face challenges that seek to tip the balance..."

Her gaze swept across the room, her voice lowering with gravity. "There are forces—like Westfield—that aim to bend this power for a less peaceful existence, for control and personal gain. They will try to disrupt what we've begun, to twist the energy of this transformation into something destructive. But we are stronger than any one of us alone. Together, we can protect what must not be lost. Together, we can ensure that this power remains a force for growth, not ruin."

The room was silent but for the faint sound of breath. Then Miriam stepped forward, her shoulders square, her expression resolute. "You've guided us through so much already, Luna. We'll stand with you."

Luna's voice rang clear and steady, and her words rippled through the room, drawing murmurs of agreement. Heads nodded, hands clasped. The collective resolve of the community began to coalesce, solidifying into something unbreakable. The pulse of unity filled the room, and in that moment, Luna knew the rhythm of her journey had found harmony with theirs.

She toned down the magnetic field around her heart, allowing the flood of thoughts and emotions to filter back in gently. Relief washed over her as she felt their collective intent—the decision to be a force for good was unanimous. Luna nodded, her heart swelling with gratitude. "Then let us prepare—not with fear, but with purpose. We will protect what is sacred, not through conflict, but through wisdom and understanding. Together, we'll light the way forward.

"The pyramid has been concealed by time, hidden so its wisdom could wait for the right moment. That moment is not yet, and we must keep its existence within our circle until the world is ready to receive its truth."

Her gaze swept across the room, lingering on the familiar faces of her closest allies—Ezra, Althea, James, Miriam. Their presence steadied her, their resolve resonating like a quiet rhythm that strengthened her own. The community had given her their trust, but this next step required the focus and coordination of those who had walked this path by her side. The weight of their collective purpose was immense, but in the unity of those gathered here, Luna felt an unshakable strength.

With time, the room began to disperse, murmurs of solidarity fading into the night as the larger group returned to their homes, carrying with them the fire of Luna's words. She motioned for Ezra, Althea, James, and Miriam to stay, their steps quiet as they gathered around a small wooden table near the head of the hall.

Ezra unfurled a large, weathered map across its surface, its curling edges and faded lines speaking of years of careful use. He placed his hand along its edge, his voice steady and measured. "I've been researching potential sites that align with known ley lines," he began, his finger tracing a path from Arkansas toward the West Coast. "Westfield has been putting out posts on social media, calling for volunteers to work at specific locations. These energy pathways have long been tied to spiritual phenomena—heightened activity, paranormal events, things like that. If Westfield Industries is targeting these areas, we need to understand why and act accordingly."

Luna leaned closer, her eyes scanning the intricate markings that crisscrossed the map like veins of energy running beneath the surface of the earth. "These ley lines," she said softly, "connect everything, like the threads of a web. If Westfield disrupts the balance at key points..." Her voice trailed off, the weight of the thought settling over the group.

James nodded grimly. "They could cause more than just localized disturbances. They could unravel connections far beyond what we can see."

Althea's voice was calm but resolute as she added, "We need to determine where they're working and how close they are to achieving their goals. If they're exploiting these sites, it could compromise more than just the energy—they could manipulate people, communities."

Miriam folded her arms, her gaze fixed intently on the map. "Then we have to be ready to move quickly. We need information, and we need a plan."

Luna's fingers grazed the edge of the map, her gaze unfocused as she reached out with her senses, trying to thread the patterns of energy that connected the sites. She closed her eyes briefly, searching for clarity—but something was missing. The flow she had grown accustomed to reading felt disrupted, fragmented, as if key threads had been severed. A flicker of frustration passed over her face, but she steadied herself, grounding in the rhythm of the moment.

"They're close," Luna said softly, her voice carrying a note of certainty. "Westfield knows the existence of these sites, of the power they hold, but they don't understand it—not fully. They're seeking it through their machines, their technology, trying to harness something they can't feel or comprehend. They're reaching blindly into forces they were never meant to touch."

Her hand hovered over the map, tracing a slow path across the ley lines Ezra had marked. "But they're not just seeking to control. They've created something... something designed to block energy, to obscure it. I can feel it—it's like a void, a place where the flow of life is silenced." She paused, her brow furrowing as the weight of this realization settled over her. "Whatever they're using, it's not natural. It disrupts the rhythm of the earth itself. That's why I can't see everything. Their technology blinds me in certain places, hiding their intentions. I can't say if they are doing this intentionally or not."

Ezra's eyes darkened, his jaw tightening as he leaned closer to the map. "If they can block energy, they might be able to control it—shape it to their will. That kind of power in the wrong hands..." His voice trailed off, leaving the thought unfinished.

"We need to find these voids," Althea said firmly, her gaze sharpening. "Perhaps it is similar to a blocked chakra, that can be cleared, or if we understand how their technology works, we can counter it—restore the balance they're trying to tip their way."

Luna nodded slowly, her voice steady but laced with urgency. "The answers are there, but we'll have to uncover them piece by piece. Westfield's technology might shield their movements, but it also leaves a mark. Their machines can't mimic the natural flow of energy. They disrupt it, and that disruption creates echoes. If we listen carefully, we'll find them."

Miriam leaned forward, her expression grim yet determined. "Then that's our path. We track the voids. We follow the echoes. And we find out what they're doing before it's too late."

Luna exhaled, the rhythm of her heart aligning with the resolve of those around her. This was their challenge—to navigate the unseen, to untangle the disruption, and to protect the harmony that held everything together. "Then let's begin," she said quietly, her voice carrying the determination of the group, a shared purpose binding them as one.

Ezra nodded, his expression resolute. "Right, then," he said, pointing to a spot in northern New Mexico. "Here is Chaco Canyon, once a major center of Ancestral Puebloan culture. It's believed to sit on intersecting ley lines, which might explain its profound historical and spiritual significance."

Luna's gaze followed his finger, a faint hum vibrating in her awareness as he spoke. "Chaco Canyon was a hub of activity and trade," she said, her voice firm with knowing. "Its alignment with celestial events reveals a deep understanding of the energies that flow between earth and sky.

The people there didn't just observe—they worked with those forces. Westfield won't be the first to seek its power."

"I only found one post on Westfield's social media about Chaco Canyon. Judging by the comments, they weren't very welcome there. Still, it might be worth checking out on the way," Ezra said, his finger shifting westward across the map. "There's much more interest in Arizona from Westfield—Sedona specifically. It's known for its vortex sites—swirling centers of energy believed to facilitate healing and spiritual awakening. One of the most active energy hubs in the world. I also found some public notices about cell towers Westfield is constructing there. Maybe they have something to do with the energy blockage," he added thoughtfully.

Miriam leaned in, her brows furrowed. "Sedona... I've heard about the peace people feel there, the pull of the red rock formations. Do you think Westfield would be after the vortexes?"

"It's likely," Ezra replied, his tone darkening. "If they're trying to disrupt or manipulate natural energy flows, Sedona's vortexes would be an obvious target."

At the mention of Sedona, Luna felt a subtle hum ripple through her senses, as though the name itself carried a vibration. "Yes, Sedona," she murmured, her voice distant but certain. "There are others there. Others who are awake, with a deep understanding of the universe's balance. They'll help us." She nodded, her focus sharpening. "Good call on the cell towers, Ezra. We should look closer at those."

Ezra's lips curved into a faint smile, his pride in his research evident. "Continuing west," he said, his finger tracing across the map to northern California, "we have Mount Shasta. It's considered one of the most powerful energy vortexes on the planet. Legends speak of hidden cities beneath the mountain and mystical beings guarding its secrets. Westfield has several towers around this area."

James raised an eyebrow, his skepticism cutting through the tension. "Hidden cities? Mystical beings? That sounds more like fantasy than fact."

Luna's soft smile didn't waver. "Many myths have roots in truth, James. Mount Shasta has drawn spiritual seekers for generations. Its energy is undeniable to those who know how to feel it. I am certain of lost cities. As for mystical beings... well, I suppose it depends on the definition. Besides all that, if Westfield is tampering there, it could destabilize far more than we can imagine."

Ezra nodded and moved his finger northward. "And here, in southern Oregon, we have the Oregon Vortex. It's a smaller site, but the energy anomalies there suggest a distortion of natural forces—an effect that might be tied to a cluster of ley lines in the region. Nothing recent from Westfield in the area, but they did put up a few more towers of theirs last year."

Althea leaned against the table, her brow furrowed. "If these places are so significant, why haven't we seen more overt activity from Westfield? Surely there'd be signs by now."

"They're working in the shadows, disguised as legitimate, ordinary technologies" Luna replied, her voice steady but edged with resolve. "Westfield has media influence. They control the narrative. What's really happening is buried beneath a layer of obfuscation. They study in secret, exploit in silence. We can't wait for their plans to be obvious—we have to stay ahead of them."

Ezra leaned back, his arms crossed. "We need more than awareness. If we can connect with the guardians, spiritual leaders, or communities near these sites, we can create a network. Vigilance is our first line of defense."

Luna placed her hand gently on the map, closing her eyes for a brief moment. The subtle vibrations of the earth's energy pulsed beneath her fingertips, grounding her thoughts. When she spoke, her voice was steady but filled with concern. "If Westfield is up to no good in these areas, it's not just the land at risk—it's the people. Many of them won't even know what's happening until it's too late."

Her eyes opened, a quiet intensity radiating from her. "We need to protect them. To make sure they're not caught in something they don't understand. If Westfield's machines can manipulate the energy here, they could cause real harm. We have to act before that happens."

Ezra glanced at her, his expression steady. "Then we start with New Mexico."

Luna nodded, her voice resolute as she laid out the plan. "New Mexico first. From there, we move to Sedona. We'll gather allies where we can and continue west. Once we reach Los Angeles, we'll get close enough to Westfield to uncover their next move."

"I can head up to Oregon and make my way south to Mount Shasta, keep my ear to the ground, and see if I can uncover anything. If I don't, I'll meet you in L.A.," James offered, his tone steady with purpose.

"I'll come with you," Althea said, her smile warm as she glanced at James. "I'll be able to sense what we're looking for, pick up on signs you might miss. Two pairs of eyes—and instincts—will serve us well."

James nodded, appreciating her partnership. "Agreed. We'll move quickly, but carefully."

The room grew quiet as each member absorbed the weight of the mission ahead. The path was uncertain, fraught with challenges, but the unity of their purpose and the guidance of ancient wisdom gave them the resolve to move forward.

Luna turned to Miriam, her gaze softening as she spoke. "Miriam, your role here is just as vital. The community needs someone to guide them while we're away—someone they trust to hold this space, to nurture the connections we've built. There's still so much work to do here. I can't think of anyone better to carry it forward."

Miriam's expression shifted to quiet pride, her hands resting lightly on the table. "I'll stay," she said, her voice calm but certain. "I'll look after the community. If Westfield comes near, we'll know."

Luna smiled, gratitude warming her features. "Thank you, Miriam. Knowing you're here brings peace."

Miriam nodded, her eyes softening. "We're all part of this. You carry the vision out there—I'll carry it here. You'll have something worth returning to."

A stillness settled over the group as the meeting concluded, the weight of what lay ahead pressing gently between them. One by one, they exchanged nods and quiet words, their purpose clear.

As Ezra rolled up the map, Miriam brushed her hand along its edge. "We've got what we need," she said. "Let's not waste time."

Luna stepped back, watching them disperse, each moving with quiet intention. Though the rest of the community had gone, their presence lingered—hopeful, uncertain, but trusting in the path she'd drawn.

She let herself exhale, just for a moment.

Just as Luna allowed herself a moment to exhale, to gather her thoughts, a familiar voice cut through the stillness, warm and tinged with mischief.

"Well, it seems I arrived just in time to witness history being made."

Luna turned sharply, her heart skipping as her gaze landed on the figure leaning casually against the doorway. Elias stood there, his ever-present satchel slung over one shoulder, his expression a mix of amusement and something softer—something deeper.

"Elias," she breathed, her face lighting up with welcomed surprise. Without hesitation, she crossed the room, her steps quick and unguarded, and pulled him into a firm embrace.

"Good timing, Elias. You missed all the hard work," Luna said with a soft chuckle, stepping back to study his face. She gently drew in her field, quieting the radiant energy around her, and looked briefly into him. Her smile deepened as a sense of clarity settled over her, like the faint hum of a string plucked within the fabric of Elias's universe. She didn't need to ask why he had come—she simply knew. The threads of his path, his choices, wove seamlessly into her understanding of the moment.

Her gaze shifted to the group, her voice carrying both light humor and unshakable gravity. "Everyone, this is Elias. He has decided to stop merely teaching history and start making it." She glanced back at him, one eyebrow raised in a playful challenge. "He's here to help us find Dr. Marin."

The room rippled with soft laughter, the tension easing for the first time in hours. Elias blinked, too stunned to speak, much less share the humor. His mouth opened slightly, then closed again as he stared at her, his expression shifting to one of quiet disbelief.

"Well," he finally said, his voice tinged with amusement, "I suppose that's right, but... how?" His words faltered, and he shook his head, a wry smile tugging at his lips. "I couldn't stop thinking about our last call. The lead I gave you—it wasn't enough. There's something bigger at stake here. I felt it, and I had to come. And besides, Dr. Marin..."

"Dr. Marin?" Ezra interjected, his brow furrowing as he crossed his arms. His tone carried both recognition and caution. "The Westfield scientist?"

Elias nodded slightly, a flicker of unease shadowing his face. "She's more than that. Beth was one of their lead researchers—brilliant, driven, obsessed with uncovering the connection between earth's energy and ancient technologies. She believed it was the key to unlocking the next stage of human evolution." His voice lowered, his expression darkening. "But she disappeared... I suspect she realized what Westfield intended to do with that knowledge—how they planned to manipulate it for control and profit. I'm hoping she went into hiding... and not something worse."

The room fell quiet again, the weight of his words settling heavily over the group. Althea tilted her head slightly, her calm voice cutting through the silence. "And you believe she'll trust us? Trust you?"

Elias exhaled slowly, his eyes narrowing in thought. "I don't know," he admitted. "But if she's alive, if she's still out there, I think she'll listen. Marin isn't someone who gives her trust lightly, but she's not blind to the truth. If we can reach her... if we can show her we're not like them..." He let the words hang, as if even he wasn't entirely sure how to finish.

Luna stepped forward, her presence a quiet force that steadied the room. "We don't need to convince her of everything all at once," she said, her tone deliberate yet soft. "The lips of wisdom speak to the ears of understanding. If Dr. Marin has seen what Westfield is capable of, then she already knows more than most. What she needs now is a path—one that aligns with what's right. That's where we come in."

Elias studied her, his unease softening as he nodded. "If anyone can convince her, it's you."

Luna's eyes met Elias's, a flicker of knowing illuminating her expression. "And if anyone can find her, Elias, it's you."

His fingers tightened on the edge of the table. "I've been trying," he said quietly. "I reached out weeks ago—no calls, no emails, no trace. She's gone underground, if she's still out there. I just hope she's okay. That we aren't too late."

Luna's expression softened, she closed her eyes and shifted her focus. Stepping closer, her presence calm but charged with intention. Slowly, she opened her eyes, and a vibrant shimmer illuminated her irises—emerald light alive with an otherworldly glow. The threads of connection had flooded her mind's eye, weaving into a web of quantum entanglement that reached beyond time and space. Elias's heart skipped a beat at the sight, as if realigned in that moment with hers, his surprise melting into cautious hope.

"You knew her well, Elias. Your memories of her are threads—threads that connect to the present, to where she is now. If you'll let me, I can follow them."

"You can... find her? From my memories?" he asked, his voice mixed with curiosity and excitement.

A faint smile touched Luna's lips, quiet confidence radiating from her. "If she's still alive, yes."

Elias hesitated only for a moment before nodding. "Do whatever you need to."

Luna reached out, her fingertips brushing the back of his hand. Closing her eyes, she steadied her breath and sank into the rhythm of the moment. Her senses expanded outward, rippling like light across a calm sea. She felt the threads of Elias's memories—faint yet vivid—humming softly beneath the surface of his consciousness. Each one shimmered, vibrating in perfect harmony with the quantum fabric of existence.

The room fell silent, the faint hum of the overhead lights blending with the steady rhythm of her breathing. Luna's awareness drifted, tracing the essence of Dr. Marin as it wove through Elias's mind: the sound of her laughter, the intensity in her eyes as she worked, the cadence of her voice as they debated theories late into the night. Each fragment pulled Luna deeper, drawing her to the faint echo of the woman who had vanished.

"She's still here," Luna murmured, her voice distant, as though carried from another plane. "Her essence is faint, but strong enough to follow." Her brow furrowed slightly as the threads grew sharper, more distinct. "I see her... near towering pines and granite cliffs, a cabin hidden deep in the forest." Her voice strengthened, certainty blooming within her. "She's near Yosemite. Northwest of the valley."

Ezra leaned forward, urgency lighting his face. "Can you pinpoint it?" He said as he unrolled the map again.

Luna's eyes fluttered open, and the room seemed to hold its breath. The shimmer in her irises intensified, alive with the undeniable pulse of the universe, like stardust swirling in the depths of her gaze. Awe rippled through the room as her glowing eyes seemed to capture the very essence of creation.

Her hand drifted to the map spread back across the table. Her fingers hovered over California, moving slowly and deliberately, guided by an unseen force. She stopped just north of Yosemite National Park, tapping a spot near the end of a secluded unnamed road.

"Here," she said, her voice resolute, the light in her eyes softening as she returned to the present. "This is where she's hiding."

The room remained silent for a beat, the weight of Luna's revelation settling over them like the final note of a song. Elias stared at her, his disbelief giving way to quiet awe. "You just... saw her?" he asked, his voice barely above a whisper.

Luna nodded. "I don't just see her, Elias. I feel her, as if I were her. She's waiting, whether she knows it or not. Now, it's up to us to find her before Westfield does."

Ezra's jaw tightened as he folded the map. "Then we move quickly. If Westfield's already operating near there, we don't have much time."

"Ezra is right," Luna said, her tone carrying a quiet urgency. "She's not safe. Her energy feels strained, like she's constantly looking over her shoulder. She knows they're closing in. She has evidence, but not what she was looking for. She feels stuck."

Elias nodded, his jaw set with determination. "I'll head out first thing in the morning. She needs to know that she's not alone and that we're on her side."

Luna stepped closer, placing a hand gently on his arm. "You'll feel her fear, her doubt. But don't let it deter you." She paused, her voice dropping to a near whisper, her words carrying the weight of truth. "She's waiting for you, Elias. She just doesn't know it yet."

Elias's eyes searched hers, processing the quiet magic of her eyes and the certainty in her words, the strength in her calm clarity. For a moment, the room felt suspended, the reality of her abilities settling over him like a revelation.

Finally, Elias chuckled softly, the usual composure in his demeanor momentarily shaken. "I see your abilities have grown beyond what I imagined."

Luna's lips curved into a knowing grin as the glow of her eyes settled to their natural beauty. "And I haven't even begun to show you."

Her gaze swept the room, landing on each of them in turn—Ezra, Althea, James, Miriam. "We all have important paths to take," she said, her voice steady but laced with emotion. "We'll soon part ways to follow them, but every step we take will shape the future. Even apart, we will be connected."

The quiet intensity of her words lingered, the group's resolve solidifying in the stillness. Elias placed a reassuring hand on her shoulder, grounding the moment. "We'll walk this path together, no matter where it takes us."

Luna nodded, her heart swelling with determination. The threads of their paths stretched before them, uncertain but bound together by purpose. As they turned their focus to the tasks ahead, Luna felt the quiet hum of possibility thrumming beneath it all. Together, they were weaving a new story—one step at a time.

THIRTY-THREE

BOUND BY LIGHT

T he pale moon hung low on the horizon, its light muted and distant, as though it too carried the burden of the night. The community had settled into a rare and uneasy stillness. Despite the fervor of the day's planning, an undercurrent of urgency hummed beneath the surface, a collective sense that time itself was slipping through their fingers. Luna stood on the porch of her cabin, the chill of the night air brushing against her skin. The forest whispered in hushed tones, the rustle of leaves and the rhythmic chirping of crickets weaving a fragile melody against the silence. It felt delicate, as if the night could shatter under the weight of what lay ahead.

She closed her eyes, her breath steady but heavy, and reached outward—not with her hands, but with the awareness that pulsed through her like a second heartbeat. The energy of the land beneath her feet thrummed in reply, the concealed power of the pyramid resonating deep within her chest. Its rhythm matched her own, a steady cadence that anchored her in the present moment. But as her awareness expanded, she felt it—the fragile threads of possibility stretching out before her, unraveling into the unknown.

At first, the visions came like faint whispers—an intangible shimmer, a shift in the fabric of reality. But then, like the pull of a tide, the threads wove themselves into something vivid, undeniable: a future etched in sorrow.

She saw the land, stripped bare and robbed of its life. The once-lush forests were replaced by industrial wastelands, their skeletal remains standing as grim reminders of what had been. Towering smokestacks clawed at the sky, spewing ash and poison that darkened the air. Their shadows stretched long and sinister, consuming the barren earth beneath them. The hum of relentless machines drowned the silence, silencing the songs of birds, while the rivers choked with sludge ran black as ink.

In the distance, a structure rose, cold and unfeeling. Its sharp angles pierced the horizon like a scar, pulsing faintly with the same energy that had once filled the pyramid. But this was no sacred beacon. It was a desecration—a grotesque mockery of balance and wisdom. The power it wielded no longer flowed with life's harmony but was twisted into chains of dominance and greed.

She observed the faces of those who controlled it—shadowy figures wrapped in opulence, their features gaunt, their eyes void of compassion. The spark of their humanity had been surrendered, dulled by the seductive illusion of convenience offered by their technology. They sat high above the desolation, their wealth growing endlessly as the masses below toiled in despair. The chasm between them widened with every pulse of stolen energy, every choice that fed their hunger for power. The unity that once connected all things had been shattered, its light now dimmed and corrupted.

Her vision shifted again, and she saw herself. Her chest tightened at the sight—her power bound, her voice silenced. Chains of light and shadow wrapped around her, their edges etched with twisted symbols of wisdom turned to weapons. Her arms were heavy, her will stifled, and her heart ached beneath the crushing weight of failure. The cries of the oppressed rang out across the dismal land, their voices sharp and unrelenting, echoing in the hollow chamber of her soul.

"No," she whispered, her voice breaking as she grasped desperately to the thread of her own present reality. Her hands trembled as she anchored herself in the rhythm of the here and now.

The vision was not fixed; it was one path among many—a warning, not a certainty. She clung to that hope, steadying herself as the dark tapestry of despair began to unravel. The brutal weight lifted as the forest returned to her senses.

Luna opened her eyes, the soft glow of moonlight bathing the world in silver. The forest's rustling leaves and swaying trees became a balm, soothing the echoes of the bleak future she had glimpsed. But the sorrow lingered, a faint shadow that would not fade. The path ahead was steep and uncertain, yet a quiet strength rose within her. The future was not fixed. The threads of fate could be rewoven.

"This is only a shadow of what could be," she murmured. "And I will not let it come to pass."

The hum of the pyramid's energy beneath her feet seemed to echo her heartbeat, a steady rhythm that acknowledged her vow. She turned her gaze toward the sleeping community—their trust in her a beacon of hope against the darkness she had seen.

With one last glance at the stars, Luna stepped back into her cabin, her spirit burning with quiet intensity. The journey ahead would test her in ways she could not yet imagine, but she would not falter. She pressed her hand against the rough wooden door, whispered into the stillness, "We will not let the light be extinguished," and stepped inside.

The cabin was silent, but her thoughts were not. The choices they made now would ripple outward, shaping the world for generations.

Luna crossed to the small wooden box on her table and lifted the lid, revealing a collection of quartz crystals nestled within. Their facets shimmered in the soft glow of the cabin, like whispers of the earth's ancient heart—a quiet promise of purpose yet to come.

She ran her fingers lightly over the stones, their smooth, cool surfaces sending a faint tingling sensation up her fingertips. Each crystal seemed to hum softly under her touch, a resonance that matched the pulse of the land beneath her feet. Guided by instinct, she selected the clearest, most vibrant stones, those whose energies sang brightest in the quiet harmony of the moment. The subtle vibrations of the crystals intertwined, creating an invisible symphony that filled the room with anticipation.

Luna knelt on the floor, arranging the chosen stones in a perfect circle before her. Sitting cross-legged, she placed her hands gently on her knees and closed her eyes, drawing a deep, steady breath. The hum of the pyramid's concealed energy surged faintly beneath the land, rising to meet her awareness like a steady drumbeat, guiding her into the rhythm of the universe.

Her hands hovered over the crystals, palms open, as the connection deepened. A gentle warmth radiated from the stones, not merely heat but an ancient resonance—alive, aware, waiting. Luna's breath slowed, each exhale a thread of her energy, weaving into the fabric of the crystals. Her mind's eye opened wide, revealing the hidden stories held within them.

Visions bloomed before her—worlds born in fire and shadow. Some crystals had risen from the depths of molten earth, forged in volcanic heat and cooled over ages, their essence shaped by the heart of the planet. Others grew quietly in deep caverns, nurtured by the slow dance of mineral-laden waters. They glowed in her vision like stars beneath the surface of the earth, an ancient constellation woven into the stone veins of Arkansas.

They remember, she thought, a reverence filling her. *They remember the first light, the first breath of the world.*

With every breath, Luna entwined her essence with theirs, threading light and intention into the crystalline core of each stone. It was no longer just a connection—it was a merging, a cosmic entanglement that transcended time and space. The crystals pulsed softly, their light deepening, glowing in harmony with the rhythm of her heartbeat.

In the stillness, the ley lines of the earth revealed themselves—rivers of luminous energy stretching across the land, vast and eternal. The crystals became anchors in this sacred web, their purpose clear: to guide, to protect, to connect.

Her voice broke the silence, soft yet resonant, each word a ripple across the aether. "May these crystals carry our light, guiding each of you through shadow and storm. Let them speak the truth of our intent and protect the purity of our mission."

The air thickened, shimmering like a veil between worlds. The walls of the cabin seemed to hum in harmony, amplifying her intent. Threads of light rose from the circle of crystals, weaving intricate patterns in the air—constellations forming and reforming in a cosmic dance. The energy pulsed brighter, filling the space with sacred intensity, before gently settling into a steady, quiet glow.

Luna withdrew her hands slowly, her eyes glowing softly in the dim light. The crystals' light dimmed but did not disappear. Their bond was complete, their connection unbreakable—a promise whispered through stone and time, born of the earth's own heart.

One by one, she picked up each stone, holding it close to her chest. She closed her eyes briefly with each crystal, whispering her gratitude before placing it gently into a small leather pouch. These were more than tools—they were pieces of her intent, fractals of her will, bound to the people she trusted most. In their hands, the crystals would serve as beacons of connection, reminders of the light they carried within.

The pouch now rested in her lap, warm with the energy of the stones it held. Luna ran her fingers lightly over the leather, a soft smile forming on her lips. "The threads are woven," she murmured to herself. "Even if the path divides, we'll remain bound to the same purpose."

The next morning, as the sun's first rays crept over the horizon, Luna gathered James, Althea, Ezra, Elias, Miriam, her father, and Eleanor in the gathering hall. The soft light filtered through the windows, illuminating their faces with a golden glow that seemed almost otherworldly. Each stood in silence, their expressions a mixture of curiosity and reverence as Luna stepped forward, holding a small pouch in her hands.

"I have a gift for each of you.... Some crystals for the journey ahead," she began, her voice soft but steady, "they carry more than hope. They carry a piece of us—threads of entangled connection that will span the distance. They are a reminder of who we are, what we're fighting for, and the light we carry within."

Luna opened the pouch and withdrew the first crystal, its facets catching the light in a delicate prism of color. She approached James, his rugged features etched with quiet strength. Placing the crystal into his weathered hand, she held his gaze. "For guidance and resilience," she said, her tone imbued with gratitude. "You are as strong and steadfast as this crystal, James. No matter where this journey takes you, trust in your strength to guide you—and all of us—back home."

James's hand closed around the crystal, his throat working as he swallowed hard. "I'll do my best, Luna," he murmured, his voice low but resolute.

Next, Luna turned to Althea, whose calm presence radiated like a soothing balm against the tension in the room. The crystal Luna handed her shimmered with a soft lavender light, its energy a perfect reflection of Althea's serene wisdom. "For clarity and wisdom," Luna said, her voice gentle but unwavering. "You've been my guide through the chaos, reminding me to breathe, to trust, and to let go. You'll bring that same light to others, Althea, illuminating their path when they need it most."

Althea smiled softly, her hand closing over the crystal as if cradling a delicate flame. "I'll carry it with love," she whispered.

When Luna reached Ezra, her heart tightened, the unspoken bond between them heavy in the air. She held his hand for a moment longer than the others, her voice lowering as she placed the crystal in his palm. "For infinite love that transcends time and space. This crystal will bring you back to me, should we ever part." Her voice wavered slightly, but she steadied herself. "You've been my anchor, Ezra. My steady ground when everything else felt uncertain. Hold onto the endless courage within—not just for me, but for yourself."

Ezra's jaw tightened, and his eyes glistened as he fought the tide of emotion rising within him. "I'll keep you close," he said softly, his voice thick. "Always."

Luna turned to Miriam, the quiet yet unwavering force within their community. Placing the crystal gently in her hands, Luna said, "For your steady heart and unwavering belief in what we are building. You've held this community together in ways that most cannot see. While I am away, keep this place safe, Miriam. You are its guardian now."

Miriam's lips curved into a small, grateful smile. "We're stronger together," she said simply. "I'll protect it, Luna—until you return."

Her father was next, his weathered face lined with years of wisdom and quiet strength. The weight of their shared journey lingered in the space between them as Luna placed the crystal into his hands. "For the will to endure and the strength to carry on," she said, her voice soft but steady. "You were the first seed of will that brought me into this world, setting me on this path. Your presence is woven into every step of my journey. This bond we share will be our compass, grounding us when the path becomes uncertain."

His large hands closed over the crystal, and his voice, a quiet rumble, broke the silence. "And I'll hold this with pride, knowing you've become all you were meant to be."

When Luna faced Eleanor, the room seemed to hold its breath. The once-skeptical leader stood with quiet resolve, her gaze meeting Luna's without hesitation. Luna placed the crystal gently into her hands, her voice firm yet compassionate. "For leadership and devotion. You've given so much of yourself to this community, guiding and protecting it with unwavering strength. Your dedication has laid the foundation for what is to come. Now, your wisdom and balance will help lead us into the future."

Eleanor stared at the crystal for a moment, the weight of Luna's words settling over her. Her lips pressed into a thin line, but her eyes softened. "I've been cautious, even skeptical of all this," she admitted, her voice steady and sincere. "But I see it now. I see the importance of what's happening—of what you're doing. My doubts were misplaced." She lifted her gaze to meet Luna's again. "You have my full support, Luna. I'll stand beside you and fight for this balance, for Everwood, and for all of us."

Finally, Luna stood before Elias, the historian whose life had been dedicated to finding the truth of the past. His usually composed demeanor softened as she placed a crystal into his hands. "For the strength to teach and inspire," she said, her voice warm with quiet reverence. "You've carried the stories of those who came before us, and now you stand at the threshold of creating your own. You are more than a keeper of history, Elias. You are the maker of it."

Elias's lips quirked into a faint, wry smile. "I'll try not to disappoint the future historians," he said lightly, though his tone carried the weight of his gratitude.

As Luna stepped back, her breath slowed, and she opened her heart fully, allowing her essence to envelop the group. A warm surge of energy rose from her chest, radiating outward like a wave of light. Her eyes glowed bright, their emerald brilliance with an intensity that seemed to pulse in harmony with her breath. The crystals in their hands responded, their facets shimmering with the same vibrant green light, threads of connection weaving through each of them.

Luna's gaze swept over the group, her heart heavy with the weight of the unknown yet lifted by the quiet strength of their unity. The connection was undeniable—a bond that transcended words, formed in the heart of the earth itself and carried forward by their collective will.

"These crystals are more than tools," she said, her voice steady, resonant, charged with meaning. "They are a promise—a connection that will guide us through whatever lies ahead. No matter the distance, no matter the challenge, these crystals will carry our light and remind us of who we are."

The room fell into a deep, contemplative silence as her words settled over them. The glow of the crystals intensified briefly, illuminating their faces with sacred light—a quiet affirmation of their shared purpose and the ancient power flowing through them.

Then, slowly, the emerald glow began to fade. The brilliance in Luna's eyes dimmed, returning to their familiar hue, while the crystals settled into their natural, quiet radiance. Yet the connection remained, woven into the very air around them—strong, enduring, unbreakable.

As the moment stretched, Luna felt the shadow of her vision lingering at the edge of her mind—a world twisted by imbalance and greed. But as she looked into the faces of her companions, she held tightly to the hope burning in her chest. The future was not yet written, and as long as they stood together, the threads of possibility could still be rewoven.

"Remember," she said, her voice firm and clear, "we carry each other, always."

The room exhaled as one, a collective breath releasing the tension of the moment. But unspoken truths lingered in the air: the knowledge that some paths would be fraught with loss, and the journey ahead would test the very core of their unity.

THIRTY-FOUR

THE ROAD UNFOLDS

The morning sky was painted in soft hues of gold and lavender as the sanctuary stirred to life. James' old pickup truck rumbled to life, its engine coughing before settling into a steady hum. Althea climbed into the passenger seat, her movements deliberate and graceful, her gaze lingering on the retreating outlines of the sanctuary in the rearview mirror.

Nearby, Elias secured the last of his bags in the back seat of his silver SUV, its metallic paint catching the morning light. He turned to Ezra, offering a grateful nod. "Thanks for the couch last night—it was more comfortable than I expected."

Ezra gave a small grin and clapped him on the back. "Anytime."

Luna stood with Elias for a moment longer, her hand resting lightly on his arm.

"Stay safe, Elias," she said softly, her voice carrying both warmth and gravity. "And trust your instincts. They'll guide you to her."

Elias gave her a crooked smile, eyes crinkling with mischief. "You mean the same instincts that had me circling the map like a lost tourist until you pointed me in the right direction?" He chuckled, pulling open the door of the SUV. "Don't worry—I'll trust my instincts and cross-check your coordinates."

His expression softened for a moment, his hand resting on the door-frame. "But really, thank you—for everything, Luna."

Luna stepped back, watching Elias's SUV roll down the dirt path until the trees began to swallow it from view. A thin trail of dust lingered in his wake, shimmering in the morning light.

Behind her, James and Althea sat in the old truck, the engine ticking softly as it warmed—a quiet signal that they were ready when she was. Luna moved to the driver's side and leaned into the open window.

"Keep an eye on each other," she said, her tone firm yet affectionate. "The two of you are going to be an incredible team out there."

James nodded, his hand briefly squeezing hers. "We'll check in as soon as we can."

Althea offered a serene smile. "We'll keep the light steady."

Luna stepped back once more, shielding her eyes as the truck pulled out, its tires rolling over the same rutted path Elias had taken. The two vehicles disappeared one after the other, their shared dust cloud slowly settling over the road like a fading signature.

Everwood fell silent again, the clearing bathed in golden stillness. Though they were heading into different missions, they all carried the same flame—and Luna could feel its warmth long after the engines had faded.

The cab smelled faintly of leather and motor oil, a grounding scent that suited James' no-nonsense nature. He tugged at the brim of his worn baseball cap, adjusting it with a practiced motion as they bumped along the narrow dirt road toward the highway.

For a while, neither of them spoke, the rhythmic crunch of tires on gravel filling the silence. Althea glanced at James, his profile set against the early morning light. His rough exterior—calloused hands, sun-worn skin, and a perpetual furrow in his brow—told the story of a man who had spent a lifetime in tune with the land. Yet there was a softness in his eyes, a depth that spoke of unspoken loss and a quiet resilience.

"You've been quiet," Althea said gently, her voice carrying the warmth of a soft breeze. "Do you regret taking on this journey?"

James chuckled low, shaking his head. "Regret? No. I don't regret much in life, Althea. Not anymore. But this...this feels different." He glanced at her briefly before returning his focus to the winding road ahead. "Feels like we're standing on the edge of something bigger than us. Can't say I'm not a little uneasy about it."

Althea nodded, her hands resting lightly in her lap. "The unknown has a way of unsettling even the strongest souls," she said, her tone calm. "But it also holds the greatest potential for growth. That's why we're here, isn't it? To face the unknown and bring light where there's shadow?"

James grunted in agreement, a small smile tugging at the corners of his mouth. "You've got a way with words, don't you?"

Althea chuckled softly, her laughter like the gentle rustle of leaves. "Years of practice. When you've guided as many souls as I have, you learn to find the right words."

"And who guides you?" James asked, his tone curious but not intrusive.

Her smile softened, her gaze turning inward. "The same force that guides us all, if we let it. The universe has a way of nudging us in the right direction, even when we don't understand it."

James nodded thoughtfully, his grip on the steering wheel tightening as they turned onto the highway. "Reckon that's why Luna trusts you the way she does."

"She trusts us both," Althea replied. "She sees the strength in you, James. Your connection to the earth, your loyalty to the people you care about. That's not something to take lightly."

The conversation lulled as the miles slipped by, the scenery shifting from dense forest to open plains. The truck's engine hummed steadily, a comforting backdrop to their shared silence. James glanced at Althea, the rising morning light catching the silver strands threaded through her dark hair, giving her an almost ethereal glow. She seemed calm—centered—but he knew the weight of their mission rested just as heavily on her shoulders as it did on his.

"You know," James said after a while, his voice tinged with humor, "this isn't exactly what I pictured for my retirement. Driving halfway across the country, chasing down energy lines and ancient secrets."

Althea smiled, her eyes glinting with quiet amusement. "And what did you picture? A rocking chair on a porch, watching the world go by?"

"Something like that," he admitted, a grin tugging at his lips. "But if I'm being honest, I think I'd get bored after a week. This... this feels like living."

They shared a laugh, the tension easing between them as the truck ate up the miles. The sun climbed higher, bathing the landscape in golden light. As they made their way northwest, the air grew cooler, the scent of pine mingling with the earthy aroma of damp soil.

Althea reached into her bag and pulled out a small thermos. "Tea?" she offered, pouring some into a tin cup she'd brought along.

James accepted it with a nod, taking a cautious sip. "Not bad," he said, though his expression suggested it wasn't exactly what he was used to.

"It's calming," Althea said with a knowing smile. "We'll need calm where we're headed."

James leaned back, his gaze fixed on the road ahead. "Think we'll find what we're looking for in Oregon?"

Althea's eyes drifted to the horizon, her expression serene but contemplative. "The land holds its own wisdom. It'll guide us to who and what we're meant to find."

James nodded, his heart steadying with her words. Despite the uncertainty of their journey, he felt a growing sense of trust in the woman beside him. They were different, yet their strengths complemented each other in ways that felt deeply aligned.

As the truck climbed a winding mountain road, the scenery became more rugged, the trees towering like slumbering titans. James turned the radio dial, landing on a station playing an old blues tune. The music filled the cab, mingling with the steady hum of the engine and the soft rustle of wind through the open windows.

James tapped the steering wheel in rhythm with the song, his eyes scanning the road ahead. "We'll need to find a spot to rest tonight," he said, his tone light but practical. "I can keep driving, but if you'd rather not sleep under the stars, we should figure out where to stop before it gets too late."

Althea smiled faintly, her eyes fixed on the horizon. "I'm not picky," she said. "A roof is nice, but the stars have their own kind of comfort."

James nodded, his grin tugging at the corner of his mouth. "Fair enough. Let's play it by ear and see what the road gives us."

For the first time in a long while, James felt a sense of purpose and belonging—a quiet reassurance that whatever lay ahead, they would face it together.

THIRTY-FIVE

A SHROUDED CONNECTION

T he golden afternoon sun filtered through the trees, casting dappled patterns of light on the ground as Luna worked alongside the community members. They moved with quiet purpose, gathering branches, moss, and stones to create a natural camouflage for the pyramid's entrance. Nearby, others arranged tarps painted in earthy tones, ensuring the entrance would blend seamlessly with the forest. Quiet conversation murmured through the group, but an undercurrent of solemnity lingered—this task wasn't just about concealment; it was about safeguarding something sacred.

The need for this precaution weighed heavily on Luna. The pyramid's presence was more than physical—it carried an energy that could be felt by those attuned to it. And if Westfield had come this far in their search, she knew it was only a matter of time before they would locate it. Earlier glimpses of possibility had shown her the destruction that could unfold if the pyramid fell into the wrong hands. Now, as she knelt before its entrance, the urgency of their work settled like a stone in her chest.

Luna brushed her hands over the cool surface of the stone, her fingertips tingling with the energy coursing through it. She whispered an incantation, her voice soft but steady, as threads of shimmering energy wove themselves into the structure. The lattice of light pulsed faintly, forming a protective barrier that felt both ancient and alive. The pyramid's steady heartbeat resonated beneath her hands, its rhythm mirroring her own, a reminder of the bond she shared with it.

For a moment, the connection comforted her. But as her work pressed on, a quiet worry gnawed at the edges of her thoughts. The energy she had woven would shield the pyramid from detection—for now. But would it be enough? Luna's visions of the future had shown her the lengths Westfield would go to, and the thought of the pyramid in their hands sent a cold wave through her.

"This isn't just concealment," she murmured to herself, her voice barely audible over the soft rustle of leaves. "It's a promise to protect what can't be replaced."

A subtle voice interrupted her focus. "Luna," Miriam called gently, stepping closer. "Is it safe to go inside? Some of us are curious... we feel drawn to it."

Luna paused, her hand still resting on the cool stone. The question sent a ripple of unease through her. She could feel the growing curiosity within the community—the magnetic pull of the unknown, the allure of the wisdom hidden beneath Pyramid Hill. Yet, with each presence inside, the energy would shift and build, like ripples growing into waves, a potential beacon for unwanted attention.

Her thoughts spiraled momentarily, but a steady, familiar resonance grounded her. "Trust them to trust themselves, Luna," her higher self whispered, the words carrying a gentle reminder that echoed through her spirit.

Luna turned to face Miriam and the others who had gathered nearby. Her voice was calm but carried an undercurrent of gravity. "The structure is strong, sound. You won't be trapped, if that's your concern. But entering the pyramid is not something to take lightly. It's a choice that must be guided by the pull of your own spirit. Only those who feel its call—who seek its wisdom with pure intent—should venture beyond the entrance."

Her words settled over the group like the quiet rustle of leaves in an autumn stillness. Some nodded thoughtfully; others exchanged uncertain glances.

"Thank you, Luna," Miriam said softly, her steady voice holding the weight of understanding. "We'll be mindful."

Luna's gaze softened as she met Miriam's eyes. "Please," she added, her tone shifting slightly, "watch over it. If you sense something is wrong—if the energy changes—no one else should enter until I return."

Miriam nodded with quiet assurance. "I will."

As the group lingered, their curiosity unspoken but palpable, Luna's attention shifted to the edge of the clearing. Standing slightly apart from the others was young Stephen, his wide, thoughtful eyes fixed on her. His father, Joseph, stood a few paces behind him, arms crossed, his face a mixture of pride and quiet apprehension.

Stephen stepped forward, his small frame brimming with a curious strength. His voice was clear, tinged with both wonder and hesitation.

"Luna... even me? Can I go inside?"

Luna felt her breath catch as she looked at him. His energy radiated in her mind's eye, bright and untamed, pulsing with a resonance that called to the pyramid like a forgotten melody searching for its next note.

But there was something else.

For a moment—just a moment—time shimmered around him. The air grew still. The forest hushed. And in the silence between his words, Luna felt a ripple move through her—not from the boy in front of her, but from something that stood behind him, or within him.

An echo.

Four pulses. Like a rhythm she couldn't place but had always known.

Her gaze flicked to Joseph, silently asking for his trust. He studied her for a moment, then exhaled, his posture easing. A small nod. He understood.

Luna knelt to Stephen's level, her voice warm but steady. "Yes, Stephen. One day soon. But not alone." She placed a gentle hand over his. "I will go with you when the time is right."

His brow furrowed, his fingers twitching with the urge to act now, to move forward without hesitation. "But I feel it," he whispered. "Like it's calling me."

She nodded, her throat tightening. "It is. And it always will be. But even the brightest stars must wait for the right moment to rise."

Again, she felt it—that fourfold pulse. A quiet resonance in her chest. Her breath caught in her throat. She didn't understand it, not fully, but it brushed against the deepest parts of her knowing.

Not yet, she thought. But soon.

"Greatness lives within you, Stephen," she said softly, the words arriving unbidden, as if spoken through her. "And when the time is right, the world will quiver in recognition."

She reached into her pocket, drawing out the amethyst crystal Althea had given her. It was warm against her palm, thrumming with a quiet pulse, still carrying the resonance of the pyramid's energy.

She placed it in his hand, curling his small fingers around it. "Take this," she said. "It holds a part of what waits inside. Let it guide you. When you are ready, I will walk that path with you."

Stephen stared at the crystal, eyes wide with reverence. He clutched it tightly to his chest, holding it as though it might slip away. When he looked back at her, his expression was no longer just that of a child's—it was something deeper, something knowing.

"I'll wait," he promised, his voice steady with quiet conviction. "And I'll be ready."

Luna smiled, her heart swelling with hope and the quiet certainty of his path. "I know you will. You have a light within you, Stephen—a light that will not only guide you but all of us, when the time comes."

Stephen nodded solemnly, his expression filled with wonder, as though he already understood the significance of what lay ahead. Joseph stepped forward then, placing a steadying hand on his son's shoulder. His trust in Luna was unspoken but unshakable.

As Luna rose, she couldn't help but feel that this moment was the start of something much larger—a seed planted in fertile soil, waiting for its time to grow.

The moment felt suspended in time, a quiet yet profound affirmation of the future they were building together. As Stephen turned to his father, clutching his crystal tightly, Luna felt a flicker of the world they were fighting for—a future where the next generation, awakened and guided by wisdom, would carry their mission forward, a collective consciousness to change and heal the planet in its time of need.

The sun dipped lower in the sky, casting a golden glow over the clearing. The work of concealment continued, but within the hearts of those present, a deeper understanding took root. The path ahead was fraught with uncertainty, but moments like these—moments of connection, trust, and shared purpose—carried the promise of a brighter tomorrow.

Luna rose, her eyes briefly meeting Ezra's across the clearing. She could feel the shared weight of their responsibility, but also the quiet resolve growing within their community. Together, they would face whatever lay ahead. And with each step, they would ensure that the light of hope and unity burned brighter than ever.

THIRTY-SIX

THE CALM BETWEEN BOLTS

T he night pressed heavily against the walls of Luna's cabin, an oppressive silence settling over the world beyond. The usual symphony of crickets had vanished, and the air hung still, as if the land itself were holding its breath. Luna could feel the shift—the protective work she had woven around the pyramid had dampened its energy, obscuring its presence from the outside world. But the ripple of that act extended further, dulling the lifeblood of the forest that had thrived in its glow. The stillness gnawed at her, a quiet reminder of the cost. Yet she held firm, reassuring herself of the necessity of her actions, even as a faint unease lingered at the edges of her thoughts.

Inside, the soft flicker of a lantern cast long, wavering shadows across the wooden beams as she and Ezra packed for their journey. Every item placed into their bags carried intention—tools, provisions, and Luna's journal, its pages brimming with symbols and insights from the pyramid. The weight of the journal felt heavier than ever in her hands, as though the wisdom it contained was pressing against her, urging her to remember what was at stake.

They worked quickly, their hands moving in rhythm as they prepared for what lay ahead. Supplies were neatly packed, plans quietly finalized. The weight of the coming day pressed heavily on their minds. Exhaustion crept in, eventually pulling them into a deep, dreamless sleep. The cabin, cocooned in stillness, seemed at peace under the night sky.

But just past midnight, Luna's eyes snapped open.

The room trembled with a low, resonant rumble, the sound crawling up from the earth and vibrating through her chest. This wasn't thunder. It was deeper, sharper, and deliberate. A ripple of awareness shot through her, pulling her upright. Something unnatural stirred outside—a storm alive with intent.

She threw off the blankets, her feet meeting the cold floor with purpose as she rushed to the door. Her breath was fast, her pulse racing like the storm had reached into her and shaken her awake.

"Luna?" Ezra stirred, his voice thick with sleep. He sat up quickly, his instincts pricking at her urgency. "What's wrong?"

She didn't answer. She flung the door open, and the storm howled to life, roaring into the cabin like a living beast. Sheets of rain slashed at the earth, and the wind screamed as lightning fractured the sky in violent streaks. The air was electric, heavy with a palpable charge that sent shivers through her skin.

Ezra scrambled for his boots, pulling them on as he followed her onto the porch. "Luna!" he shouted over the storm's fury, his voice barely cutting through the chaos. "What is this?"

Luna stood motionless, her hair whipping wildly around her face, rain soaking her to the skin. Her eyes narrowed as she stared into the roiling stormfront, her senses tuned to its charged energy. This wasn't chaos—it pulsed with intention, its rhythm calculated and unnervingly alive. She could feel its cadence, like an unnatural heartbeat thrumming against the earth.

"This isn't a normal storm," she murmured, her voice steady despite the chaos around her. "I can feel it. It's them. It's Westfield."

Ezra's jaw clenched as he moved beside her, shielding his face from the lashing rain. "Are you sure?"

Luna raised her hands slowly, palms open to the storm as if catching its chaotic energy. Her breath steadied, and her eyes fluttered shut, the world around her dissolving into raw sensation. Rain lashed her skin, its rhythm merging with the storm's pulse. Each crack of thunder was a heartbeat, each flash of lightning a jagged thread of intent woven into the fabric of the tempest. She extended her awareness, threading through the currents of wind and rain, tracing their chaotic dance back to its source.

The physical world faded, replaced by a vast, shimmering web of energy. Pulses of light traveled along unseen pathways, guiding her deeper into the storm's memory. She followed the vibrations, feeling the storm's essence unravel beneath her touch, revealing its history.

"This storm isn't natural," she whispered, her voice distant and hollow, her mind far from the present. "It's crafted—built to disrupt, to test."

In her mind's eye, the storm's threads led her far beyond the horizon to towering structures bristling with antennas, each one crackling with stolen energy from the sky. Beneath the cold hum of fluorescent light, engineers moved with frantic precision in an industrial labyrinth, monitoring the storm's progress on glowing consoles. Data streams reflected in their eyes as they adjusted dials, their intent focused yet fraying at the edges.

She saw the machines—the generators manipulating the atmosphere, whipping the wind into a frenzy, bending nature to their will. It had started as a controlled experiment, but the balance had tipped. When the storm crossed the veil of energy Luna had cast around the Pyramid, something shifted. The currents warped. The system destabilized. What they had built with cold precision now roared with untethered fury, no longer responding to command. The storm had slipped their grasp, its energy spiraling into chaos—*and someone had noticed.*

Her senses snapped back, the storm's history burning in her mind like an echo that refused to fade.

"How can this be? They're searching," she said, her voice sharpened by understanding. "They're testing capabilities... *my capabilities?* They want to see how far they can push—see if someone can stop it."

Ezra's expression darkened, his eyes scanning the churning skies. "Can you stop it?"

Luna nodded, her jaw tightening as she weighed the choice. "I think I could stop it," she said, her voice low. "But if I do, I reveal myself to them. If I don't... the storm will run its course, burning itself out. They've lost control of it now. It's dangerous—someone could get hurt."

Her eyes flicked to Ezra, emerald and fierce, shadows of worry lurking beneath the determination.

Her head snapped back to the sky. A searing bolt of lightning split the clouds, striking not more than a hundred feet away in the heart of the community. The ground shuddered beneath them, the air thick with ozone and raw power. Luna didn't flinch. Her glowing eyes tracked the bolt's path with precision, her entire being locked into the storm's energy. She knew exactly where it would strike—knew no one would be harmed.

The lightning's radiant reflection danced across her face, giving her an otherworldly beauty, fierce and unyielding. "Such power," she said, her voice low and steady, "and they use it to tear at the fabric of nature. To dominate what they don't understand."

Ezra, on the other hand, instinctively recoiled, his pulse spiking at the close call. His eyes darted toward the still-smoldering ground, then back to Luna, his heart pounding in his chest. "Luna," he urged, stepping closer, his voice tight with concern. "Come inside. This storm... it's too dangerous."

But Luna's gaze remained locked on the storm above, her expression calm, almost serene. The glow in her eyes softened, and the wild threads of power she had been holding began to dissipate into the wind.

Ezra placed a steadying hand on her arm, his touch grounding her. "Let it pass. Don't give them what they want. The safest thing anyone can do is get inside." He said, hinting for her to come back in.

Luna exhaled, her body relaxing as she let the last tendrils of the storm's energy slip from her awareness. She nodded, the tension in her shoulders easing. "You're right, Ezra. It'll pass," she said softly.

Closing her eyes once more, her senses brushed against the storm's threads one last time. She felt its energy pulsing wildly—unstable, chaotic, and waning. With a deep breath, she released her focus, letting the storm's erratic rhythm fade into the distance.

Turning back toward the cabin, the rain still lashed at her, but her voice cut through the storm with quiet strength. "We'll help with any cleanup in the community before we go. But this is our signal. We need to move forward, or they will come to us."

Ezra met her gaze, the weight of the storm reflected in his eyes. "Then we move at first light," he said firmly. "The next step starts tomorrow."

Together, they stepped back into the cabin, the storm's roar echoing in their ears as the door shut behind them. Outside, the maelstrom raged on, its fury stretching into the night, but inside, the next step of their journey was already unfolding.

Inside the cabin, the storm's growls were muted, its ferocity reduced to a distant echo. Yet its energy lingered in the air, crackling faintly, like an unspent charge. Luna shed her soaked clothes, her movements deliberate but heavy, the weight of the night pressing against her shoulders. Wrapping herself in a towel, she sat on the edge of the bed, her damp hair clinging to her flushed skin. Her breaths came unevenly, the storm's chaos still echoing in her chest.

Ezra moved quietly nearby, wringing out his soaked shirt and draping it over the back of a chair. His gaze drifted to Luna, and for a moment, he simply watched her, his expression a mixture of concern and quiet admiration. The soft flicker of lantern light danced across the room, accentuating the vulnerability etched into her posture and the strength that had carried her through the storm.

"You scared me out there," Ezra said finally, his voice low and rough with emotion. He stepped toward her, the floor creaking faintly beneath his weight. "The way you stood in that storm... like it couldn't touch you. Like you were part of it."

Luna lifted her gaze, a thoughtful smile touching her lips. "For a moment, I was," she murmured. "The storm and I... we were the same. Its chaos, its power—it's all connected." Her voice dropped to a whisper, almost reverent. "It felt so alive. There is such beauty in the chaos. Every surge of electricity felt like it was part of me, charging through the air, weaving everything together."

Her breath grew heavier as she recalled the rush, the moment she merged with the bolt of lightning, striking the ground as one with it.

Ezra knelt before her, his hands brushing lightly over hers. The warmth of his touch cut through the lingering chill of the storm, grounding her in the here and now. "I can't imagine what that feels like," he said, his voice steady, filled with awe. "But I can see it in you. You're still carrying its energy. It's like it's part of you now."

His hand traced the length of her forearm, his touch gentle yet deliberate. Luna's breath hitched, a thrill rushing through her body like a spark dancing across her skin.

"Is it that obvious?" she murmured, her voice soft and trembling, charged with both vulnerability and exhilaration.

Ezra's gaze dropped to her lips, his breath warm against her skin. The air between them seemed to hum with electricity. Slowly, tentatively, Luna tilted her head, her lips hovering just above his—a silent question, a whispered promise.

Ezra closed the distance, his kiss soft at first, almost careful, but it deepened with every second. The taste of rain lingered on her lips, mingling with something unspoken, something ancient and powerful. His hands cupped her face, his touch tender yet certain, as though grounding her not just to the moment, but to him.

Luna's hands found their way to Ezra's bare shoulders, his skin warm and firm beneath her fingertips. His body radiated heat, a stark contrast to the cool air that lingered from the storm. She traced the curve of his shoulder, feeling the quiet strength that had carried her through moments of doubt and fear. But now, there was something more—something raw and untamed. A heat, a passion that surged like a flame, burning away every shadow that clung to her thoughts.

Ezra inhaled sharply as her touch lingered. His hands slipped down to her waist, steady and deliberate, pulling her closer until their bodies melded in perfect alignment. Her legs draped over his, locking them into a slow, unspoken dance of trust and desire.

Their kiss deepened, the air around them thick with warmth and electricity. Their breaths mingled in the small space between them, each exhale charged with an intensity neither could deny. The storm's chill melted beneath the fire of their connection, replaced by a current far more potent.

Ezra's fingers brushed along her spine, his touch sending shivers through her. His lips moved against hers with growing urgency, yet every movement remained grounded in reverence—as if he were afraid this moment might slip away like a fleeting dream.

Luna pressed herself closer, her fingers tangling in his damp hair, holding him in place. The world outside ceased to exist, the weight of their mission fading into nothingness. All that remained was this: the undeniable truth of their bond—a love forged through trials, trust, and the unyielding promise to face whatever lay ahead, together.

When they finally parted, their foreheads rested gently against each other, their breath coming in ragged harmony. Ezra's voice, low and rough with emotion, rumbled between them. "I'll follow you anywhere, Luna."

Luna's lips curved into a radiant smile, her eyes glowing with an inner light. "And I'll never stop leading us toward the light," she whispered, her voice a vow wrapped in warmth.

The storm outside had passed, leaving only the soft patter of rain against the cabin roof. But within their quiet embrace, a new kind of energy swirled—fierce, steady, and unyielding. It wasn't born of chaos, but of love, trust, and the promise of a future they would build together.

THIRTY-SEVEN

THE GRAVITY OF INTENTION

T he first light of dawn crept over the foothills, bathing the landscape in soft hues of gold and amber. The storm had cleared, leaving the air crisp and filled with the scent of wet earth and pine. Luna stood by the cabin window, her gaze lingering on the shimmering drops of rain that clung to the glass. She couldn't help the small, secretive smile that played on her lips, her heart carrying a quiet warmth that lingered from the night before.

Ezra emerged from the small kitchen, handing her a steaming cup of herbal tea. "That's quite a smile you have," he remarked, his tone teasing but gentle. "Care to share the secret?"

Luna glanced at him over the rim of her cup, her smile deepening. "Perhaps, there is a secret," she replied, her voice light and enigmatic. "Or perhaps it's just a good morning."

Ezra chuckled, pulling on his jacket as he stepped closer. "Well, whatever it is, I'll take it. That smile is infectious. Come, we've got a bit of work to do before we head out."

The two of them stepped outside, the world glistening in the aftermath of the storm. The community had already begun to stir, with small groups gathering to assess damage. Luna and Ezra made their way down the main pathway, greeting neighbors as they passed.

Stephen and Joseph stood near the gathering hall, the boy enthusiastically recounting how the storm sounded like a giant roaring beast. Luna ruffled his hair as they continued on, her heart swelling with affection for the boy's unyielding spirit.

The golden morning sunlight filtered softly through the canopy, casting dappled patterns on the forest floor as Luna and Ezra approached the edge of the community. There, sprawled across the roadway, lay a massive tree, its roots twisted and gnarled as though wrenched from the earth in protest. A group of community members gathered around it, their voices low, a mixture of frustration and determination rippling through the air as they debated how to move such a colossal obstacle.

Ezra surveyed the scene with practiced focus, rolling up his sleeves. "Well, looks like we've got some heavy lifting to do," he said, stepping forward.

Luna hung back, her gaze fixed on the fallen giant. Its immense trunk sprawled across the narrow road, defiant and immovable, like a sleeping beast too large to stir. Yet something in her awoke—a memory from the earth, when ancient stone had moved not with force, but with intention. The memory didn't feel like hers alone. It came from a deeper well of knowing, as if whispered from beyond time by those who had once walked this land with knowledge modern minds had long forgotten.

She took a step forward. "Wait," she said quietly.

Ezra turned to her, his brow creased. "What is it?"

Luna placed her hand gently on the bark, its surface cool and uneven beneath her fingers. "This isn't about strength or force. It's about cohesion and alignment." She turned to the group. "Everyone, please—step back. Just in case."

A few exchanged glances, hesitating.

"Seriously," she added, her voice firmer now. "Give me some room, I see what must be done, but I don't know how the tree will respond."

Slowly, they backed away, forming a wide semi-circle around the scene. Even little Stephen, who'd been bouncing with nervous energy, moved to his father and took his hand, wide eyes never leaving Luna.

Luna knelt beside the tree, closing her eyes and drawing in a long, steady breath. The world fell away.

A warm pulse beat behind her closed eyelids—a slow, golden rhythm that seemed to rise from the earth itself. The memory became vision: stone monoliths rising into sunlit skies, hands carved symbols into rock that resonated with sound, and minds attuned to the flow of the universe. The ancient ones had known—had remembered—that reality was vibration, and matter only illusion.

A current of knowledge surged through her—not learned, but remembered.

She pressed both palms flat against the trunk. The bark pricked her skin, grounding her. Her awareness sank into the tree, diving past cells and fibers, deep into the atomic sea beneath. She could feel it all now—the chaotic spin of electrons, the constant shimmer of movement where nothing ever touched. The tree vibrated with its own ancient music, deep and slow, like the drone of a didgeridoo echoing through time.

Electrons spun in chaotic rhythm around nuclei, countless microcosmic orbits forming the illusion of solidity. Yet Luna could feel them—those spinning points of energy, each vibrating in its own pattern.

Her consciousness wove through them until she found the tree's center of gravity—its point of balance within the earth's embrace. There, she felt the dissonance, the randomness of atomic spin. Through will alone, she began to impose order—not by force, but by resonance and rhythm.

Her breath slowed. Her hands glowed faintly.

The electrons began to spin in unison, synchronized along a single axis—first in the tree's core, then expanding outward, harmonizing with the surrounding matter. In the earth below, she mirrored the process but reversed the spin, creating magnetic polarity. Through the collective spin, the scale of resistance shifted from the microcosm to the macrocosm of the tree's existence.

A hum, once felt only by Luna, grew louder—audible now. The air around her buzzed faintly, like the charged stillness before a lightning strike. Static danced across her skin. Her hair lifted from her shoulders.

Then it happened.

With a gentle thoom, the tree bounced upward, as if lifted by invisible hands, and hovered waist-high above the road. A collective gasp broke the silence.

"Ohhh wow," Stephen whispered, his eyes wide as saucers. "It's floating..."

Joseph gripped his shoulders protectively, but even he couldn't look away.

Ezra took a slow step forward, eyes locked on the impossible sight. The immense trunk floated, unmoving but untethered, vibrating gently like a held breath.

Luna stood, breath steady, the golden glow fading from her hands. "Now," she said softly, "help me guide it."

Ezra stepped forward and pressed his hands to the trunk. He exhaled sharply—its weight was still there, but it no longer resisted. It moved like a log on water, buoyed by unseen forces.

The others joined, awe still etched across their faces. Together, they guided the massive tree to the side of the road, then they collectively stood back and watched the spectacle before their eyes.

Luna released the resonance gently. As her connection faded, the ordered spin began to dissolve, and the natural chaos of the material world resumed. The hum ebbed into silence. The light faded.

Then—thud.

The tree crashed down with a forceful finality, sending a tremor through the ground that rippled up through their feet. The sound was deep and resonant, like thunder muffled by soil. A flock of nearby birds startled from the trees, wings fluttering into the sky.

Ezra staggered slightly, his eyes wide. "Well... it was floating."

"Until it remembered what gravity was." Luna added.

Stephen tugged at his dad's shirt, practically bouncing. "That was awesome! Did you see that? It floated!"

They stood motionless for a long moment, stunned.

"You did that," Ezra finally said, wonder woven into every word.

Luna flexed her fingers, residual warmth still lingering in her palms. Her gaze drifted to the tree, now resting peacefully beside the road. "It's amazing," she said softly, "what a little will and harmony can do when you stop fighting chaos and start listening to it."

She looked up at the trees around them, the wind just beginning to stir their leaves. "Nature holds so much quiet power... patterns, rhythms, beauty we've forgotten how to see. Sometimes all it takes is remembering how to move with it instead of against it."

Ezra nodded slowly, the weight of her words settling over him like the morning sun. No more questions. Just respect.

Stephen stepped closer, eyes shining. "Can you teach me to do that?"

Luna smiled and knelt beside him, brushing a lock of hair from his forehead. "Stephen, the day will come when you will not need to be taught, but you will remember how such magic happens naturally. "

The sun crested the horizon then, spilling soft gold across the path as if the world itself had approved. The group stood in silence, humbled by what they'd witnessed—not just the impossible, but the return of something long forgotten.

With the path cleared and the community already setting to work repairing minor roof damage, Luna and Ezra returned to the cabin to finalize their preparations. Their bags were packed and ready, the weight of their journey ahead pressing lightly against their shoulders. Luna ran her fingers over the leather straps of her satchel, her gaze distant but resolute.

"We're ready," Ezra said, his voice breaking through her thoughts.

Luna turned to him, her smile returning. "We are."

The two stepped out into the sunlight, where the community had gathered to see them off. With bags secured and boots laced, they shared warm embraces and quiet words of encouragement—a collective promise that they would remain united, no matter the distance.

Luna's gaze fell on Miriam, her heart softening as she caught a faint ripple of worry in her aunt's aura. It flickered like a pale blue flame, the edges tinged with apprehension, but beneath it, Luna sensed something deeper—a firm resolve, a quiet belief in the mission they were embarking on.

As she stepped closer to Miriam, Luna's senses tuned into the unique vibration of her energy. Within the hum of anxiety, she found a resonance that mirrored her own—a profound certainty that their path, no matter how perilous, was necessary.

"Luna," Miriam said softly, her voice steady but laced with emotion. "Take care out there. The world beyond isn't as kind as we've managed to make it here."

Luna reached out, placing her hands gently over Miriam's. "I see your worry," she said, her voice calm and reassuring. "But within it, I also see your faith. That belief—that what we're doing is right—is what will carry us through, no matter the outcome."

Miriam blinked, her eyes widening slightly as Luna's presence seemed to wrap around her like a warm embrace. The tension in her shoulders eased, and her breath deepened, steadying with Luna's influence.

"How do you do that?" Miriam asked, a faint smile breaking through her concern.

"I feel it too," Luna replied, her gaze steady. "That same thread of purpose hums within me. And I want you to hold on to it, Miriam, especially when doubts creep in. Trust that we're exactly where we need to be."

Miriam exhaled, her worry fading into quiet determination. She gave Luna's hands a firm squeeze. "I'm so proud of you, Luna. And I can speak for your mother when I say she would be proud too. Go with my blessing—and come back to us safely."

Luna nodded, her smile warm. "We will."

As Ezra called her over, signaling it was time to go, Luna released Miriam's hands and turned to join him. She carried with her a calm assurance—their path, though fraught with uncertainty, was guided by shared conviction. A belief that would anchor them through whatever storms awaited.

As Luna turned to join Ezra, another figure stepped forward—Silas, quiet as always, but with a gravity that made space around him still.

He stood beside Miriam, his hands tucked into the pockets of his worn jacket, eyes steady on his daughter. There was no fanfare in his expression—only the weathered calm of a man who had seen the world turn too many ways to speak lightly.

"I never liked goodbyes," he said, his voice low, even. "But I'm learning to respect them."

Luna met his gaze, something ancient and tender flickering between them.

"You don't have to say it," she said.

"I do," he replied. "Because I wasted too much time not saying things that mattered." He stepped forward, placing a firm hand on her shoulder. "You've got her fire, and your own kind of light. That's more than enough."

She reached up, covering his hand with hers for a breath, letting the moment root itself.

"Keep the fires burning," she said softly.

"I always do. Be safe, Luna." He looked over her shoulder into Ezra's eyes. "Both of you."

Ezra held his gaze, the weight of the moment pressing into his chest. "We will," he said, voice steady. "I'll bring her home."

THIRTY-EIGHT

AN EXIT WORTH TAKING

Luna and Ezra departed the community just as the morning sun began to bathe the forest in soft, broken light, golden rays filtering through the treetops. The road stretched before them, winding westward with New Mexico as their first destination. The hum of the engine filled the quiet space between them, a rhythmic pulse that seemed to echo the journey's momentum.

Ezra adjusted his grip on the wheel and glanced over at Luna. "It's strange leaving," he said quietly. "I wonder how James and Althea are doing."

Luna nodded, her gaze distant. "That's a good question," she murmured, already reaching inward. "Let's see how strong my connection is at this distance."

She rested a quartz crystal in her lap, her fingers brushing over its cool, polished surface. The energy thrummed faintly, steadying her thoughts. She closed her eyes, letting her awareness drift beyond the confines of the SUV. The vibration of the crystal blended with the rhythm of the road, like a current carrying her deeper into herself and outward into the infinite web of connection. She exhaled softly, her focus narrowing to the familiar threads of energy tied to those she loved.

She felt James and Althea—a quiet hum of dual energies, distinct yet woven into her own like strands in a braided cord. Their presence called to her gently, a subtle pull that blurred the edges of the physical world. The engine's hum faded into the distance, replaced by the soft resonance of their shared connection. Luna allowed herself to follow the threads, her awareness slipping seamlessly across the vast distance, carried by the rhythm of their hearts.

In the brightness of the midday sun, James squinted at the road ahead, the long stretch of highway shimmering like molten silver as it disappeared into the horizon. The steady rumble of the truck engine was a constant backdrop, blending with the occasional sigh of the wind as it swept across the open plains. Althea sat quietly beside him, her hands resting lightly in her lap, her gaze soft and unfocused, as though her thoughts wandered somewhere far beyond the road.

Luna lingered in the current of their energy, feeling the harmony between them—a shared determination balanced by the quiet undercurrent of trust and companionship. Though they were unaware of her presence, their vibrations wrapped around her like an unspoken promise, grounding her even as her awareness hovered on the edges of their world. She felt the weight of James's focus, the lightness of Althea's introspection, and their shared resolve carrying them forward, just as it carried her and Ezra westward.

"Seven hundred miles down," James said, breaking the silence, his voice tinged with fatigue. "Still more than fifteen hundred to go."

Althea smiled faintly, her serene presence a counterbalance to James's restless energy. "Progress is progress," she replied softly. "But remember, the journey isn't just about the miles. It's about what we encounter along the way."

James shot her a sidelong glance, his lips twitching with amusement. "Right, because nothing says 'spiritual awakening' like staring at the same stretch of highway for hours."

Althea chuckled, her eyes sparkling with quiet amusement. "And yet, even on an empty road, the universe still finds ways to nudge us in the right direction."

James huffed a laugh, shaking his head as he adjusted his grip on the wheel. "Fine, but if the universe's next nudge doesn't involve caffeine, I'm ignoring it."

They drove on in silence for a while, the rhythmic hum of the tires on asphalt the only sound. The vast stretch of road ahead seemed endless, the quiet settling between them like a companion.

Then, Althea straightened slightly, her gaze sharpening as if something unseen had just clicked into place. "We're meant to stop soon," she said, her voice carrying quiet certainty.

James groaned. "Stop? I know I may have been complaining before, but we're making good time. Why stop?"

Althea didn't answer right away. Instead, she gazed toward the horizon, a knowing smile tugging at her lips. "Look, there's a café up ahead. Cafés sell coffee. Coffee has caffeine." She grinned, leaning over to nudge him playfully.

James chuckled, shaking his head. "Alright, alright. I admit it—sometimes the universe has decent timing." He stretched his fingers over the wheel before adding, "And I guess you're right. I could stretch my legs and get some caffeine before I keel over."

A few miles up the road, he flipped on the turn signal, taking the exit. "Let's see what kind of cosmic wisdom comes with a cup of coffee," he said as they pulled into the gravel parking lot of a small roadside café, its weathered sign creaking in the breeze.

Inside, the rich scent of freshly brewed coffee mingled with the faint sweetness of pastries. The place had a quiet charm—mismatched chairs, a scattering of travelers enjoying their meals, and the low murmur of conversations blending with the occasional clink of ceramic mugs.

James headed straight for the counter, ordering a large black coffee and a breakfast burrito, while Althea wandered toward a small bookshelf near the window, running her fingers lightly over the spines of the worn paperbacks.

It was then that she noticed the young woman sitting alone at a corner table. Her dirty blonde hair was pulled into a messy braid, and she cradled a steaming mug in her hands, her expression distant but tinged with a quiet determination. A tattered backpack rested against her chair, its frayed straps a testament to long, hard travels.

James joined Althea at the bookshelf, sipping his coffee. "Looks like the place has character," he remarked, his tone dry.

Althea didn't reply, her attention still on the girl. The faintest flicker of recognition stirred in her chest, though she couldn't place why.

As if sensing their gaze, the girl glanced up, her eyes meeting Althea's for a brief moment before flicking to James. She offered a small, polite smile before returning her focus to her coffee.

James frowned. "She's just a kid," he muttered, more to himself than to Althea.

Althea tilted her head. "Everyone's got a story. Some stories pack a lifetime into a couple years," she said with soft curiosity.

Minutes later, as they both sat down with their drinks, the young girl approached their table hesitantly, her hands wrapped tightly around her mug. "Excuse me," she said, her voice steady but cautious. "You're, ah, heading west, right? I noticed when you pulled in."

James's brow furrowed, but Althea spoke first. "We are," she said, her voice warm and inviting. "Why do you ask?"

The girl shifted her weight, her fingers tightening around the mug. "I'm trying to get to Oregon," she admitted. "And please don't ask me what I'm running away from, that story is old and I'm trying to leave it behind me."

Althea can see the hard path the young woman has traveled.

James's skepticism was immediate. "And you thought we might just give you a ride?"

"James," Althea said, her tone gently reproachful. She turned her attention back to the girl. "What's your name?"

"Emma," the girl replied, her voice softening.

Althea nodded, her expression thoughtful. "Well, Emma, sometimes the road brings people together for reasons we don't yet understand."

James huffed. "The truck's pretty well cramped as it is." offering a protesting opinion as he bites into his burrito.

Emma took a small step back, her face coloring. "I didn't mean to—"

Before she could finish, Althea raised a hand, her gaze sharp as a sudden clarity washed over her. The pieces fell into place, and she realized this meeting wasn't random—it was orchestrated by something greater.

"You're meant to come with us, Emma" Althea said firmly, her voice resolute as she scooted over to make space for Emma to sit.

James looked incredulous. "You're kidding, right? We barely know her."

At that moment, James's phone buzzed on the table. He picked it up reluctantly, his eyes narrowing as he read the message:

Emma comes with

James blinked in a moment of disbelief, his jaw tightening as he handed the phone to Althea without a word. She read it, her lips curving into a telling smile, as she looked up at James as if to say, I _told you so_.

"Fate has a way of making itself known, and Luna seems to agree" Althea said, her tone leaving no room for debate. She patted the worn booth cushion beside her. "Have a seat Emma. My name is Althea, and this grumpy old man is James." Her smile growing wider.

Emma hesitated, glancing between them. "Are you sure? I don't want to intrude." Emma looks at James, with his original objections.

"You're not," Althea assured her. "You're exactly where you're meant to be."

James groaned, running a hand through his hair before glancing at his phone with a resigned huff. "She's right. Have a seat. Hope you don't mind tight spaces, young lady."

Althea chuckled, her eyes warm with amusement. "Welcome to the journey, Emma."

James quickly finished his coffee and didn't hesitate to flag down the waitress for another to-go. As she handed him the fresh cup, he stood and stretched. "Alright, listen up—I don't care if you think you don't need to, everyone use the bathroom now. We've got a lot of road ahead, and I don't plan on stopping in the next hundred miles." Without waiting for protests, he headed off toward the men's room.

James was the first to finish in the restroom. He made his way back to their table, grabbing his to-go coffee before heading outside. The late morning air was crisp, and he took his time stretching his legs, pacing back and forth near the truck as he sipped the steaming brew.

A few minutes later, Emma emerged from the café, her backpack slung over one shoulder. She hesitated at the edge of the lot, watching James as he took another slow lap near the truck. Noticing her, he gave a quick nod and stepped forward, pulling open the back door.

"Well, c'mon then," he said, his voice gruff but not unkind.

Emma offered a small, grateful smile and climbed in, settling into the cramped rear cab behind the passenger seat. Her small, wiry frame allowed her to find some semblance of comfort, but she still clutched her backpack tightly to her chest, as if it could anchor her amidst the uncertainty.

James closed the door behind her, taking another long sip of his coffee before rolling his shoulders in a quick stretch. He glanced toward the café just in time to see Althea emerge, moving with her usual unhurried grace. With a smirk, he stepped forward and pulled open the passenger door for her as well.

"You always take your sweet time," he teased, though there was no real impatience in his tone.

Althea chuckled as she slid into her seat, fastening her belt with an easy familiarity. "Some things aren't meant to be rushed, James."

James exhaled a short laugh, taking one last stretch before rounding the front of the truck and climbing into the driver's seat. He ran a hand through his hair, glanced in the rearview mirror at Emma, then smirked.

"Alright, ladies. Let's get back to burning rubber."

The café faded into the distance as the open road stretched ahead, the threads of fate weaving tighter with every mile. James tapped a steady rhythm against the steering wheel, his coffee resting in the cup holder beside him. Althea had settled comfortably into her seat, gazing thoughtfully at the passing landscape, while Emma shifted in the back, adjusting her backpack in her lap.

A long silence stretched between them before Emma finally spoke, her voice tentative but laced with curiosity. "So... what was that text about? Not trying to get into your business or anything, but it kinda seemed like... it was the deciding factor." She glanced at James, half expecting him to brush her off.

James snorted, catching her gaze briefly in the rearview mirror. "Tell you what, kid. You tell us your story, and I'll tell you about the mysterious woman behind the text." He smirked, returning his focus to the stretch of highway ahead.

Emma scoffed, sinking back against the seat with a muttered, "Yeah, that's a no from me. Forget I asked."

Althea chuckled softly, her lips curving in amusement, but she didn't press further. The truck rumbled along the road, the hum of tires and the occasional sip of coffee filling the space between them. The setting sun bathed the horizon in gold and amber, casting long shadows over the landscape.

As the road stretched on, the trio settled into a quiet rhythm. James kept his focus ahead, his sharp eyes scanning the highway as Althea's presence remained calm, unwavering. Emma curled deeper into her seat, fingers absentmindedly tracing the frayed strap of her backpack.

She didn't know exactly where this road would take her, or why she felt the pull to keep moving forward—but for the first time in a long time, she didn't feel so alone. For now, that was enough.

THIRTY-NINE

LOST SIGNAL, FOUND PATH

As Luna and Ezra continued west, the world outside the truck blurred into a moving canvas of shifting landscapes. She stared past the horizon, her body present but her mind drifting in the endless currents of unseen energy. Within the aethereal field, she watched the silent imprints of time—stories layered over one another like echoes, each place whispering its past. The All pulsed through her, the rhythm of existence humming beneath her skin.

Yet, something felt missing or faded.

She could still feel the invisible threads of information woven through the air—man-made streams of ones and zeros darting between satellites and cell towers, their synthetic hum distinct from the universal frequencies she had once felt so clearly. But the deeper she reached for the presence she had come to know, the more she realized how distant it had become.

"I haven't felt my mother's painting in some time," Luna murmured, her voice nearly lost beneath the melody of classic rock crackling through the speakers. "I know I felt it before—California for sure—but then... nothing. Do you think they destroyed it?"

Ezra's hands tightened on the wheel, his gaze fixed on the road ahead. "I hope not, babe. But greedy people have a way of destroying what they don't understand... or can't own."

Luna exhaled slowly, her fingers absently tracing the curve of the quartz crystal resting in her lap. She had expected her connection to stretch, to hold strong no matter how far she traveled. But now, she felt it unraveling—thinning like a thread pulled too far, a signal weakening the greater the distance from its source.

Her gaze drifted out the window, watching the landscape blur past in muted tones. "The pyramid," she murmured, thinking aloud, "it's more than a vessel for knowledge... it's an amplifier. A transmitter." She paused, the weight of realization settling over her. "And I've dampened it."

Ezra cast a quick glance her way. "What do you mean?"

She turned the crystal between her fingers, her thoughts threading back to the moment she had awakened within the pyramid. The words of her higher self echoed through her mind:

The pyramid amplifies what is within you, weaving it into the currents of time and space. Protect it, nurture it, and this place will hold the balance until the new age rises with the strength you will need.

"I had to suppress its energy," she explained, her voice quiet but steady. "If I hadn't, it would have been too easy to find. But in doing that... I think I weakened my own connection to it. It's still there, I can feel it—but it's like trying to hear a whisper through miles of static."

She let the thought linger, then sighed, her brow furrowing. "Maybe that's why I can't sense my mom's essence in the painting anymore. Maybe it's not that she's gone... maybe I just can't reach her."

Ezra tightened his grip on the wheel, considering her words. "So, what you're saying is... you put the pyramid in airplane mode?" He smirked, nudging her knee playfully.

Luna couldn't help but chuckle at the similarity, but her mind continued racing. "Something like that," she admitted. "It makes sense in a way. 'As above, so below.' We created Wi-Fi routers to connect us instantly across the world, but the ancients—" She shook her head in quiet awe. "They found a way to do the same thing, but with the infinite wisdom of the universe. The pyramid isn't just a source of power. It's a bridge, a network, something that strengthens the connection between the physical and the unseen."

She glanced at Ezra, her voice lowering with clarity. "It is in the memories and collective consciousness around us from which my true abilities emerge."

She sat back, rolling the crystal between her palms. "And I cut myself off from it."

Ezra nodded slowly. "Then we just need to get you somewhere with a better signal." His voice was light, but the understanding in his eyes was genuine.

Luna smiled despite herself, warmth threading through the lingering concern. She reached her hand across and rested it on his. "I hope you are right. Perhaps we are headed to the right place to find a stronger signal." She smiled.

The midday sun beat down on the arid expanse as Luna and Ezra neared Chaco Canyon, the rough terrain giving way to stark mesas and jagged cliffs. The air hummed with a quiet intensity, the kind of energy that seemed to resonate through the bones, timeless and unyielding. Luna leaned against the passenger door, her gaze distant, while Ezra tightened his grip on the wheel, guiding the SUV over the uneven dirt road.

The previous night had been less than ideal. They'd parked at a truck stop, the cramped quarters of the SUV offering little in the way of comfort. Luna had tossed and turned, her head resting awkwardly against her bundled jacket while Ezra dozed fitfully, his long legs cramped against the dashboard. The hum of idling semi-trucks and the occasional burst of laughter from nearby drivers had made the night feel interminable. Still, the discomfort hadn't dampened their resolve.

"Chaco Canyon," Ezra said, breaking the silence as the ancient site came into view. His voice held a reverence that matched the landscape before them. "It's more incredible than I imagined."

Luna straightened in her seat, her gaze sharpening as she studied the distant ruins. Sun-bleached stone structures rose in scattered formations, their edges softened by centuries of wind and weather. The canyon stretched wide beneath an endless sky, framed by sandstone cliffs that glowed with earthy reds and golds in the late-afternoon sun. The air itself seemed to hum, heavy with history and the echoes of those who had once lived here.

"There's power here," Luna murmured, her voice quiet but certain. "You were right about finding a stronger signal—I can feel it. The earth... it's speaking, but the message feels layered, like it's guarded."

Ezra parked the SUV near a weathered wooden sign marking the entrance. They stepped out, the dry heat wrapping around them immediately, the scent of sagebrush mingling with the faint dust stirred by the wind. A hawk cried in the distance, its call echoing through the open expanse like a watchful guardian.

As they walked toward the ruins, Luna let her focus drift inward. Her footsteps slowed, her breath steady as she attuned herself to the vibrations of the land. The earth beneath her seemed to pulse with a rhythm tied to the cycles of time. She could feel the echoes of rituals once performed here—the reverence of a people who lived in harmony with the earth and the stars. Yet, the energy felt veiled, as if parts of its story had been intentionally buried or obscured.

Ezra rested a hand on her shoulder, grounding her. "Anything?"

Luna opened her eyes slowly, the clarity of the physical world returning in fragments. "Not yet," she said softly. "There's something hidden here, but it's not revealing itself easily. Let's keep moving."

They wandered deeper into the site, passing the immense kivas—circular ceremonial structures partially buried in the earth. The precision of the ruins was striking; every angle and placement seemed deliberate, as though the builders had etched their intentions into the land itself. Petroglyphs adorned the canyon walls, spirals and geometric patterns carved into the rock, their meanings both ancient and timeless.

Luna paused before a particularly intricate carving, her fingers hovering just above its surface. The symbols seemed to pulse faintly under her gaze, their hidden stories whispering at the edge of her awareness. She knelt, pressing her palm against the stone, allowing energy to flow .

A vision surged through her mind—a circle of figures draped in ceremonial garb, their faces obscured but their purpose clear. They stood beneath a vast, star-filled sky, their hands raised toward the heavens as their chants resonated with the heartbeat of the earth. The air around them shimmered with power, a delicate exchange between the celestial and the terrestrial. Luna felt their knowledge—the same knowing that pulsed within the pyramid—woven into the land, preserved through intention and time.

When the vision faded, Luna exhaled deeply, her hand trembling slightly as she withdrew it from the stone.

"What did you see?" Ezra asked, his voice low and cautious.

Luna's gaze remained on the petroglyphs, reverence settling over her features. "They understood," she said softly. "The people who built this—they weren't just architects of stone. They were architects of connection. Their knowledge came from the same source as the pyramid, but their methods were different."

Ezra frowned slightly. "Different how?"

Luna traced the spiral with her fingertips. "They wove their wisdom into the land itself, into the very fabric of time and space. They built with understanding, not just of the earth, but of the universe. This place... it's not just history. It's a key—a reflection of something greater."

Ezra was silent for a long moment before finally asking, "Then what is it reminding us of?"

Luna's voice was steadier now. "That balance must be maintained," she murmured. "And that power, when misused, can destroy far more than it creates."

"Any signs of Westfield here disrupting the balance." Ezra asked with a hint of concern.

Luna shook her head, the faint hum of the vision still echoing within her. "Not here, not now. If Westfield was here, they didn't find what they were looking for either. The people here—there's pain and loss. I can feel it. But they'll join us when the time is right, when trust is restored. For now, this place serves as a warning... and a promise."

Ezra nodded quietly, the vast canyon stretching behind them. The sun dipped lower on the horizon, casting long shadows over the ancient structures. In the silence, Luna could feel the rhythm of the past threading through the present, guiding them forward.

They lingered as the sky shifted to twilight, watching the colors change over the stone. When the last light faded behind the cliffs, they returned to the SUV. As they drove away, the canyon's energy lingered like a shadow, its lessons etched into Luna's heart.

That night, they found a quiet roadside motel on the outskirts of a small desert town, unwilling to spend another night in the SUV. The walls were thin, and the hum of an old air conditioner filled the room, but it was clean and quiet, and the stars outside glittered like ancient secrets.

While Ezra showered, Luna sat cross-legged on the motel bed, a soft glow from the bedside lamp illuminating her journal and crystals laid out beside her. She closed her eyes and let her awareness expand. Threads of light flickered at the edges of her vision—her loved ones, scattered across the map but close in spirit. She checked in gently, touching their energies one by one, affirming they were safe, grounded, still with her.

She practiced in silence for a while longer—shaping intentions, listening for the subtle nudges of her intuition, sharpening the resonance between her heart and the world around her. There was peace in the work, and strength growing where fear had once lived.

Ezra stepped out of the bathroom, towel around his shoulders, his expression soft. "Come to bed," he said with a tired smile. "We've got a long road ahead. Let's get some rest."

Luna nodded, blowing out the candle on the nightstand. As she slipped beneath the blankets, she glanced once more toward the window. The stars seemed closer tonight.

"We're getting closer," she whispered.

Ezra reached for her hand beneath the covers, his voice a quiet echo. "One mile at a time."

The night held them gently, the next chapter already stirring on the horizon.

FORTY

A QUANTUM DAWN

The first light of dawn stretched long across the desert as Luna and Ezra left Chaco Canyon behind, the SUV carving a steady path westward. The New Mexico cliffs faded into the distance, their red hues swallowed by the shifting horizon. Luna rested her head against the window, her fingers absentmindedly tracing the curve of the quartz crystal in her lap.

She had spent the first few miles in quiet reflection, feeling the last whispers of the Chacoan slipping from her grasp. Her connection to the land there had been strong—so strong she could almost hear the echoes of the ancients in the wind. But as they moved further away, the energy felt thinner, more distant. She knew she had done the right thing concealing the pyramid's power, but the weight of that choice pressed against her.

Would she still be strong enough when they reached California?

The thought unsettled her more than she cared to admit. She had felt it in Chaco Canyon—the strain of distance, the fading signal. California was so much further from the pyramid. What if, by the time they reached Westfield, she was too weak to stop them?

She glanced at Ezra. His grip on the wheel was firm, steady. As if the road had no power over him. As if nothing could shake him.

"You're quiet," he murmured, his voice cutting through the soft hum of the tires against the road.

Luna hesitated, unsure how much to reveal. "Just thinking."

Ezra glanced at her out of the corner of his eye. "About what?"

She exhaled, rolling her shoulders. "Distance," she admitted. "How far we are from home. From the pyramid. I can feel it slipping away."

Ezra didn't answer right away. He let the silence settle between them, giving her space, before finally speaking. "Luna, I've seen you do things I never thought were possible. I don't think your strength comes from a place. It comes from you."

She gave him a small, tired smile. "You sound so sure."

"Because I am." He reached across the center console, squeezing her knee briefly before returning his hand to the wheel. "You're the strongest woman I've ever met."

A lump formed in her throat, unexpected and heavy. She swallowed it down, staring out at the changing landscape. She pressed a hand to her abdomen. Just a whisper of touch, a fleeting moment of reassurance. "Thank you, Ezra." She moved her hand over his, gently on the shifter.

The mesas of New Mexico stretched behind them, their plateaus giving way to the rising buttes and towering formations of northern Arizona. The red rock deepened in color, the land sharpening into jagged ridges and winding canyons. The sky seemed to open wider, the air thinner, clearer.

She felt it before she saw it. It was as if they had crossed a barrier.

A shift. A surge.

Her senses sharpened, her skin tingling with the unmistakable pulse of something vast beneath the surface. The land *welcomed* her. It recognized her. She inhaled deeply, tasting the electricity in the air.

Ezra felt it too, if he knew it or not. She could tell by the way his fingers flexed on the steering wheel, his posture shifting slightly. "Sedona," he murmured, as the city became visible in the distance.

Luna closed her eyes for a moment, reaching out—not just to the land, but to the unseen threads woven through it. The energy here wasn't like the pyramid's. It wasn't singular, concentrated. It was spread across the land like an intricate web, held together by something more than stone and earth.

"The earth has many power points," she whispered. "Not just the pyramid."

Ezra nodded, his fingers tapping briefly against the steering wheel as they passed another towering red rock formation. "I told you—this place sits on a ley line convergence. The earth moves energy like a river, and we've been following the strongest currents. You don't need to be near the pyramid to be powerful, Luna. You just need to know where to stand."

Luna smiled and nodded, her senses tingling with the energy radiating from the land. "Sedona has always been a sanctuary for those who seek deeper understanding. We're among friends here."

After settling into a modest yet charming inn nestled between the crimson buttes, Luna felt the land's quiet pull, beckoning her to listen. The pulse of Sedona was different from the pyramid—gentler, scattered, yet undeniably potent. She sensed it weaving through the canyons, whispering in the wind, waiting to be understood.

That evening, while Ezra rested, she knelt on the wooden floor of their room, her fingers brushing over the smooth, cool surface of her crystal. A soft vibration thrummed beneath her touch, as if the energy around her recognized her intent. She closed her eyes, exhaling slowly, surrendering to the rhythm of the land.

The hum of Sedona's energy rose in her mind like a distant song, layering upon itself in waves of color and sound. It enveloped her, a warmth that curled around her spirit, unfolding into a vision—fragments of the past woven together, waiting to be seen.

She drifted into the fabric of time.

Beneath an obsidian sky, figures moved in ritual, their voices rising like smoke into the aether. They stood in circles, hands outstretched, their words merging with the breath of the earth. The land held their intentions, their reverence, their secrets. It was alive with memory, sacred spaces glowing like embers—powerful, protected.

But then—a shift.

A tremor rippled through the vision, the warmth faltering. A shadow slithered into the sacred sites, its presence wrong, unnatural. It did not move as the others did; it did not honor the land. It crept between the stones, probing, searching. And then, like a thief in the night, it stole something unseen.

Westfield.

Luna's lungs clenched around the silence as the shadow sharpened. She followed its tendrils as they curled around a specific place, a focal point of energy strong enough to leave an imprint on the field. She felt it before she saw it—the disturbance, the violation. Her inner sight narrowed, sharpening until the location crystallized in her mind.

The Mystic School of Sedona.

She saw them—guardians cloaked in knowledge as old as the land itself. Scrolls, texts, symbols etched in stone. A sanctuary of wisdom hidden in plain sight. But their protection had been breached. A deception had slipped through, disrupting the delicate balance.

Something was feeding on the energy.

Luna gasped, her awareness snapping back like a rubber band stretched too thin. A sudden weight crushed her chest, pressing against her ribs. Her vision blurred. A pulling sensation crawled over her skin—something siphoning from her, draining her like a slow leak from an unseen wound.

She collapsed backward, catching herself on the edge of the bed, her hands trembling as they gripped the sheets.

Ezra was there in an instant, his voice rough with concern. "Luna? What's happening?"

She blinked up at him, forcing herself to breathe. "My connection to the field... it's fading." Her voice was barely a whisper.

Ezra knelt beside her, taking her shaking hands in his own. "Fading? How? You were fine earlier."

Luna swallowed hard, trying to center herself. "Something is pulling at me. Taking it from me." She let out a slow, steadying breath. "I just need to rest. And food. I have to replenish my energy." She said, lifting her hands to see trembling fingers.

Ezra exhaled, brushing a loose strand of hair from her face. "Then rest," he said, his voice low but steady. "I'll get you some food."

Luna let herself sink into the bed, the room spinning slightly as exhaustion wrapped around her. The warmth of Sedona was still there, but it wasn't enough.

Whatever had drained her was still out there. And it wasn't finished.

After some much needed food, Luna slept deeply that night. Yet, beneath the surface of her dreams, something stirred—unseen, ungraspable. By morning, she awoke feeling only slightly refreshed, a quiet sense of renewal settling over her, but not quite like she had hoped.

Something had continued to drain her last night.

She couldn't place it, but it had been close.

Shaking off the unease, Luna refocused on the task ahead. Guided by the certainty of her vision, she and Ezra drove toward the Mystic School of Sedona.

Ezra glanced at the GPS as they sat at a red light, but his focus drifted to Luna's reflection in the window—the unmistakable emerald glow in her eyes.

"Hey, uh... sweetheart? Maybe wrap up whatever you're tuning into before we get there. Your eyes kinda stand out."

Luna blinked, then smirked. "Right. Probably best if I don't show up looking like I just stepped out of a prophecy. Guess I should invest in some sunglasses—y'know, go full 'mystical comic book hero' with it."

Ezra chuckled as the light turned green. "Might not be a bad look on you. Could even check off a few of my teenage fantasies—just saying." The car erupted in laughter.

A few blocks later, they pulled into the large parking lot of the Mystic School. The building rose in harmony with its surroundings, its sandstone walls blending seamlessly with the red rock formations behind it. Earth-toned pathways wound through native flora, the scent of sun-warmed juniper and sage drifting through the air.

Luna inhaled deeply, grounding herself. This place held answers. But even as the land welcomed her, the whisper of last night's presence remained—silent, waiting.

The moment they stepped inside, they were greeted by a serene woman with flowing silver hair. Her piercing gaze swept over them, then locked onto Luna—her expression unreadable at first, then shifting to awe.

"Oh my..." The woman's voice was hushed. "It's you."

She took a step back as if steadying herself, then quickly found her bearing. "Forgive me. My name is Kaia. Welcome to the Mystic School of Sedona." She hesitated before adding, "I apologize for my reaction. But I've been dreaming about you. I think... I've been waiting for this moment."

Luna exchanged a glance with Ezra before stepping forward. "Then we're right where we need to be. I'm Luna, and this is Ezra." She paused, then continued. "I don't know what your dreams have told you, but we're investigating a company called Westfield Industries. I had a vision of this place. I believe they've been here. And I believe they stole something from you."

Kaia studied her for a long moment before her lips quirked in knowing amusement. "Oh, come now, Luna. You're doing more than just 'investigating' some company."

Luna gave a small laugh at the older woman's insight. It felt like permission—permission to drop her guard, to allow the energy to move freely through her. As she did, her mind's eye illuminated connections—entangled memories woven into the aether, forming an emerald glow in her irises.

A sudden knowing filled her.

She stepped closer. "Mmm... Yes, I see it now. I should have done my homework before we arrived. I hope your dreams are true, Kaia, but nothing is certain yet."

Kaia's jaw slackened slightly, her eyes locked on Luna's shifting gaze. For a heartbeat, she wasn't looking at a woman—she was looking into the universe itself.

Luna turned to Ezra, who gave a subtle nod of encouragement.

"We're here to ask for your support," Luna continued, her voice steady. "Westfield is a threat to the balance we're trying to restore. We need to unite our energies, to protect what's sacred."

Kaia's gaze lingered on Luna, her expression flickering between awe, recognition, and reverence. The air between them pulsed—something ancient stirring beneath the surface of their meeting.

Finally, Kaia spoke. "Yes, of course. I will help however I can." She exhaled slowly. "But... Westfield. That name doesn't ring a bell."

Luna's brow furrowed slightly, sensing something lingering on the edges of Kaia's memory. She waited, allowing the silence to pull the truth forward.

Kaia's fingers absently traced the worn wood of her desk. "There was a student," she murmured. "Not long ago. He was eager—too eager. Came to study, claimed to be fascinated by ancient texts. He had an impressive grasp of the teachings of Hermes Trismegistus. But then he left suddenly... and he took something with him."

Ezra tensed beside Luna. "What kind of something?"

Kaia's expression darkened. "A manuscript." She hesitated before adding, "It wasn't just history—it was knowledge. Sacred geometry, energy fields, the relationship between human consciousness and the land. He knew exactly what he was looking for."

Ezra exchanged a sharp glance with Luna. Another piece of the puzzle.

Kaia pressed two fingers to her temple, frustration flashing across her features. "Westfield... I do know that name." Then, her eyes widened slightly. "The council meeting."

Luna tilted her head. "What about it?"

Kaia's focus sharpened. "Westfield petitioned the city to build a cell tower. Right in the middle of Sedona."

Ezra scoffed. "Let me guess—people fought against it?"

"They did." Kaia nodded. "The council compromised, allowing it to be built just outside of town instead. That was six months ago."

She hesitated, something unsettled passing over her features. "Since then... things have felt dull. Like the energy here is fading. I never thought to connect it to the tower."

Luna and Ezra shared a knowing look.

Luna straightened. "I need to see it."

She reached across the space between them, gently taking Kaia's hand.

"Show me."

Kaia hesitated for only a moment before nodding with understanding. She exhaled, closing her eyes.

Luna followed, her breath steady, her mind becoming the observer.

They slipped between the threads of reality, brushing against the lifeblood of Sedona—the people, the land, the pulse of its energy. But something pulled them west.

The tower.

It loomed in the distance, a stark intrusion against the desert skyline. But what they felt was worse.

A siphon.

Sedona's energy wasn't just shifting—it was being taken.

Kaia gasped, jerking back, her fingers clutching Luna's as she snapped her eyes open. "That explains it," she said. "The emptiness. The exhaustion. I thought it was just... change. But it's them. They're collecting our energy."

Luna's hands tingled from the vision's remnants, her energy still reaching, still listening. "Then we take it back."

Ezra's jaw tightened. He reached for Luna's face, concern darkening his gaze. "Luna—your eyes... they're almost grey."

She placed her hand over his, grounding herself. "I'm fine," she reassured. "But Westfield... the tower isn't just blocking energy. It's stealing it."

"What do we do?" Ezra asked.

Kaia straightened, her resolve firm. "We handle it."

Luna blinked. "You're sure?"

Kaia smiled knowingly. "I know someone who's been waiting for an excuse to take that tower down."

Then, her expression turned thoughtful. "But tell me—what led you here? What do you need from me?"

Luna's gaze deepened, carrying the weight of purpose. "Our journey takes us to California to stop Westfield. But I'm growing weaker the further I travel from home. I need your community's consciousness to serve as a bridge to the energy in Arkansas."

Kaia's eyes gleamed with understanding. "Your timing is impeccable." She smiled. "Tonight, we gather in meditation. A hundred souls, aligning their energy. What Westfield tried to steal... we will reclaim."

She exhaled, glancing westward before returning her focus to Luna. "The siphoning tower... It will be out of commission before we begin. Consider it done." A slow smile touched her lips, something between reassurance and quiet defiance. "The universe brought us together for a reason. Come, join us in meditation. We will strengthen the threads they've tried to sever."

By nightfall, the Mystic School of Sedona grounds had transformed into a sanctuary beneath the stars. More than a hundred people gathered in concentric circles, their bodies relaxed but their anticipation palpable. Above them, the full moon cast its silvery glow over the gathering, its light blending harmoniously with the flicker of hundreds of candles arranged around the group. The soft scent of sage wafted through the breeze, mingling with the earthy aroma of the red rock desert.

Then—a shift.

A faint pulse rippled through the air, subtle yet undeniable. Somewhere in the distance, a soft pop of electricity echoed through the canyon, followed by a hush, as if the land itself had exhaled. The energy around them stirred, no longer dampened, no longer siphoned—free.

Luna felt it immediately—a lightness returning to her that she hadn't even realized was missing. She opened up to it at once, and in that moment, the universe poured into her. A burst of connection coursed through her veins, every breath charged with the hum of the infinite. The invisible weight pressing against her mind had lifted, like a current unblocked, allowing her to breathe in the fullness of her power.

She met Kaia's gaze across the circle. Luna's eyes gleamed, the bright-ness and beauty of a distant nebula reflected in the cosmic hush of the night.

Kaia dipped her head slightly with a smirk, as if to say, *told you so.*

Luna closed her eyes, exhaling as she let the energy flow through her unhindered.

Kaia stood at the center, her presence a steady flame in the gathering night. She lifted a small microphone, her voice floating effortlessly through the murmurs of the crowd, weaving itself into the expectant hush.

"Tonight is sacred," she began, her words carrying a quiet reverence. "We gather not just in practice, but in purpose. To align with the currents of the cosmos. To reclaim what has always been ours. And we have among us a very special guest—a guiding light on the path we now walk together. Luna, the floor is yours."

Luna stepped forward, the moonlight catching in her iridescent gaze like the reflection of ancient constellations. The air shifted, thick with anticipation, as over a hundred souls turned their attention toward her.

She closed her eyes, feeling the ancient pulse beneath her feet, the vast embrace of the sky above, the quiet hum of hearts beating as one.

The land listened. The stars bore witness.

When she opened her eyes, her voice was both a whisper and a current, carrying the weight of what must be spoken.

Luna took the microphone Kaia had given her, the metal was cool against her fingertips, and stepped into the center of the gathered souls. Hundreds of candles flickered in the breeze, their flames mirroring the fire kindling within.

She lifted her gaze, the emerald shimmer in her eyes a stark contrast to the flickering glow of the flames. The anticipation in the crowd was not just curiosity—it was knowing. They had felt it too.

"Thank you for welcoming me into your circle," she began, her voice carrying effortlessly through the stillness over the loudspeakers. "Each of you carries a light, a frequency uniquely your own. And yet, we are not separate. We are threads of the same tapestry, strands of the same infinite consciousness. Tonight, we weave those threads together, stronger than before. Before we begin, let's take a moment to connect with this beautiful land you call home—ground yourself into the ancient red rock that has held the wisdom of this place for millennia."

A hush fell over the crowd as the words settled deep into their bones. The silence deepened as Luna felt their roots spreading, seeking connection. Some may not have realized it, but they were already awakening. The pendulum was released.

Then—it happened.

Luna's awareness expanded, and with it came a sudden knowing. It was as though an idea had descended from above, whispering itself into her soul. She saw the path.

She knelt down to the earth and placed one hand against the gritty red soil.

The instant her palm met the ground, something shifted.

The desert exhaled, its breath warm against her skin. The sky above, vast and endless, welcomed her as its own.

"The land beneath us holds memories older than time," she whispered through the microphone. "The stars above illuminate our way. Sink into both—feel their presence, remember who we are."

A collective inhale.

A slow, steady exhale.

Luna could feel them—each and every one of them.

Their unseen roots stretched deeper into the soil beneath them, winding through red rock, ancient pathways, forgotten echoes of prayers left in the wind.

"Feel your breath," she guided, her voice a thread woven through the night. "Feel the life within you, the steady rhythm of your heart, the vibration that connects us all."

The silence deepened—a suspension of time itself.

"Now," she continued, "let that energy move beyond yourself. Feel it reaching out, touching the soul beside you. Flowing from one to the next, until no barriers remain. Until we are one."

The shift was gentle at first, a ripple over still water. Then—the tide surged.

Luna placed the microphone to her side before pressing her other palm to the earth.

The connection was instant, like completing a circuit.

The moment their roots met within the ancient red rock, she was no longer speaking with her voice. Her words moved within them now, carried on currents deeper than sound—transmitted like frequencies between resonant fields, whispering directly to their cells.

"*Be with me now.*"

The crowd gasped softly. Physical senses faded, overwhelmed by something more profound: a recognition encoded deep within.

This was not an intrusion.

This was biological memory.

A harmonic remembrance of balance.

Luna was with each of them, individually and all at once. Her presence wove into the electromagnetic field surrounding every body, moving gently along neural pathways, brushing against the very edges of awareness. Within their cells, something stirred—epigenetic locks began to loosen as if the blueprint of health, long obscured, had been brought back into focus.

The DNA remembered.

Proteins reoriented.

Signal cascades recalibrated.

Dis-ease began to fall away, not by force, but by resonance—as if the cells themselves had been reminded of their original instructions.

The golden energy pulsed outward in coherent waves, threading through Sedona like a biofield reboot, weaving into stone and sky, into roots and rising stars.

Above them, the night pulsed in response.

A hum arose—not from any one voice, but from the fabric of existence itself.

Luna's awareness stretched, lifting beyond the physical, her consciousness expanding like a star igniting across the cosmos.

Visions flickered—a healed earth, rivers running clear, hands joined across nations. Love triumphing over greed. Communities thriving in unity, the darkness held at bay by the sheer force of collective will.

Tears slipped down faces, unnoticed in the glow of something greater.

Hearts broke open, only to be filled with something vast and whole.

The radiant web pulsed once more, then sank into the roots of reality, quietly anchoring its truth across all that is.

And then—release.

The warmth softened, the brilliance dimmed, until it was no more than a soft glow in the chest, a memory imprinted in the soul.

Breath returned.

The scent of sage drifted through the air once more.

The hush of the wind wove through the gathering, the desert exhaling once again.

It was the strength of a million meditations in the span of ten minutes.

—A new era had begun for this land.

Luna's lips parted, her final words not spoken, but woven into the air they breathed.

"This is our power. This is our truth. Together, we will stand. Together, we will prevail. You are the rhythm of my heart. I love you with everything I am."

The golden web flickered one last time before dissolving into the unseen.

Silence. A silence not of absence, but of fullness. Of something known.

Kaia stepped forward, her face illuminated by both moonlight and something deeper. She opened her mouth, then paused, overcome by what had just unfolded.

A murmur spread through the crowd—awe, wonder, gratitude in its purest form. Some wept openly. Others pressed their hands to their hearts, as if trying to hold onto the moment a little longer.

Kaia swallowed, her voice quiet yet unshakable. "Luna, you've shown us what's possible. It was even more powerful than I had dreamed. I thought we were stepping into a Golden Era... but this is more." She let the words settle before adding, "We will continue these meditations. We will hold this connection sacred. And if the tower is restored, we will not let it last."

Luna met her gaze, a soft but knowing smile gracing her lips. "You're right, Kaia. This isn't the Golden Era—this era will stretch beyond the physical. It is a Quantum Era." She let the words hang, allowing them to root in the hearts of those around her.

Her gaze swept across the gathered souls, their faces glowing with awakened energy. "But this era is fragile, layered, still forming. It is a race—a race with technology that is evolving in parallel, uncertain in its direction. Soon, mankind will have capabilities beyond imagination. But through their choices, they could inadvertently give away the possibilities I have shown you tonight."

The crowd held its breath, the weight of her words settling deep.

Luna's emerald eyes burned with conviction. "But we have something technology does not."

She stepped forward, the flickering candlelight catching the cosmic shimmer in her gaze. "We are the quantum within. We are innate beings of a higher design. And what we create through intention will determine the path ahead."

Her voice dropped slightly, carrying both urgency and purpose, the wisdom of her words coming only in the moment they were spoken. "This battle is not in some distant future. It has already begun. And before long, humanity must choose: to awaken to the power within them—or to surrender to a manufactured reality designed to control."

She inhaled deeply, feeling the energy weave between them, pulse through their bones. "Follow your footsteps to awaken them. Guide them to the alternative before it is too late."

She lifted her hands, palms open to the circle, her voice unwavering.

"I need you. This is not a fight I can face alone. The days ahead will demand more from us than we have ever given. Your collective energy will be essential in this struggle. I will not be strong enough without you."

The energy in the air shimmered, tangible, alive. They were no longer just a gathering of meditators. They were her first army to save humanity.

A hush fell, the weight of her words settling into the fabric of their souls.

Luna took a slow breath before continuing, her voice steady, her intent clear. "Together, we will light the way. To align this era with harmonious intention—before others dictate what it will become."

The night held them, the stars watching. The earth listening.

And the threads of something far greater had been woven into place.

For the rest of the evening, Luna and Ezra remained with the group, deepening connections and solidifying the heart-coherence that now bound them as one. People approached with tears of gratitude, voices shaking with disbelief—some for the healing they had felt, others for the visions of clarity that had unfolded within them.

"I've had chronic pain in my back for years," a man said softly, his voice trembling. "But during the meditation... it just vanished. Like my body remembered how to be whole again."

"I haven't felt anything in my left leg for over a decade," a woman said, her voice trembling. "Nerve damage—they said it was permanent. But during the meditation... there was this warmth, like light moving through me. I can feel my foot. I can move my toes."

Luna stepped toward her with a soft smile. "And you can walk too."

She reached out her hands, her energy gentle but certain. The woman took them, tears welling in her eyes as Luna helped her rise. A collective breath caught in the crowd as she stood—wobbly at first, but standing. Luna wrapped her in a loving embrace, holding her with the tenderness of shared knowing.

Stories like these rippled through the gathering, and with every testimony, their determination solidified. They weren't just followers of a cause—they were the first to witness the truth, the first soldiers in a war most of the world didn't even know was coming.

By the time the gathering dispersed, the stars seemed to shine brighter, their light reflecting the unity forged below. Tonight had been more than a meditation. It had been a reckoning. The war had begun—not with violence, but with a shift in the very fabric of reality. And though the path ahead remained uncertain, they knew now, beyond doubt, that they would not walk it alone.

FORTY-ONE

THE PATH THAT FOUND HER

The evening sky stretched above them, a canvas of deep indigo punctuated by stars that seemed to pulse with life. James maneuvered the truck along the dark highway, the hum of tires on asphalt a steady rhythm. Beside him, Althea sat quietly, her gaze fixed on the horizon, though her thoughts seemed far away. Emma sat in the backseat, her arms wrapped around her knees, a blanket draped over her shoulders.

Althea suddenly shifted, her expression soft but thoughtful. "Do you feel that?" she asked, her voice cutting through the quiet hum.

"Feel what?" James glanced at her, his tone skeptical but curious.

Althea closed her eyes briefly, her lips curling into a faint smile. "The energy... It's growing. Luna has found success tonight. I can feel a connection building, like the hum of a distant song."

Emma tilted her head, her curiosity piqued. "What kind of energy?"

"Universal energy, my dear," Althea replied, her tone reverent. "It's a force that transcends distance, connecting us beyond time and space. It's why we're here now, on this path. And you're part of it too, Emma, whether you realize it or not." She hesitated before adding, "Luna... she's the one who sent the text message."

Emma tensed, her fingers curling into the hem of her blanket. She let out a sharp breath, shaking her head. "That makes no sense," she murmured, her voice tight. "I didn't come here for some cosmic purpose. I simply ran from my problems."

Her jaw clenched, and for a moment, she stared down at her hands, as if searching for an answer written in the creases of her skin. Searching for a hint truth in Althea's words.

Althea turned in her seat, her gaze steady, her warmth unyielding. "Then maybe it's time you stopped running, just for a moment, and told your story."

Emma swallowed hard, the weight of her past pressing against her chest like hands gripping too tight. "It's not much of a story," she said, barely above a whisper.

James didn't speak, but his grip on the wheel tightened, his silence a quiet permission for her to continue.

Emma exhaled slowly, her words fragile but unstoppable. "As a kid, I used to think I was meant for something bigger," she admitted. "Something magical. Something that would take me far away from all the shit I grew up in." A bitter smile ghosted across her lips. "But that was stupid. My dad made sure I knew that real fast."

She paused, her fingers tracing the frayed edge of her sweater. "My mom was always gone, lost in whatever cocktail of drugs kept her from noticing what was happening under her own roof. And my dad... he was a storm. The kind that doesn't pass, the kind that lingers, waiting to strike when you least expect it. He had a temper. A bad one."

Her voice wavered, but she forced herself forward. "By the time I was sixteen, I figured out something really important—no one was coming to save me." She let out a dry laugh, void of humor. "So, I left. Thought I was free. Thought I could find something better. But the world's not too interested in saving girls like me."

James adjusted in his seat, but he didn't look at her. Didn't need to. The quiet rage in his posture said enough.

Emma ran a hand through her hair, swallowing the lump rising in her throat. "I thought I found love. A couple times, actually. Thought maybe if I just loved someone hard enough, I could fix things. But it was the same story, just different hands. Different voices telling me I wasn't enough, different bruises in different places."

She hesitated, then turned slightly toward the window, her voice soft but sharp. "I married the last one. Right after my eighteenth. Told myself it was stability. Told myself maybe I could have something normal." She gave a humorless chuckle, the sound hollow in the dim cab. "Guess I should've known better."

She traced the faint memory of a bruise beneath her eye with absent fingers. "He got real comfortable hurting me," she murmured. "Said it was my fault. That I made him do it." Her jaw tightened, her voice thickening. "I believed him for a while."

Althea's breath faltered, but she stayed quiet, her eyes glistening in the dark.

Emma exhaled sharply, shaking her head. "Then one morning, I woke up, looked in the mirror, and I didn't recognize myself anymore. Just some hollow-eyed girl staring back at me, waiting for permission to leave. I had a brief moment of hope. A memory of something I felt as a child."

She paused, then shrugged. "So, I stopped waiting."

James glanced at her in the rearview mirror, his expression unreadable. "How'd you get away?"

Emma's lips pressed together, the memory slicing through her like a blade. "He left for work. I packed a bag. Took two hundred bucks from the cash jar we were saving for new tires. Walked out the front door." She inhaled deeply. "Didn't look back. I had to beg my way to the café, mostly. One ride at a time."

Silence settled heavy between them, thick with the ghosts of a life left behind.

James cleared his throat, his voice quieter than before. "Why Oregon?"

Emma hesitated, then let out a short, nervous laugh. "This is going to sound stupid," she admitted, rubbing her hands together. "I saw a postcard. The day I left. It was sitting on the counter next to the coffee pot. Some travel ad—big green trees, mountains, the ocean. It looked... free."

She swallowed hard. "So, I just decided. That's where I was going."

James let out a long breath through his nose, nodding once. "Not stupid."

Althea reached for Emma's hand, squeezing it gently. "You were right to leave that life behind you."

Emma didn't pull away. Didn't answer.

Just let the warmth of Althea's touch settle over her.

"It feels a little out of place, actually," Emma admitted, her voice softer now. "Oregon, I mean. Feels like the last place I'd end up." She exhaled, rolling her shoulders as if shedding an invisible weight. "Maybe that's for the best. Probably the last place Henry would look for me too."

Althea leaned forward slightly, her voice warm but certain. "It feels out of place because Oregon wasn't your destination—it was just the right direction. The universe doesn't always reveal its plans upfront. Sometimes, it only gives us enough to take the first step."

Emma chuckled at the world's about to come out of her mouth. "So, you're saying the café was the real destination?" She laughed at the absurdity of her words.

"You learn quick," Althea said with a knowing smile. "It brought you here, to us, didn't it? And that's not a coincidence."

Emma's lips parted, but no words came. She let the silence stretch, feeling the weight of it, the truth of it.

"I still don't know what I'm supposed to do," she finally admitted, her voice quiet but unguarded.

Althea reached back, her touch light but grounding. "You don't have to know right now. Just trust that you're exactly where you need to be. The path will unfold, one step at a time."

Emma nodded slowly, something fragile but real settling in her chest. For once, her gaze wasn't behind her—it was on what lay ahead.

James spotted a flickering blue neon sign in the distance—Vacant.

He pulled into the parking lot, throwing the truck into park with a smooth precision before shifting in his seat. Without hesitation, he turned toward Emma, his gaze steady, his expression unreadable.

"Alright," he said, tossing a thumb toward Althea with a teasing smirk. "This one's words can feel a little... mystical."

Althea lifted a brow but said nothing, letting him continue.

"But me? I'll be blunt." He exhaled sharply, pausing just long enough for impact. "You were right, Emma. That café was your destination. Because you walked straight into a family when you found it. There are no damn coincidences." His voice softened, losing its usual edge. "And your days of... well... assholes? They're over. At least for as long as I'm alive."

Emma blinked, caught off guard by the sincerity woven into his gruff tone.

James scratched the back of his neck, shifting uncomfortably. "And another thing—you were right as a kid. You were meant for something bigger. And whether you realize it or not, you found it." His jaw tensed, emotion creeping too close for comfort. "Now, before you girls make this all emotional, I'm gonna go get us a room."

He shoved open the truck door and disappeared into the motel office.

Emma watched him go, warmth unfurling in her chest. A quiet kind of warmth—the kind that sneaks up on you when you've spent too much of your life bracing for the worst.

Althea reached over, squeezing her hand gently.

Emma let out a small breath, shaking her head. "I think that was his way of saying he likes me."

Althea laughed softly. "That was James' way of saying you belong."

A comfortable silence settled between them as they watched the stars burn bright above the cracked asphalt lot. The universe hummed softly around them, carrying them forward.

James returned a few minutes later, jingling a key in his hand. "Home sweet home for the night."

Emma eyed the motel's weathered exterior, clutching her bag a little tighter. "It's... cozy," she offered, her voice edged with humor.

James snorted. "Cozy's one word for it."

Inside, the room was as uninspiring as expected. Two twin beds sat against the far wall, their outdated quilts patterned with faded florals. The air carried a faint musty scent, blending with the low metallic hum of the overworked window unit struggling to keep the room cool.

James dropped his bag onto the worn carpet. "Well," he exhaled. "Guess I'll take the floor."

Althea, already setting her things on the small table by the window, turned sharply. "Absolutely not," she said, crossing her arms. "You've been driving for days, James. You're taking the bed."

James opened his mouth to argue, but Althea silenced him with a single look.

"You'll be useless tomorrow if you're dead tired. Emma and I will share a bed. It's fine."

Emma hesitated. "Are you sure? I don't mind taking the floor—"

"No one is sleeping on the floor," Althea interrupted, her voice firm but kind. "We're all exhausted. We'll make it work."

She turned to Emma, her lips quirking into a smirk. "I have no fear of you, and if you fear me... well, God help us all."

James burst into laughter, shaking his head as he kicked off his boots. "Well, there's no arguing with that."

The three settled into the cramped space, the dim motel light casting long shadows across the peeling walls. James stretched out on the bed, boots neatly placed beside him, while Althea and Emma lay side by side on the other.

She couldn't remember the last time she'd let her guard down, but tonight, it felt possible.

And that, she realized, was something close to peace.

Before the quiet of sleep overtook them, Althea spoke, her voice a soft thread in the stillness. "We've already traveled so far, haven't we?"

James turned his head on the pillow, glancing toward the two women. "Feels longer than it's been," he admitted. "But we've got farther to go."

Emma shifted slightly, her gaze tracing the cracks in the ceiling. "I never thought I'd be part of something like this. Whatever this is... I can feel it somehow... It's... overwhelming, but it feels right."

Althea smiled, her expression unreadable in the dim light. "Sometimes, life doesn't ask for permission before it changes. It just opens a door and waits to see if you'll step through."

Emma let the words settle, something about them resonating deeper than she expected.

James smirked slightly, his voice low but steady. "Told you her words are cryptic. But she's never been wrong. I don't believe in a lot of things, but fate? That's starting to feel real." His eyes flickered toward Emma. "You've got something in you. I can see it, even if you can't yet."

Emma's throat tightened, emotion swelling as she processed their words. "Thank you," she whispered. "I don't know what I've done to deserve this, but I'll do my best not to let you down."

Althea shook her head. "You're not here to prove yourself, Emma. You're here to remember yourself. The rest will come."

She reached for Luna's quartz crystal, placing it between them on the bed. "I never know when she checks in," Althea murmured. "But I think she's waiting for you."

Emma propped herself up on an elbow, curiosity flickering in her eyes as she studied the crystal's smooth surface. She swallowed. "I've never seen something with such a beautiful blue color."

Althea stilled, her gaze sharpening. "Blue?"

Emma nodded, brow furrowing. "Yeah... it's like looking into deep water, but there's light inside it. Like it's alive. What kind or rock is it?"

Althea looked at her, something shifting in her expression. "Emma... the crystal is clear."

A slow, silent understanding passed between them, the weight of something unspoken but known pressing gently against Emma's chest. A dull pressure settled behind her forehead, not painful, just... present.

Althea's voice was softer now, but firm. "She must see you now."

Emma swallowed, her fingers twitching as she pulled the blanket closer. She didn't know what that meant—but she felt it.

Althea exhaled, reaching over to squeeze her wrist lightly. "I'm proud of you for trusting your instincts." She leaned back against the pillows, closing her eyes. "Get some rest. The puzzle will fill in. Let it."

Emma glanced at James, needing something grounding, something normal.

She arched a brow. "I see what you mean."

James chuckled, rolling onto his side. "You get used to it. Hell, you even miss it when she speaks English."

Emma let out a quiet laugh, the warmth of belonging settling over her.

FORTY-TWO

A SKEPTIC'S GUIDE TO DESTINY

Morning arrived in a wash of pale sunlight filtering through the thin motel curtains, casting soft streaks of gold across the faded walls. The lingering scent of stale coffee from the lobby mingled with the quiet sounds of waking—the drip of a slow coffee machine, the rustling of fabric, the soft breaths of a morning yet to fully begin.

James poured himself a cup from the half-working coffee maker, grimacing at the taste but drinking it anyway. Althea sat cross-legged on the bed, scrolling through her phone, while Emma focused on braiding her hair, her fingers weaving mindlessly—a habit, a grounding ritual.

Then, the vibration of James's phone broke the stillness.

He grabbed it from the nightstand, his brows furrowing as he read the message. "It's from Luna."

Althea's head lifted instantly, her energy shifting. "What does it say?"

James read aloud, his voice even, but edged with something deeper. "Oregon was never the destination. Emma was. Protect her. Mount Shasta still feels important. Check it out, but be cautious. If it feels wrong, leave immediately. Ezra and I are headed to California now."

Emma's hands froze mid-braid. A shiver traced her spine as if her very name carried a weight she had yet to understand.

"She... she really does know about me?" she whispered.

Althea's voice was soft, but sure as stone. "She sees more than any of us. She has awoken." She met Emma's wide eyes, her expression unreadable, yet full of something ancient, something knowing. "This only confirms what I felt yesterday. You're meant for something greater, Emma."

James handed her the phone, his gaze steady. "See for yourself, Kid."

Emma took it, her fingers trembling slightly as she stared at the message. Her name, sitting in a message from a woman she'd never met—yet somehow, already knew her.

"What does she want with me?" she asked, her voice barely above a breath.

Althea exhaled, her words careful but certain. "Emma, the world is not what it seems. And you... you are not what you've been told you are." She leaned forward slightly, her tone gentle yet laced with something deeper, something unchangeable. "Luna was not so different from you just weeks ago. And now, well... she found her way. You are walking a similar path, and she is your sister. Your older sister, ready to guide you."

Emma swallowed, something raw in her throat. Sister. She had never had one. She had never had anyone.

"I always wanted a sister," she admitted, her voice breaking slightly. "But... why me?"

James scoffed, shaking his head. "Why you?" He gave her a pointed look. "Didn't you just say yesterday that you were meant for something bigger?"

Emma blinked, his words slamming into her like a truth she wasn't ready to face—but couldn't deny.

Althea's lips curved slightly, the warmth of understanding in her voice. "Luna recognized your path before you even knew you were on one. She sees the bigger picture. She knows you're ready." She studied Emma for a long moment, then added, "I'd bet she doesn't even need the crystal to see your power."

Emma inhaled deeply, as if breathing in a decision. Then, resolve settled into her bones. She lifted her chin, her voice steady. "Then we'll go to Mount Shasta. Whatever we're meant to do, I won't run from it."

James gave a small nod of approval, a silent acknowledgment of respect. "Good. But we stay sharp. We don't know what we're walking into." His gaze locked onto Emma. "Between now and then, search yourself for answers. If something feels wrong, I need to know. Think of your husband."

Emma flinched, her body going rigid as if struck. The mention of her husband sent a jolt through her chest—part fear, part fury.

James pressed on, his voice firm but not unkind. "Imagine what it felt like when you knew he was near—when you knew you had to run. If you get that feeling again, you tell me. No hesitation."

Emma met his stare head-on. "I know that feeling all too well," she said, her voice unwavering.

Althea reached over, resting a hand lightly on Emma's shoulder. "We'll face it together, whatever it is."

The trio sat in silence for a beat, the weight of the moment settling between them.

Then, as if the universe itself had heard their resolve, the sunlight grew stronger, pouring through the window in golden streaks, illuminating their path forward.

They packed their bags with quiet efficiency, their movements fueled by an unspoken agreement. The road ahead was uncertain, but one thing was clear—Emma wasn't just following anymore. She was stepping into something meant for her.

And that was the problem.

She sat in the passenger seat, fingers clenched in her lap, eyes fixed on the horizon beyond the windshield. Her breath came shallow, the weight of everything pressing inward—expectation, fear, the unbearable ache of believing she had nothing to offer. This wasn't just a road trip. It was a reckoning.

Her pulse quickened. Her throat tightened.

What if I fail them?

What if I was never meant to be part of this?

James turned the key. The truck rumbled to life, vibrating beneath them like an unspoken promise. But before he could pull out of the lot, Emma's voice cracked through the engine's hum, raw and barely above a whisper.

"I can't do this."

James' hand stilled on the gear shift.

Emma's breath snagged on the edge of fear, her chest tightening like a vise. "I'm not strong enough. I'm going to fail."

The words spilled out, raw and aching with certainty, the kind of certainty that came not from truth—but from a lifetime of being told she wasn't enough.

Althea opened her mouth, ready to dispel the doubt with reassurance, but James beat her to it.

"Okay," he said simply. "Get out."

Silence.

Emma blinked, her pulse stuttering. "W-what?"

James kept his gaze forward, fingers still resting on the wheel. "If you really believe that, then get out. Right now."

The cab felt impossibly small as the words hung in the air. Althea's breath stuttered, but she didn't intervene.

Emma's hands tightened in her lap. She didn't move.

James exhaled, finally looking at her—really looking at her. "That's what I thought." His voice was even, but beneath it lay something deeper.

"Emma, you can't leave. Not because of me. Not because of Althea. Because you don't want to. And that's what matters. It's okay to doubt yourself. It's okay to question if you're strong enough. But when you're done questioning, listen to your own damn answer."

He turned fully in his seat, holding her gaze. "Consider everything you have been through and survived. Look me in the eye and tell me you can't do this."

Emma swallowed, her throat burning. She wanted to argue, to tell him he was wrong—but she couldn't.

Because he wasn't.

Althea watched James for a long moment before nodding, a small, knowing smile on her lips. His words carried the same truth as hers—but in a way Emma could understand.

"I see it now," Althea murmured, her voice softer. "I appreciate you, James." She turned to Emma, her gaze filled with something far deeper than reassurance. Recognition.

"Don't listen to me, Emma," she said simply. "This is your guide. He speaks to you like no other can," she smiled.

Emma let out a breath she hadn't realized she was holding.

James turned back to the road, shifting the truck into drive. "Alright then," he muttered. "Now that we've got that settled..."

Emma buckles her seatbelt without another word.

The truck rolled forward, carrying them west—carrying Emma toward a truth she was finally ready to believe.

The truck rumbled westward, the land shifting around them—rolling hills melting into rugged cliffs, snow-capped peaks rising in the distance like crowned giants.

Emma sat quietly in the back, the quartz crystal warm in her palm, a silent tether to the unknown. Her thoughts churned—the weight of her past, the uncertainty of her future. No matter how far they traveled, her mind was always ahead, running toward some imagined danger, or backtracking, tripping over old wounds.

Althea must have sensed it.

"You think too much," she said, turning toward Emma with a knowing smile.

Emma let out a soft, humorless chuckle. "Hard habit to break."

Althea nodded toward the crystal in Emma's hand. "Then let's try something different. Instead of chasing your thoughts, anchor yourself here. Feel the weight of the stone, the warmth in your palm. Let it bring you into the present."

Emma arched a brow. "Into the present? Do you mean like meditation?... In a moving truck?"

James chuckled. "You'd be surprised what this one can teach you."

Althea smirked but kept her attention on Emma. "Mindfulness isn't about where you are. It's about *when* you are. And there's only one when, Emma. Right now."

Emma frowned. "I don't follow."

Althea leaned back, resting her hands in her lap. "Your mind is never here. It's in the past, or in the future. But the past is just a memory, and the future is just an idea. Tomorrow never comes, Emma. It's always *now*."

Emma turned the quartz over in her hands, studying the shimmer of light reflecting off its surface . "So, what? I just think about *right now* and suddenly I'm enlightened?"

Althea laughed softly. "No, you *stop* thinking about anything. Thinking is the veil that keeps you from feeling the truth of the present moment. You don't need to find peace. You need to *let go* of everything that isn't peace."

Emma sighed, shifting uncomfortably. "And how do I do that?"

"Start with your breath," Althea said simply. "Close your eyes."

Emma hesitated but then complied. The truck rumbled beneath her as she settled into the seat.

"Feel the air as it moves in... and out," Althea guided, her voice gentle, steady. "Not forcing, just noticing."

Emma inhaled, and for the first time, she actually paid attention to what it *felt* like. The cool air filling her lungs. The warmth as she exhaled. The slight pause in between. The rhythm, steady, unchanging.

"Now, listen," Althea continued. "Not with your mind. With your body. Feel the weight of yourself in the seat. The vibration of the tires on the road. The wind pressing against the windows."

Emma did. And suddenly, she noticed things she'd never paid attention to before—the steady vibration of the engine beneath her fingertips. The warmth of the sun filtering through the glass. The quiet rhythm of her own breath, steady and present, no longer lost in the noise of her thoughts.

The storm of her mind softened into a quiet lake.

"Good," Althea murmured. "Now let everything else fall away. The past, the future—drop it. Be here. In the only moment that has ever existed."

Emma focused. At first, her mind resisted, pulling at distractions. But then—stillness.

She was not the pain of her past. She was not the fear of tomorrow. She just *was*.

A strange warmth bloomed behind her forehead, a gentle pressure that wasn't quite physical. It pulsed, faint but undeniable.

Emma didn't fully understand it. But she *felt* the first tickle of awakening.

And as the miles stretched behind them, she no longer felt like she was just running.

She was *becoming*.

Then—James exhaled a long, exaggerated breath and stretched. "I'm glad you two are bonding here, but in my present moment, all this deep breathing is gonna put me to sleep," he said, breaking the silence.

Emma's eyes snapped open. "Oh, yeah, definitely don't do that." She shook out her arms, rolling her shoulders dramatically as if to *physically* shake off the meditation. Then she reached forward over the center console, cranking up the radio. A rock song blared through the speakers.

"There," she said, grinning at James. "Emergency anti-meditation protocol activated. You stay awake, and I avoid becoming one with the cosmos while still trapped in this truck." She laughed.

James chuckled. "Much appreciated."

Althea just shook her head with an amused smile, slightly readjusting the volume. "You do realize you can be present *and* listen to music, right?"

Emma smirked, leaning back into her seat. "Baby steps, Althea. Baby steps."

James shot her a look in the rearview mirror with pride and appreciation, then over to Althea. "Alright, wise one. Mount Shasta... You ever been there?"

She shook her head, her eyes thoughtful. "No, but I've read about it. People call it a spiritual vortex, a place where the veil between worlds is thin. It's a gathering point for those seeking enlightenment, a beacon for the awakened."

James grunted, his hands steady on the wheel. "Sounds like our kind of place. Let's just hope it's not crawling with Westfield types."

Emma's brow furrowed at the mention of Westfield. "I probably should have asked this before but, what exactly are we walking into?"

Althea turned in her seat, her voice calm but serious. "Mount Shasta is powerful, Emma. It draws people from all walks of life, those seeking answers, healing, or purpose. But power like that also attracts those who would exploit it. Luna's warning wasn't just about Westfield's presence—it's about the energy there. If it feels wrong, we leave. Simple as that."

Emma nodded, her grip tightening on the crystal. "I just... I want to do this right. I want to be ready."

James glanced at her through the rearview mirror, his tone softening. "You are ready. Don't overthink it. Just trust your instincts. But remember, this is a recon mission, we are just trying to get a sense for the area, see if Westfield or anyone else is up to no good, and then we meet up with the rest down in Los Angeles."

The road stretched on, winding through dense forests and rocky outcroppings. They stopped briefly at a roadside diner, grabbing sandwiches and coffee to fuel their journey. The atmosphere was light, punctuated by James's dry humor and Althea's gentle encouragement. Even Emma found herself laughing, with the weight of her past lifted.

As they neared Mount Shasta, the landscape became more striking. Majestic pines lined the road, their emerald needles shimmering in the midday light. The air grew cooler, tinged with the fresh scent of cedar and earth. A sense of anticipation settled over them, the mountain's magnetic pull undeniable.

Emma leaned forward, her voice filled with quiet wonder. "It's beautiful."

Althea smiled, her gaze fixed on the towering peak ahead. "It is. And it's more than that. It's a place where clarity finds those who seek it."

They rolled into the small town of Mount Shasta as the sun dipped behind the towering peak, casting long shadows over the streets lined with quaint shops, cafés, and crystal-laden storefronts catering to both locals and seekers alike. The town pulsed with a quiet, lingering energy—a place where the mystical and the mundane coexisted in an easy rhythm.

James pulled into a parking space along the main strip, exhaling as he shut off the engine. The silence that followed was almost jarring after hours of road noise.

"Finally," Emma groaned, stretching her legs before even attempting to climb out. She raised her arms overhead and winced as her muscles protested. "I swear, ten more minutes in this seat and I would've fossilized."

James cracked his neck and rolled his shoulders as he pushed the driver's side door open. "I'm officially too damn old for long hauls."

Althea smiled but said nothing, instead stepping out and taking in their surroundings. The air was crisp, carrying the scent of pine and distant woodsmoke.

Luna had described this place as a hub of energy, a crossroads where the veil thinned—but right now, it just looked like a picturesque mountain town with a heavy dose of esoteric flair.

They started walking, letting the town reveal itself to them.

Emma trailed her fingers over the rough brick of a shopfront, taking in the colorful window displays—tarot decks, aura photography, a sign promising "Ascension Workshops." It was both fascinating and overwhelming.

James took the lead, scanning the sidewalks as if expecting trouble. "If anything feels off, we regroup immediately," he muttered.

Emma arched a brow. "Are we expecting a rogue band of crystal-wielding mystics to ambush us?"

James just grunted. "You joke, but I've seen weirder things."

They wandered past cafés and local art shops, ducking into the visitor center for maps and local history. But no one spoke of anything unusual. There were no obvious signs of Westfield's presence, no whispers of stolen artifacts. Just friendly smiles, pamphlets on hiking trails, and an older woman at the counter who cheerfully explained ley lines like she was reciting the local weather.

After nearly an hour of exploring with nothing to show for it, Emma sighed. "So, what's the plan? We can't just wander around hoping for divine intervention."

Althea slowed, her eyes narrowing as something across the street caught her attention.

A bookstore, tucked between a café and a crystal shop.

Sacred Journeys.

She tilted her head, a familiar pull stirring in her chest.

"There," she said, nodding toward it. "Let's try there."

The trio stepped into the bookstore, the scent of aged paper and incense wrapping around them like a familiar spell. Shelves crammed with books on mysticism, healing, and lost civilizations stretched to the ceiling, the atmosphere thick with new-age reverence and tourist intrigue.

Behind the counter, a woman with auburn hair braided and adorned with tiny crystals watched them with a knowing smile.

"Welcome," she said, her voice soft and melodic. "The mountain has been waiting for you."

Emma's eyebrows shot up. "Me?"

The woman nodded slowly. "You carry a light, one that will soon awaken fully. Trust in the path before you."

Althea and James exchanged a glance—James struggling to contain an eye roll, while Althea remained intrigued.

"We're here to learn," Althea said. "Anything you can share about the mountain's energy? Or any recent... disturbances?"

The woman's smile wavered. "The energy is strong, but it's been restless lately. Disruptions." She hesitated, lowering her voice. "Some say it's natural. Others... feel it's interference. Be cautious, especially if you go near the sacred caves."

Emma felt a shiver crawl down her spine. The woman's words carried weight. Or at least, they were meant to.

Then, her eyes landed on a stack of brochures by the entrance.

Her lips twitched.

"You're full of shit."

Althea blinked. "Emma—"

"Sorry, but it's a sham story. She says that to everyone to boost tours of the caves."

James doubled over laughing. "I can't believe she called it before you did, Althea!" He pointed, gasping for breath. "She saw through it in seconds!"

The woman sighed, unfazed. "Look, lady, 80% of my customers want to hear that. I just... give them what they're looking for."

Emma crossed her arms. "What about the other 20%?"

The clerk smirked. "They get the truth."

Emma tilted her head. "Then let's start over. We're the 20%. Give us the real weird shit."

The woman tapped her nails on the counter, considering. "There really isn't any to be honest. Only thing that comes to mind is that storm back in February. Came outta nowhere, rolled over the mountains east of here. Freak thing—news covered it for weeks. Three people died." She shrugged. "Outside of that? Just your usual curiosity seekers."

James grinned and raised a hand.

Emma slapped him a high-five without hesitation.

James shook his head, grinning. "I was so wrong about you, kid."

Emma smirked. "I know."

Althea sighed, offering the poor clerk a nod of apology. "Thanks for your time."

Outside the bookstore, the crisp mountain air felt heavier than before. Emma tucked her hands into her jacket pockets, rocking on her heels as she processed what they'd learned—or, more accurately, what they hadn't.

"So," she said, glancing between James and Althea, "what now?"

James blew out a breath, rubbing the back of his neck. "Well, that was underwhelming."

Althea frowned. "Three people died, James."

He held up a hand. "I didn't mean it like that. I just... I expected something bigger. Like missing hikers or government cover-ups. Not a freak storm from months ago."

Althea's expression softened, but her voice remained firm. "Abandon expectations and see the path in front of you."

James huffed a small laugh. "Yeah, yeah. You're right." He looked back at the bookstore with a smirk. "Still, I gotta say... Emma calling that scam out in two seconds? Highlight of my day."

Emma grinned. "What can I say? I have a low tolerance for bullshit."

Althea shook her head with a chuckle but then turned serious. "I don't think we should ignore this. That storm wasn't normal. Luna has already told us that Westfield was behind the storm that hit Everwood. If it wasn't natural, then something—or someone—triggered it. We need to know who those people were."

Emma let out a sigh. "Guess that means we're digging into public records next, huh?"

James groaned. "Of course it does." He glanced around the street. "Alright, first things first—food, coffee, then finding the cheapest half-decent motel we can crash in."

Althea smiled. "Now that's a plan I can get behind."

Emma stretched, rolling her shoulders. "Fine. But if we're doing this, I call dibs on the first shower. Non-negotiable."

James smirked, already heading toward the truck. "We'll see about that, kid."

As they piled into the truck, the neon signs flickered to life across town, the mountain looming behind them. The storm's mystery lingered in the back of their minds, waiting.

And in the quiet hum of the truck's engine, the threads of fate continued to weave.

FORTY-THREE

WHEN SCIENCE MEETS FAITH

The SUV's engine rumbled softly as Elias wound his way up the narrow mountain road. Shadows from the towering pines stretched across the cracked asphalt, their limbs like stoic giants guarding the ancient secrets of the Sierra Nevada. The air outside was crisp, tinged with the faint scent of pine resin and damp earth. Inside the vehicle, however, the atmosphere was heavy with thoughts and memories.

Elias tightened his grip on the steering wheel, his knuckles whitening as the road curved sharply ahead. His mind wandered back to his time with Dr. Beth Marin, when she first started with Westfield. She had been a force of nature—brilliant, determined, and unyielding in her pursuit of truth. He remembered their late-night discussions, the hum of lab equipment in the background as he helped her piece together fragments of ancient knowledge found in frequencies. Beth's excitement had been infectious, her mind leaping from one revelation to the next with a passion that left even him breathless.

But it was her quiet moments that lingered with him the most. Those rare instances when she let her guard down, her voice soft as she spoke of the potential their research held—not for power, but for healing, for balance. She had trusted him, confided in him her growing unease as Westfield's true intentions seemed to shift.

Elias glanced at the GPS. He could only find one cabin where Luna identified she would be. He could only hope that Luna's gift was truly as accurate as she made it seem.

"She's going to be here," Elias murmured under his breath, his voice a quiet affirmation against the hum of the engine. He reached into his jacket pocket and pulled out the quartz crystal Luna had given him. Its faint, pulsing glow offered a sense of calm, a reminder that he wasn't alone in this. The crystal hummed softly against his palm, its energy resonating with the rhythm of the mountain's ancient pulse.

The landscape shifted as the road ascended, the dense forest thinning to reveal glimpses of snow-capped peaks in the distance. Elias let out a slow breath, his thoughts sharpening as the journey neared its end. The weight of his mission pressed against him, but he welcomed it. Every mile brought him closer to the answers they so desperately needed—and to the person who held them.

He could almost hear Beth's voice in his mind, the determined cadence of her words as she unraveled the mysteries of their shared work. There was no turning back now.

Ahead, the road curved once more, revealing a break in the trees. The sun dipped low on the horizon, casting the mountains in hues of gold and crimson. The coordinates were close. Elias's pulse quickened, his heart thudding in time with the crystal's steady vibration.

"This is it," he muttered, the cabin's silhouette finally coming into view beyond a stand of old pines.

The first step of many.

The gravel crunched beneath Elias's tires as he pulled up to the secluded cabin, its weathered wood blending seamlessly with the dense forest. He cut the engine, the hum fading into the soft rustle of wind through towering pines.

For a moment, he sat in silence, his grip tightening on the steering wheel. It had been years since he'd last seen Beth, but there was no time for hesitation—no point in rehearsing words that would never come out the way he planned.

Before he could even knock, the door creaked open.

"Elias?"

Beth stood in the doorway, her presence unchanged yet strikingly different. Age had traced subtle lines across her skin, but it had done nothing to diminish her radiance. If anything, she had only grown into it, an effortless beauty that defied time itself.

Her hair, a deep chestnut touched with strands of gold, cascaded loosely over her shoulders, catching the fading sunlight like polished copper. Her eyes—sharp, unreadable—held the weight of knowledge few could bear. A soft, worn jacket rested over her casual clothes, but nothing about her felt ordinary. She was a presence, a force that existed beyond the passage of years.

Elias exhaled. "Beth."

Her lips curved in a faint smile, but the concern in her gaze did not fade. "After all these years, you show up at my door? What are you doing here? How did you even find me?"

Elias hesitated before stepping forward, his satchel slung over his shoulder. "Through the help of a very powerful friend—Don't worry, we can trust her... I'm sorry, but I had to find you. There's something you need to know... about Westfield."

"I'm sure I can trust your friend if you say so, but if you can find me, so can they." Her expression darkened, and she motioned for him to come inside. "I guess we don't have time for pleasantries. Come on in, old friend."

The cabin's interior was cozy but cluttered, its shelves overflowing with books, journals, and scattered research papers. A small fire crackled in the hearth, casting flickering shadows on the walls. Elias dropped his satchel onto a chair, his eyes scanning the space before settling on a corkboard filled with notes and photos connected by strings of red thread.

"You've been busy," he remarked, gesturing to the board.

Beth followed his gaze, her arms crossed. "You don't survive by being idle, Elias. Now, tell me—what brought you here?"

"It's my friend, Luna. Something profound is happening to her. Her DNA—it's changing, evolving in ways we once only theorized. The possibilities we talked about all those years ago? They're no longer speculation. They're real. And Westfield knows it. They found her. They sent a spy into her community. A painting was stolen—not just art, but a vessel of wisdom. And it's not just that. Ancient alchemical texts have gone missing from Sedona. The world stands on the edge of something extraordinary, a shift unlike anything before. But Westfield isn't just watching—they're moving, and whatever they're after could jeopardize everything. We can't stand by. We have to act. Now."

He hesitated just a moment, his voice softening. "Luna is Margaret's daughter. You might remember her from college—we all crossed paths more than once."

Beth's eyes lit with a flicker of recognition. "Ah, yes—Margaret." A small smile tugged at her lips. "I recall whenever you couldn't be found, it was because the two of you were off somewhere, lost in thought. The library, the cliffs, wherever there was silence enough for theory and wonder."

Beth's eyes lingered on him, the memory of Margaret still fresh in her expression. "You mentioned a painting…" she said slowly. "Westfield's fixation on artifacts hasn't changed, it seems?"

She turned toward the board, her fingers tracing one of the criss-crossed strings with absent precision. "Herold Westfield was always fascinated by the Hermetic principles, as you know. In college, he was obsessed with mastering them. I tried my best to teach him—but he lacked patience, discipline. When traditional methods failed, he turned to technology, looking for shortcuts to harness universal energies. And, he is finding them."

She hesitated, her fingers curling into a fist. "Over the years, as our capabilities grew stronger and faster, his obsession turned into madness. That's why I left."

Elias leaned forward. "What were they doing?"

Beth's voice grew heavy, tinged with bitterness. "With his quantum computers, he was able to develop machines to manipulate natural frequencies—to tap into the Earth's energy, disrupt ecosystems, even control weather patterns." Her lips pressed into a thin line. "It could've healed the world. But Herold didn't care about that. No profit. No power. That was the end of it."

Elias's breath hitched. "Luna was right, then." He exhaled sharply, shaking his head. "A storm hit the community she's from. It wasn't nat-ural—she said it felt manufactured."

Beth's expression darkened. "Then it was Westfield. I'd put money on it. They're testing their reach, pushing boundaries. And now they're after anything that can enhance their control, or hinder their progress."

Elias sat back, the weight of her words pressing down on him. "If Westfield has the painting... where would they keep it?"

Beth's gaze sharpened. "Herold's private collection."

Elias frowned. "A vault?"

Beth nodded. "Not exactly. More like a fortress. He hoards relics, man-uscripts—anything that might give him an edge. If the painting's there, it's not just a trophy—it's a weapon in his eyes."

Elias's pulse quickened. "Then we stop him. We expose him. If we can retrieve those items—"

"It's not that simple." Beth interrupted, her voice low, resolute. "West-field's influence runs deep. I've been collecting evidence, but I've had to stay hidden. They tried to kill me once. I barely escaped. If they find me again, they won't fail." She said with intensity and caution.

Elias's jaw tightened. "Then we don't give them the chance." He leaned forward, his voice measured but firm. "We work together. Bring this to light before it's too late."

Beth studied him, searching his face for hesitation. She found none.

A small, knowing smile ghosted her lips. "You've always been stubborn." But the steel in her eyes didn't waver. "If we do this, we need a plan. Bulletproof. Something their lawyers can't bury and their deep pockets can't make disappear. I haven't found that yet."

Elias extended his hand across the table. "Luna can help. I'm sure of it. Come with me, meet her. She'll find the missing pieces in your research. Together, we take down Westfield."

Beth glanced around, her cabin filled with months of work—pinned notes, faded journals, artifacts stacked in controlled chaos. "Look at this place. It would take me a month just to pack up and sort through it all. Can't Luna come here?"

Elias chuckled. "She doesn't need any of it. She just needs you." He held out his hand. "So, what do you say?"

Beth's hesitation lasted only a second. Then, her grip tightened around his. "She really has such a gift?" She paused, searching his eyes for the truth.

Elias reached into his pocket, retrieving the smooth quartz crystal that had become a silent tether to Luna's presence. Without a word, he placed it gently in Beth's palm.

She arched a brow. "What's this?"

"Luna's essence is entangled within it," Elias said, his tone steady, certain. "Humor me. Pretend it's a magic 8-ball. Ask it if you should come with me—then feel the answer."

Beth exhaled sharply, half-amused, half-skeptical. But curiosity won. She closed her fingers around the crystal, letting its cool weight settle in her palm.

At first, there was nothing.

Then—warmth. A pulse, faint yet unmistakable, thrummed through her skin. It wasn't a voice, not exactly. More like a whisper of knowing—a quiet pull in the depths of her being.

Beth's breathing fractured under the moment of acceptance.

She had spent years doubting, questioning, distrusting everyone and everything. But this? It was different.

It felt like truth.

Slowly, she opened her eyes, meeting Elias's steady gaze.

"Fine," she said, her voice softer now, almost reluctant. But the resolve was there. "We do this together." A smirk ghosted her lips. "I sure hope this Luna chick is everything you make her out to be."

Elias chuckled, tucking the crystal back into his pocket. "You'll see for yourself soon enough."

Beth barely had a moment to process his words when his phone buzzed.

One new message.

Elias glanced at it, then smirked and turned the screen toward her.

Beth's stomach flipped.

Thank you for your trust, Beth.

Her fingers curled instinctively, a rush of heat crawling up her spine. "What the hell—" she stopped herself, exhaling sharply. She wasn't sure whether to be unnerved or reassured.

A long pause settled between them.

Beth's skepticism battled against the quiet truth stirring in her gut.

She met Elias's gaze, her throat tightening. "I hate to admit it," she muttered, "but I think that was all the proof I needed."

Elias grinned. "Told you."

The fire crackled softly in the hearth, its flickering light casting shifting shadows against the walls.

The battle hadn't even begun—but in that moment, they both knew there was no turning back.

FORTY-FOUR

TIDES OF PURPOSE

The sun hung low on the horizon as Luna leaned back in her seat, her phone pressed to her ear. The hum of the road filled the quiet space between her and Ezra as the SUV sped down the highway. On the other end of the line, Elias's voice crackled through the speaker.

"So, Herold's private collection," Luna said, her voice calm but tinged with frustration. "That's where the painting is?"

"Almost certainly," Elias replied, his tone steady but laced with urgency. "Beth says he guards his collection obsessively. His home in Malibu is like a fortress—top-tier security, but also, a status symbol. If the painting's there, it's not just hidden; it's being flaunted with all his other relics."

Luna sighed, her fingers drumming lightly on her knee. "I've been trying to connect with it, to see where it might be, but there's something... blocking me. It's like its energy is buried, muffled. Herold must have it surrounded by something that severed its connection to me."

Beth's voice chimed in, her tone sharp and focused. "Westfield isn't careless, especially when it comes to objects of power. He's also paranoid—likely using shielding technology to mask the painting's frequency, whether he knows of your capabilities or not. If you need to connect with it, you'll have to get closer. Or disable the tech, which means getting inside Westfield Headquarters, Downtown L.A."

Luna exhaled, her fingers tightening around her phone. "Beth, thank you again. I can't tell you what it means to have you with us." She hesitated, choosing her words carefully. "I believe the painting's secrets are tied to me alone—like my mother designed it that way. But I can't be sure. If Westfield's tech is advanced enough... could it unlock the embedded memories without me?"

Beth frowned, considering the question. "Herold's latest quantum computers are remarkable, Luna. They should be solving cancer, not chasing power. I'd be surprised if he's actively developed something to crack the painting's secrets, though. His arrogance wouldn't allow him to believe human consciousness could achieve what you're describing. But..." She sighed. "It's not impossible. If he's thrown enough money and minds at the problem, he might have found a way."

Luna exchanged a glance with Ezra, who kept his eyes on the road but nodded in silent agreement. "Then the target is Herold," she said firmly. "We'll meet in Santa Monica. It's close enough to Malibu to plan our next steps without drawing too much attention. We can determine if the headquarters is necessary from there."

"Good call," Elias said. "Beth and I will head out first thing in the morning. We should be there by late afternoon."

"We'll book a SpotStay," Luna added. "Ezra and I will get there ahead of you and start working on a strategy. Once you arrive, we'll finalize everything."

Beth's voice softened slightly, her gratitude evident. "Be careful, Luna. If Herold's protecting the painting this fiercely, he knows its value, even if he hasn't unlocked its secrets. He'll stop at nothing to keep it—and to stop anyone who gets in his way."

"I know," Luna replied, her voice resolute. "But we're not just anyone and we aren't alone. We've come too far to stop now."

After a brief exchange of goodbyes, Luna ended the call, her mind already racing with possibilities.

She dialed Althea immediately. The phone rang only once before Althea's familiar, steady voice came through.

"Luna," Althea greeted, her tone calm but expectant. "We've been waiting to hear from you."

"How far are you from Mount Shasta?" Luna asked without preamble.

"We put Mount Shasta in the rear view mirror this morning," Althea replied. "We managed to learn about a storm they had back in February—really strange one, killed three people, all struck by lightning. Two of them were Westfield employees: Alden Falkridge and Ryan Carter. They were working a crew stationed at the Westfield Towers project nearby. It must have been them... It gave us an eerie feeling, so we got out of there. We're already heading south to you. Where do you need us?"

"Ryan Carter..." Luna murmured, the name pulling threads of insight from the aether. Her breath caught. "Ryan was their target. A potential whistleblower... They murdered him."

Silence hung in the air, heavy with the weight of realization. Luna let it settle before continuing, her tone sharpening with resolve. "You were smart to leave. Trusting your instincts may have saved you. I need you in Santa Monica. The sooner I get everyone back together, the better I'll feel."

Her voice softened for a beat, then strengthened again. "Elias and I spoke, He is bringing Dr. Marin with him. The painting's likely in Herold Westfield's private collection, which means Malibu. Ezra and I are already on the road. We don't think Westfield's unlocked its secrets yet—that he's discovered the existence of the pyramid. But we have to get it back before he does."

As Luna was finishing, Althea tapped the screen, turning on the speaker. There was a brief pause before Althea responded, her tone measured. "Understood. We are on our way?"

"We're booking a place near the coast. I'll send you the address once it's confirmed. Please be safe." Luna said with worry.

In the background, Luna heard James's voice, sharp and teasing. "What's she got us doing now?"

Althea chuckled softly before responding to him. "We're heading to Santa Monica."

Emma's voice came through next, quieter but curious. "What's in Santa Monica?"

Luna smiled faintly, feeling something stir within her—something familiar.

"Your next step, Emma," she said gently. "You're part of this now. More than you realize."

The moment she spoke, she felt it again—a presence, something vast, layered beneath Emma's energy. Something vital. Something inevitable.

Ezra must have sensed her shift in focus.

"I'll drive through the night if I have to," James interjected, his tone resolute. "We'll get there."

"Good," Luna replied. "But be careful. The closer we get to Westfield, the more dangerous things will become, and if they will go after one of their own.... Trust your instincts, and don't hesitate to listen to them."

"We'll be there, Luna," Althea assured her. "And we'll be ready."

After exchanging a few more details, Luna ended the call and leaned back in her seat, her fingers briefly pressing against the smooth surface of the crystal resting on her lap.

"What stole your attention there?" Ezra asked, keeping his eyes on the road but casting a quick glance in her direction.

Luna hesitated. "Emma..." She exhaled, trying to grasp the feeling, but it slipped through her thoughts like mist. "There's something about her. Something I recognize, but I can't place it yet. She is important, I just don't know how."

Ezra's jaw tensed slightly. "She reminds you of yourself, doesn't she?"

"Maybe...This just became much more serious. I'm worried that I am putting everyone in danger, but I know this is the right path." Luna said, looking over to Ezra.

Luna took a deep calming breath and found reassurance in the air.

"They'll be here soon," Luna reassured herself , her voice steady and confident. "It's all coming together, Ezra. We're not alone in this any-more. We have Everwood, Sedona, and now Emma and Beth. That's our strength."

Ezra nodded, his gaze turning toward the distant horizon. "Then let's make sure we're ready when they arrive."

Far ahead, the Los Angeles skyline shimmered under the late afternoon sun, its spires of glass and steel piercing the hazy horizon. Luna gazed out the window, watching as the distant city slowly grew sharper with each passing mile—a gleaming promise of answers and danger intertwined.

By the time they reached Santa Monica, the city was alive with its usual buzz of activity—tourists meandering along the promenade, street performers weaving music into the salty air, neon signs flickering to life. They navigated the winding roads until they pulled up to their Spot-Stay—a modest yet charming beachside retreat.

The white stucco walls and sun-bleached wooden deck stood in stark contrast to the intensity of their mission, offering a temporary illusion of peace. Luna snapped a picture and texted Althea and Elias with the address.

Inside, the space breathed with openness—large windows welcoming the ocean breeze, the distant rhythm of waves a grounding force against the chaos looming ahead.

Luna dropped her bag by the couch and moved with quiet purpose, setting up her workspace at the dining table. Her journal and crystals were arranged with careful precision, each item placed with intention next to her laptop.

Ezra carried their bags into one of the bedrooms and then took a detour to the kitchen, returning after with two steaming cups of tea. He placed one beside her and pulled out a chair, his gaze steady as he watched her work.

"What's the plan?" he asked.

Luna cradled the tea in her hands but didn't drink. Her focus remained on the quartz crystal, its cool surface warming under her touch.

"First, I'll try again to connect with the painting," Luna said, her voice steady but resolute. "I might not pinpoint its exact location, but I should at least sense its surroundings—enough to confirm it's in Malibu. If Herold sees its value, he'll have it secured, not destroyed. I need to be sure before we risk anything. If it's gone, there's no point in walking into the lion's den."

Ezra nodded, his expression thoughtful. "And if that doesn't work?"

Luna exhaled slowly. "Then we wait for the others. Work on a new plan."

The steady crash of waves filled the space between them as Luna closed her eyes, shifting her focus inward. The crystal in her hand pulsed faintly, its energy syncing with the rhythm of her breath.

She reached out, her consciousness stretching beyond the walls of their temporary home, searching for the faintest trace of the painting's presence.

A flicker—sharp, cold—brushed against her senses, her mothers face flashed in her mind's eye.

But as quickly as it appeared, it was swallowed whole, buried beneath an oppressive, suffocating void.

Luna's brow furrowed. Her grip on the crystal tightened. Her thoughts and concerns clouding her focus.

Ezra leaned forward, his voice careful, measured. "Anything?"

Luna opened her eyes, frustration simmering beneath her usually steady expression. "It's there, Ezra. I can feel it, but it's buried.

Whatever they're using to block its energy is strong." She paused, trying to put it into words. "I've been practicing my connection with man-made signals, but this... this is just static. Nothing but interference."

Ezra placed a reassuring hand on her shoulder. "We'll figure it out. Everything happens for a reason. You'll see it when you need to."

Luna studied him for a moment, then nodded, her resolve solidifying. "We will. This is just the beginning."

Her gaze drifted past the window, out toward the endless horizon. The sun hovered low, casting long shadows as the first strokes of sunset painted the sky. Soft oranges and blush pinks spread like watercolor across the canvas of fading blue, the Pacific shimmering in reflection, alive with the promise of twilight still far off.

A small smile curved her lips.

"Come, Ezra. Let's walk down to the shoreline."

She reached out her hand.

Ezra hesitated only a second before intertwining his fingers with hers, allowing himself to sink into the moment, just for a little while.

The sun hung low in the sky, casting long golden beams across the tranquil waves of the Pacific. The rhythmic crash of the ocean filled the air as Luna and Ezra strolled barefoot along the sandy shoreline. The evening breeze played with Luna's hair, and for a brief moment, the weight of their mission seemed to fade under the embrace of nature's timeless beauty.

Luna paused, her gaze fixed on the horizon. The expanse of the ocean seemed to stretch endlessly, its surface shimmering like liquid gold. She tilted her head slightly, her fingers grazing her temple as she allowed her senses to open. The energy of the planet flowed through her like a current, faint but persistent, whispering echoes of Earth's earliest history.

She saw flashes—primordial seas churning under a violet sky, single-celled organisms bursting into life, and the delicate dance of evolution unfurling across eons. But the connection was faint, as if filtered through a veil. She sighed softly, her hand falling to her side.

"Can't quite reach it?" Ezra asked, his voice gentle.

Luna shook her head, a faint smile tugging at her lips. "It's like trying to hear a song through a wall. It's there, but distant. The distance to the pyramid is too far." A hint of worry crawled up her spine. A simple knowing that if she faced Herold now, she wouldn't stand a chance.

Ezra nodded, his hand finding hers. "Even if it's faint, it's still incredible. You see things no one else can. That's why we're here, Luna. To protect that gift, so others can find it."

Luna squeezed his hand, drawing strength from his quiet support, not willing to ruin the moment with her concerns. They continued walking, the silence between them filled with unspoken understanding.

As they reached a stretch of beach where the sand met jagged rocks, Luna stopped abruptly. She turned to face Ezra, her heart pounding. The warmth of the setting sun painted his features in a soft glow, and she took a deep breath. The looming uncertainty demands her to say what needs to be heard.

"Ezra," she began, her voice steady but laced with emotion. "There's something I need to tell you," she continued, her palms resting on her abdomen.

He looked at her, his brow furrowing slightly in concern. "What is it?"

She hesitated for only a moment before the words tumbled out. "I'm..... we are pregnant."

Ezra's eyes widened, his mouth opening in surprise. For a second, he said nothing, his expression unreadable. Then, a slow, radiant smile spread across his face. "You're serious?"

Luna nodded, her own smile forming. "I felt it the very moment the spark ignited within me. It was magical." She paused as the memory filled her with joy. "It happened the night of the storm, I wanted to tell you immediately, but it didn't feel right then... it feels necessary now."

Ezra pulled her into a tight embrace, his laughter warm and full of joy. "Luna... this is amazing. You've just given me the greatest news of my life."

Luna leaned into him, her eyes shimmering with emotion. "Even with everything happening? The danger, the uncertainty..."

Ezra pulled back just enough to look into her eyes. "Especially with everything happening. This is a reminder of why we're fighting—for the future, for hope."

Before Luna could respond, Ezra knelt down on one knee, his hand reaching into his pocket.

She felt the ripple of excitement pass through her.

"Ezra..." she whispered, her voice thick with emotion, already knowing, but still deeply moved.

He held up a simple but elegant ring, the diamond catching the last rays of sunlight. "Luna, you've changed my life in ways I can't even begin to describe. You've shown me a world I never thought possible. I want to be by your side for all of it—for every challenge, every triumph, every moment. Will you marry me?"

Tears welled in Luna's eyes as she nodded, her voice trembling. "Yes. A thousand times, yes."

Ezra slipped the ring onto her finger and rose to his feet, pulling her into a kiss just as a voice crackled over a nearby loudspeaker.

"Congratulations, lovebirds!"

They broke apart, startled, and turned to see a lifeguard standing in his tower, grinning as he waved. Luna and Ezra burst into laughter, waving back before sharing another kiss.

As the sun drifted lower, deepening the sky's palette from soft peach to rich amber, Luna felt a sudden surge of energy. It wasn't her own—it came from afar, a wave of power strengthening her connection to the aether.

"The meditation group," she murmured, her eyes widening.

Ezra tilted his head. "What's happening?"

Luna closed her eyes, allowing the energy to flow through her. The faint veil she'd felt earlier began to lift, and for a moment, she saw the Earth's beauty in vivid clarity—the intricate patterns of nature, the harmony of life's interconnected web. She reached out with her mind, pulling Ezra into the vision.

He gasped softly as the world around them seemed to dissolve into light. They stood together in a vast expanse of stars, watching galaxies swirl and dance. Below them, Earth glowed with an ethereal light, its pulse synchronized with their own.

"This is what we're fighting for," Luna said, her voice reverent. "Not just for now, but for all that's possible."

Ezra squeezed her hand, his voice steady. "And we'll do it together."

The vision faded, leaving them standing on the darkened beach, the waves lapping gently at their feet. The moment felt sacred, a promise not just to each other but to the world they sought to protect.

FORTY-FIVE

A NAME REMEMBERED

T he sun had dipped behind the mountainous horizon to their right, leaving the highway cloaked in darkness, the faint glow of the truck's headlights carving a narrow path through the night. The low hum of the engine was steady, a stark contrast to the brewing energy within the truck's cabin.

James focused on the road, his hands firm on the wheel, while Althea sat with her eyes closed, her hands resting gently in her lap. Her breath slowed, her awareness reaching outward.

Then—a ripple seemed to pass through her.

She inhaled softly, her lips parting as something vast stirred within her.

"Hmm..." She exhaled, tilting her head. "Something is happening."

James shot her a glance, his brow furrowing. "What's happening? Is it Luna?"

Althea's eyes remained closed, her mind tracing the energy shift. "No... it's different." A pause, then a deepened awareness. "The meditation group—their energy is strengthening Luna. But this..." Her voice dropped to a whisper. "It feels closer. More personal. Almost like Luna is here."

From the backseat, a sharp inhale.

Emma stirred beneath her blanket, her body tense as if awakening from a deep dream. A shiver ran through her as unseen threads of energy coiled and unraveled along her spine.

Her breath came fast.

Her fingers curled against her knees.

"I feel it too," she whispered, voice unsteady. "It's like... she's calling to me. But it's not just her."

James' grip tightened on the wheel, his gaze flicking to the rearview mirror. "Emma, you alright back there?"

Emma shook her head, pressing her palms against her temples as if trying to contain the energy surging through her. A tingling warmth spread from her core, radiating outward in waves that shimmered beneath her skin. It wasn't painful—just overwhelming, like liquid light pouring into every cell, expanding her from the inside out. Her chest heaved in response, eyes wide as her pupils dilated, her body trembling under the weight of it. "It's too much... but it doesn't hurt. It's like—" she gasped, her voice quivering with awe, "like I'm blissfully being pulled apart and made whole at the same time."

Althea twisted in her seat, her gaze soft but urgent. "Emma, what do you see?"

Emma squeezed her eyes shut. Stars. Infinite, luminous, burning stars. They spun and spiraled, their gravity pulling at her, filling her lungs, her bones, her very being.

She gasped. "I see... a planet being born."

Her voice trembled, awe lacing her words. "Light—bright, warm, endless. It's forming, shifting... and there's someone there." Her chest fluttered with the weight of recognition. "She holds the same energy as Luna... but older, deeper. Like the source Luna came from."

James swore under his breath, easing off the gas. "Nope. Nope. Not doing this while I'm barreling down I-5 at seventy." He flipped on the blinker and pulled onto the shoulder, the tires crunching against the gravel. "I'm all for cosmic revelations, but let's not have the universe rearrange itself while I'm trying to keep us between the lines."

The instant the truck stilled, Emma threw open the door, stumbling onto the cool earth. The night air hit her like an electric charge, grounding her, yet sending ripples of energy through her veins.

She dropped to her knees, gripping the damp grass as if it were the only thing tethering her to the physical world. The earth beneath her pulsed.

The visions surged.

Althea knelt beside her, placing a steadying hand on her back. "Breathe, Emma," she murmured, her voice soft but strong. "Let it flow. Don't fight it. You're strong enough."

Emma gasped for air, but Althea's words reached her, wrapping around her like an anchor. The chaos slowed. The light in her mind took shape.

She saw her.

A figure standing in the vast cosmic expanse, radiant and ancient, watching with quiet knowing.

The name slipped from Emma's lips like a whispered truth remembered from another life.

"Solara."

The moment the name was spoken, everything clicked into place.

James crouched nearby, frowning. "What's a Solara?"

Emma turned to him, her face tear-streaked, but her eyes shining. "I don't know." Her voice trembled, caught between wonder and certainty. "But it's her. It's Luna. It's me." She exhaled shakily. "I can't explain it, but… it's like we are two halves of something greater."

The stars in her vision flickered, aligning.

And somewhere deep within the cosmos, something stirred—not in remembrance, but in recognition.

Althea's hand stilled on Emma's back, her expression thoughtful, eyes tracing something unseen. "You're opening a door that's been locked for lifetimes. That kind of remembering—it doesn't come gently."

Her voice softened, steady and grounding. "Feel the ground beneath your fingers. Recognize your hands, your arms, your body… you are here, Emma. This moment is yours. Return to it."

She paused, her hand warm against Emma's spine. "Accept what you now know to be true—and breathe. Gently."

Emma's breath slowed as the torrent of knowing began to subside, her trembling easing as Althea's words sank in. She swallowed hard. "It feels too big," she murmured, voice raw. "Like I'm standing on the edge of something vast, and if I step forward, I won't come back the same."

James huffed softly, crouching beside her. "You won't," he said, matter-of-fact. "That's kind of the point."

Emma turned to him, her expression a mix of apprehension and reluctant amusement. "Helpful, James."

He smirked, but his tone softened. "Look, you don't have to have all the answers right now. Whatever this is, whatever you're becoming—you're still you, Emma. The rest? Let it happen when it happens."

She blinked, her tears drying as something steadier flickered in her eyes. Not quite certainty, but a willingness to step forward despite the unknown. "Thank you," she said quietly, her voice finding its balance. "I don't understand it all yet, but I trust it—and I clearly can't ignore what's happening. Luna needs me."

Althea gave a slow nod, her gaze knowing. "Trusting it is enough. For now."

James exhaled, pushing himself up and brushing the dirt from his knees. "Alright, let's get back on the road before someone mistakes us for a roadside cult."

Emma huffed a laugh, the sound surprising even her. She stood slowly, drawing in a deep breath—her first, it seemed, in this new reality. The air tasted different, crisp and alive, like the world had been rinsed clean. For the first time, she felt tethered not by fear, but by purpose. She climbed back into the truck, her body still humming with the remnants of her vision, her mind stretching toward something just out of reach. As the truck rumbled onto the highway, the night itself seemed transformed—the stars sharper, the air charged, as if the universe had shifted to meet her at the threshold of something greater.

From her seat, Emma whispered one final time, the name laced with reverence and familiarity.

"Solara..."

FORTY-SIX

AETHER & CODE

L una sat at the dining table, cross-legged and serene. Her hands hovered over a quartz crystal, her breath slow and steady, her energy weaving through the air like a whisper. She smiled as the sparkle of her engagement ring stole her attention briefly.

Ezra leaned against the counter, arms crossed, watching her with quiet admiration. She had changed since they first set out on this journey. There was a radiance to her now—something soft yet unshakable, like the steady pull of the moon over the tides. It wasn't just her power, though that was undeniable. It was the way she carried it—without arrogance, without fear. She stood rooted in purpose, her presence a quiet promise that even in the face of uncertainty, balance could be restored.

The air around Luna shimmered, almost imperceptibly, as she reached out—not with her hands, but through the unseen threads of energy that connected her to the world beyond sight. Her breath slowed, deep and rhythmic, guiding her inward while her awareness expanded outward, untethered from the physical. She could feel the resonant energy from the Sedona meditation from the previous night still fueling the strength of her will.

It no longer surprised her how naturally this came. Her regular practice had reshaped hesitation into certainty, like muscles strengthened through repetition. Where once there had always been a moment of resistance—a threshold she had to press through, like a leaf breaking the surface tension of still water. But now, she slipped effortlessly into the aetheric current, her consciousness gliding through the fabric of space-time as though it had been waiting, eager to welcome her like an old friend.

Luna smiled faintly, eyes closed, heart open. *This is what trust feels like.*

Her consciousness stretched outward, brushing against the subtle hum of life—the slow pulse of the earth, the gentle sway of tree roots beneath the soil, the faint auric glow of every living thing.

The world was a symphony of energy, and she was a welcomed conductor—no longer merely hearing its song, but composing herself within its melody, each breath a note in perfect harmony.

She focused her intention, honing her awareness into a sharp, singular thread: *The painting. Find the painting.*

Immediately, the world shifted. Energy currents realigned, guiding her like a magnetic pull beneath the surface down paths carved by memory. Shapes flickered at the edges of perception—outlines of streets bending and stretching like liquid fractals, voices echoing in fragmented whispers, the pulse of lives rippling through space and time. Each moment held its mark, and Luna followed the thread her mother had woven into the painting itself, like tracing the scent of lavender long after the flower was gone.

The trail led her toward the coast, the distant hush of ocean waves blending with the faint pulse of life along the shoreline. She drifted past winding roads and hillside villas, her mind's eye sweeping across sunlit ridges and shadowed canyons until the energy sharpened—vibrating with recognition.

Westfield.

The name surfaced, sterile and cold. She drifted to the estate's edge, feeling the disturbance in the field. Something synthetic masked the energy flow.

A scramble field.

Rather than push through, Luna moved like water—sinking beneath, into the earth's memory. The ground, loyal only to what touched it, held the imprint. The trees—slow, rooted witnesses—remembered her mother's essence woven into the painting.

She followed the echo to the gates. The memory pulsed like a final note: the painting had passed through.

"It's there," she whispered. "Hidden, but not forgotten.

The shimmer around her flickered as her awareness began to retreat, the strain of holding the connection brushing faintly against her senses. Not because she lacked strength, but because she had found what she came for. There was no need to push further.

She exhaled slowly, centering in the quiet afterglow of connection.

"They think it's secure," Luna muttered. "But the land itself remembers. And now... so do I."

Ezra's brow furrowed. "Westfield," he said, the name carrying weight. "Beth mentioned they've perfected ways to block frequencies. But it looks like they underestimated what's truly possible—underestimated you."

A knock at the door interrupting her thought. "They're here" Luna smiled as Ezra moved to answer it, revealing Elias and Beth standing on the porch.

Elias greeted them with a warm smile, but Beth lingered just behind him, her gaze sharp, scanning the street before stepping inside. Her presence was guarded, her movements precise—always assessing, always aware.

Luna's heart swelled with gratitude at the sight of them. "Elias," she said, stepping forward with open arms. "It's good to see you."

His smile softened as he embraced her briefly. "You too, Luna."

Luna turned her attention to Beth, who held herself a touch too stiffly, her expression careful. Luna didn't meet Beth's skepticism with resistance—only warmth.

"Beth," Luna said gently, "you're safe here."

Beth hesitated, as if weighing the truth of those words, then gave a small nod. "I trust you, Luna. But safety's relative when it comes to Westfield."

"Fair point," Luna admitted.

Ezra shut the door behind them, locking it securely. "Maybe. But we're stronger together. Whatever danger's out there, we're safer facing it as a team. Now, let's sit down and get to work."

The group settled around the dining table, the air shifting as the conversation turned serious. Luna spoke with ease, catching Elias and

Beth up on her struggle to connect with the painting, but confirming it went into the mansion within the last few days. Beth listened intently, her fingers tapping lightly against the table, her eyes narrowing as she took it all in.

The tension in Beth's posture remained, but something had shifted—subtle, cautious.

She hadn't come here for comfort. She'd come expecting deflection, half-truths, maybe even denial.

Instead, she found Luna—unshaken, welcoming, open.

And against that quiet certainty, doubt struggled to hold its ground.

Beth's fingers drummed against the table, her expression sharp with calculation. "If the shielding tech is what I think it is," she said, "then it's not just blocking the painting's energy—it's scrambling it. Disrupting the signal, making it harder to pinpoint or connect with. It's one of Herold's newer toys, designed for situations exactly like this, believe it or not."

She exhaled, shaking her head. "Herold has always known the potential in us. Let's just hope he doesn't see this coming so soon."

Luna watched her carefully. There was something in Beth's voice—frustration, yes, but something deeper, something personal.

Without breaking eye contact, Luna reached across the space between them, her hand hovering just above Beth's wrist. "May I?"

Beth blinked, caught off guard by the quiet request. She hesitated, then gave a short nod, irritation still tightening the corners of her mouth. "If it'll help, sure."

Luna's fingers brushed Beth's skin—light, deliberate. The connection ignited like a spark catching dry tinder.

Beth inhaled sharply, her body tensing for a moment. But then—she stilled, her gaze locking onto Luna's eyes.

Emerald light flickered within Luna's irises, like sunlight catching on dew-drenched leaves. The glow deepened, swirling with fractal patterns that pulsed in sync with the rhythmic beat beneath Beth's skin. Her breath hitched, but she couldn't look away. It wasn't just light—it was coherence, the synchronization of quantum states, each flicker reflecting the entanglement forming between them.

Luna's consciousness extended, her focus sharpening like the lens of a telescope. She didn't push into Beth's mind; instead, she attuned herself to the vibrational signature of Beth's memories—information encoded within the quantum field surrounding her. The body didn't just store experiences in neurons and synapses; it imprinted them into the energetic fabric of existence, like footprints in soft earth.

With practiced precision, Luna stabilized her mental field, maintaining quantum coherence as she tuned in to those imprints. The emerald shimmer in her eyes brightened, each pulse collapsing probability waves into clarity.

Fragments appeared—disjointed at first, like glimpses through an ancient kaleidoscope. But as Luna refined her focus, the threads of memory began to weave together.

Beth's breath wavered, caught between memory and moment. The hum of fluorescent lights in a sterile lab. The faint glow of encrypted files on a flickering screen. A whispered conversation behind closed doors. Sleepless nights spent chasing truths that didn't want to be found.

But the resonance didn't stop at conscious recollection.

Luna dipped deeper, into the quantum substrate where experiences encoded themselves into cellular vibration. The past wasn't confined to the mind; it lived in the body, etched into the energetic blueprint beneath flesh and bone.

The images sharpened. Long afternoons spent dismantling radios and rebuilding them, Beth's small fingers deftly twisting wires, her father's quiet pride watching from the doorway.

Luna saw her career within Westfield, the pride she felt for the work she had done, until her first brush with Westfield's darker side, when curiosity turned to realization—they weren't just observing the world. They were observing her. Tracking her. Calculating probabilities.

A sharper thread vibrated, pulling Luna closer. She plucked the string, and the memory unfurled like a ripple through still water. A speeding car. A dropped hot dog. The near miss that had once seemed like chance. But beneath the illusion of randomness, Luna saw the driver's face—tight with disappointment, not relief. A *mission failed.*

Beth hadn't been paranoid. She'd been right. They had tried to kill her.

Luna didn't just *see* Beth's story—she *felt* it, absorbed the emotional charge imprinted within each moment. The weight of isolation. The cold clarity of survival. The relentless pursuit of truth.

Beth inhaled sharply, her body tensing as the connection deepened. But Luna, practiced now, recognized the threshold—the point where awareness risked becoming intrusion. She softened her focus, allowing the quantum coherence between them to unravel naturally.

With deliberate grace, Luna withdrew her hand, the emerald shimmer in her eyes dimming with each blink until they returned to their usual striking green.

The energy between them thinned, like mist dissipating in the morning sun, but its imprint lingered—an echo neither could ignore.

Beth stared at her, wide-eyed and unsteady. Her voice was barely a whisper. "What was that?"

Luna met her gaze, a quiet understanding passing between them. "Your DNA doesn't just hold your genetic code—it holds your experiences, your knowledge, your fight. I just... listened to the story it needed to tell me."

She hesitated for a moment, her expression softening. "I'm sorry you had to live like that—to always be watching."

Beth exhaled shakily, running a hand through her hair as if to ground herself. "That's... unsettling."

Luna's lips curved slightly, not quite an apology but not without compassion. "I know. But as you said, it would've taken a month to pack up all your work." A beat passed, the weight of the moment settling between them. "It's useful in the right moments."

Beth blinked, her sharp mind already working through the implications. She no longer looked at Luna as an anomaly, but as something more—something dangerous, but also... necessary.

Finally, Beth let out a breath that sounded like surrender. "Well," she muttered, shaking her head, "guess I don't need to show you my notes, then."

Luna's smile softened. "No. You've already shown me more than enough. Thank you, Beth."

Luna turned back to the task at hand, her expression sharpening. "We go around Herold's tech. If I can't connect with the painting directly, I'll use the energy web to access Westfield's servers. The information we need is there—proof of what they're doing, and maybe even a way to disable their shielding."

Beth's eyes widened slightly. "You can do that?"

Luna gave her a faint but knowing smile. "I've been practicing."

Elias leaned forward, concern flickering behind his steady gaze. "Are you sure? Wont this leave you vulnerable?"

"I'll be fine," Luna replied, her voice firm but not dismissive of his concern. She didn't lie—she knew the cost, knew the risk of stretching too far. But this wasn't about hesitation.

It is time for action.

"This isn't just about me," she continued. "It's about all of us—and the world Westfield is trying to control."

Ezra placed a hand on her shoulder, grounding her with his presence. "We'll be here. Whatever you need."

Luna exhaled slowly, nodding.

Because now, thanks to Beth, she had everything she needed to begin.

Luna took a few moments to drink some water and recenter herself. When she felt ready, she closed her eyes and exhaled, slow and deliberate, as if releasing herself into something greater. She knew this would take time. She couldn't force it, couldn't rush what needed to unfold naturally.

The room faded away. Her awareness sank downward, past the wooden floors, past the foundations of the house, down into the waiting embrace of the earth.

She reached deep.

Roots formed beneath her, unseen but powerful, stretching through layers of soil, weaving through bedrock, seeking something older, something steady. She felt the hum of the land beneath her, the ancient pulse of the earth's memory.

Then—she reached further.

Deep within the earth's crust, she found it. A ley line, faint, but beautiful and radiant with life.

A vast lattice of energy crisscrossed beneath the surface of the world, pulsating like veins of liquid fire, connecting places of power, history, and intention. Luna tapped into this network, letting its raw strength pour into her, letting it ground her, fortify her in this journey.

She became a coherent part of the current.

Her breath deepened, her pulse slowing to match the rhythm of the land itself. The energy of the earth wasn't just beneath her now—it was within her.

From the soil below, golden light spiraled upward, twin currents weaving around each other in a perfect double helix. The energy flowed through her core, rising like breath drawn from the earth itself. Each turn of the spiral brushed her chakras, not as separate points but as a continuous river of awakening, clearing, aligning.

At her crown, the light unfurled, spilling into the infinite sky above. Earth and cosmos met within her, no longer distinct but one seamless current—life flowing through life, creation folding into itself.

Luna exhaled slowly, as the infinite, unconditional love soothed her into the moment, dissolving the last remnants of separation.

The others remained silent, watching as pure bliss bloomed across her face—expressions only a physical form could convey.

The air changed.

It was subtle at first—a faint pressure shift, a charge building in the atmosphere, like the moment before a storm breaks. The light in the room dimmed, the edges of reality softening, as if the space between the physical and the unseen had grown thin.

Luna opened her eyes.

They glowed—an intense, emerald brilliance, not just light but coherence, a harmonic resonance with the aether itself. The glow didn't flicker or waver; it was steady, absolute, the unmistakable signature of mind, body, and field perfectly aligned.

Her gaze sharpened, piercing through layers of existence. The room remained, but overlaid with it was something more—a shimmering lattice of energy, threads of possibility stretching into the infinite. Time fractured into glimpses of what was, what is, and what could be, all folding into a single, lucid now.

Luna wasn't seeking alignment. She was alignment. The bridge, the current, the observer and the observed, all bound by the same luminous thread.

She lifted a hand over the laptop, fingers hovering just above the surface. Where before she had reached for the pulse of the earth, she now reached for something else—something constructed, coded, contained within the fabric of a man-made web.

As *above, so below.*

A fractal of a similar design, created by the created. The paths became clearer. Decoding was no longer a matter of breaking through. It was a matter of finding the pattern in the rhythm.

The transition was seamless, as if flipping a switch from nature's ancient current to the sharp, artificial hum of digital pathways.

The ley lines blurred into fiber optic cables.

The pulse of the earth became the rhythmic flow of data streams, signals racing through an invisible aether.

She became the conduit between two webs of the same design: one born of nature, the other of human innovation.

The screen of the laptop flickered, its glow shifting erratically as if struggling to keep up with what was happening.

Beth leaned forward, unable to hide her intrigue. "She's…" Beth trailed off, her voice almost reverent. "She's accessing the web!"

Her fingers twitched slightly, as if itching to confirm what her instincts already knew. Luna was moving through encrypted networks—not with code or keystrokes, but with pure energy and intent. Her mind acted as a transceiver, receiving and translating the digital language directly—streams of ones and zeros unpacking themselves not as data, but as meaning. She wasn't just accessing the system; she was communing with it, decoding structure through intuition, as if the network itself had become an extension of her nervous system.

Ezra watched with narrowed eyes. "It's incredible," he admitted. "But it's going to take a toll on her." The warm loving presence Luna gifts to the space around her dimming quickly. His jaw tightened, his hands flexing at his sides. "She knew it would." he said as the unmistakable look of bliss on Luna's face shifted.

But none of them moved to stop her progress.

Luna's face grew pale, her breath shallow, the brightness of her eyes fading. A sheen of sweat glistening on her brow as she pushed deeper into the cold, lifeless corridors of the digital realm. It was nothing like the aether. There was no warmth, no rhythmic pulse of life, no boundless flow of creation. Here, everything was rigid, jagged—static lines of code pulsing like artificial veins, sharp and unyielding.

The resistance was unnatural, almost violent. A machine's attempt to reject an intruder that did not belong, demanding her to disconnect.

She endured.

The deeper she went, the more it hurt—not like the strain of stretching one's consciousness into the infinite, but the suffocating grip of something that did not breathe, did not feel.

Then—a break.

An understanding found her. An observation collapses the barriers.

The screen burst to life, lines of encrypted data unraveling before her in a cascade of stolen secrets—documents, emails, blueprints filled the screen. Westfield's crimes laid bare. A victory carved from something cold and hostile.

Her next breath was jagged, her vision blurred.

"Got it," she rasped, holding on for a beat—her speed eclipsed only by the laptop's limits.

The moment she spoke, the severance came like a violent snap.

Her senses recoiled, like being ripped from ice into burning air. Her body convulsed slightly, breath staggering, as if she had surfaced too fast from deep waters.

The room returned in a rush—the scent of salt air, the warmth of Ezra's presence, the solidity of the earth beneath her feet. But her body felt hollowed, as if something foreign had scraped against her soul and left her raw.

Instinctively, she reached for the connection that had once flowed so effortlessly, but the thread was gone, frayed and distant, like the memory of warmth after the fire burns out.

Luna sagged inward, breath shallow. She had pushed too far, and now the earth—her greatest ally—lay just out of reach.

Beth leaned over her shoulder, shifting the laptop, her eyes scanning the screen. "This is more than I ever hoped for," she murmured, her voice distant, unaware of the cost Luna had just paid. "This will destroy them."

Luna barely heard her.

Her strength buckled. She slumped back, her head falling against Ezra's shoulder, the sensation of flesh, warmth, life—almost shocking after the cold abyss she had just endured.

"Luna." Ezra's voice was there, steady, grounding, but tinged with worry. His hand brushed damp strands of hair from her face. "Talk to me. Are you okay?"

Her fingers twitched, trying to hold onto something real.

"I'm... fine," she whispered, though her voice was fragile, unconvincing. "Just... need a moment."

Elias and Beth exchanged a glance, concern flashing between them, but Luna lifted a weak hand and found a gentle smile. "Don't worry," she murmured, as if trying to convince herself as much as them. "This is worth it. We have what we need."

Ezra didn't argue. He simply scooped her into his arms, cradling her carefully, as if she might slip away if he loosened his grip. He carried her to the couch, lowering her gently and pulling a blanket over her cold, frail frame.

"You've done enough for now," he said firmly. "Rest."

Luna let her head sink into the cushion, but even as her body stilled, her mind buzzed—a mechanical hum clinging to her, lingering like static in her veins.

She had traveled through the infinite. She had touched the breath of the universe itself.

And yet, of all the places she had ever reached, the digital world had been the most inhospitable, the most lifeless.

If ever given the choice—the aether, always.

FORTY-SEVEN

THE SPACE BETWEEN SECONDS

A heavy stillness hung in the Santa Monica SpotStay, broken only by the quiet rustle of papers and the low murmur of voices. Golden light slanted through the windows, stretching long shadows across the floor as the sun dipped toward the horizon. The group sat hunched around the dining table, their focus sharp, their tension tangible.

Beth spread out a rough map of Herold's Malibu estate, smoothing its edges with practiced precision. Elias leaned against the counter, arms crossed, his gaze hard and calculating. Ezra sat at the table, his fingers drumming absently against the wood as Beth began breaking down the near-impossible task before them.

Luna, however, was absent from the discussion, at least in presence.

She lay curled on the couch in the adjacent room, her body still heavy from the cold, artificial grasp of the digital world. The warmth of Ezra's touch, the sound of the ocean outside, the rhythm of real life—it began to recalibrate her, pulling her back into balance. But exhaustion lingered, her mind still coated in the static residue of what she had touched.

Faint voices drifted from the next room, indistinct at first, blending with the hush of waves. Then—a shift.

A word. A name. *Herold.*

The conversation sharpened, no longer background noise but a beacon cutting through the fog of fatigue. Luna stirred, the weight of sleep peeling away as the energy in the room changed—focused, urgent.

The moment she caught the phrase "*access points,*" her body reacted before her mind could catch up, muscles tensing, heart kicking against her ribs. Awareness snapped into place, fragile but undeniable.

She sat up slowly, blinking against the dimming light, her breath steady but purposeful.

A pause in the conversation.

Beth had just finished outlining Herold's private security, and Ezra was frowning, his skepticism palpable.

Then, Luna's fingers grazed the edge of the map.

"What about access points?" she asked, her voice still laced with sleep, yet charged with something deeper.

The others turned, startled by her sudden presence. She hadn't announced herself, hadn't made a sound—she had simply arrived at the table, as if drawn there by gravity itself.

Beth hesitated, then pointed to a side entrance on the blueprint. "This service entrance might be the least monitored. It's used for deliveries and staff, so it's not as heavily guarded when not in use. But it's still not easy. The locks will require clearance, and the cameras are likely monitored in real time."

Ezra exhaled through his nose. "And the painting?"

Beth tapped a smaller wing of the structure, branching off from the main estate. "Here. This is his private collection. Reinforced walls, limited access. It's a vault, basically. And if the painting is in there, it's going to be protected."

Elias leaned back, jaw tight. "So, we're breaking into Fort Knox?"

Luna sat straighter, her fingers trailing over the lines of the map as if deciphering something beyond the ink.

"It's doable," she murmured, almost to herself.

Ezra scoffed, shaking his head. "Doable? Seriously?"

Luna didn't answer. Instead, her gaze flicked toward the hallway, focus narrowing like the edge of a blade. Without a word, the bedroom door at the end of the hall slammed shut with a sharp crack. The sound ricocheted through the room, startling everyone. Elias flinched, Ezra shot to his feet, and Beth's hand flew to her chest.

"What the hell?" Elias muttered, eyes darting toward the empty hallway.

But Luna was already moving. While their attention hung on the door, she slipped around the table, each step fluid, soundless. By the time their puzzled gazes swung back, she stood on the opposite side, arms crossed, unshaken.

"I can do it," she said quietly, the weight of certainty in every word. "But I need Everwood and Sedona."

"Nice distraction Luna... But, It isn't so much your ability that has me worried. It is the danger you are walking into." Ezra said with intense

"That's why I need Sedona and Everwood. I'll need a lot more than a few slamming doors." Luna explains.

Beth's brow furrowed. "Sedona, I get. But Everwood? Why them?"

Luna inhaled deeply, grounding herself in the weight of the secret she was about to reveal.

"There is a pyramid there," Luna continued, her voice a steady hum of insight. "One from a long-lost time, but it's more than a structure—it's a key, a stabilizer in the quantum field. It holds a coherent frequency, like a tuning fork resonating with the Earth's own harmonics. But the further I get from it, the more the signal scatters. Sedona alone isn't enough."

She paused, then let the deeper truth settle into the room like a slow-burning flame.

"I won't break in—I'll step between moments. I'll find the space between seconds, the sliver of 'now' that doesn't truly exist in time. It's there the laws begin to bend. Using the bridge between Everwood and Sedona, I can hold myself in that gap just long enough to be in and out before anyone ever realizes I was there. It won't be force or stealth. It'll be resonance, precision... and presence."

She looked up, meeting each gaze in turn, the certainty in her voice sharpening.

"I need both communities to accomplish this. Sedona's vortex amplifies energy, magnifying the pyramid's frequency and extending its reach. It's Hermetic polarity—two forces, equal and opposite, creating balance. Everwood transmits the strength of the pyramid, Sedona stretches that signal across space. Together, they form a bridge—an energetic corridor that reconnects me to the pyramid's field."

Silence stretched between them, heavy with the enormity of what

Luna was asking. Beth's jaw slackened as the connection clicked into place, logic threading itself through intuition in a way that almost made sense. *Almost.*

Ezra's jaw tensed. "That's a lot of people, Luna."

She nodded. "And that's exactly why it will work. Everwood has been training for this. Sedona's energy flow is naturally aligned. Together, they can strengthen the connection—create something stable enough for me to work through."

Beth leaned back in her chair, arms crossed, eyes sharp with scrutiny. Like she was testing the hypothesis, running variables in her mind, searching for weak links.

"And if it doesn't work?" she challenged. "If the signal collapses? If the energy scatters instead of stabilizing? What's the contingency plan?"

Luna exhaled slowly. "Then I go in alone. Find my connection within the earth like I did tonight."

Ezra's fingers curled into a fist against the table. "That's not an option. It's too dangerous." He paused. "We call the press, and the cops. We expose what we uncovered, and recover the painting after they have raided the place."

"I'd rather not expose them until I have mom's painting back, but okay. I can see that being a safer option." Luna agreed reluctantly.

Beth's smirk was small but deliberate. "Then we make sure plan A works."

"Let's start making phone calls. I'd want to do this in the dead of night and we need to coordinate that. People will need to be rested and ready. We may need to give them a couple of days. I probably need that too." Luna gave clear instructions.

FORTY-EIGHT

LIGHTNING IN THE REARVIEW

The Santa Monica SpotStay hummed with focused urgency, the air crackling with the weight of everything they were setting into motion. Scattered maps, open laptops, and hastily scribbled notes cluttered the table—a physical manifestation of the storm they were preparing to walk into.

Luna sat cross-legged at the head of the table, her voice calm yet commanding as she spoke with Kaia, coordinating the collective meditation.

"We are scheduled to meet in two hours for our meditation," Kaia confirmed, her tone crisp but steady through the speaker. "I'll gather everyone then. That's when I'll explain the plan—what we're channeling, why it matters. They need to understand what they're holding space for. After tonight we will rest for the day, until you are ready."

Luna nodded. "Good. If they're aligned in intention, the energy will flow cleaner. No resistance."

Across the room, Ezra leaned against the counter, his voice low as he relayed instructions to Miriam. Every detail had to click into place—Everwood and Sedona synchronized, their focus sharp when the moment arrived.

Meanwhile, Beth and Elias huddled over a laptop, exchanging sharp whispers as they pieced together the final steps of their plan to expose Westfield in case they needed to rely on plan B. Files stolen from the servers scrolled across the screen, evidence waiting to be unleashed. Beth's fingers flew across the keyboard, her movements precise, relentless.

The room was alive with motion—not frantic, but purposeful.

Ezra's conversation faltered. His brow furrowed as he pulled the phone from his ear, glancing at the screen. For a moment, something shifted in his expression—sharp, unreadable. He exhaled slowly, rubbing his temple before pressing the phone back to his ear and speaking quickly into the receiver.

"Miriam, I'll have to call you right back." His voice remained calm, but Luna caught the subtle edge behind it.

As he ended the call, Ezra glanced at the screen, his grip tightening for just a fraction of a second before he handed the phone to Luna.

"It's Althea," he said, his voice low but weighted.

Luna pulled the phone to her ear, her other hand still holding Kaia on the line.

"Kaia, hang on a second."

The air in the room shifted, a current of unspoken tension threading between them.

Ezra didn't need to say more. Whatever this was—it was important.

Luna held the phone tightly, her pulse quickening. "Althea?" she answered, her voice steady but urgent. The crystals—they should have warned her. But the strain of pulling Westfield's files had drained her too deeply, dulling her awareness. She hadn't checked, hadn't felt the usual hum of connection that kept her tethered to her allies.

"Luna," Althea's voice came through, raw with tension, the faint crackle of static underscoring her panic. "We're an hour out, but we've got a big problem."

"What's going on?" Luna pressed, her connection to the aether flickering faintly as she strained to sense the disturbance.

"A storm," Althea said, her voice rising. "It came out of nowhere. It's not natural, Luna—this isn't just bad weather. I'm sure it's Westfield. It's like they're trying to stop us before we can get to you."

Luna felt a chill creep up her spine. She closed her eyes, reaching out with her energy, following the thread that binds her to Althea, but Luna was still too weak and the vast distance stretched her thin. The storm was faint at best—a distant, chaotic ripple she couldn't grab hold of. "I can barely sense it," she admitted, her voice tight with frustration. "I'm too far away to stop it."

James's voice cut in, sharp and steady. "This thing's gaining on us, Luna. It's not just a storm—it's targeting us. Lightning's hitting the road behind us. We're barely staying ahead of it."

Luna locked eyes with Ezra, the worry evident on her face. "Westfield's using the storm to try and eliminate them," she said grimly.

Beth leaned forward, her analytical mind already piecing together the mechanics of the situation. "If they're controlling it, the storm isn't autonomous," she said. "The tech needed to generate and maintain something like this isn't portable—it's centralized."

Luna caught on quickly. "At their headquarters," she said, her tone resolute. "It has to be."

Beth nodded. "Exactly. If we can stop the tech at the source, the storm collapses."

Luna relayed the information quickly. "Althea, Beth says it's being controlled from Westfield Headquarters downtown. You need to stay ahead of it no matter what. I'll do everything I can to help."

Althea's breathing was steady, though strained. "We'll keep moving, but we can't outrun it forever."

Luna didn't waste a second. "Kaia, did you hear all that? Change of plans. We need you as soon as possible. As many people as you can gather."

Kaia hesitated only for a breath, but Luna could hear the understanding in it.

"I'll do what I can," Kaia said quickly. "But the full group won't be ready in time. I'll gather as many as possible."

Althea, listening on the other line, exhaled sharply. "That'll have to be enough. We need help ASAP!"

Luna closed her eyes, steadying herself. It had to be.

Because the storm was coming. And it was coming for them.

As the call ended, Luna looked at the others. Her pale complexion betrayed her frustration. "Lets call Miriam back, we will need them now too. Kaia and the group will do what they can, but it won't be enough without stopping it at the source."

Beth's lips pressed into a hard line. "Then we go to the source. We don't have time to wait for anyone else."

Elias rubbed the back of his neck. "You're talking about storming one of the most secure buildings in LA. This isn't a stealth mission—it's a suicide run."

Beth's gaze hardened. "If we don't do this, Althea and the others won't make it. We don't have a choice. We can't let more people die to this psychopath."

Ezra straightened. "She's right. They're family. We have to move fast."

The SUV tore through Los Angeles, weaving between cars as the emergency broadcast crackled over the radio.

"This is an emergency weather alert. A powerful storm system is approaching the greater Los Angeles area, bringing extremely strong winds and severe lightning. Residents are advised to seek shelter immediately. Secure all outdoor items and stay indoors away from windows. If you are driving, pull over to a safe location and avoid trees or powerlines. Stay tuned to this station for updates and safety instructions."

Elias cursed under his breath as they passed cars pulling to the shoulder. The road ahead was still clear, but a faint, unnatural glow on the horizon warned of the storm's encroachment.

Beth leaned forward from the backseat, her laptop open. "If I'm right, the servers controlling this will be on the lower levels. It's where they keep most of their experimental tech."

"And if you're wrong?" Ezra asked, his knuckles white against the wheel.

"Then we'll improvise," Luna said, her voice cutting through the tension. She clutched the quartz crystal in her lap, her energy sparking faintly against the stone. "We'll find a way."

Elias glanced at her, his voice low. "And what if you can't handle it?"

"I don't have a choice," Luna replied. Her voice carried a steely edge, but Ezra caught the faint tremor beneath it. "They're counting on us."

With that, Luna closed her eyes to center herself. A sudden realization that this could be the point of failure that resulted in the vision she had of a dark and desolate future. "Luna..." Ezra began again. she quickly lifted her finger to her lips, demanding a moment to connect and center.

He silenced his nerves, knowing it is the only thing he could do for her. Luna blocked out all distractions until it was time for action.

The air inside the truck was thick with tension, a sharp contrast to the howling storm outside. Rain battered the windshield in relentless sheets, each drop a deafening impact against the glass. Lightning ripped through the night sky behind them, illuminating the twisting highway in stark, unnatural flashes. James gripped the steering wheel, his jaw set as he guided the truck through the worsening chaos.

"Hold on," he muttered, his voice barely audible over the cacophony of thunder and pounding rain. He swerved sharply to avoid a sedan that had pulled off onto the shoulder, its hazard lights blinking feebly through the deluge.

Althea braced against the dashboard, eyes flicking to hazard lights blinking along the shoulder. "They're pulling off. Maybe we should—"

"No," James snapped, his knuckles whitening on the wheel. "This storm isn't just unnatural—it's after us. If we stop, we're not just sitting ducks—we're putting anyone near us in danger."

Althea nodded, her lips pressing into a thin line. She knew he was right, but the relentless storm was unlike anything she'd ever encountered. The wind screamed against the truck's frame, making it groan in protest. Another burst of lightning struck terrifyingly close, the blinding flash illuminating Emma's pale, anxious face in the backseat.

Emma clutched her blanket tightly, her breath shallow and uneven. Eyes closed, fingers tracing frantic patterns in the air, she searched for something unseen. When she spoke, her voice trembled with urgency. "We have to keep going. I have to get to her."

James gripped the wheel tighter, jaw clenched. "Emma, I'm doing everything I can, but this storm—"

"Luna needs us." Emma cut in with urgency, her tone hard. "If we stay ahead of it, we have a chance. If we stop, we don't."

Thunder cracked overhead, drowning James's muttered curse. Cars peeled off the highway, hazard lights blinking like panicked heartbeats. The few drivers still pushing forward swerved blindly, their headlights fractured by the relentless downpour.

The storm closed in fast. Forked lightning carved the sky, each strike unnervingly precise. A towering pine tree exploded into splinters, fiery shards whipping past the truck. Wind tore roadside signs from their posts, flinging them across the pavement like jagged projectiles. James swerved hard, tires skidding through standing water.

"This storm is unreal," Emma rasped, bracing herself against the seat, her senses opening to the storm itself. "It's pushing us back. Trying to keep us from her."

James didn't glance away from the chaos ahead. "Well, let's hope this old beast can outrun whatever the hell 'it' is."

"We're not outrunning it," Emma said, her voice sharp with conviction. "But it's slipping. I can feel it—the storm's fighting against something. Nature's pushing back, rejecting the weapon they've twisted it into."

For the first time, James hesitated—not from doubt, but from the sudden, fragile hope threaded through Emma's words.

He pressed the accelerator, the engine growling as the truck lurched forward.

The wipers thrashed uselessly against the torrents, the road dissolving into a shimmering haze. Emma's grip loosened on the blanket, her focus turning inward. She could still feel it—a faint pulse of energy tethering her to Luna, a fragile thread cutting through the storm's fury.

Althea's gaze flicked to James. "We'll make it. We have to."

James didn't answer. He couldn't. The leather groaned beneath his clenched hands as the truck barreled through the storm, lightning casting jagged shadows across the dark horizon. Doubt gnawed at the edge of his thoughts, but beneath it, something else stirred.

Belief.

Because failure wasn't an option. And neither was stopping.

Forty-Nine

The Stage was Set

T he SUV screeched to a halt outside Westfield Headquarters, its towering façade gleaming ominously in the city lights. Against the storm-darkened sky, the building pulsed with life—power incarnate in glass and steel. Luna stood at the base of the steps, her breath steady but shallow as she prepared herself.

"This is where it ends," she said, her voice resolute.

Ezra lingered a few paces behind her, his jaw tight and his fists clenched. "You can't do this alone," he said firmly, his voice cutting through the roar of the wind.

Luna turned to him, her expression calm but confident. "I am not alone... I never am. You've seen what Westfield's capable of. If anything happens to me—"

"I'm not leaving you," Ezra interrupted, his tone unyielding. "Not now, not ever."

Luna hesitated, her heart aching at his words. "I need you to stay here, Ezra," she said softly but with finality. "If something goes wrong. Call the cops... Call the press... Make them pay."

Ezra's protest was written across his face, but before he could argue further, Luna placed a hand gently on his chest. "Please," she whispered. "Trust me."

Reluctantly, Ezra nodded, his hand brushing against hers before letting it drop. Luna turned, her silhouette briefly illuminated by another bolt of lightning as she ascended the steps. Ezra watched her disappear through the imposing glass doors, his resolve hardening. He waited a moment longer, then slipped after her, the weight of unspoken fears pressing down with every step.

Inside, the sterile corridors of Westfield Headquarters hummed with a cold, lifeless energy. The decor was sleek and modern—polished marble floors reflecting the soft glow of recessed lighting. Expansive walls flickered with high-tech displays, flowing streams of data cascading in elegant patterns. But something was off. The usual pulse of surveillance—the watchful eyes of security feeds—was conspicuously absent.

Luna paused in the grand entrance, her gaze drawn to the floor-to-ceiling windows dominating the far wall. A cluster of people—employees, visitors, even the few security officers she expected to challenge her—stood motionless, faces turned toward the storm raging beyond the glass. Thunder rumbled, and another flash of lightning illuminated their silhouettes, like statues carved in the moment of wonder and dread.

Why aren't they stopping me? She thought, stepping deeper into the lobby. No clipped demands for identification. No hurried radio chatter. Just the low thrum of technology and the faint crackle of rain against glass.

Luna moved with quiet purpose, following the path Beth had mapped for her—left at the information desk, through the archway beside the abstract sculpture, and toward the central stairwell. Yet, it wasn't just Beth's directions guiding her now. The deeper she ventured, the more her intuition sharpened, like a sixth sense snapping into focus.

The energy shifted.

A warmth, subtle but growing, tickled the edge of her awareness—the unmistakable resonance of Sedona. It pulsed like a heartbeat beneath her skin, amplifying her senses, threading clarity into her thoughts. And with it came understanding.

This isn't neglect.

The empty corridors. The unchallenged passage. It was intentional. The security wasn't lacking; it had been *removed*, like a stage cleared for a final act.

Her breath knotted beneath her ribs as the truth crystallized in her mind's eye—Herold was waiting. Not somewhere deep in the maze of offices and labs, but just ahead, in a vast control room humming with purpose. He wanted her to come. He'd *designed* it this way.

Luna's pace slowed, her pulse steady despite the rising dread. Her awareness stretched outward, brushing against the walls, the floors, the very air itself. And there—like a flicker of light behind her closed eyelids—she caught the faint, unmistakable essence of her love.

Damn it, Ezra. He was far behind, careful, but not far enough to escape her notice. She knew better than to turn, to warn him. Any ripple of attention would be like blood in the water. Herold's trap was already set. The only choice now was to spring it on her own terms. Luna felt a moment of trust, that this was meant to unfold this way. Fear for Ezra shifted to confidence.

Drawing a slow breath, Luna stepped forward, shoulders squaring as the hallway widened into an expansive threshold. Beyond it, lights glowed softly, the rhythmic hum of computer servers barely masking the presence she knew awaited her.

She didn't hesitate. She walked into the trap knowingly.

Luna stepped into the cavernous room, breath steady despite the weight of the moment. The space was stark, almost clinical, its minimalist design a deliberate contrast to the chaos outside. Walls of matte black metal curved inward, like the ribcage of some mechanical beast, while the floor shimmered faintly with embedded circuitry, veins of light pulsing in sync with the rhythmic hum of machinery.

But it was the screens that dominated the space—dozens of them, stretching from floor to ceiling, plastered across the far wall like a digital mosaic. They flickered with live feeds, each one displaying a different vantage point: bustling city streets, deserted back roads, private homes, and remote wilderness. Some locations were recognizable; others, impossibly intimate. Luna's breath faltered when her gaze landed on one feed in particular—the storm, captured from above, swirling like a living thing. Beneath its shadow, headlights cut through the rain: James' truck, tires biting into slick asphalt, weaving through the chaos.

At the heart of it all stood Herold Westfield.

He was tall, lean, and composed, his posture that of a man who never questioned his authority. His sleek, charcoal-gray suit fit like a second skin—not fabric, but an advanced weave that shimmered subtly under the cool overhead lights. Thin lines of circuitry traced the cuffs and lapels, nearly imperceptible until they flickered with an occasional pulse of light, like veins carrying power instead of blood.

But it was his face that held her attention. Time had sharpened rather than softened him. Silver threaded through his dark hair, neatly combed back, while lines around his mouth and eyes spoke of a man who smiled rarely and meant it even less. A slim headset curved around his temples, blending into his skin, projecting translucent displays across his eyes—data streams, environmental metrics, and, Luna suspected, everything about her.

With the slightest tilt of his head, the floating screens rearranged themselves, lines of text and shifting diagrams obeying his silent command. His fingers—adorned with sleek, ring-like receptors—moved in subtle, practiced gestures, manipulating the holographic interface with effortless precision. It wasn't magic. It was mastery—technology so advanced it danced on the edge of intuition.

To his left and right stood two men, weapons drawn but hanging low, almost relaxed. They weren't expecting a fight out of Luna.

He smiled, thin and knowing. "Luna," he drawled, his voice smooth and dripping with condescension. "Right on time. I was starting to wonder if you'd lost your nerve."

Luna stepped forward, chin high, the emerald glow in her eyes flickering like a warning. "If you've been watching me, then you know why I'm here."

Herold chuckled, the sound vibrating through the room like the distant roll of thunder. He flicked two fingers, and one of the holographic displays expanded, showing a magnified feed of the storm swirling outside. Lightning forked across the screen, illuminating the chaos he had summoned into existence.

"Oh, I know exactly why you're here," he said, stepping forward, the receptors on his fingers pulsing faintly as the screens around him shifted again. "You think you can stop me. That your quaint little gifts and ragtag band of followers stand a chance against real progress."

He gestured lazily, and another screen blossomed into view—Sedona. The meditation group, bodies still, faces serene, caught in the act of channeling energy into the web that connected them all. "Everwood. Sedona. Your precious alignment of universal energy and wishful thinking. Impressive, for what it is. But you're playing checkers while I'm rewriting the game itself."

Luna didn't flinch. Instead, she stepped forward, slow and deliberate, drawing their attention with every measured stride. "Progress?" Her voice cut through the hum of technology, calm but edged with disdain. "You mean control. Manipulation. Turning nature into a weapon because you're too blind to see you're fighting the very thing that gives life."

Herold's gaze tracked her, the receptors on his fingers flickering with faint pulses as he instinctively adjusted his interface. The two guards shifted subtly, eyes narrowing as Luna moved—not toward him, but around him, circling the room like a predator studying its prey.

Screens flickered in her periphery—Sedona's meditation circle, the storm's relentless pursuit of James' truck, even the empty hallway she'd just walked through. *Ezra will come.* The thought sharpened her focus. If they kept looking toward her, they'd miss his presence.

"Life bends to those strong enough to shape it," Herold countered, his voice smooth but taut. "Quantum fields, energy currents—they're tools, Luna. Tools I've mastered and perfected."

Luna kept moving, circling the room like an orbiting moon, each step deliberate, pulling their attention further from the entrance. "Tools?" she echoed, her tone sharp. "You're drowning in tools, Herold. So much metal and code—and still, you're blind. You've surrounded yourself with technology so advanced, it's dulled your perception. You can't see the very power you're chasing. You never did."

Herold chuckled, the sound dry and calculated. He flicked two fingers, and a screen shifted to show the storm again, the eye tightening as it tracked the faint glow of headlights—James' truck, still fighting its way forward.

Herold barely seemed to blink before a bolt of lightning hammered the pavement twenty feet ahead of the speeding vehicle. Tires screeched as the truck swerved, narrowly avoiding disaster.

"Ah," Herold mused, lips curling into a satisfied smile. "My aim is improving, Luna." His eyes narrowed, tracking her movement. "On the contrary... I understand its power perfectly. And I should thank you, really. This—" he gestured broadly at the room, the storm, the flickering streams of data "—has been the perfect proving ground. Real-world application. Uncontrolled variables. All thanks to you."

Behind him, the massive wall of screens flickered to life, displaying the SUV just around the corner outside. The footage sharpened as the image zoomed in, centering on Beth.

"And look at the bonus you've brought me," he said with a sneer. "I see you found that little rat, Marin. I've been looking for her."

Luna's steps faltered, just for a heartbeat.

Herold smiled, catching the hesitation like a predator scenting blood. "You didn't think I cleared security out of kindness, did you? Most of the usual staff were liabilities—predictable, fallible. I sent them home. Only my personal team remains." He nodded toward two guards, who straightened, grips tightening on their weapons. "Trusted. Efficient. Silent."

His fingers twitched, and a new screen blinked to life—Everwood, seen through some unseen surveillance node. It is as if Herold's computers could see the unseen as she could. Luna's chest tightened.

"Your little evolutionary sideshow is fascinating," Herold said, his tone laced with triumph. "But you're late to the game. I've spent years refining this—tracking, manipulating, optimizing technology. Not as a bridge, but as a leash. And every bit of it powered by the same energies you hold sacred."

Luna's jaw tightened, but she kept her pace steady, pulling their focus further from the door. *He doesn't understand the impeccable timing of the universe.* That, she realized, was a weakness.

"You're using this storm as a test run," she said coldly.

"A successful one," Herold confirmed. "And not just the storm. Once this ends, I'll have everything I need—optimized protocols, real-time adjustments under stress. The next generation of control. Thanks to you."

Luna kept moving, her path curving away from the entrance, toward the bank of screens displaying the storm. The flickering light caught the emerald glow in her eyes, intensifying as she passed one monitor after another. She didn't need to see the door to know Ezra was out there, waiting for the chance she was quietly carving for him.

The guards' attention followed her arc, one glancing toward Herold for confirmation, the other distracted by the shifting displays as Luna's movement triggered subtle changes in the holographic interface.

Herold's headset flickered as more data streamed across his lenses—Luna's heart rate, her thermal signature, spikes in electromagnetic activity surrounding her. He frowned, receptors twitching on his fingertips.

Herold's Ego continued. "While your mother was chasing vibrations and earthbound fantasies for her silly painting, I was building a network that stretches beyond borders, beyond sight. Your crystals, your meditations—they're breadcrumbs compared to the systems I've designed to harness the same forces. You feel energy, Luna. I command it."

Luna's fingers brushed the edge of the console, and she paused, holding his gaze. "Command it?" she murmured, voice soft but steady. "No. You cage it. Force it. Strip it of its nature until it snaps back at you."

Luna straightened, the emerald light in her eyes flaring. "And when it does, Herold, it won't care how many screens you hide behind."

Herold's eyes gleamed behind the floating code. "I don't think so Luna. I'll crack that code too. That charming little town of yours? Everwood. You've hidden something there, haven't you? Something deeper than crystals and good intentions. You think I don't see the anomaly? The spike in geomagnetic resonance every time you push past your limits? I may have been a little late to take an interest in you Luna, but whatever you're protecting, I'll find it."

He leaned in, the hum of his technology vibrating in the air between them. "Once I'm done with you, I'll peel back Everwood's secrets layer by layer. And no one will be left to stop me."

The trap snapped shut around her, silent and final. A brief flash of her desolate vision solidified in her mind's eye. But Luna didn't panic—she didn't move. Her breath steadied as she quickly rose above the poles of fear and courage, her awareness stretching outward—not just into the room, but into the currents beneath the surface of reality. The storm. The universal life force, humming like strings beneath a bow. The strength from Everwood and Sedona surged through her, anchoring and igniting what was to come.

Ezra's presence lingered on the edge of her awareness, a shadow moving carefully behind the walls. He was here.

Luna squared her shoulders. "You've underestimated one thing, Herold."

He arched a brow, receptors flickering with another surge of data. "And what's that?"

Her emerald eyes burned brighter, locking onto his.

"This isn't just me standing against you, Herold. It's the will of something far greater—an end written into the design unfolding before you."

Luna took another step forward, slow and deliberate. "You think you're playing god, Herold, but you've lost sight of what it even means to be human. The connections you dismiss—the love, the unity—that's where real strength lies. Not in circuits. Not in control."

Herold's eyes darkened, the fleeting amusement draining from his face. The receptors on his fingers pulsed red, as if mirroring the spike in his frustration. "Spare me the lectures," he snapped. "I've spent my life ensuring mankind's survival—my survival. And you? You're a relic. An evolutionary sideshow clinging to obsolete ideals."

Herold sneered, his grip tightening around a sleek, metallic device in his hand—a weapon forged from stolen knowledge and corrupted science. It was compact, almost elegant, the grip molded to his palm like it belonged there. Extending from the barrel-like core was a thin, disc-shaped emitter, pulsing faintly with alternating bands of blue and violet light.

He turned it over slowly, savoring the moment. "Enough talk Luna, time to turn your little adventure into a memory I'll soon forget."

The air thickened, dense with an unseen force. Luna could feel it vibrating at the edge of perception—an unnatural hum that prickled against her skin, reaching for something deeper, something essential.

Herold smiled, raising the weapon casually, his finger brushing the trigger. The emitter disc swirled faster, light bending around its edges like heat off asphalt.

"This," he said, voice laced with triumph, "is my masterpiece. A set of frequencies so precise it disrupts the human essence itself. Not just nerves or cells—the core of what makes you *alive*. Intense exposure leading to pain, sickness..." He tilted his head, eyes gleaming as if studying prey. "And death, written off as natural causes. No trace. No proof. Just... silence."

The weapon gave a faint, rhythmic pulse—like a heartbeat in rage.

Luna gritted her teeth, instinctively reaching out, not physically but through the energy field she'd come to master. If she could connect with the weapon's frequency, she might have a chance to disrupt it before he pulled the trigger.

And then—*movement*.

A shadow slipped into place behind Herold.

Ezra.

Herold's focus was locked on Luna, blind to the danger. But Luna saw it. Ezra's gaze caught hers—a flicker of understanding. A promise.

"You'll never win, Herold," Luna said, voice low but steady as she shifted subtly, drawing attention further from the door.

Herold snorted, raising the weapon another inch. "And why's that?"

Luna exhaled slowly, grounding herself in the web of energy still surging from Sedona and Everwood. It pulsed through her like a second heartbeat, the collective bond magnifying her awareness.

"Because you don't understand... impeccable timing."

Ezra moved.

Fast.

Herold's smirk faltered as Ezra lunged, shoulder slamming into him with enough force to knock the weapon sideways. The emitter flared, but

Herold recovered too quickly, the receptors on his fingertips flashing red as he recalibrated with a twitch of his hand.

The weapon swung around.

Ezra's eyes widened.

The trigger clicked.

An unnatural stillness gripped the room—then the weapon flared.

No sound came, nothing audible to human ears. But Luna *felt* it—a ripple in the fabric of the air itself, like a tremor vibrating through bone and marrow. Her senses, sharpened by the web of energy flowing from Sedona and Everwood, caught the invisible assault as it sliced through the space between them.

The air shimmered in its wake, like heat rising, but fractured—chaotic. Waves of destructive vibrations scattered outward, warping the light, distorting the very particles they passed through.

Ezra froze, eyes widening as the wave slammed into him.

His body buckled and fell to the floor.

Luna's world tilted.

"No!" The cry ripped from her throat as he hit the ground, motionless. His chest barely rose, his hand twitching once before falling limp.

Herold stepped back, the weapon still humming in his hand. He didn't bother to look at Ezra. "Ha! How is that for timing? Your little hero thought he could play in the big leagues," he drawled, voice cold, clinical. He took a slow step closer, eyes gleaming. "Let's see how far your precious love gets him now."

Luna was already moving, dropping to her knees beside Ezra, hands trembling as they pressed against his chest. His skin was cool, his pulse fluttering weakly beneath her fingertips.

His life force flickered, like a candle betrayed by the wind.

Her mind raced. She could *feel* what the weapon had done—frequencies calibrated to disrupt the delicate quantum entanglement of life itself. Not just nerves or cells, but the energetic blueprint that made Ezra, *Ezra*. It was unraveling him from the inside out, like threads pulled from a tapestry until nothing remained.

"Stay with me," she whispered, panic cracking through her voice as she leaned closer. Instinctively, her heart's magnetic field surged outward, wrapping around him in waves of warm, golden energy. "You're not leaving me."

The room faded—the guards, the humming weapon, Herold's smug grin. There was only Ezra's dimming light and the desperate pull of connection.

Her energy reached deeper, brushing against the memory held in the blueprint of his cells—the quiet intelligence written into every strand, every fold of him. Not a miracle, but a reminder. A spark of instruction whispering: this is what you are.

But it wasn't enough.

Come on, Ezra...

The air thickened, the tension sharp and electric.

Then—a pulse.

Faint but unmistakable.

A tremor danced on her exhale. The tether from Sedona flared brighter, the resonance deepening. Somewhere, far beyond this sterile room, the pyramid's field rippled outward, reconnecting through Everwood's crystalline grid.

The meditation had reached its peak of what they could provide—the collective energy feeding into Luna, strengthening her, holding her up even as her body shook with exertion.

Herold's eyes narrowed, receptors flashing amber as he processed the spike in electromagnetic activity surrounding her.

"Enough of this," he snapped, irritation breaking through his composure. He raised the weapon once more, the emitter spinning faster, glowing like the eye of a storm.

Luna didn't hesitate.

She closed her eyes and inhaled deeply—not just oxygen, but the very energy woven into the fabric of existence. This was more than herself. More than the here and now. She reached—not with her hands, but with her consciousness.

Into the earth. The rhythmic pulse of the planet, ancient and unwavering, grounding her in the resonance of all life into the aether. The formless potential where thought and matter intertwined, where reality bent to the will of intention into the connection. The energy web of Everwood and Sedona, amplifying the circuit like a conductor in a cosmic symphony.

Herold's weapon hummed with artificial interference, a discordant vibration attempting to overwrite the natural harmonics of the universe. But the Hermetic laws were absolute—resonance amplified, and energy followed intention.

Luna's breath steadied.

Vibration. Rhythm. Correspondence.

Her consciousness sharpened, eyes still closed as she observed the vibrating particles around her—the molecules of air, the subtle electromagnetic hum of the walls, even the biological rhythms pulsing through Herold and his guards. Everything moved. Everything flowed.

And at the heart of it all, she found the still point—the quiet center where vibration met will.

Luna reached into the field, gathering the scattered frequencies like gravity pulling dust into a star. Swiftly in the absence of time, she shaped them, condensing the formless potential into a dense, throbbing sphere of pure energy. It floated before her, not light, not heat, but *possibility*—particles held in perfect superposition, vibrating in sync with her intention.

The weapon in Herold's hand flickered, the disc emitter wavering as if sensing the shift in the field. He frowned, receptors on his fingertips glowing red as he recalibrated. "What the hell are you—"

Luna opened her eyes.

The sphere pulsed, synchronized with the natural rhythm of the universe. Not destruction. *Coherence.*

She exhaled and released it.

The shockwave exploded outward, not a sound, but a force—a tidal surge of perfectly harmonized energy collapsing probability into certainty.

The air warped in its wake, rippling like water, distorting light into fractured prisms. Herold's guards barely registered what was happening before the wave hit them. Their bodies jerked as the frequencies scrambled their nervous systems, muscles locking and limbs giving way.

The weapon in Herold's hand sparked violently. The emitter disc fractured with a high-pitched whine, scattering shards of metal and glass across the floor. He staggered, hand smoking, receptors flickering as the system failed to recalibrate.

Herold stumbled. His guards crumpled. Monitors shattered and died, the marble beneath them fracturing under the force.

Luna barely registered any of it.

She turned, heart pounding, and returned her focus to Ezra.

The energy web pulsed, flowing through her, into him. She didn't just give—she synchronized, matching her vibration to the fragile hum of his life force.

Where his energy had frayed, she wove it back together. Where his pulse had weakened, she amplified it. Her hands pressed against his chest, not healing him—*reminding* his body how to heal itself.

Ezra exhaled.

A shallow, unsteady breath at first—then another, deeper this time. His skin still held a ghostly pallor, but his presence steadied, anchored back into his form.

Luna pressed her forehead against his. "I've got you."

Herold's voice cut through the electric hum of the air, ragged with disbelief.

"You think this changes anything?" He staggered upright, eyes wild, ego unable to comprehend what had just unraveled before him. "You're a fool if you think you're leaving here alive!"

Luna rose to her feet, Ezra still cradled in her arms. The storm outside raged, but within her, the rhythm had already shifted.

"You've underestimated love, Herold." Her voice was calm, absolute. "You've underestimated the force of connection—of creation itself."

Herold shouted orders, his voice splintered by panic. But the guards barely stirred, dazed by the shockwave. The weapon lay in ruin, its disc emitter cracked, flickering like a dying star.

Luna didn't stop to fight. She moved, her will pulsing outward in rhythmic waves, lifting Ezra with effortless grace. It wasn't strength. It was resonance—vibration aligned with the world around her, resistance falling away like mist before the sun.

She moved fast, weaving through fractured corridors and dying light, the crumbling edges of Herold's empire yawning behind her.

There was no time for triumph.

Only the need to get Ezra to safety.

FIFTY

THE COLLAPSE OF PROBABILITY

O utside, the storm roared. Lightning carved jagged veins across the sky, but the wind barely touched her.

The SUV screeched to a halt at the curb.

Elias reached back and threw open the back door, eyes wide with alarm. "What happened?"

"No time," Luna gasped, carefully lowering Ezra onto the back seat. His breathing was shallow but steady, skin warming beneath her touch.

She gripped the edge of the door, eyes narrowing as she glanced back at the tower. Herold's silhouette flickered behind the shattered glass of the control room, receptors on his hands pulsing like a heart grasping at its last desperate beat.

"Drive. Now."

Elias didn't hesitate. The tires screeched as the SUV sped away from the building into the stormy night.

Luna knelt beside Ezra in the backseat, her hands trembling as she placed them on his chest. His breathing was shallow, his face ashen. She pressed her forehead against his, her tears falling onto his skin. "You're going to be okay," she whispered, though her voice cracked with doubt. "You have to be." Ezra continued to struggle, his eyes closing as he drifted towards the pull beyond the physical.

The SUV barreled through the rain-slicked streets, its tires screeching as Elias navigated the labyrinth of abandoned vehicles. The storm loomed ominously above them, flashes of lightning illuminating the chaos within the vehicle. Luna's trembling hands pressing firmly against Ezra's chest. She focused all her remaining strength on stabilizing him, to counter the pull into the aether, to keep him with her. The warmth of Everwood and Sedona's collective energy flickering like a fragile flame within her, helping her to maintain his heartbeat.

"Stay with me," Luna murmured, her voice choked with emotion. Ezra's pallor deepened, his breathing faint and uneven. Her tears mingled with the storm pounding outside, desperation clouding her thoughts.

Beth twisted in her seat, her expression a mix of concern and fear. "We need to keep moving," she urged Elias. "Herold won't stop, not after this."

"I know," Elias replied, his grip tightening on the wheel. His jaw was set, his eyes scanning the road for any sign of safety. "Hang on!" He shouted, stepping harder on the gas.

Suddenly, a blinding flash of lightning struck the asphalt just ahead of the SUV, the crackling sound of the earth itself splitting open. The vehicle jolted violently, the tires losing grip as the engine sputtered and died. The SUV coasted to a halt, steam rising ominously from the hood.

"What the hell was that?" Elias shouted through the high pitch scream of Beth beside him, slamming the steering wheel in frustration.

Beth's eyes widened as she turned to look behind them. Her voice shook. "It's him."

Through the rear window, Herold Westfield emerged from the building's imposing entrance, his silhouette jagged against the backdrop of the storm's fury. Rain lashed against his sleek, form-fitted suit—its fabric woven with shimmering threads of conductive material, now flickering faintly like a dying circuit. His once-polished appearance had unraveled, hair plastered to his forehead, face taut with unbridled rage.

But it was the headset that truly marked him as dangerous.

The slim, curved frame hugged his temples, lenses projecting holographic displays across his eyes—real-time data streams, environmental metrics, and dynamic targeting grids flickering in chaotic patterns.

Herold's fingers twitched, receptors pulsing red as he manipulated the storm itself. His weapon now wasn't something he held—it was the sky above, the raw force of nature bent to his will.

He flicked his hand forward, the holographic display narrowing to a single point.

Lightning cracked.

The bolt hammered the pavement barely ten feet from the SUV, asphalt exploding into jagged shards.

Herold grinned, wild and manic, rain streaming down his face. His aim was still imperfect—nature resisted full control—but he was close. Too close.

Behind him, several guards spilled out of the building, their suits slick with rain and weapons drawn, moving with mechanical precision through the downpour.

Herold didn't seem to care. His focus remained locked on the SUV, fingers dancing through the air as he recalibrated, the quantum headset glowing brighter with each adjustment.

"Luna," Ezra rasped, his voice barely audible. His hand weakly gripped hers, his eyes fluttering open just enough to meet hers. "Run."

"I'm not leaving you here, alone." Luna said firmly, her gaze snapping to meet his. "Don't you dare ask me to."

Herold's voice cut through the storm like a mad man, amplified by a portable speaker built into his wearable tech. "You can't outrun the storm, Luna!" he bellowed, his voice barely audible over the roaring wind. "Not when I *am* the storm!"

Luna straightened, her energy flickering weakly but still burning with unrelenting determination. As she gently eased Ezra back against the seat, her gaze fell on his jacket. Her fingers moved instinctively, reaching into the inner pocket where she knew it would be—the crystal she had once given him, now faintly warm to the touch, as if it had been waiting for this moment.

Without hesitation, she pressed it briefly to her forehead, eyes closing as she drew a breath and deepened the connection—her energy threading into the crystal, reawakening its resonance. Then, in a gesture as deliberate and sacred as a blessing, she touched it gently to Ezra's forehead.

"For clarity," she murmured, her voice steady despite the chaos outside.

She moved the crystal downward, laying it over his heart with reverence. The rhythm of her breath matched the subtle thrum of energy between them.

"For strength."

Luna then took Ezra's hand and placed it over the crystal resting against his chest. Her fingers laced through his, holding it firmly in place.

"I'm here with you," she said quietly, her voice thick with emotion. "I'll be with you... always."

She leaned in, pressing her forehead to his for a moment—a quiet benediction—before she pulled back, her resolve hardening once more.

"Stay here," she said softly. "I'll handle this."

"No," Ezra croaked, his hand tightening slightly. "Don't go."

Luna turned to Beth and Elias, her voice low and urgent. "Keep him alive. Do whatever it takes."

Before they could protest, Luna stepped out of the SUV into the torrential rain. The storm swallowed her immediately, the wind whipping her hair around her face as she squared her shoulders against the oncoming threat. Herold stopped twenty yards away, his cruel smile illuminated by another flash of lightning.

"You're resilient," he said mockingly. "I'll give you that. But resilience won't save you."

Her gaze flickered across the street. The storm had emptied the sidewalks, but behind fogged windows and cracked doors, faces watched. Shopkeepers, pedestrians—everyday people caught in the crossfire of Herold's ambition. Phones were raised, lenses glinting through the rain. The world was already recording.

Luna's focus sharpened. "Look around you, Herold."

Her voice cut cleanly through the storm's roar, commanding without force. Herold blinked, momentarily thrown off by her tone.

"This is your legacy," Luna continued, gesturing to the fractured pavement, the scorch marks from lightning strikes, the wide-eyed witnesses peering from shelter. "Not a visionary. Not a savior. Just a deranged man with armed guards, wielding weather like a blunt weapon to strike down his enemies. This is what they'll remember."

Herold's manic grin faltered. His gaze swept the street—the shattered asphalt, the horrified onlookers with recording phone's pressed against a windowpane.

Luna stepped closer, voice low but cutting. "Put the weapons down, Herold. Or do you really want the world to see you like this?"

His jaw tightened. For a moment, he stood motionless, headset flickering as data scrolled across his lenses. Calculating. Always calculating.

Finally, with a flick of his fingers, the guards hesitated—then lowered their weapons.

"Cameras don't change the outcome," Herold muttered, rain dripping from his brow. "They'll never charge me. How do you convict someone for an act of God?"

Thunder rumbled overhead, as if to punctuate his claim. He lifted his hand, ringed fingers twitching as he shaped another bolt within the swirling clouds.

"That's the beauty of it, Luna. No fingerprints. No trace. Just a storm—an unfortunate, tragic storm."

Luna stood her ground, energy humming just beneath her skin. She could feel the rhythm of the universe pulsing through her—Vibration, Rhythm, Correspondence—all aligning in perfect harmony.

Herold took a step forward, voice dropping into something colder, more measured. "And don't fool yourself into thinking I'm your only enemy. There are others—people just as capable, just as ruthless. People who will gladly bury this story and hide the truth. Give it a week, and it'll be forgotten in the tabloids of conspiracy theories."

His lips curled into a sneer. "You're fighting more than me, Luna. You're fighting an entire system built to erase you."

Herold flicked his fingers to zoom in from above, trying to find her precise location to strike her down.

Luna closed her eyes, centering herself as she felt the collective energy surge one last time. She whispered softly, "Emma... I need you."

Herold sneered. "Goodbye, Luna."

But then, the faint roar of an engine broke through the storm's din. Headlights pierced the rain as another vehicle careened onto the scene, skidding to a halt behind the SUV.

James threw open the driver's door before the truck had fully stopped, his boots hitting the wet pavement with a determined thud. Without hesitation, he sprinted toward the SUV. Althea followed, her coat flaring behind her as she moved, focus narrowing to the backseat, where Ezra laid.

And then Emma emerged.

She stepped out slowly, rain plastering her hair to her face. But it wasn't the storm that held her attention—it was the field of energy shimmering faintly around her, drawn from something far deeper than the earth. Her eyes, wide and unyielding, glowed with an inner light—the unmistakable imprint of Luna's presence burning behind her gaze, as if a piece of that same flame now lived within her.

Luna's head snapped up, her exhausted eyes locking onto Emma. An invisible thread seemed to pull at them, drawing Emma forward.

Herold's fingers twitched, the ring-like sensors glowing faintly as he recalibrated. The SUV stood in the crosshairs now, a cluster of vulnerable targets—Elias, Beth, James, Althea, Ezra. Herold's hand lifted, guiding the storm's fury toward the easier prize.

"No point wasting precision," he muttered, narrowing the targeting grid.

Lightning coiled above, drawn into a tightening spiral.

That's when Emma stepped forward.

"Stop."

The word wasn't shouted, but it cut through the chaos like the eye of the storm—calm, centered, undeniable.

Herold's hand froze, sensors flickering amber with hesitation. His gaze snapped to her, recognition dawning behind the frustration etched into his face.

Herold laughed, sharp and incredulous. "The hitchhiker? That's rich. Who the hell are *you* to command me?" His finger hovered over the virtual trigger, the storm above crackling in anticipation, waiting for his final command.

But Emma wasn't looking at him—she was looking at Luna. And in that instant, the world shifted and time slowed.

A golden thread of energy ignited between them, stretching through the air, vibrating with an ancient knowing. The storm's deafening roar dulled to a low hum, as if reality itself had stepped aside.

The streetlights flickered, dimming—not for the world around them, but within *their* perception, time nearly stopped. The veil had thinned, and they were no longer bound to the physical world.

The ground beneath them shimmered, then dissolved into cascading light. Time folded inward, the linear unraveling into something deeper—something *true*.

The cityscape peeled away, fragmenting into threads of energy, into quarks and stardust, into the silent void from which all things are born. Their awareness stretched outward, touching the quantum memory field—the *Akashic Record*, the aetheric imprint where past, present, and possibility converged.

The storm, the streets, the glassy towers—all of it vanished, replaced by an endless ocean of stars. Nebulae spiraled in radiant plumes, galaxies breathed with cosmic fire, and beneath it all pulsed the rhythmic vibration of creation.

Luna and Emma came together at the center of this celestial canvas, their forms luminous and radiant. Around them, the quarks of creation danced, vibrating with the pulse of the universe. They saw each other—not as they are today, but as they had been, countless eons ago.

Memories unfurled in a cascade of light. They were no longer human but beings of pure energy, born from the same nebula at the dawn of existence. They had danced together in the cosmic womb, their energies entwined as they shaped solar systems, birthed stars, and seeded the first sparks of physical life across the galaxies. They were creators, siblings in the truest sense—two halves of a perfect balance, yin and yang, will and creation.

Their shared history was a symphony of light and sound, each memory a note in the grand composition of existence. They saw the worlds they had formed together, the civilizations they had nurtured and guided from above, and the moments of love and loss that had defined their journey.

And then, they saw the moment of separation. The pain of being pulled apart, their energies split to fulfill their destinies in different forms. They saw the countless lifetimes they had lived, always searching, always yearning for the other. And now, at this moment, they were whole again, after more than fifty thousand years of separation.

The memories dissolved, not with a jolt, but with a gentle unraveling—as if the stardust of their shared past had begun to drift away on an unseen current. The warmth of celestial light receded, replaced by a creeping chill that kissed their skin. The hum of the cosmos faded into the steady patter of rain on asphalt, each drop a tiny drumbeat calling them back. The scent of ozone and wet pavement bloomed in Luna's senses, grounding her in the now. The street reformed around them like fog lifting from a dream—blurry edges sharpening into glass, stone, and storm. But something had changed.

Luna and Emma stood at the epicenter of an invisible force, their energies perfectly aligned, resonating in harmonic balance.

The Hermetic Principle of Vibration echoed through them: *Nothing rests; everything moves; everything vibrates.* The collision of their fields created more than resonance—it created *coherence*, a quantum entanglement that bridged the divide between thought and form.

For everyone else, only fractions of a second had passed. But within that sliver of time, the laws governing matter and energy had momentarily bent.

In the quantum field, every possibility had existed at once—victory, defeat, surrender, destruction—a chaotic sea of potential, unobserved and unclaimed. But when Luna and Emma aligned, their consciousnesses merged into a single point of awareness, like a lens focusing scattered light into a piercing beam.

The Hermetic Principle of Mentalism revealed itself: *All is mind.*

They didn't just witness reality—they *defined* it.

Probabilities collapsed in rapid succession, each choice narrowing the field, each shared intention pruning the branches of possibility until only one path remained: coherence.

Order.

The wave became particle. Potential became form.

And the world *shuddered.*

The force of their unified observation bent the quantum fabric outward, like gravity distorting the edge of a star. Reality folded inward, then rebounded outward in an electromagnetic pulse—a shockwave born from the collapse of uncertainty into certainty.

The air shimmered as the pulse expanded, spherical and undeniable. Streetlights flickered and burst in quick succession, glass raining down like crystalline confetti. Storefront windows fractured, spiderweb patterns racing across their surfaces before they exploded outward with sharp cracks.

Car alarms blared and died in an instant, electrical systems fried by the surge. Even the storm faltered—thunder rumbling like a confused question, the wind stuttering as if the atmosphere itself had momentarily lost its rhythm.

Herold staggered back, his quantum headset sputtering, holographic projections glitching and collapsing like a corrupted file. The ring-like sensors on his fingers flickered violently, then dimmed, leaving his hands twitching uselessly.

But the true force wasn't in the destruction. It was in the *feeling.*

The EMP passed through bodies like a pulse of truth, not painful but undeniable—a harmonic vibration that resonated in the chest, rumbled through the bones, and left behind an eerie clarity, like dawn breaking over a long-forgotten landscape.

The collapse of probabilities had left only *now.*

Luna and Emma turned toward Herold, their combined presence more than physical. They were will and creation entwined, the pulse of the cosmos made manifest, standing in the stillness left behind by the unraveling of uncertainty.

Herold's eyes widened, disbelief etched into every line of his face. His footing faltered, the storm above flickering as his control fractured, no longer tethered to the systems that had once obeyed his every command.

For the first time, he didn't look like a man commanding nature. He looked like someone nature had already marked for retribution.

The sisters glowed with a celestial brilliance, their forms shimmering like twin stars caught in perfect orbit. Emma lifted her hands to the sky, and guided by Luna's will, the thick, churning clouds above unraveled into gentle streams of rain.

The storm didn't simply *fade*—it *transformed*, its ferocity collapsing into tranquility as if the very rhythm of nature had recalibrated. Each raindrop shimmered faintly, infused with the hum of creation, resonating with the fundamental vibration of the universe.

But the rain wasn't just water. It was *information*—a quantum transmission entangled with the unconditional love radiating from Luna and Emma's unity. The same force that had birthed the EMP now rode the falling droplets, soft but undeniable, a reminder that even the most chaotic energy could be restructured into peace.

Herold's guards faltered.

The first raindrops kissed their skin, and something shifted—a subtle rewiring, not of mind, but of *heart*. The cold certainty that had driven their obedience cracked, like brittle glass under gentle pressure.

Possibilities bloomed.

The Hermetic Principle of Polarity alive within: *Everything is dual; opposites are identical in nature, but different in degree.* Fear and love, not separate forces, but extremes of the same vibration.

The frequency of fear—once sharp, commanding, absolute—began to soften, unraveling like a tightly wound thread. With each raindrop, the vibration shifted along the spectrum, sliding toward its opposite pole. Cold dread warmed into quiet connection. Aggression dissolved into peace. Isolation gave way to unity.

It wasn't force that disarmed them, but *alignment*—a gentle recalibration of the heart, proving that what once seemed unchangeable was merely one side of a greater whole.

Hands that had gripped weapons so tightly now trembled, uncertainty blooming where orders had once rooted. The threat of violence flickered and dimmed, replaced by something more profound: *choice*.

The rain fell softly, and with it came clarity.

Luna and Emma's light expanded outward as they stood hand in hand, not as force, but as invitation—an offering of a world no longer bound by fear, but shaped by love's infinite potential.

One by one, the guards lowered their weapons, their gazes shifting from Herold's failing command to the radiant certainty standing before them.

Herold's breath came in ragged gasps. His headset flickered, data streams glitching across the lenses. He tore it off and hurled it aside, the rings on his fingers dimming as the last vestiges of his technological control sputtered out.

"This isn't over," he hissed, stepping forward, rain streaking his face like tears he'd long forgotten how to shed. "You think you've won? You think love—peace—can undo what's coming?"

Luna held his gaze, unshaken. "It's not about winning or losing, Herold. It's about evolving—about what humanity can become when we embrace unity and possibility. You don't have to fight this. Let us help you."

For a fleeting moment, Herold froze.

But the darkness within him was too deep, his choices already woven into an inescapable pattern.

The Hermetic Principle of Cause and Effect stirred within the moment: *Nothing happens by chance. Every action creates a chain of consequences—some seen, some unseen.*

This was Herold's reality. Every decision, every manipulation, every calculated move had led him here. He had not stumbled into destruction; he had built it, step by step, believing himself untouchable. But now, standing in the rain, stripped of his power, he faced the consequence of every action.

And he could not accept it.

His lip curled into a bitter snarl. "You still don't get it, do you?"

In a flash, he lunged for the gun one of the guards had abandoned. His fingers closed around the grip, slick with rain, as he whirled back toward Luna, barrel rising with practiced efficiency.

"This war doesn't end with me," Herold spat, eyes wild. "You think this changes anything? There are others—stronger, smarter. They'll bury you. Bury all of this."

His finger tightened on the trigger.

Before the shot could ring out, the sky answered.

It didn't arc aimlessly, nor was it drawn by Herold's fractured technology. It struck with *purpose*, as if guided by intention.

For the briefest moment, Emma's gaze sharpened, her breath steady despite the chaos around her. Her fingers twitched, almost reflexively.

The bolt hit him directly.

The world went white.

Herold's scream was swallowed by the thunderclap, his body arching violently as the energy coursed through him. The gun clattered from his grip, spinning into a puddle as smoke curled from his suit. For an instant, his form seemed to flicker, caught between matter and energy, like a particle collapsing from superposition into finality.

When the light faded, he collapsed to the ground.

Still. Silent. Gone.

The rain fell heavier, steam rising from the scorched pavement around his lifeless form. The guards stood frozen, weapons forgotten, eyes wide with disbelief. There was no need for confirmation. The universe had made its choice—or had *she*?

Emma stood rooted to the spot, rain streaking her face. Her expression was unreadable, but in her eyes, the faintest ember of knowing flickered before it, too, faded.

Luna exhaled slowly, the glow surrounding her and Emma softening into something quieter, more enduring.

"You were right, Herold," she murmured, gaze steady on his motionless body. "Polarity must exist. Darkness will always push against the light. But when you chose the darkness, you also chose your end."

For a long moment, no one spoke.

The battle had ended. But the war—the one Herold had warned of, the one fueled by those still clinging to power, fear, and control—had only just begun.

FIFTY-ONE

IN THE RAIN, WE REMEMBERED

The rain didn't stop. It fell steady and warm, no longer cold and punishing, but soft—cleansing. It washed over the streets, mingling with the faint shimmer of residual energy left behind by the EMP. The sharp edges of the storm had dulled, leaving behind something quieter, more intentional.

Luna and Emma stood side by side, hands still joined, their bond unbroken. The glow that had once radiated from them had dimmed, settling inward—no longer a beacon, but an ember, steady and enduring.

Around them, the world stirred.

The people who had sheltered in nearby shops and doorways now stepped hesitantly into the rain, drawn not by curiosity, but by something deeper—an unspoken pull, like waking from a long-forgotten dream.

Shopkeepers peered out from beneath awnings. A mother clutched her child's hand, guiding them into the open street. An elderly man, his cane forgotten, stood still as the rain soaked his clothes, his face upturned to the sky.

It wasn't force. It wasn't magic. It was *recognition*.

The EMP had done more than disable technology—it had fractured the rigid constructs that kept hearts closed and minds tethered to fear. And now, under the gentle fall of unconditional love, the pendulum swung into the light.

Luna watched in silence, the weight of the moment pressing gently against her chest. *Not victory*, she realized. *Awakening.*

Ezra lay in the backseat of the SUV, his breathing steadier beneath Althea's watchful hands. Elias stood nearby, rain dripping from his chin, his eyes flicking between the street and Luna, as if searching for confirmation that this was real.

Beth, ever the skeptic, lowered her phone, the screen dark and lifeless from the EMP. She didn't seem to care. Her gaze had softened, the furrow in her brow smoothed by something resembling hope.

Luna turned to Emma, their eyes meeting with quiet understanding.

"It's not about us fixing this," Luna murmured, her voice low and sure. "We're not here to force change. That's not how this works."

Emma nodded, rain tracing paths down her cheeks. "We're here to ignite it. To remind humanity of what it's capable of. The potential was always there. Now it's stirring."

Just the rain—soft and steady, as if the sky itself wept not in sorrow, but in release.

The people standing in the street didn't speak at first. Some tilted their heads, eyes closed, as though savoring a long-lost sensation. Others reached out, palms upturned, letting the rain pool in their hands, as if holding something fragile and precious.

And in each heart, something shifted.

A young woman near the edge of the sidewalk blinked up at the sky, her face softening from disbelief into wonder. She turned to the stranger beside her—a man she had nearly collided with while running for cover minutes before. Without hesitation, she reached out, clasping his rain-slicked hand. He didn't pull away. Instead, he squeezed it gently, a quiet acknowledgment passing between them.

Laughter, hesitant at first, rippled through the air. A child darted out from beneath an overhang, arms outstretched, spinning in the downpour. His mother, who moments ago had clutched him tightly in fear, now stood smiling, her hands falling to her sides as she watched him dance.

Emma exhaled, her gaze sweeping across the street, watching the threads of connection weave themselves back together. "Mm, yes," she murmured, voice soft with wonder. "The pendulum swings."

Luna's smile matched hers, soft but certain. "Change doesn't happen in an instant," she murmured, watching as two strangers—once wary, now smiling—embraced beneath the falling sky. "But this is the spark. The first ripple. Step by step, the collective will awaken."

The rain kept falling, steady and warm, as the city took its first breath in a world quietly, undeniably changed.

Everwood—One Year Later

From a distance, the land looked unchanged. The forest stretched endlessly, its towering oaks standing as timeless stewards beneath the vast sky. The morning mist curled between the branches, weaving its delicate veil over the hills, obscuring what lay beyond.

But for those who knew how to see—for those whose hearts had opened to the rhythm of the unseen—the illusion shimmered.

Like the surface of a still lake kissed by the wind, reality rippled, bending the light. The dense woodland softened, giving way to something luminous, something waiting. And then, as if the earth itself exhaled, the veil lifted.

The pyramid stood, fully revealed. Radiant with purpose and wisdom.

No longer buried beneath the weight of time, it gleamed in the golden light, its smooth stone whispering of long-forgotten hands that once carved its sacred geometry. Reminders of times past pulsed faintly along its surface, breathing in rhythm with the land, their ancient wisdom awakening with each passing moment. Though hidden from those who would exploit it, to those who sought with pure intent, it called—a beacon for the wandering, the awakening, the seekers of truth.

At its base, Everwood flourished.

Paths wound through gardens bursting with life, where lavender and sage perfumed the air, and vines draped over wooden archways like nature's own scripture. The river sang its endless hymn, its waters shimmering beneath the midday sun, carrying the echoes of whispered prayers and unspoken dreams.

Within the sanctuary, life unfolded in harmony.

Beneath the shade of a great oak, Althea sat in quiet meditation, her presence a stillness that rippled outward, guiding those gathered around her. By the river's edge, James and a group of newcomers shaped the land with careful hands, constructing a wooden bridge that would serve as both passage and symbol—a connection between what was and what would be.

Near the heart of it all, before the great pyramid, Luna and Emma stood before a gathering of souls, their voices weaving a tapestry of truth. Their hands moved with quiet grace, bending light into form—shifting strands of radiant energy into fleeting shapes that spoke without words. Spirals of golden filaments intertwined, blooming like sacred geometry made visible, each pattern a reflection of the concepts they shared.

They spoke not of doctrine, nor of rigid teachings, but of *remembrance*. Of the pulse within the earth that mirrored the one within their chests. Of the light woven through all things, seen and unseen—the connective tissue of existence itself.

The figures they shaped in light shimmered with shifting forms—an ouroboros circling itself, a flame that burned both hot and cold, a coin spinning endlessly on its axis, revealing neither face nor tail.

"Truth was never meant to be carved in stone," Luna said softly, her fingers coaxing the light into the shape of a Mobius strip, its surface endless and without edge. "When held too tightly, it fractures into half-truths—rigid and blind. Real truth breathes. It bends. It holds contradiction without breaking."

Emma nodded, weaving the light into a pair of mirrored masks—one smiling, one serene, both dissolving into a single shape. "The return isn't about discovering what's right. It's about learning to sit with what is—beyond duality. To feel the knowing that lives between the opposites."

The crowd watched in silent awe, not merely hearing, but *feeling* the resonance of the words—the vibration of truth expressed not as command, but as invitation.

And as the final strands of light unraveled into the air, the message lingered: *The answers were never out there. They had always been within.*

Luna's gaze lifted for a moment, her breath catching as something unseen stirred within her. A warmth bloomed in her chest, soft and knowing. She placed a hand over her heart and closed her eyes.

And there he was.

Ezra.

The morning light filtered through the newly built cabin windows, casting warm, golden hues over the small room. The gentle creak of the rocking chair filled the silence, rhythmic and steady. Ezra leaned forward, his gaze soft as he traced the tiny fingers curled around his own. Overhead, hanging just above the crib, was The Shift—Margaret's final masterpiece, alive with the energy she had poured into every brushstroke. The golden threads woven through its swirling depths seemed to pulse in the morning light, as though carrying her presence forward, cradling the next generation in its warmth. A mother's legacy. A grandmother's love. A piece of her, still watching, still guiding.

From the corner of the room, the radio murmured, its low static giving way to a clipped but urgent voice.

"*Breaking news—another victory for prosecutors today as the tenth guilty verdict is handed down in the Westfield scandal. Among those convicted is Caleb Marlowe, charged with multiple counts of fraud, identity manipulation, and the trafficking of culturally significant artifacts. Authorities say Marlowe played a central role in a series of high-level thefts and financial schemes stretching across several states. Today's sentencing marks a pivotal step in unraveling the broader web of corruption tied to Westfield's inner circle, though officials suggest further indictments may follow.*"

The voice faded into the background, swallowed by the soft creak of Ezra's rocking chair as he settled beside their child. Across the room, Silas sat quietly, his weathered hands resting on his knees, his gaze drawn to the tiny life before him. He exhaled slowly, not from exhaustion, but reverence—a quiet gratitude blooming in his chest. For second chances. For forgiveness. For this impossible, miraculous new beginning.

Luna smiled, her heart swelling with the profound knowing that this—*this*—was the future they had created.

They had arrived.

Yet, far beyond the sanctuary, across lands untouched and cities humming with the restless stirrings of awakening souls, others were feeling the call. Other sanctuaries were forming. The veils were thinning. The whispers of ancient places, once silenced, had begun to rise.

The shift is here.

Awakening is not about becoming something new, but remembering what you have always been. The path is not found outside of you—it is uncovered within.

-The Beginning...

THANK YOU FOR READING

Dear Reader,

Thank you for spending time with The Shift: Discovering Inner Evolution. I'm deeply honored you chose to walk this journey with Luna—and with me.

This story was written from a place of personal transformation, spiritual curiosity, and a desire to create something that stirs the soul. If it resonated with you, moved you, or made you reflect—I'd be truly grateful if you'd take a moment to share your thoughts.

Your review doesn't have to be long. Just a few honest words can make a huge difference in helping other readers decide if *The Shift* is right for them.

If you feel called to share your experience, I'd love for you to leave a review—on Amazon, Goodreads, or wherever you found your copy.

Amazon Review /
Goodreads Review

The Shift is just the beginning.

Book Two of the Inner Evolution Series is already in motion, continuing this journey of remembrance, awakening, and soul-deep transformation. I'd love for you to be part of it.

With gratitude,

J.W. Pressler

ACKNOWLEDGEMENTS

Every moment matters.

Every conversation, every book, every seemingly insignificant inter-action has the potential to shape who we become. Over the years, I've learned from so many. Through direct teachings, shared stories, unex-pected challenges, and quiet inspirations. To capture all of it here would be nearly impossible... and probably better suited for an autobiography.

What follows is only a fraction—a trail of the clearest breadcrumbs I can trace back to this book. These are the insights, inspirations, and teachers whose influence is unmistakably woven into The Shift. Their words, wisdom, and presence helped shape the ideas on these pages and helped shape me in the process.

I wrote my first book when I was just a teenager. Unfortunately, that book was lost before it could be published. Looking back, I realize it wasn't just the story that was missing—it was the experience and wisdom that the following 25+ years would give me.

Still, the idea never truly disappeared. As I grew, explored, and expand-ed spiritually, the concept kept resurfacing, whispering to me through different moments in my life.

During that journey, I discovered the work of Eckhart Tolle. His books, The Power of Now and A New Earth, were more than just pages of wisdom—they were lifelines. In a world often steeped in stress and noise, they offered stillness, clarity, and truth. They became a foundation of my spiritual growth and personal peace for the better part of a decade.

In my late twenties, I felt an intense desire to write again—not just to entertain, but to bring attention to ideas that I believed could help change the world. But life happened. A demanding career, the need to earn a living, and all the responsibilities that come with adulthood kept me from even starting.

Now, I see that all of it was for a reason. There are no coincidences.

Back then, I thought I understood life—how it worked, what it meant, and what my place in it was. As it turned out, I was still waiting for the right coincidence to awaken me, the one that would reach into the quiet spaces I hadn't yet explored.

That next cycle of awakening began with Becoming Supernatural by Dr. Joe Dispenza. His work offered a gateway I hadn't known I was searching for—a bridge between science and spirituality. Through his lens, I saw how ancient wisdom could be made visible through neuroscience, how consciousness and the quantum field were not abstractions, but tools of transformation. His teachings on epigenetics radically shifted how I viewed the human body, DNA, and the power of thought to shape our biology. It was as if he gave language to things I had long felt but could never explain.

Through continued interest and discovery, I found my way to André Duqum's Know Thyself podcast—a sacred space of open dialogue, wisdom, and wonder. Through his intentional conversations, André introduced me to an entire community of thinkers and seekers. It was through his podcast that I encountered Gregg Braden, whose work deepened everything I had begun to explore. Gregg took that spark of interest and fanned it into something cosmic—expanding my curiosity into the realms of quantum physics, lost civilizations, timelines far older than we're taught, and the interconnected nature of our existence. Many of the ideas scattered throughout this book were seeded by the questions he encouraged me to ask.

I'd been meditating for years—tuning into stillness, finding presence—but it was Dr. Dispenza's practices that helped me take it deeper. His approach gave me a new way to see things. It helped me connect thoughts and emotions with intention—to picture the life I wanted and actually feel it, like it was already real. That shift changed everything. It gave me a way to move through pain, uncertainty, even hope—with purpose. I started to see that the world around me wasn't just happening to me. It was responding to who I was becoming inside.

At the same time, his work also revealed something unexpected about myself. While I could access deep emotional states, I often struggled to visualize clearly. The vivid inner landscapes he described—seeing the life you wanted in perfect detail, living it in the mind's eye—remained elusive for me. I could only catch fleeting impressions. For a time, I worried that I was broken, that I wasn't meditating "properly." Eventually, I came to suspect I might have a degree of aphantasia—a reduced or absent ability to form mental images. But in time, I realized: I simply experience the world differently. Where some create through visions, my mind prefers words. My thoughts take shape as language and emotion, and through that, I can experience the unseen. Perhaps this is what drew me to writing.

Through my continued meditation practice, I began to notice my own shift. My thoughts were no longer just internal—they were becoming reality. Intentions once whispered in quiet became visible in form. Small and subtle recognitions, but no less profound or confirming. I was observing, in real-time, the coalescing of unseen energy into lived experience.

One summer night in 2024, as I lay in bed listening to sound frequencies—white noise, binaural beats, anything to soften the ever-present tinnitus I'd carried since my time in the Army. I don't remember what I fell asleep to. But I'll never forget what woke me: a voice, calm and clear, speaking truths that aligned with everything I had believed but had never been able to fully articulate.

By what seemed like pure coincidence, an audiobook had started playing as I slept. It was The Kybalion.

That night, my perception of the world changed forever—yet again. It was as if all the pieces I'd gathered along my journey had finally clicked into place. The Hermetic Principles articulated with elegant simplicity and logical precision what I had been intuitively living, learning, and sometimes struggling to define. It gave language to the unseen forces I had felt for years and offered clarity to truths that had only previously brushed the edges of my awareness.

What struck me most wasn't just the wisdom—it was the timing. This book had existed for over 75 years before I was born. It had always been there, quietly waiting. And yet, I had never once encountered it. Not in passing conversation, not on a bookshelf, not in a stray search result. It found me only when I was ready.

I can't help but mention how fitting the axiom from the Kybalion is: "The lips of wisdom are closed, except to the ears of understanding." The truth doesn't shout. It waits—until your ears, your heart, your being are ready to receive it.

From that moment forward, my meditations deepened. My inner world became more structured, more meaningful. I began to see purpose in the everyday, rhythm in what once felt random, and design where I had seen only chance. The Kybalion didn't give me something new—it helped me remember something eternal. For that, I will be forever grateful.

As I continued my journey, I committed to regular meditation—sometimes multiple times a day—and I began to feel a familiar shift. Subtle patterns surfaced, ones I recognized from past seasons of life where depression had crept in. Only this time, something was different. I didn't fall into them. Instead, I observed them. I was aware of the cycle, aware that my energy was shifting—not downward, but outward. What had once been a time of withdrawal was now something else entirely.

I realized I was transitioning from a season of deep internal reflection and spiritual integration into one of external creation. The frequency I had been tuning into for so long was ready to take form. And that's when the inspiration to write returned—not as a random urge, but as a natural extension of the work I'd been doing within.

The ideas I'd collected over the years, the questions, the fragments of truth—they all began to rearrange themselves. A foundation formed. Then a structure. And before long, that structure blossomed into The Shift—the story that had always been there, waiting to be written.

It is my hope and intention that this book be a "coincidence" in a reader's life—The Shift that sets the pendulum in motion on a path of discovery they never knew was possible. If that becomes the case for even one person, then I will find myself incredibly successful. I hope that person is you.

I'd settle for a "not bad" as you turn the last page too. :)

And finally, to my wife, Yvonne—thank you.

The journey from first draft to final page was a long one, and it demanded more of me than I anticipated—time, focus, and energy pulled from our already full life. You gave me the space to disappear into the world I was building, the patience to stand beside me when I was lost in it, and the grace to let me follow it through.

This book may have my name on the cover, but your support is in every page.

I am grateful for everything this journey has given me—for the insights, the growth, and the chance to create something that I hope inspires others as much as it has transformed me.

Thank you—for reading, for exploring, and for being part of this with me.

With gratitude,

J.W. Pressler

ABOUT THE AUTHOR

Life has a way of shaping us, often in ways we don't fully understand until we look back and connect the dots. For Joe Pressler, every challenge, every turn, and every so-called coincidence was part of a greater journey—one that led him here.

A U.S. Army veteran and civil service employee with over 20 years of combined federal service, Joe carries a deep appreciation for life's meaning, its interconnectedness, and the quiet wisdom found in presence.

Writing, for Joe, is more than self-expression—it's a form of exploration. A way to weave together lessons learned and insights still unfolding. Through his words, he explores the landscape of emotion, energy, and the space where the seen and unseen meet. His storytelling blends grounded experience with spiritual inquiry, inviting readers to feel deeply, think openly, and remember who they truly are.

This book is part of that journey—an offering from the heart, and a reflection of the deeper truth that we are all connected.

Stay connected and up to date with future work From J.W. Pressler at www.yjpresspublishing.com